This city is home to exceptional people blessed or cursed with abilities through scientific or biological experimentation, abilities that have changed the face of law enforcement. For every simple gang banger or convenience store robber, there was a being capable of throwing cars like bags of trash, deflect bullets with a wave of the hand, or leap across the rooftops as if playing hopscotch.

The business of creating tools to deal with these "Exceptionals" is a lucrative one. One of the largest, most powerful defense contractors in the world, Corp Hudson, specializes in the development of weaponry for law enforcement and the military for the sole purpose of taking down the most powerful of targets. Corp Hudson seeks to corner the market on developing combat tools by taking their research to the next level: the development of human-weapon hybrids strong enough to defeat any enemy force. But before Corp Hudson can move forward with their ambitions of creating the perfect superhuman army, they need to study one unique subject...a subject that, unlike all other Exceptionals, was mysteriously born with her abilities.

She uses her abilities for one purpose: to make as much money as she can by sabotaging the efforts of Corp Hudson and companies like it, doing what she can to keep the corporations from dominating the world with their oppressive power. The streets know her as the most dangerous, most beautiful, and most elusive bandit of them all, the criminal underworld's top go-to girl, Nia Black. But Corp Hudson has another name for her:

Target Omega.

"INTRUDER ALERT. INTRUDER ALERT."

Time stopped for Dr. Kane Romedrux. He and his employer were merely talking outside of his building. Then the alarm cut off the prepared speech Kane Romedrux been spouting to his employer, and suddenly all his rambling about his security and his accomplishments became meaningless.

The repeating computerized voice stifled all attempts the researcher made at explaining himself. All Romedrux could do was stare meekly into the eyes of his benefactor, the powerful and formidable Maxwell Hudson.

The alarms were joined by flashing orange lights that shined through every window of the building. It was at that moment that Hudson spoke a single line to the trembling scientist.

"Why are you still standing here?"

Electronic sliding doors swooshed open and Dr. Romedrux stormed into the foyer. The alarm that was a whisper before became a full on scream, the entire building a menagerie of rushing security officers and pulsating lights.

Romedrux bellowed to the security personnel with strength and poise that belied his humility, and though his orders were redundant, speaking them instilled the scientist with a sense of authority. *He* was the lord of this castle, and no intruder would get away unpunished, especially since the situation gave him the opportunity to impress Mr. Hudson.

"Block all the exits! Secure the examination rooms! You, come with me! To the vault!"

As guards took their positions in the corridor leading to the heart of the building, Romedrux slowly looked backward at the array of windows that made up the entire front wall. Staring back at Romedrux through the tinted glass was Hudson, silent and still as a monolith, with his arms folded as if he *needed* to express how domineering his presence was. Romedrux quickly ran down the hall, joining his guards.

Romedrux trembled with fright, realizing that there was only one thing any intruder could have been after.

No…the prototype! Not now! Not with Mr. Hudson here!

Hudson commissioned Kane Romedrux to develop a new kind of weapon, one made to aid law enforcement with the apprehension of targets that—for various reasons—proved too powerful for conventional arrest methods. A weapon meant to take down *exceptional* beings.

Romedrux was so proud of his security that it must have taken an 'exceptional' person to breach it. Telling himself that was all he could do to reassure himself.

Romedrux and his accompanying guard reached the vault within the building's inner sanctum. It bore a twelve-inch-thick titanium steel alloy door, resistant to any form of demolition. The only reliable means of entry was through the correct sequence of numbers entered into a keypad to the door's immediate left, followed by a retinal scan and voice verification.

Romedrux rushed ahead and jabbed the keypad with his index finger, punching in a special code only he knew that would bypass the security system completely.

As the massive circular door grinded aside, Romedrux's heartbeat hammered his chest, his mouth became dry and his eyes watered. He thought of what might happen to him if Hudson discovered his corporation's newest device was in danger. Maxwell Hudson's power and influence were commanding enough to move mountains. This kind of mistake could destroy a man's life.

Romedrux stopped trembling when he peered into the curved slit between the vault door and its frame. He spotted something, an image that both brought him ease and made his hair stand on end at the same time.

The weapon was still there.

In the hands of an intruder.

And the intruder was quite a sight indeed.

A curvaceous woman stood before them, young and short, yet her stance exerted dominance and strength that belied her appearance. She wore a tight leather jacket and pants laden with compartments and pockets. Her narrow brown eyes matched the unwavering stare of the guard in such a manner that he was as taken aback by her beauty as he was by her brazenness.

She was standing directly under an open ventilation shaft, its grate carelessly cast away on the floor. The intruder moved carefully and methodically, lifting the weapon from its shelf, despite clearly being aware of Romedrux's presence.

Dr. Romedrux and his guard entered the vault, and with every step, Romedrux felt more assured. The thief could not go back through the vent without becoming an easy target, and the only other exit was the vault door itself, which the guard blocked.

Sliding the device into a satchel, the thief turned about and faced Romedrux with controlled, graceful, confident movements. If the bandit were at all concerned about their presence, it didn't show.

"I guess you got me," the thief grinned, apparently amused.

The guard recognized her immediately. He read the papers and saw composite sketches of her on the news, but never imagined that he would be face-to-face with her. She was an infamous and dangerous criminal, pursued heavily but for some reason never caught.

"Doctor," the guard began, leaning towards his boss, muttering in a low voice. Then Romedrux's eyes widened.

"Are you certain? Alert everyone!"

"All units," the guard immediately spoke into his radio. "*Target Omega* is on the premises. Repeat. *Target Omega* is on the premises."

A fuzzy voice crackled back over the radio. "Copy that. All units are in position."

Target Omega! Romedrux thought. *Of all the luck! It's her...the one Hudson's been searching for! This is my chance!*

"Who sent you to this facility? How did you know about the weapon?" Romedrux growled, his overwhelming sense of zeal inspiring him to stand firm in the face of his feared intruder.

"Yeah, right," she sighed. "Like I'm gonna tell you that."

"Well it doesn't matter; you'll never escape with it," Romedrux asserted with a laugh, though it was more nervousness than condescending. "I have guards all over the building. Every exit is covered. There's no way out. Don't throw your life away for nothing; just return the prototype, if you please."

The woman smiled. Then her stance went taut.

She pressed her toe to the floor and before anyone could utter another breath, she'd already *soared across the room* through the air—her knee colliding with the guard's skull at blinding speed!

The guard fell to the ground lifelessly, his stumbling body taking Romedrux along with him. Romedrux swung his head toward the shelves where all his special projects and prototypes were stored—minus Corp Hudson's weapon and the woman. He looked in the other direction and stared in horror as he saw the woman heading down the corridor, the satchel containing the stolen prototype weapon securely in her grip.

Romedrux was flabbergasted. *How did she move so fast?*

The scientist's face reddened with every passing second. His emotions outweighed his strength, but he had to do something. He had to stop her. His future depended on it.

He snatched the walkie-talkie from his defeated guard's belt and screamed into it.

"All units! *Get her!*"

Sentries from other posts in the building ceased guarding the exam rooms and rushed toward the vault, their footsteps rumbling.

Racing through the narrow halls of the building, breezing past various offices and research rooms, the thief threw the satchel over her shoulder.

A platoon of guards appeared before her in the hallway. They wore heavy black helmets and armor with Kevlar and metal accouterments, with large gauntlets and shin guards.

One guard's face tightened as he closed his fists and raised his gauntlet, a chrome cylinder rod twelve inches in length protruding from a slot above his knuckles. The rod crackled with electricity as his partners mimicked him, producing shock rods of their own and assuming fighting stances.

"Hold it!" he roared.

The thief's small grin stretched into a full smile as she secured the satchel's strap diagonally across her chest. She tightened her fists, relaxed her knees and wagged her finger at them, *daring* them to step forth.

It was then that they learned why she was feared so. There was something about her, something exceptional. A juxtaposition of limitless confidence and razor-sharp skill; stories of her battle prowess were qualified with adjectives like *remarkable, unstoppable, invincible*. And she reveled in that reputation.

The first guard to accept the challenge darted at the thief. He swung left, she swayed right and he hit nothing but air. He swung right and she swayed left; again, he missed his mark. He bared teeth like a beast, let out a growl of frustration and raised his shock rod high in the air. He barreled it down toward her head with enough aggression and fervor to rip a hole in a wall. But for all his bravado, he was dramatically slow to the thief, who simply stepped sideways as his arm connected with the floor, cracking the tiles beneath their feet in a flash of sparks. He turned to the woman now above him as her body swirled around; her boot smacking his head with enough force to propel him from the floor into the wall behind him. He slinked back down to the floor and stopped moving.

Two of the remaining three guards charged her, planning to flank her and give her no place to dodge. But she rushed forward and became a whirlwind of flying fists and feet amid a storm of sparks hitting every surface except her body. She dodged back, buried her palm into one guard's throat, her elbow in the chest of the other; swayed to the side, ducked another attack and countered with a knee strike to the belly and a double high kick to the face.

It almost looked choreographed.

She sent the second guard sailing head first to the floor with a leaping axe kick, dodging a low thrust from the third guard at the same time. She landed, crouched and swung her leg around, taking the third attacker's feet out from under him with a sweeping kick that send him crashing on his back, his skull hitting the floor first.

She instantly outstretched her other foot to answer the would-be surprise attack from the last guard. Her foot collided with his gut with force fueled by his own rushing momentum. He stumbled back further than expected, falling on his butt, unable to comprehend why the heel of such a small woman cost him his balance.

Then he felt like a building crashed upon him. Before he realized what was happening the thief smashed into him from above, slamming both knees into his torso like an avalanche, cracking the floor underneath.

She rolled backward off her last opponent and stood up straight. Leaving her attackers squirming on the floor, the thief continued her flight, eventually making her way to the foyer.

She sprinted ahead and sharply turned left, away from the main entrance, rushing toward the window-wall.

Drawing one of the two handguns she carried from holsters resting at the small of her back, she opened fire and left spider-web cracks all over the windows.

She sprang and tucked through the air and crashed through the weakened window like a wrecking ball in a brilliant explosion of glass.

As shards showered the ground like crystal rain, the man named Hudson turned and glared at her. She landed a few feet away from him on the sidewalk and quickly trotted away, vanishing into an alley on the side of the Romedrux Labs building.

Hudson slowly approached the alley, looking inquisitively into the shadows.

He heard a metallic jingling, then a low-pitched grumble. Then a blinding light flashed in his face and he immediately lunged backward.

A silver motorcycle leaped from the alley, its engine's deafening growl shaking the air as it smashed aside garbage cans and frightened stray cats. The sport bike came to a brief stop inches from the rear of Hudson's limo, perpendicular to the lengthy automobile and facing the open road. The curvy rider twisted around and grinned at the outlandishly tall businessman, flashing a smile that pierced him like a dagger. It was a smile of confidence and victory, a smile of fearlessness. This young woman not only paid his presence little heed, she seemed to recognize how that frustrated him. She reveled in that. Slapping her goggles over her eyes, her engine roared like a lion as her bike rocketed away and disappeared into the sunset.

Hudson slowly walked in her direction, shards of glass crumbling under his alligator skin shoes. Watching her through the billowing smoke of her engine with a guttural breath, he slid his hand into his pocket and drew a cellular phone. He made a call, and glanced at the building's front door as the silhouette of a short man came into view behind it.

8

Moments later, the main doors slid apart and there was Romedrux, stumbling to a stop as Hudson clasped his phone shut. The scientist backpedaled. He saw the fierce, hardened face of Hudson and the wisp of smoke from a motorcycle long gone.

There was no saving face. Kane Romedrux's eyes went wide and his mouth fell agape as he shifted focus from Hudson to the open road and back again. The thief was long gone, along with the prototype. Romedrux knew it.

He'd failed Hudson.

Maxwell Hudson slid thin leather gloves on, and Romedrux trembled as Hudson's chauffeur opened the rear passenger door of the limo.

"Dr. Romedrux. If you would, please join me inside my limousine. I have decided to move up our discussion regarding your future with Corp Hudson."

Several blocks away, the leather-clad young bandit glanced at the satchel over her shoulder, the weight of the bag's contents satisfyingly pulling against her as she sped across the roads, the streetlights and flickers of traffic blurring on either side.

She smiled. *That's one less weapon you'll be putting in the hands of some punks on the street, and another fat payoff for me.*

A SOFT MISTY RAIN blanketed the streets one quiet, cloudy night. Inside the *Jazz Hall*, a sophisticated nightclub downtown, the atmosphere was alive with music and merriment. The faithful, fancy suit and cocktail dress-wearing patrons that attended the performance that evening cared nothing for the wet weather. They would never miss a live performance from Bobby Styles, the club's proprietor and master of the saxophone. Filling the air with calming, tranquil tunes, the sax, played expertly by one of the region's favored musicians, subtly augmented by bass notes and light drumming in the background from the band, created an ambiance of coolness and grace.

The languorous music of Bobby Styles and his jazz band held every patron in the club in a state of perpetual hypnosis like a siren. Some gazed because Bobby was the source of the music and an inspiration to those who wanted to express their own musical gifts, but many of the women looked upon him for a different reason altogether. He was a smooth-looking brother, draped in a teal silk shirt just thin enough to show the bulges of his chest, his lack of an undershirt blissfully apparent to every woman examining him. His faded haircut, sharp moustache, and clean features drew the eyes of every woman to him, leaving them unsure whether to focus on his soulful eyes or hardened pectorals.

The Jazz Hall's front door creaked open and the bouncer showed in a woman, tightly holding a satchel. She harvested the brief attention and lingering looks from most of the men present, including Bobby. The way her appearance demanded attention defeated Bobby's music from top to bottom.

The young woman looked like the star attraction of a hip-hop video. She wore a form-fitting black jacket partly opened. A golden pendant adorned with an opal stone sat around her neck and dangled, deliciously and tantalizingly, just above her cleavage. A tight leather miniskirt, gossamer panty hose, and black leather boots with short heels completed her outfit. Her short black hair, perfectly styled in a smooth, silky bob, curved from the peak of her head and slid across her rounded cheeks like a waterfall, a scant few locks intentionally slid within the frames of her tinted glasses.

The woman looked toward the Jazz Hall's bar and the familiar man behind it. Her smooth, graceful walk and rhythmical footsteps were as melodic to onlookers as the saxophone in the air, as if the sumptuous music were her own theme song.

Her eyes met those of the bartender, an older black man in a white button shirt, his sleeves rolled up to his elbows as he expertly mixed various drinks. The woman eased her thighs across a barstool directly in front of the bartender, a seat one gentleman was more than happy to vacate for her. The bartender immediately prepared a glass of light drink and placed it before her.

"Your usual, Nia," the bartender smiled warmly.

"How you doin', Marc?"

Marc Benson was the bartender and owner of the upscale nightclub. He came along when Bobby's Jazz Hall was desperately in need of funds and on the verge of shutdown. In exchange for majority ownership of the property, Marc kept the club open and allowed Bobby to continue playing his music full time while he handled the club's business affairs.

Marc befriended Nia and always seemed eager to hear her stories of adventure. He was no stranger to tales of gunfights and fisticuffs over money and power. The club was host to many colorful characters—hit men, robbers, gangsters and small-time hustlers always gathered at the Jazz Hall, mingling like salt in water with the regular, more lawful patrons. The Hall was one safe, relatively public place where shifty, shady and downright crooked folks could meet and discuss business safely. They respected Marc, because he treated them equally. In fact, much of the Jazz Hall's success, once Marc took over,

11

came from the good rapport he developed with the big-spenders of the criminal underworld. Marc learned a great deal about the clandestine affairs of the city's seedy underbelly, knowledge he often shared with his favorite patron, Miss Nia Black.

"I'm cool, sweetheart. You?"

"Never better. Had a good time the other night."

"I heard," Marc looked away briefly and nodded toward another customer, taking an order for wine. He turned back to Nia.

"One of these days, you're going to get in a lot of trouble messing with the big man."

Nia grinned. "That's what I do, boo. I take risks. But look, I came here tonight to—"

"To see Bobby, like the rest of the sisters here. Right?"

"Come on, Marc, you know he's got a girl," Nia blushed.

"That's not what I asked you."

Nia smiled. "Seriously man, did my contact get here yet? I had this thing long enough. He needs to hook me up."

"You mean Charlie? I think I saw him..." Marc looked around. "Yeah. He's sitting up front, next to your favorite seat. He looks a little agitated though. Be careful. Something ain't right about him tonight."

"You know me, I'm always careful," Nia spun on the barstool and turned away from the bar, tightly grasping the bottom of her skirt to keep it from riding up as she hopped off the seat.

Nia walked toward the center stage, weaving through the other tables until she made her way to the table nearest to the stage, where the man named Charlie Ross sat. His impatience was evident in his wide, baggy, reddened eyes as they followed Nia's every move. Missing the dress-to-impress code by a mile, his shabby brown sport jacket, dingy hair and stubble-ridden face stood out amongst the sharp suits and sequined dresses filling the club. He did seem agitated, incessantly checking his watch and repeatedly sipping his vodka. It looked like something had him spooked.

Nia sat down on the only other chair at Charlie's table and placed the bag she was carrying on her lap. As Nia slid her jacket off and exposed her halter-top, she turned to the sexy saxophonist with a wink and puckered her full, luscious lips at him. Bobby grinned and continued to play his music with seemingly increased fervor, as if her presence empowered him. He finished his set and began anew, this time with an increased tempo, the band following suit with stronger drums and deeper bass notes as another performer, a man who called himself 'Silk' appeared on stage spouting poetry.

"I never get tired of this place," said Nia in a whisper, leaning forward and sliding off her tinted spectacles. Charlie's eyeballs slid down, his vision diving into the chasm created by her breasts.

Charlie abruptly reset his gaze forward when he realized Nia was staring into his eyes.

"Having a good time?"

"Yeah, yeah, whatever, Miss Black," he stammered with every word. "Look, do you have it?"

Nia squinted back at him. "Come on, man, how long have we been doing this? Have I ever messed up?"

She lifted the satchel from her lap and placed it on the table. Charlie opened it and peered inside. The prototype weapon sat within with nary a scratch on it, even maintaining the luster from the last time its metal housing was buffed.

"Wow, you're unbelievable! I mean, you've done some great things before, but getting into that lab without getting spotted, then getting past all that security …you've outdone yourself, kid!"

"I know, right?" Nia grinned. "If you could only have seen the look on Hudson's face when he looked at my little behind jettin' with this thing. You could tell he was *mad!* Eyebrows all twitching…"

Nia calmed down after she noticed Charlie clearly tuned out.

"So, you got my money?"

"W-what's that now?"

"My *money*, Chuck."

"Oh, right," the man chuckled. "I almost forgot."

"Come on man, don't play. Let's get this done."

Two days had passed since Nia fought her way out of Romedrux Labs with Corp Hudson's experimental weapon, and she was fed up. Nia was tired of carrying such a hot piece of property for far too long. Usually after Nia lifted something for him, Charlie met up with her the same night with her payment to make the exchange, freeing Nia from any liability. Then Charlie and Nia would part ways until the next time he wanted her to nab something for him, Nia waiting patiently for the telltale page from her first contact in the fencing game. This time, Charlie offered neither explanation nor apology for the delay, and this irked her.

"You wanted the prototype from Romedrux Labs, and I got it," said Nia. "I could just leave it in your care and let certain people know who has the big man's recently stolen new toy. And you could have every hitter in the city hunting you down. Everybody on the street knows who you are, Chuck. Nobody out there knows how to find me. I don't need the loot from you as much as you want to keep living and breathing."

"Now, there ain't any need in getting like that. Your money's right here!"

Charlie shuddered when hissing from surrounding patrons telling him to shush blasted him like missiles. He angrily lifted a silver attaché case from underneath the red tablecloth and slammed it upon the table, as if he meant to antagonize everyone else. His drink capsized but Nia managed to lift hers before it ended up wasted on the table and floor. She accepted the attaché, spun it around so the locks faced her and unlatched it, slowly and subtly, avoiding noise, and glanced inside without opening it completely.

Then she slammed the case shut.

She wasn't stupid. She had seen all makes and models of money, and this wasn't close to any of them. The case contained the work of a clearly amateur counterfeiter.

"Charlie, what the hell is—?"

But Nia shut her mouth when she noticed the round, black metal hole aimed at her. Charlie stared at Nia, his forearm rested on the table, his fingers coiled around a Smith & Wesson 340PD.

Nia immediately focused on the weapon. It was a tiny, lightweight revolver perfect for concealment, and Charlie was clearly just itching to pull it out. She noticed how he had to make subtle adjustments in his grip to keep the gun steady. She saw his finger hovering slightly away from the trigger, ready to pull it. He was serious.

But that wasn't why she sat still. She was fast enough and skilled enough to reverse the situation with a flick of her wrist. The gun would then face the hunter instead of the hunted.

Then Charlie would gasp…

Then someone would notice, see the gun, and some woman would scream…

Then everyone would run in every direction trying to get away from the danger…

Then chaos would explode and the relaxed atmosphere of the Jazz Hall would give way to a scene akin to the movie *Titanic*, just after everyone realized the ship was sinking.

Marc would be pissed. Cops would case the joint every other night thereafter. The Jazz Hall's attendance would drop dramatically—the shadier clientele would have to find a safer place to hang out. No more complimentary drinks for Nia, if she could even show her face there *at all* after the fiasco.

Play it cool, Nia told herself. *Keep it chill.*

Charlie spoke with a slight chuckle. "I was trying to tell you that you're made. I gave away your location here to those guys who're looking for you. That's why I waited. You know what happens to people who cross the Corp. You know that better than anyone, don't you?"

Nia looked toward Marc, who subtly shook his head. She knew Marc expected her to hold back from attacking Charlie in the middle of Bobby's performance. Nia had to do her best to stay docile until she could get outside and do her thing. But if Charlie decided to attack, nothing would stop things from going crazy.

"Charlie, how could you do me like that? You're the one that got me started in this game! And now you're going around making deals with Vincent, throwing me under the bus?"

Holding the gun steady, Charlie stood up and snatched the bag out of Nia's grip.

"Look, there are some people you just don't screw with. Hudson is one of those people. You've been messing with the big man for too long, and frankly, he's sick of it. His people found me and offered me a big payoff, way bigger than what I could even pretend to hope to get for this weapon on the street. Don't be mad at me. It's business. I go where the money goes, you know that."

Nia Black sighed. "Can't trust nobody. So now what?"

No one seemed to notice what was going on at the table in the front row. The performers were that good; Bobby Styles, blowing skillfully and stylishly into his saxophone with his eyes calmly shut, the poet uttering lyrics in cadence with the music. It didn't hurt that Charlie held his small gun close enough to his body that even someone looking from the side probably couldn't tell what exactly the black object was in the dimly lit hall, and would most likely take it for a cell phone.

For his part, Bobby knew what was up—he couldn't miss it since Nia and Charlie were sitting closer to the stage than anyone else—but he knew not to react. Nia could handle it.

Charlie took advantage of the moment. Holding the bag tightly, he wormed his way out of the hall, shoving his pistol into his pocket. He turned back to Nia with a snide smile.

"I'm going to return this thing. Hudson's guys will be outside waiting for you. Don't keep them, kid."

Nia remained at her table, tightly gripping the tablecloth as she bit her lip. She could have been upon Charlie in a second. But after one bad incident in the past, Marc told her nicely, *chill here whenever you want, just don't start no mess up in here.*

She had to take deep breaths just to remain civil. It was one thing for Charlie to set Nia up. She expected that to happen eventually.

What truly pissed her off was that Nia had nothing to show for what she did but a stack of counterfeit cash.

Outside the club, Charlie made his way to his black sedan, parked some distance down the block. On the way toward his car, Charlie noticed Nia's ride, a powerful and exotic silver sport bike. He checked out the vehicle with a smile.

She's done for, he thought; he considered hotwiring it and keeping it for himself. But he didn't actually know how to ride a motorcycle, so he let that idea go. Just to add insult to injury, he kicked the motorcycle over and roared into laughter as it clanged on the ground.

Another man approached, flinching at the clang of the bike hitting the asphalt. He was a stocky African-American man, his haircut low and sharp, eyes covered in dark shades, wearing a blue suit.

"Vincent Marks," Charlie grinned. "Now, what kind of an asshole wears sunglasses at night?"

"Why did you kick over that motorcycle?"

"What do you care? It's not your bike!"

"Never mind. Give it to me," Vincent retorted, muttering curses under his breath. Charlie did as ordered, placing the satchel in Vincent's hands. The gentleman opened it and examined the contents.

"All right, good. Now, she's in there, right Ross?"

"Just like I said, the girl always comes here after a job. So you've got the weapon, and you've got the girl. Can I get my money and go already?"

Vincent shot a glance toward the parked van behind him and nodded.

Then on cue, a half-dozen men in combat gear, carrying rifles, burst on the scene. Charlie gasped as the soldiers surrounded him and aimed their weapons.

"I thought you'd be smarter than that, Ross," said Vincent. "I mean, you bought some info about the weapon, you sent your best girl to snatch it so you could fence it, on the same day that Mr. Hudson himself—my employer, I might add—is touring the facility. She embarrasses his security and gets away right in front of my boss with one of his most important projects, all because of you. You thought we'd *reward* you for that?"

Charlie snarled. "What the hell, Marks! We had a de—!"

Then a blunt force struck him between the neck and shoulder, and Charlie Ross collapsed to the ground. The soldiers flex-cuffed his wrists.

Another soldier approached Vincent and spoke low. "Media blackout is in effect. Local law enforcement's been ordered to stay out of the district and disregard any calls from this area until we say otherwise. You've got the floor, Mr. Marks."

Vincent nodded. "Good. We have the prototype back. Get everyone ready. Next comes Nia."

NIA BLACK FINALLY calmed down, and allowed Bobby's music to soothe her. Soon, she became less concerned with Charlie's warning, and she leaned forward, returning the gaze from the saxophonist. Nia didn't even wonder how the night would turn out. She had other things on her mind, like whether or not Bobby had been working out. It looked like it.

Bobby snatched his sax from his lips when a deafening BOOM from outside—a gunshot—interrupted the peace. Immediately, frightened patrons leaped from their seats and scrambled for the exit. People were running, shouting, crouching, and cursing in every direction. Then, finding logic among confusion, someone must have realized how foolish it was to go in the same direction that the blast came from, and slowly people settled back down in the center of the club, taking positions under tables and crouching near the bar.

As the other patrons' panic and inquisitiveness killed the calm ambiance, Nia finally stood from her seat, straightening her skirt with a sigh. The noise was the telltale sign; the time for relaxation was over. It was time for action. Like a light switch, her calm instantly became edge, her reflexes got primed and ready, and her mind switched to the battle to come.

She lifted her jacket from the back of her chair, securing a pair of silver-plated semi-automatic pistols within its inner pockets. Throwing the jacket on her shoulders and sliding her arms into her sleeves, she approached the door, the one calm element among the pandemonium of the club as she ambled in the midst of their chaotic behavior. A dozen people took a dozen actions between each one of Nia's soft and graceful steps. She drew one of her pistols as she closed in on the club's main entrance, taking care to keep the people inside the club from seeing it and getting even more excited. Before she

19

could grab the knob, a powerful voice amplified by a bullhorn called her attention.

"NIA BLACK. I KNOW YOU'RE IN THERE. YOU KNOW WHO I AM AND YOU KNOW WHY I'M HERE. COME ON OUT. WE DON'T WANT ANY INNOCENTS HURT."

Nia stopped.

Vincent! So you decided to come after me yourself, she thought. *Damn it.*

"Hold up, Nia."

A man's deep voice caught her attention. Bobby approached Nia from behind, accompanied by Marc.

"Bobby, what's the deal?" asked Nia. "Why are you off the stage? You should keep playing so everybody calms down!"

"I had a feeling something was up," Marc said.

"So why didn't you say anything?"

"You know how it is, Nia," Marc grinned. "That's your thing. I ain't trying to step on your toes. 'Sides, I told you he was acting nervous, didn't I?"

Nia rolled her eyes.

"Go out through the back. I don't want you getting hurt," said Bobby.

Nia smiled. "Hurt? By *them?* That ain't nobody but my old boyfriend. Nice guy and all, but he's in the wrong line of work."

"Look, you're not fooling anyone, Nia," Marc said. "I know you're upset. I saw it in your eyes when you found out Charlie made a deal with Vincent. Hudson's been after you for a while now, and you know he's serious if he sent his number one guy after you, especially given your history with him."

"Vincent ain't the problem," Nia groaned. "It's what Vincent might have brought with him that I'm worried about. He's the only one Hudson lets play with the big toys. Look, I'm going to go out there and draw his attention away from the club. Clear it out or lock it up or whatever you're going to do. Just know it's going to get hot out there."

"Be careful, all right? I want you to make it home tonight," begged Bobby.

Nia snickered. "Why, Bobby, I didn't know you cared."

"Yes you did," Bobby finished as Nia kissed his cheek. She turned and headed for the rear of the club.

"Good luck, girl; you're going to need it," added Marc.

"Hey, you watch yourself out there, you hear me?" yelled Bobby.

Nia blushed as she walked off, overcome with elation. "You boys...I feel so loved."

Soon Nia found her way to the back alleys behind the Jazz Hall and positioned herself between the battered garbage cans, examining the distance between her position and the top of the building. All was quiet save the humble sounds of droplets hitting the ground and the scrambling of stray felines looking for scraps.

The air behind the club contradicted its classy interior with the scent of garbage, urine, and spilled alcohol. Nia's face cringed as she held her breath, the various odors merging into a pungent aroma that bored into her sense of smell like a drill. She stopped moving and listened to the air, picking up the sounds of humming engines and boots grinding into the asphalt.

She locked her focus on the edge of the Jazz Hall's roof. She crouched and sprang upward, grinding her heels in the cinderblock wall behind her, and then springing off of it, launching herself to the gravel-covered surface of the roof. She straightened herself out and stealthily approached the edge of the roof, overlooking the narrow street, and saw several armed soldiers flitting about. They were taking triangular attack positions in front of the club with assault rifles aimed at the door, their jeeps forming a half circle around the bit of street in front of the Jazz Hall, blocking anyone from entering or exiting. Nia shook her head.

Why did it have to be you, Vincent? You're Corp Hudson's head of security. Couldn't you have sent one of your yes-men out here? I don't want to hurt you, but I will if I have to.

Nia glared at Vincent. He had a bullhorn in one hand and a flashlight in the other. He walked about while he spoke into his amplifier, looking left and right, clearly uncertain of Nia's precise location.

"NIA. WE DON'T WANT TO HAVE TO BUST INTO THAT NIGHTCLUB, BUT WE WILL AND YOU KNOW THAT. WE KNOW HOW MUCH YOU LIKE THAT PLACE, THANKS TO YOUR FRIEND, CHARLIE. I WOULD LIKE FOR YOU TO SURRENDER SO IT DOESN'T HAVE TO GET NASTY."

Damn, Nia muttered to herself. *I can't let them hurt any of those innocent— oh shoot; I forgot it was raining. Now my hair's going to get all frizzy. I have to make this quick, or I'll be right back in the hairdresser's tomorrow.*

"Mr. Marks!" one of the soldiers suddenly shouted. "Up there, on the roof! It's her! It's Nia Black!"

Vincent looked up and aimed his flashlight. The soldiers aimed their weapons, all of them staring at Nia as she stood straight up on the roof.

"What's up, Vince?" Nia yelled. "Is this how your boss handles business? You come down here with all these armed soldiers, scaring all the innocent people in the club, barking orders to them like you're still in the military just because a man behind a desk told you to?"

"That man pays my bills," Vincent shouted back. "Not to mention all the other great things he does for this city. I'd gladly follow his orders if it means keeping the peace. But not you; you're just a little girl with guns who never grew up. You refuse to understand that you can't just do whatever you want in this world."

"Yeah, you're always calling me immature and all types of names," Nia griped. "You never showed me any respect at all…no wonder we're not together anymore."

"We're not together anymore because you put this…street life over our relationship. You had me. You didn't need to keep robbing people and blowing things up for pocket change. You wouldn't have had to work a day in your life, but instead you kept causing trouble. And when one of those people you robbed happened to be my boss, I couldn't ignore it."

"I'm not meant to be somebody's little woman, Vincent!" Nia squealed. "You wanted me to become your happy homemaker, but I can't live like that! My freedom is all I have, and I won't let anyone take that away from me, not even you."

"Okay, Nia," Vincent sighed, "This is getting too dramatic, and my men are starting to laugh at our little soap opera, so let's change the subject. Fact is I'm not out here to argue about our relationship right now. I've got orders to bring you to the big man. Now, are you going to come down from that roof peacefully or are we going to have to bring that nightclub down, right out from under you?"

Nia rolled her eyes. "Man, please. I could just go back the way I came behind the building and you'd never even know which way I would go after that. Left, right, into another building, down the sewer, whatever…you blow it up if you want to. It'll be on your boss' hands if you do."

Vincent smirked, and then snapped his finger. Two of his men approached him, dragging a third man along with them.

"You're so worried about innocent people," Vincent said, "What about this guy?"

"Charlie? Do whatever you want to him. He's the whole reason I'm in this mess."

"Well, that's only partially true. Fact is, he didn't want to help us, but it was his life, or yours. We got to him, he begged for his life, we made a deal.

You know how it is. But hey, we have him, we have the weapon you stole, and we have you right here too. So come on down, or your little friend will pay for working with you."

"Give it a rest already!" another voice shouted from inside a van behind Vincent. "She's not buying it!"

"Whoa, wait a minute, Gunner," Vincent began.

Nia started hearing a whirring sound. Her heart started pounding.

"Vincent! Get away from the van!"

Instinctively, Vincent did so. So did his men, dropping the limp Charlie to the ground.

Nia clasped her palms to her mouth, her eyes wide in shock as she watched a screaming torrent of bullets rip through the van from inside. Charlie Ross' body danced in place, horrifically shredded with hellfire.

A boot-clad foot smashed aside the van's bullet-riddled rear doors. A shirtless, muscular man with freshly crew cut, platinum-dyed hair leaped from inside and landed on the street, splashing water mixed with oil and blood as his boots hit the asphalt. He was wearing the pants and boots of a military uniform, but nothing else. But what really caught Nia's attention was what appeared to be a *mini-gun* grafted in place of the man's left forearm, and a bandolier with a seemingly endless strand of bullets wrapped around his bicep, feeding into the weapon.

The man walked toward Vincent, grasped the handle of the mini-gun attachment with his right hand, and raised it toward Nia.

"What the hell do you think you're doing, Gunner? You were brought here only as support," Vincent griped. "You were only supposed to come out if things got out of hand!"

"Things *are* out of hand, Marks," said the man known as Gunner, "You two would be talking back and forth all night if I didn't do something. You can spend all the time you want clearing up your little issues *after* we bring her in."

Nia tightened her fists and flashed teeth. She was seeing red.

Her initial plan was merely to escape. But when she saw what happened to Charlie, how callously Gunner killed him, and how he nearly killed Vincent and who knows who else, Nia needed to make sure he couldn't harm anyone else.

She reached behind her back, coiling her fingers around the two gun handles sitting in her holsters.

"Mr. Marks!" one of the soldiers shouted as he and his comrades aimed their rifles toward the roof. "She's going for her guns!"

"What?" Vincent growled. "No, no, damn it, Nia!"

Vincent turned and ran behind the van as Nia aimed her Baby Eagles at the soldiers down on the street. The soldiers opened fire at Nia, and she raced to the side.

The soldiers' bullets chattered against the roof's edges, leaving holes in the brick and cinderblock, sending plumes of dust and smoke flying into the air.

Not one bullet came anywhere near Nia.

Nia aimed her guns and crossed her arms over one another, firing back at her attackers. Each one of her shots tore through a soldier's leg, arm or shoulder, sending them tumbling to the ground and their rifles skittering away.

She noticed that Gunner stood in the middle of the fray, looking down at the street with his mini-gun arm at rest, as if waiting for something.

Then, as Nia took out Vincent's last guard, Gunner immediately lifted his head and looked toward Nia with a frantic glare in his eyes.

"Now that the peanut gallery is out of the picture, we can have some real fun."

Nia ejected the empty clips from her pistols and reloaded them, raised one of her Baby Eagles and fired. Three shots pounded into Gunner's shoulder, red droplets diluting in puddles of rain on the street. With each shot, Gunner staggered back.

Then he stood straight again.

Nia's eyes went wide. He wasn't hurt at all.

"Yeah," Gunner smiled. "I like it when they put up a fight. See, they gave me something, baby. Something that makes my muscles real dense, and I don't feel much pain either. Something about subduing my nerves or something. Not even you can do anything to me, girl…me, on the other hand, well; I think I can do a whole lot to you."

Hudson…turning people into living weapons, Nia thought, seething. *He just gets more and more disgusting.*

Gunner drew one foam rubber earplug from his pocket and pushed it into his left ear canal. He repeated the action using the same hand—the only hand he *could* do it with, plugging his right ear. He pulled a small trigger on the underside of his gun-arm, and with a subtle whir, the mini-gun's multiple barrels began spinning.

Then he opened fire.

His weapon screamed like a siren and the laser-like shots tore through the stone and brick buildings like a weed whacker.

Nia leaped from the roof, somersaulted in the air and landed on the sidewalk, immediately sprinting out of the way, as Gunner tilted his weapon in her direction and continued to fire, a chain of exploding cars and leaping sparks erupting behind her as she shielded herself from flying debris with her arms. The thundering force of the weapon quivered the air.

"Run, bitch! Run!" Gunner clamored.

Nia circled around Gunner as he traced her with his gunfire, the high-powered bullets from his weapon tearing through everything in their path, from the passenger cars on one side of the street to Vincent's jeeps on the other.

"Gunner!" Vincent screamed. "Not our cars, you idiot!"

"Huh? I can't hear you! The gun's too loud!" Gunner shouted back as his shots shredded more vehicles.

Nia leaped behind an SUV as Gunner's shots chattered on the other side, the vehicle trembling with every bullet.

Nia exhaled. *This ain't never going to end until he blasts my ass into confetti or until I find a way to stop him.*

Gunner turned toward Vincent, his spinning weapon slowly grinding to a halt. "What, man? You want her down, don't you? Just let me do my job!"

"You're shooting our vehicles, you moron," Vincent said. "Let me handle this!"

"Forget it! You didn't bring me here just to watch y'all have your little soap opera. My job is to take the bitch down, and that's what I'm going to do!"

A truck tilted a bit toward Gunner with a tinny squeak. Something hit the top.

Vincent looked up.

"Gunner—!"

But it was too late.

Nia Black pounced from the roof of the SUV.

Gunner saw the sole of a heeled boot speeding toward his face. Before he knew it, with a *whap* his head jerked backward and he slid across the wet asphalt on his bare back, his gun grinding across the ground in a wave of sparks.

He shook his head and looked forward, seeing the blurry image of a small woman charging toward him. He immediately climbed to his feet and wildly swung his gun arm out like a massive club, his arm whooshing through the air. Nia, her heels skidding against the wet asphalt, swung back her spine and bent under his attack like a limbo dancer. The mini-gun sailed just above her lips, the pull of its wake nearly yanking hair from her head. His arm clanged on the ground behind him, the overwhelming momentum of his brazen attack throwing him off-balance.

Nia saw her opening and immediately unleashed an onslaught of strikes to his body. She punched him, kicked him, elbowed him in the jaw, leaped and kicked him, but all she did was knock him around like a bobble-head; he never once lost his balance.

Vincent Marks could only stare with his fists clutched.

When Nia stopped, Gunner turned to her with a sick grin on his face. He didn't even bleed this time.

Nia frowned.

He began to heft the gun-arm again for another melee attack.

She took a breath, stared into Gunner's eyes and winded her foot back.

She swung her foot toward her enemy; it met its mark with a sickening *thump*, and he stopped in his tracks.

Vincent cringed.

Gunner's face went blank as Nia's foot slammed into his groin with the force of a 9-iron, crushing his testicles flat. All use of his appendages failed at once and he stumbled to the ground, every action and every thought muted by a throbbing that spread throughout his body. He'd never felt such pain before. It was as if someone dropped a cinderblock square on his manhood, and he could only beg and plead in his mind for the pain to cease, groaning in misery and clutching himself as best he could.

"I figured you wouldn't have your nerves 'subdued' down *there*," Nia said.

Her face as fierce as a lion, she turned her attention to Gunner's left arm. She raised her pistol, pressed it directly on his forearm just at the breach between his arm and the gun. The heat still present on the barrels sizzled on his skin. Gunner grunted and glared at Nia.

"Oh, you ain't hurt yet," Nia grumbled.

She pulled the trigger!

Gunner howled in agony as the bullets *eviscerated* his flesh, his blood spattering on the ground, raining on the street and Nia's legs.

"You felt *that*, huh?" Nia screamed. "Stupid-ass gave up your humanity to be turned into a walking gun—and the damn experiment didn't even *go through* all the way?!"

Nia sheathed her pistol, took the mini-gun apparatus in both hands and pulled with all her might, pressing her boot into Gunner's chest.

With one solid yank, Nia *tore* the mini-gun from his arm, blood and sinews flailing in the air and spilling on the street.

She took the weapon in both hands, winded up and swung it like a golf club, smashing it into Gunner's head and sending him flying across the street! He crashed back first into a ruined automobile and crumbled to the ground in a bloody pile.

Finally, Nia dropped the mini-gun on the ground and slammed her foot into the barrels, stomping it out of shape until the weapon was nearly unrecognizable.

Nia instantly shot an icy glare at Vincent Marks.

"These are the kind of people you work with? This is what you gave up on us for? This is what you call 'keeping the peace'?"

Vincent stood in silence.

"If anything, I'm the one doing *good* out here," Nia continued. "You're the one who's afraid to see real life."

Nia walked toward her bike and lifted it from the ground. She sighed in relief, realizing the only reason it survived Gunner's onslaught was because someone knocked it over and Gunner's shots passed over it.

"Damn repair shop is going to charge a fortune for these dents, and I ain't even get no money tonight."

Vincent seethed, and pulled out his Beretta.

"Nia. Stop!"

She swung her leg over her bike, started the engine.

"Nia...I'm warning you."

Nia looked Vincent in the eyes, and shook her head. She slapped her goggles on and took off.

Vincent sighed and lowered his gun before turning to his soldiers, who were still squirming on the ground, groaning in agony.

"Pick yourselves up. Let's head back. I've wasted enough time here. At least we got the prototype back."

The men dragged themselves to what vehicles remained after Gunner's brazen attacks. Vincent stood still, watching the road where Nia's bike had long since vanished.

NIA BLACK drove into the backstreet leading to a run-down neighborhood. While the city government made pledges to attack urban blight and clean up the city's look, it was hard not to doubt their sincerity when passing through neighborhoods such as this one.

Condemned and dilapidated houses lined the back streets. Every other corner was a hangout for local hoods and drug dealers. The air reeked of marijuana, gun smoke, and alcohol. The sounds of gunfire and sirens ran rampant. The police could barely make a dent in the criminal element here, filled with people most uncooperative and unfriendly toward law enforcement. While there was a lot to dislike about the area, it also made for a perfect haven for a wanted criminal like Nia.

As she rode through the back streets of the ghetto, ignoring the lewd comments of the many street thugs gawking at her body as she passed them, and greeting the lower-class mothers and children she saw every day, Nia wondered if it would ever change. Those in power too often ignored areas like the inner city in favor of focusing on developing the nicer parts of town and helping the rich get richer. Every time she passed through, she thought of ways she herself could try to make things better.

But those thoughts quickly faded when she finally reached her home, Nia's innate selfishness taking over. As much as she cherished the thrill of the action that filled her nights, she always looked forward to rest and relaxation in her room after a hard night of dealing with her shady affiliates and ruthless enemies. She eagerly anticipated her bed, where she would be able to forget the day's events easily, clearing her mind for the next day, the next mission.

Nia parked her bike behind Bobby's black jeep, stepped off and secured it with a steel chain to protect it from the local hoods; hardly necessary given her reputation, but better safe than sorry, she always thought. She approached the door and entered the modest home where she was renting her room. As she stepped in and quietly shut the door, she could hear yelling from upstairs, where Bobby and his girlfriend, Nia's landlord, lived.

Uh oh. Sounds like trouble in paradise, again... Nia thought with a groan. *Those two stay arguing.*

It all started a year ago.

After Nia Black broke up with Vincent Marks, she moved out of his apartment and sought a steady home. She spent many nights bouncing from motel to motel, but soon grew tired of it.

Nia could not obtain an apartment the conventional way; she was a wanted criminal. She couldn't risk any background investigations or credit checks. What Nia needed was someone she could trust, someone who would need her as much as she needed a place to stay.

But her search led nowhere that day. She was tired and needed to relax. She happened upon the Jazz Hall. Acting on impulse, she stopped her bike and walked inside.

Dozens of tables filled the hall, yet less than half of the seats were occupied. It was unusually quiet for a nightclub. The few patrons in attendance sat quietly, sipping their drinks, muttering amongst themselves as barely noticeable instrumental jazz tunes filled the air.

Nia looked toward the far end of the hall and saw a gorgeous man playing a saxophone on stage.

His music was generic and uninspired. The look upon his face said he didn't want to be there.

She sighed, took a seat, and ordered a drink.

Then the musician glanced at Nia, and his face lit up.

Nia watched his eyes flow across her body like a scanner. His cheeks expanded and his grip tightened on the saxophone's keys. It was as if an all-new music track was suddenly downloaded into his brain. The monotone atmosphere livened up. Customers began to rock their heads to the increased fervor of the music, some even rising from their seats to sway their hips in rhythm. People who overheard the music from outside came in to investigate. Within two hours, the Jazz Hall was packed. The bartender couldn't keep up with the drink orders. The calm atmosphere became merry; a veritable celebration.

Closing time fast approached, and Nia got ready to leave. However, she figured she'd at least introduce herself to the suddenly gifted musician.

The two met after the club closed, and they talked for an hour, became fast friends.

He told her his name was Robert Styles, but everyone called him 'Bobby'. Jazz music was all he knew; he opened the Jazz Hall as a way to express himself to the people. But the club wasn't cost-effective enough—especially lately—to win the battle against the expenses he took on when he and his girlfriend moved into her parents' old house.

He couldn't believe what happened when he laid eyes on Nia. At least that's what he told her. He said there was something about her that just made him want to play; ignoring all the sheet music he studied, expressing himself from the heart.

Nia thought he was simply blowing smoke, trying to get in her pants.

Bobby suddenly mentioned that he and Charlene, his girlfriend and the woman who legally owned their house, were planning to rent out a room. Bobby's focus was on the club; his girlfriend was a nurse who did as much overtime as she could, and they still needed help. It was their last resort to get some extra cash.

Nia smiled an inviting grin. It wasn't long before she was following Bobby's black jeep on her bike, flying through the back streets of until they pulled up to a modest home deep in the inner city.

The next thing Nia knew she was shaking hands with Charlene Wright; tall, and slender, with round, worrying eyes and a sharp tongue. She was a tough, mature woman who'd seen a lot in her lifetime; Nia could tell. She wondered how she must have looked to Charlene, Nia's skin-tight half-top and hip-hugging jeans barely able to contain her curves.

And there was Bobby, presenting Nia like an adorable stray cat he just couldn't bear to leave outside.

Charlene was ready to send Nia packing on first sight. Nia could see it in her eyes.

Nia imagined what Charlene must have been thinking: some short, stocky young thing parading around the house in T-shirts and panties around *her man* while she was at the nursing home cleaning up after the elderly; that was the last thing she needed to be worrying about.

So Nia reacted. She dug deep in her pocket and drew enough cash to cover three months of the rent Charlene asked for.

The silence seemed to last for an eternity after that. Then Charlene smiled. And Nia moved in.

She stayed out of their business and went about her own. In fact, Nia was rarely ever there at all, except early in the morning when she slept. But lately, Nia noticed that whenever she *was* home, she heard Charlene's paranoid assertions and accusations more and more often, along with Bobby's *extremely* patient attempts to calm her down. Charlene accused Bobby of staying out late, spending time with 'groupies', sometimes even hinting that Nia herself was one of them.

Nia found the whole scenario hilarious. She found Charlene hilarious. In Nia's opinion, Charlene was the average pain-in-the-neck, over-attached

34

girlfriend who would end up ending her own relationship with her own bad attitude before any outsider had a chance to come between them.

Nia entered her room, a den of thick plaster walls containing naught but a dresser, a television, a twin bed, a small washroom, and a lamp. She overheard voices from above.

"Bobby, we *are* having this conversation! Don't you dare ignore me! I'm talking to you!"

That's what makes people call us bitches, Nia thought with a sigh. She was able to hear the explosive exchange above her quite clearly; due in no small part to Charlene's loud, grating voice. Nia was impressed because Bobby managed to stay relaxed under fire from Charlene's ranting even after the violence outside the club. *If that was me,* Nia thought, *Charlene would have caught an open-handed slap in the mouth.*

"Charlene, I'm sick of this. I just got home from a gig; there was shooting all over the joint…you ain't even asked me if I'm all right or nothing. Soon as I walk in the house, nag, nag, nag…"

"She was there, wasn't she? Answer me!"

"Why? What difference does it make?"

"Why do you have lipstick on you? Why is she always at your gigs when I have to work?"

"Look, she does her own thing. I ain't tell her to come! It's not like I decide what nights I'm going to perform! That's Marc's call now, you know that!"

"Is she even paying the rent? You act like you don't know where she works, but she always got the rent, right? Or are you just saying that because she's paying you some *other* kind of way?"

"Charlene, kill that noise," Bobby muttered softly with added bass. "You're the only one I—"

"Don't try that smooth shit with me…you spend more time talking to her than you do me! You see her every night while I'm waiting for your behind to come home. I think she's the one blowing your saxophone!"

"'Lene, I'm going to bed. You done lost your mind. Ain't you got to go to work or something?"

Silence for a moment.

"Yeah, whatever. You lucky I need this overtime."

Nia shook her head, listening to heavy footsteps thumping around above her. She sighed again and slid out of her skirt, pantyhose, and top, changing into an oversized T-shirt. Nia dimmed her lamp until its white light became a soft tan glow. She lit two sticks of incense, inhaling the soothing essence and relaxed with a deep breath. Sliding open a drawer near her mattress, she fished out a small box and emptied its contents in her palm. One round at a time, she reloaded her pistols, placing them under her mattress before resting her head on a pillow. She switched off her lamp and lay on her bed, eyes wide as Charlene's hollering continued.

An hour passed. Nia curled up inside her comforter, her eyes wide open. She stared out the window at the starry night sky and listened to the creaking of the house settling and crickets flitting about outside. Silence had since fallen over the room above. Nia let out a deep exhale.

About time Charlene went to work!

The floorboards creaked just outside her door, followed by a subtle knock. Nia quickly threw aside her blanket and opened the door without turning on the light, allowing her visitor to enter.

"Finally. I was getting sick of waiting."

"I had to make sure she was out," he muttered back. "You know how hard it is to play when you sit in the club looking all good like that? I was thinking about you all day."

"How hard do I make it, baby?" Nia whispered, stroking Bobby between his legs. "Ooh, I see…"

"Nice shirt," he whispered.

"You should like it," Nia whispered back. "It's one of yours. You left it in here the other night. I almost put it in with my laundry. Charlene would've had a fit."

"Let me help you with that," he muttered seductively, lifting the T-shirt off her, her breasts tumbling down from under the shirt and bounding against his chest. He reached behind Nia's neck, moving aside her hair and fumbling for the lock that secured her pendant.

Nia grasped his wrists and pulled his hands away. Bobby groaned.

"You know I never take off my mom's pendant," Nia said. "It's the only thing I have of hers. It's what keeps me going…"

"I'm just sick of the damn thing scratching me up and getting tangled in your hair. But if you gotta keep it on, keep it on, I guess."

"I'm just not trying to lose it. But, let's not get off the subject," Nia said softly, wrapping her arms around Bobby while kissing him on his face and neck.

Their lips came together; their tongues dancing as their hands slowly stroked every inch of the other's skin. Nia slid her fingers across his steely muscles, stroking his bulging pectorals, his shoulders, his biceps and triceps. She wrapped her hands around Bobby's wrists and slowly guided his palms down from the sides of her face, across the curvature of her breasts and around her taut nipples, down past her abdomen as they reached their destination in front of her thong. Bobby tunneled his fingers within her panties and between her legs. He pressed against her with his left hand and took hold of Nia's butt with his right. Nia placed her hand on Bobby's head and gently pressed down, easing him into a crouching position, his hands sliding down across her legs with her panties in tow.

Nia crossed her fingers against the back of Bobby's neck as his hand pressed against her back. Lifting her and laying her upon the bed, Bobby smiled at Nia as he looked upon the curvaceous plane of her body from the bottom up. Nia returned his smile, glaring as the moonlight glinted of every curve of his muscle mass as she watched his mouth approach her, his hands slowly parting her legs. Bobby's soft, hot breath caressed her warmth, which was now wet with anticipation. He moved gently through her perfectly trimmed hair with his tongue to expose her for his pleasure.

She hissed. A rush of excitement and pleasure shot from between her legs throughout her body as Bobby's tongue massaged her. Nia's eyes rolled back and she writhed in glee as Bobby's head swerved back and forth between her legs, his tongue moving slowly, then quickly, with long strokes and short darts. Every movement brought her more pleasure than the last. Even the subtlest of motion from Bobby shot through her body like a tidal wave of ecstasy, a rush of euphoria stimulating every nerve as she thrashed about like a snake, moaning and groaning.

Nia sat up and rubbed her fingers against Bobby's strapping back muscles, sliding her fingers across the undulations of his body, her breathing a rapid squeal as Bobby pressed his tongue deeper between her legs.

Heaving and practically gasping for air, she threw her head back again. Bobby climbed on the bed with her as she gently parted her thighs. Nia reached across to touch and stroke Bobby's rigid manhood as it trembled in full erection. With her other hand, Nia drew a condom from between her mattress and bed frame. Grinning in excitement, Nia rolled the condom along until it was in place, rubbed her fingers up and down from the head down and smoothly guided Bobby inside of her.

Nia tightly shut her eyes and inhaled sharply as Bobby thrust forward. He wrapped his arms around Nia's back, rolling over until she straddled him. Bobby stared in joy at Nia's beauty, clawing her hips and butt as she rocked her hips back and forth, her breasts swinging around as she bounced up and down upon him using the bed as a spring as he slid in and out of her. She shut her eyes and her mouth opened gently, one hand feverishly flying through her hair as the other pressed on Bobby's torso, her soft breaths escalating into full-on screams of ecstasy as she contorted about. Minutes later he too climaxed, groaning with pleasure, satisfied he had pleased her.

The two collapsed into a passionate embrace, their limbs intertwining as their breaths slowed to a satiated pace.

Nia's eyelids slowly slid apart, her room fading into a blurry view around her. She stroked Bobby's forearm, which was tightly wrapped around her, his hand clawing her breast as he pulled her deeply into his embrace. She could feel every up and down of his gentle, heavy breathing as he slept soundly.

She was still trembling from the pleasure. Nia climbed out of Bobby's grip and forced herself to sit up, peering at her alarm clock.

5:02…damn, this boy better get out of here.

Nia prepared to do what she did every time they got together, what she hated to do. She had to wake Bobby up and shoo him out. But waking such a sound sleeper out of a state of total comfort wasn't what bothered her most about it.

Nothing felt better to Nia than having Bobby's muscular, chocolate body clutching hers all night long. Nia was more than capable of taking care of herself, but something about Bobby's arms coiling around her in the night gave her a sense of security that she hadn't known in a long time; like no matter what happened, she would be all right. It agonized Nia to accept that Bobby would leave her alone to give that warmth, that strength—that *love*—to someone else, someone who she felt didn't appreciate him and certainly didn't deserve him.

"Bobby," she gently shook Bobby's shoulder. "Bobby, wake up. You need to get back in your bed."

He grumbled incoherently. His body trembled slightly; he let out a pleasant moan. Then he started to snore.

"Bobby, wake up!" Nia shook him harder. "Baby, it's five o'clock."

Bobby finally stirred and twisted until he could see behind himself, glaring at the piercing red digital display of Nia's electronic alarm clock through his blurred, lethargic vision. With an irritated grunt, he lifted himself out of bed and searched for his clothes. He didn't want to leave the warm spot he nestled into bed any more than Nia wanted him to get up.

"You know, she's not stupid. Sooner or later she's going to catch you. What you gonna do if she comes home early?"

"That woman sleeps like the dead when she gets in. You could crash your bike into the front door and she wouldn't even notice."

Nia smiled, sprawling herself across his back and wrapping her arms around him, resting her chin on his shoulder. "By the way, what's up with the deal you got going with Marc? How long has he been running the club now?"

"You know how Marc came through and helped me keep the club open with that loan, right? For a while I've been trying to buy my share of the club back from him, you know what I mean, saving up my money and what not. I mean, Marc's cool and all, but he's the one in control of my club. We have an argument one day and he could—legally—toss me out."

"Bobby, if you need some help with money…"

"Nah, girl," Bobby raised his hands. "I know you got it like that, but if I take it from you, I'll never feel like the club is mine, know what I mean? But check this—I've got some producers coming through the club in a couple of days. They're looking to hook me up with a record deal for my jazz music. If everything goes the way I hope, I'll have way more than what I need to pay Marc off and get my club back!"

"Damn, Bobby! You're about to blow up!" Nia cheered. "You're going to be making as much money as I do in a minute!"

"Oh, damn!" Bobby suddenly flinched as if he'd just been hit. "Speaking of money…Marc told me to give you a message earlier. You got a call from somebody called 'Double-D'."

Nia tore herself away from him. "You telling me this now?! It could have been important! …All right, I gotta call him."

"Sorry; I didn't get a chance to tell you before! You were out there having target practice or something."

Nia sat up in her bed, picked up the landline phone and rapidly dialed a number. After three rings, a lady's voice answered the phone.

"Darien Drakonis' office. It's after business hours. Who's calling?"

Nia rolled her eyes. "Who else calls at this time in the morning, Xara? It's me. Didn't Double-D want me for something?"

A pause. "Yes, of course. We thought you were unavailable. We were going to contact one of your competitors."

"Well I am available. I'm always available for pretty boy, you know that. Not like the way you're available though."

"We need you to do something for us. Will you meet with us on the waterfront?"

"Yeah, sure."

"Immediately?"

"'Immediately?'" Nia repeated. "Like, right now?"

"That is what 'immediately' means, yes."

"It's like five o'clock in the morning. You know I don't like coming outside in the morning."

"Mr. Drakonis will make it worth your while. He's been wanting to meet you for some time now."

"Oh, for real? He's coming out himself?" Nia's face lit up. "I've always wanted to meet him face-to-face too. I like knowing exactly where my money comes from."

"Meet who?" Bobby grunted. Nia shushed him with her hand.

"Then you'll get your wish. He has something he wishes to impart to you personally. See you soon, Miss Black."

The line clicked.

"Damn! It's all early and shit..." She hung up the receiver and laid back on Bobby's chest. He wrapped his arms around her again, exploiting another opportunity to touch her body. Nia folded her arms atop Bobby's hands, taking comfort in his embrace.

"Yo, who is that guy? You got a thing for him or something?" Bobby inquired.

Nia sighed. "It ain't like that. Darien Drakonis is the vice president of this company called Drakonis, Inc. They're kind of like Corp Hudson, but they're not psychos turning people into machines. They deal with computers and stuff. Of course, they got all sorts of dirty deals on the side just like everybody else. They're just another bunch of clients to me."

"The way you was talking about that boy, it ain't sound like he's just another client. I was starting to wonder if I had some competition up in here..."

"Darien's just nice, that's all. He doesn't bullshit me like other people try to do," Nia laughed. "Anyway, you better hurry up and get out of here before your girl gets home and notices your big sexy body ain't in that bed."

"Right, right," Bobby placed a hand upon Nia's cheek, staring, mesmerized in her eyes. She grasped Bobby's shoulders and pulled him close to give him another kiss.

"You be careful, all right?"

"Bobby, sweetheart, I'm always careful. Look what I have to come home to," Nia smiled as she stroked his muscular body. "Now get your ass back in your bed!"

Bobby soon dressed and stealthily left Nia's room. He crept up the stairs, nary making a sound as he tiptoed across the bare wooden floors. He was unsure how long Charlene might have been gone.

When he reached his bedroom, he heard the front door close tight. Bobby immediately jumped in the bathroom and turned on the shower.

Then Charlene, groggy and barely coherent, stepped inside the bathroom wearing her nursing scrubs. She walked stiffly with her eyes almost shut; it was a hard night at the nursing home, even when she worked fewer hours. Noticing the shower running, she drew back the curtain, catching Bobby scouring his butt.

"Yo, what are you doing?!" Bobby flinched from the cold blast of air that rolled over him. "You're gonna make me splash water all over the floor!"

Charlene rubbed her eyes once again, and then looked directly into Bobby's eyes. "Why are you up so early? Trying to get those hoochies' crabs off?"

"You're funny," Bobby turned around, back to his shower. "No, I couldn't sleep, so I figured I'd get an early start on fixing those shingles you keep bugging me about."

"Oh," Charlene's eyebrows furrowed as she swiftly yanked the shower curtain closed. "Whatever…"

AFTER A QUICK SHOWER, Nia searched her drawer for an outfit. She selected a black leather sleeveless top and matching pants, donned a silver chain belt and picked out a pair of matching leather boots. Finishing by styling her hair as best she could with a brush and curling iron, she grabbed her equipment, placing it inside of a plush teddy bear backpack. She threw on her leather jacket and the backpack, left the room, locked it behind her and hopped on her sport bike, ready for her meeting with Darien Drakonis.

Speeding southward, Nia came to a stop at an intersection, sitting behind numerous tractor-trailers as the light turned red.

She sighed. *This light takes forever to change.*

Nia glanced to the side and looked at a diner with a scant few customers sitting inside partaking in breakfast. One man was sitting by the window, facing away, his broad shoulders and chiseled features catching Nia's eye.

Hmm. Not bad... she thought. *Wonder what he looks like from the front.*

The man must have felt the eyes upon him, because he looked over his shoulder a few moments later, his eyes meeting with Nia.

She smiled. *Cute...*

The man gasped as he took in the sight of the young woman sitting on the rumbling motorcycle. Nia expected a smile.

But when he jumped to his feet and turned to face her, it was Nia's turn to gasp.

He had a shiny badge affixed to his chest.

Nia rolled her eyes. *Here we go.*

She watched as the police officer scrambled from his seat, leaving his coffee and donut behind and slapping his partner on the shoulder, pointing toward Nia.

Nia glanced at the traffic light. *Still red.*

The two raced for the exit door of the diner. They pulled out their side arms and yelled at her.

Screw it...

Nia throttled her bike and sped around the 18-wheeler in front of her, speeding off, cutting between two passing cars like an arrow.

It didn't take long before Nia heard sirens behind her.

The cops gave chase, hollering, one radioing for backup while the other incessantly demanded Nia turn off her engine and pull over.

She rolled her eyes at the thought.

As she swerved between two more sedans and rounded a corner, she realized that she needed to end this chase as quickly as possible. She couldn't lead them to Darien Drakonis...not if she ever wanted to do any work for him again.

Then she saw it—her ticket out.

At the end of an upcoming intersection, a large oil truck was backing toward a house, no doubt preparing to pump oil into a residential heating unit. The driver climbed out and trotted toward the house's front door.

Nia whipped out one of her Baby Eagles as her bike screamed toward the cross-section of the street.

She fired two shots and hit the gas tank of the truck, and it erupted into flames as it leaped off the street. The driver cringed in fright and raced away from the inferno.

The oil truck fell back down to earth an instant after Nia slashed through the flames, a burning wall of metal crashing directly in front of the police car. The officer behind the wheel floored the brake and the car power-slid to the side, stopping short of the smoldering metal of the oil truck.

The essence of flames and oil slowly wafted from Nia's senses as she flew further away from the scene.

Now it's off to the pier...time to get paid. That's how I like to start my day!

Nia reached the waterfront and parked, amid the guttural horns of tugboats and ocean liners. The rain of the previous night left a dense fog over the venue and the morning air was heavy and moist.

Nia arrived a few minutes early, yet several people awaited her, standing near two parked black sedans with tinted windows. As she turned off the bike and pressed her feet to the ground, her boots clacked on the cobblestone road.

Nia immediately recognized the lone woman in the group as Xara St. Croix, her contact within Drakonis Inc. She was a lean, athletic woman with a straight and narrow face, her long, shiny auburn hair complementing her light brown skin and dark brown suit. Her professional attire did little to disguise the fact that she had the spirit and inclination of a fighter, and was just as dangerous as the wide-standing, muscular bodyguards in black suits and sunglasses that stood around her like pillars, if not more.

There was a tall, Puerto Rican man in glasses standing among the group, observing quietly. Nia didn't recognize him, and he didn't look like a bodyguard. But Nia's attention went elsewhere when a striking albino man wearing a cashmere turtleneck sweater and slacks emerged from behind the bodyguards, outstretching a hand in Nia's direction.

All eyes fell on him like he was the man of the hour.

"Nia Black," said the handsome young man. "It's nice to finally meet you in person. I'm Darien Drakonis."

"I know," Nia said with a smile, but without accepting his hand. "You're either on TV or in the paper or on the internet every day for some reason or another. They keep talking about the succession like your father's on his deathbed."

"It's because I'm the public face of the company now," Darien explained, withdrawing his hand. "Though my father is still in complete control of Drakonis Incorporated and I'm little more than a figurehead, he thinks I represent a fresh young perspective that makes our business partners more comfortable. The media, of course, runs with it and wants the business world to believe I'm trying to replace him. Nothing could be further from the truth."

"So tell me, what's so important that you came out here yourself? You sure you want to risk your adoring public seeing you with a dangerous girl like me?" Nia said, folding her arms and balancing on her hip, her body forming an elegant S-curve.

Darien smiled. "So beautiful. I thought it was long overdue for us to meet face-to-face, since you have done so much fine work for us in the past."

A glint of sunlight started to eat through the fog, cutting across the sky, reminding Nia that time was ticking forward.

"Enough with the compliments. I'm not a big fan of being outside during the day, so what's up?"

"It's about Corp Hudson, naturally. As you know, Drakonis sees them as something of a rival, though Hudson is admittedly so large and powerful that we are nothing more than mosquitoes compared to them. I'm hoping to shift things in our favor. I need you to break into the Hallegan security firm. Xara?"

Xara immediately stepped forward, drawing a rolled up paper from inside her jacket. She outstretched it on the hood of one of the sedans and Nia leaned over, peering at it.

It was a printout of a floor layout, with exits, elevators and the like clearly marked.

"This is the 37th floor of the Hallegan building, where their security department monitors the workstations of the employees in the other parts of the building. We need you to retrieve a disc from…"

Darien pointed out a room in the center of the floor.

"This room. Hallegan is developing a new security system for Corp Hudson. They deal in defense contracting, but a new form of electronic security system encroaches on our market. We can't allow the Corp to become a monopoly and drive us out of business. Therefore, you breach Hallegan and remove their main systems disc, and Hallegan will have to spend their time and resources recovering their own system before they can be trusted to make something for Hudson. Does that make sense?"

Nia rolled her eyes. "Get in there, take a disc, and get out, right? Okay. You got my money?"

Darien looked back at one of the bodyguards and nodded his head. As if a switch on his back were pressed, the bodyguard immediately stepped forward and drew a metal clip from his jacket, several crisp hundred dollar bills clasped together.

"That's double the usual fee," Darien said with a smile. "Consider it a bonus because you have made my day already, just by being here and looking so lovely."

"You better be careful," Nia giggled, counting the money. "Ain't that your girl right there?"

"Oh, Xara knows I'm a hopeless flirt. But she also knows she's the only one for me. Don't you, Xara?"

Xara stood still, unmoved.

Darien's face fell. "Oh well. We haven't had breakfast yet...maybe that's making her feel down. With that, we should be going. Meet with Xara in the usual place with the item and we will have more work for you."

Nia wrapped up the blueprints, folded the poster into a neat little square and placed it inside of her inside pocket, before turning toward her bike.

"Thanks, Double-D. Nice meeting you and all that. See you later!"

She leaped upon her motorcycle and drove off.

Darien turned toward his sedan. One of the bodyguards opened the rear driver's side door for him, he sat inside. The Puerto Rican man in glasses climbed in the rear passenger-side door, sitting next to Darien Drakonis.

"Thank you," he said, handing Darien a digital tablet. "The person you were looking for, the one with that item you're interested in…everything we know about her is in here."

"Finally…I can't say I'm not reluctant to go through with this, but my treasure will be worth the loss. It's been a pleasure doing business with you, Mr. Alvarez," Darien said, shaking his hand. "Good luck."

"To you as well, Mr. Drakonis."

The Puerto Rican climbed out of the sedan and backed away as they drove off. He drew his cell phone and walked toward a sporty blue coupe parked some distance away.

AT DAYBREAK, once empty roadways slowly filled with roaming vehicles, and people embarked upon the daily metropolitan ritual of school and business commutes.

Nia Black swerved around cars and trucks on her bike, enjoying the advantages of a motorcycle as she again became withdrawn by her thoughts.

It'd be real messed up if Charlene tossed that boy out. If it wasn't for Bobby, I don't know where I would have ended up living. I was lucky to meet him. He doesn't care what I do, as long as the bills are paid. But I wish he wasn't with that skinny, irritating-ass bitch. He needs to just tell her the truth and be out…with me. He know he'd rather have all this plushy body next to him every night instead of that skin-and-bones chick.

Nia chuckled to herself when she thought about Charlene. Nia was certain Charlene felt a twinge of envy every time she compared herself to Nia, wondering how Bobby sized up the two of them in his mind. Between Nia and Charlene was a powder keg of animosity, and there was no telling when it would finally reach critical mass.

Or was there?

When Nia finally returned home, the sound of plastic crashing against a hardwood floor jerked her attention to a second-story window of the house, the window of her landlord's bedroom. Charlene and Bobby were visible through the window, darting back and forth, and objects flailing through the air. Many other neighbors had gathered in front of their home as spectators of yet another of their fierce arguments, the air heavy with Charlene's screaming voice. This time, she was loud enough that Nia didn't even have to enter the house to hear. Her heart jumped when she heard

Charlene's words, the warning Nia gave Bobby after their rendezvous ringing dangerously true.

"Tell me you weren't in her room last night! Go ahead and lie!" hollered Charlene. "Tell me you're not *fucking* that skank! I knew you were in her room last night when I caught you showering her funk off of you this morning. You don't ever get up that early!"

Damn, Nia thought. *I told that boy she ain't stupid…*

"Listen to me, Charlene," responded Bobby, his voice trembling. "You got it all wrong…"

"No, *you* got it wrong, thinking you're going to sit up in *my* house and play me…"

Uh oh, Nia thought, racing into the house. *This is getting serious…she's about to kick his ass out—and that means I'd be out too!*

Nia crept into Bobby and Charlene's room and immediately ducked as a vase shattered into a thousand shards against the wall near the bedroom door.

She calmly picked up the shards of broken pottery as she looked around. Apparently, the two were going at it for quite some time. Bobby's clothes had been tossed from the drawers to the floor, and several objects littered the floor including broken drink glasses, a clock and his pillows.

"And what you want, *ho*?" Charlene snapped toward Nia, staring tear-drenched daggers at her at first sight. "You want him, your broke ass can have him. Hope you're happy together living on the damn street, 'cause you're both getting the hell out of here!"

"Charlene, why you trippin'?!" Bobby gasped. "I told you why I got up so early!"

"Yeah, I remember what you said; your punk ass was too scared to even look me in my face while you were telling me that shit," Charlene stammered.

Bobby suddenly turned away from Charlene to Nia with a look that said *follow my lead.*

"Where were you last night, Nia? I was worried when you didn't come home; I checked your room but you weren't there."

"...I had to go see my boyfriend," Nia answered. "He called me last night, talking about how he got into a fight with his brother again, and I had to break it up. That boy is such a punk..."

"Yeah, whatever," Charlene muttered, rubbing her eyes. She was so certain Bobby betrayed her that she couldn't fight her tears. But Nia herself had never shown animosity or clear dishonesty toward her. Charlene didn't know what to think. She said the first thing that entered her mind.

"Where's my rent at? I want to see it!"

"Here," Nia immediately drew five hundred dollars from her jacket pocket—from the cash she'd just gotten from Darien—and gently placed it in Charlene's hand with a slow smile, belying her repressed frustration.

"Happy? That's for this month and next."

Charlene stared in shock at the crisp bills sitting in her palm. Usually, Bobby collected Nia's rent. At least that's what he'd told her.

Nia figured Charlene was anticipating a geyser of excuses about how she had to wait until the weekend or the first of the month or some other date to give her any money, and must have been shocked to see Nia draw so much cash on demand.

"Where the hell did you get all this from?" Charlene gasped. "Where did she get this, Bobby? Did you give this to her just to shut me up?!"

"Bobby! You ain't told her what I do?" Nia laughed, continuing her façade. "No wonder she's all agitated! She probably thinks you're letting me stay here for free and we're messing around behind her back. People get suspicious when you keep things to yourself, Bob. You gotta be clear about these things."

Bobby's eyebrows shot up.

52

Nia turned to Charlene. "Girl, I'm a dancer. You can't tell? I mean, I don't get naked, but the little bit I do wear shows enough to pay the bills, you know what I'm saying?"

Nia chuckled and initiated a mock dance routine. She laced her fingers together, outstretched her arms as if she were grasping a pole, and stuck her butt out, pivoting her hips about in a half circle. She hummed the chorus of one of her favorite R&B songs for good measure.

Charlene stared at her, still furious with watery eyes and quivering lips.

"You know, I didn't want to tell you because you know how some sisters get about that sort of thing," Nia went on. "'Oh, she's a dancer; she must be some kind of ho; going to have all types of nasty-ass men up in here', but trust me, it ain't like that. I always thought you knew though, especially after all the money I gave you when we first met. I'm surprised Bobby never told you. That's not something I would keep from somebody *I* was with."

Bobby gave Nia a sour look.

Charlene continued to wipe her tears as Nia approached, placing a hand on her shoulder in a gesture of friendliness.

"You were with your boyfriend last night?" Charlene muttered, looking Nia in the eyes.

"Come on now, we're sisters, right?" Nia said, returning her stare. "You got yourself a good man there. I'm definitely not that kind of girl that looks to mess up somebody's relationship, especially after everything you and Bobby have done for me."

Then Nia glanced at Bobby and rolled her eyes dispassionately with a look that hinged on disgust. "I mean, Bobby's all right and all, but compared to *my* man ...girl, please! You ain't got a thing to worry about. Trust."

Charlene turned to Bobby, whose hands burrowed in his pockets, his head hanging like a scolded child. Charlene's mood finally lightened.

"I'm sorry, Bobby."

"It's cool, you had your reasons, I guess," Bobby muttered, reaching over and kissing her upon the cheek. "I forgive you, though. Let's clean this room up."

Nia folded her arms, turned and left the room, marching down the steps.

That eye contact stuff only works on nervous people, girlfriend. I'm so used to lying it's not even funny.

Nia returned to her own room, looking at the clock.

It's only like seven-thirty...why do people like getting up so early? I might as well go back to sleep. What time does Charlene go to work again? Bobby needs to give me some attention for what I just did for his ass...

Nia Black was a night person. It had to be quite a job to get her to go out in the morning. It took a great deal to get her to rescind her rule about daylight, but that didn't stop her from hating it. Daytime was her time to sleep, to stay invisible.

Nia kicked off her boots, turned on her television and flopped on the bed as the morning news started. Unable to doze off immediately, she figured she'd allow daytime television to bore her into lethargy.

"GOOD MORNING. THIS IS MIKE MORRISON REPORTING. THIS ONCE BEAUTIFUL AND PEACEFUL MORNING ERUPTED IN ABSOLUTE CHAOS HERE IN THE SOUTHWEST SECTION OF THE CITY," said the newscaster.

Nia smiled, remembering the brief police chase.

Ooh, Nia thought with a giggle. *There's my work. I sometimes even amaze myself with how good I am! Go, Nia! Go, Nia!*

"AND THIS EVENT ENDED IN TRAGEDY AS WELL," continued the news. "JANE SIMON IS ON LOCATION. JANE?"

Tragedy? What the...

The screen switched to a close up of the same street Nia sped past on her bike on before shooting the oil truck. The camera swept across the disaster area until a female reporter panned into view, turning away from the site of the blast.

"WHEN THE OIL TRUCK EXPLODED, THE FLAMES SPREAD FROM THE STREET TO MANY NEARBY HOMES. WHILE MOST OF THE RESIDENTS WERE AWAY, SOME WERE OCCUPIED. UNFORTUNATELY, SOME OF THEM SUFFERED SEVERE BURNS AND SMOKE INHALATION."

Nia sat up in her bed. *I...nobody was anywhere near that truck...I made sure...*

Nia shot to her feet, her eyes quivering as she stared at the television, watching as the helicopter-bound camera swung around the sorry pile of crumbled bricks and smoldering wood from above. She thought of how it must have felt to the people inside the homes; to be minding their business at one moment, the walls around them shattering into flames the next...

Nia did her best to keep innocent people out of her crosshairs. Abiding by that rule was her way of justifying her actions and maintaining a sense of conscience during her criminal activities. As long as the only damage came to her target's financial holdings, it was no big deal.

But this time, she was in too much of a hurry—only thinking of herself, only about doing whatever it took to keep being paid.

What if they end up permanently disabled? What if they die? What if they were only kids, their lives just getting started? Nia couldn't handle the thought of her actions cutting some good person's life short, especially people no older than she, and the notion scared her to death.

At that moment, for the first time ever, Nia began to doubt herself.

Nia quickly shoved her feet back into her boots and charged for the door, grabbing only her key chain, leaving her phone and her weapons behind. She hopped on her vehicle and roared away from the house quickly, her bike's engine growling louder and more guttural than ever. The street shook as her engine deafened everything else, setting off car alarms as her bike rumbled down the block.

The Jazz Hall was only open after 8 p.m. During the early morning hours, Marc resided alone in an apartment on the second floor of the building. He passed the time by peacefully preparing his club for the patrons who would flood in for the evening, cleaning the bar and organizing his selection of drinks in the dark atmosphere. It was outlandish to expect any sort of visitors in the dawn hours. No wonder he was startled when he heard a motorcycle engine roaring and gaining in volume until the noise ceased, directly outside the door of his club.

Nia reached the Jazz Hall in record time and charged inside, headed for the bar. Marc was cleaning the shot glasses with a napkin. He glanced at Nia with a surprised look when she stepped inside; the bright corridor of sunlight flowing through the doorway, nearly blinding Marc, whose eyes had long since adjusted to the dimly lit interior.

"What are you doing here this time of day? I thought you only came out at night," said Marc, squinting.

"I need to talk to somebody."

"Okay, I'm here. What's up, sweetheart?"

"Something's bothering me. You know how I usually get when I do my thing, most of the time, I'm loving it. But this time was different. You know about that oil truck explosion? That was me. I was trying to get away from the cops...I needed a way to get them off me, and I...people got hurt because of me."

"Did they die?"

"The news said they were in critical condition or something," Nia stammered. "I'm sure they'll be okay, I think they will. I mean..."

"Okay then, no harm done, right?" Marc said, his apathy clear in the cold silence that followed.

Nia didn't look convinced. "I don't feel right about hurting innocent people. I got too hasty. It ain't my thing to involve people who ain't got nothing to do with it."

"So what, you're saying you care about somebody other than Nia Black now?" Marc looked away as he set his glasses neatly on the racks below the bar. "What's next, going out to save people like a super hero or something?"

"It ain't all like that," Nia stammered with a nervous laugh. "But right now I got respect on the streets because I mess with Hudson. I mess up his deals, steal his stuff and piss off his troopers. The people love that about me. But if innocent people get caught up in what I do, I just know I'm gonna lose that respect. They're gonna say I'm a loose cannon...that I don't give a damn who gets hurt. I might hurt a client's cousin or sister or mom or something and they'll think I don't care. And if I ain't got my respect, I don't get my jobs. I'm thinking I should quit blowing stuff up. Maybe if I just do jobs that don't hurt anybody, like, just the robberies..."

Marc looked as if he were going to say something. But he stopped, and suddenly tunneled below the bar. When he rose back up, there was a newspaper in his grip. He tossed it and it flopped on the bar in front of Nia. The paper was folded open to the business section.

"Read the headline there," said Marc.

Nia leaned upon the bar, folded her arms under her chest and stared at the paper.

"'GENIUS DAUGHTER INHERITS POSITION OF DECEASED SCIENTIST'," Nia read aloud. "So what?"

"That 'genius daughter' is Chelsea Romedrux, the daughter of Dr. Kane Romedrux," Marc explained.

"Who?"

"...Romedrux? Don't that sound familiar?"

"Not really."

Marc groaned. "Look at the picture then…what about the building? Doesn't *that* look familiar to you?"

Nia glared at the black-and-white photo on the newspaper page. She studied it for a moment.

"Oh! That's the place where I looted that weapon from the other night! Ha, I made the news twice in one week! That's what's up!"

"Except for one thing," Marc muttered. "Because you got away with that weapon, Romedrux lost his job. In fact, he worked for Hudson; he might have lost a little more than that, because of you."

"Me? But I ain't done nothing to that man!"

"Are you sure?" Marc continued. "Think about it. You broke in and stole the gun. You beat Romedrux's security and you got away, right in front of Hudson's face. Isn't that what you said? Then the guy who designed the weapon, who was supposed to be *protecting* the weapon for our favorite corrupt defense contractor, turns up dead. Why do you suppose that is?"

Nia fell quiet.

"There's no right way to do wrong, Nia."

Nia hung her head and sighed. Then the chime of her pager startled her.

"That's my contact. I have to go," Nia said. "He's got the information I need so I can do this job…"

Marc folded his arms. "You don't have to do this. Look at yourself, Nia. You're so beautiful. You shouldn't be living your life like this."

"What do you mean?"

"You have the skills and the smarts to do whatever you want. Don't waste your life as a criminal. Every bad guy goes down sooner or later, and that goes for bad girls, too."

"But…"

"But *nothing*," Marc interrupted. "There could be people plotting against you, setting you up to take a big fall at any moment. People you already know, people you think are your friends, or people you don't even know exist, anybody could be looking for a way to bring you down. Pay attention to what's going on around you. Look at every detail. You can't just keep floating through life. You gotta learn to watch your head. You gotta start acting like you know what you're *worth*."

"It's something to think about," Nia said as she headed for the door. "Thanks, Marc."

"My pleasure, sweetheart," Marc mumbled, returning to his scrubbing and polishing as Nia stepped back onto the streets.

THE WINDS grew chilly and rapid in the autumn night. The corporate offices of Hallegan Security had closed down, with only a scattered few security guards patrolling the lobby. Hallegan's employees filed out of the building as another business day ended.

Nia Black spent the better part of the day planning and preparing, using the blueprints of the building and her own research to devise the perfect scheme to breach the Hallegan Building. When the sun descended beneath the horizon and shadow-laced cumulus clouds blanketed the sky, her time had come.

The first task was to get into the building. With its lobby and loading entrances guarded by highly trained, rotating security personnel, Nia felt entry from the ground was simply more trouble than it would have been worth.

She could have easily blasted her way past the guards, just as she did at Romedrux Labs. But the time it would have taken her to reach the thirty-seventh floor from the bottom—especially since it would have been too risky to use the elevators—would give the guards enough time to marshal the authorities and trap her. No entry from the ground. That left only one option. She had to break in from above.

A nearby office building that towered above many other ones sat next door to the Hallegan building. The company was adding another wing to its corporate headquarters. It was still under construction and was presently little more than a sky-high grid of steel girders and winch-operated elevators. Construction workers busied themselves here at daytime; at night, the site was vacant and gated off. The construction site was the key to Nia's approach.

From a brisk dash, Nia lunged over the wooden barricade that barred access to the site and accessed a freight elevator, reaching the soaring peak of the building in a matter of minutes.

Nia stood on the far edge of the building's roof, the open sky yawning below her, wind slashing through her hair, the company's neon logo beneath her reflecting on her leather getup. She squinted as she gazed at the building in front of her, Hallegan's corporate headquarters.

Nia analyzed the distance between the two buildings. *Not all that far, not for me anyway,* she thought. She brought along a grappling hook with a magnetic head for rappelling across great distances, but Nia wouldn't need it immediately. She had a far more efficient means of getting to the Hallegan building.

She slid her goggles over her eyes and took a few breaths, backpedaling from the edge of the roof. She then sprinted forward with all her might, outstretched her arms and sprang from the roof with all the strength her powerful legs could muster.

Nia speared through the air like a javelin, across the yawning breadth between the two towers of steel and glass, easily several hundred feet vertical of the street below...

And seconds later, Nia's palms slapped the rooftop of the Hallegan building and she tucked into a roll and came to rest. She stood up, swept dust from her hair and looked back at the roof she jumped from—now hundreds of yards way and above her.

Nia examined the front of the Hallegan building as the echoes of traffic moaning from below and the groan of the wind filling the air around her. She had to rappel down three floors to get to number thirty-seven.

Now, she thought, *it's time to use this thing.*

She unhooked her grappling gun from her belt. It was a high-tech device; the grappling gun used gas-powered propulsion to fire one of two magnetic heads across great distances, with the second head intended to secure a hold at the point of origin, if needed.

The device was the key to Nia getting into the Hallegan tower—and her way back out. She could have tried a roof access doorway, but it was highly likely the door was alarmed, so she needed to breach from outside by rappelling down from the roof. And there was no way she could leap back up to the building, so when she'd finished inside and needed to get out, Nia would use her grappling gun to go back the way she came.

Nia affixed one magnetic end to the edge of the Hallegan building, swung her legs over the edge and began to lower herself hand over hand. She extended the cord as needed until she counted down to the 37th floor, her objective near.

Using a power-driven screwdriver, Nia effortlessly removed the bolts that secured one of the windows. Nia kicked the window after unscrewing it, sending it plopping upon the carpet inside the building. Swinging and lunging into the room with a perfectly silent four-point landing, she pressed her fingers and toes to the carpeted floor, raising her head and scanning the area like a predator seeking its prey. Nia lifted her goggles and looked about, comparing her surroundings to the blueprints in her hand. It was the correct floor.

She turned about and jerked the wire still dangling outside of the building. It was the key to her escape, so she needed to ensure it remained stable.

Nia hardly expected to have such an easy time breaking into the headquarters of a company specializing in advanced security.

According to the diagram Darien Drakonis gave her, the thirty-seventh floor of the Hallegan building held the company's most crucial computer equipment. The layout was a perfect cross with a single cube dead center. Several doors along every wall in every corridor led to a different computer room, but Nia's target was the room in the middle of it all, the room marked on the blueprint earlier.

In the center of the floor is the chamber where the network administrator, or whatever, is. In there is the computer with the Main Systems Disc. I just need to get to it. Piece of cake, Nia thought as she examined the area.

Though darkness enveloped the floor, cut only by the faint glow of the moonlight outside, Nia was able to see the details and obstructions before her, or the lack thereof. Nothing but a clear path of blank walls, nondescript doors and bland carpet lined her path.

She found that perplexing. The only form of opposition presented to Nia was the presence of two wall-mounted cameras, one directly above her and another at a corner of the cross. Nia couldn't outwardly tell if the cameras were on or not. Though clearly mounted on swivel bases, the cameras were not moving. They just leaned inertly on their pedestals.

Forgetting the cameras, Nia reached in her pack and drew a can that sprayed odorless aerosol. She suspected perhaps there were invisible lasers barring the otherwise unassuming hall. She pressed her pointer on the nozzle and swayed her wrist back and forth, filling the hall ahead of her with enough mist to create a fog.

Nia frowned.

Nothing.

She was eager to go leaping and somersaulting through an otherwise impregnable array of beams, averting any chance of setting off alarms while being incredibly graceful in the process. She was genuinely upset.

All that exercise for nothing.

Nia switched her way toward the room in the center of floor thirty-seven with a twisted look on her face, annoyed that she had to give up her *Mission: Impossible*-styled plan of infiltration. She approached the door and subtly graced the knob with her palms—testing for more traps in an almost paranoid way—before quickly grabbing and turning it.

The door was unlocked. Nia pushed her way into the room and examined the area.

This is where their main systems disc is? Nia wondered. *This place looks like a storage closet or something.*

The chamber was a spacious square. Aged, dusty computer terminals were stacked atop each other amidst the shadows against the walls. It was far too packed and musty to house a high-end computer that would hold a 'Main Systems Disc'—there wasn't even a chair in the room, and all sorts of alarms were going off in Nia's head.

Did I count the floors wrong? No way. Maybe the hard part was just getting in.

She spotted the only fully assembled PC in the rear corner of the room, and sighed with boredom.

I thought it would be a little more difficult than that. Oh well. The easy jobs are the best jobs. No bruises and no torn-up clothes to worry about.

Nia approached the computer and glanced upon it.

What the hell?

She noticed a yellow sticky note affixed to the monitor. Neither the monitor nor the hard drive tower connected to it was receiving any power. Nia peeled the paper off and read.

'CONGRATULATIONS FOR MAKING IT THIS FAR. WE ARE IMPRESSED WITH YOUR SKILL. HOWEVER, A LITTLE CONSTRUCTIVE CRITICISM FOR YOU: YOU'RE TERRIBLY NAÏVE. IN CASE YOU HAVEN'T FIGURED IT OUT YET, THIS IS A TRAP.'

The paper slipped from Nia's fingers and her eyes went wide.

The lights shot on at once, irritating her eyes. Nia found herself surrounded by soldiers, clad in black uniforms and ski masks, wearing padded suede shoes, and bearing nightsticks. They flooded the room, and Nia found herself covered on all sides.

The time for stealth was over. She spun around, dashed out of the computer room and rushed toward the window she originally jumped in from.

She only brought a single, suppressed pistol with her for self-defense, preferring to travel lightly for a stealth mission. She wasn't expecting this kind of trouble. And for that, for not expecting this, Nia cursed herself. Even if she put one of her ten bullets in one of her attackers, she would run out of ammo long before she would run out of foes.

Run. That was her only choice.

Masked men appeared from every corner of Nia's vision, lunging toward her. And each one that attacked Nia Black learned the hard way why she was such a hard target.

They watched helplessly as a young woman easily half their size took hold of their torsos and hurled them away like bags of trash, thrust her palms into their chests, reversing their and momentum with strength and agility that belied her diminutive, stocky body, knocking them aside like a linebacker rushing through a defensive line. For every soldier that threw himself at her, another flew away, crashing into the walls, slamming into the ceiling, or collapsing to the floor like used up rag dolls.

Nia grew confident. They couldn't stop her. Nia charged through the straight corridor leading back to the open window. She saw the window growing ever closer, the lifeline of her grappling cord wagging in the wind, taunting her, the open sky waiting for her to fly away through it—

Suddenly a massive force struck Nia across the belly! She stumbled backward, away from the window, and skid across the carpet. Nia recovered and looked ahead, and when she looked at the man that brought her down, her eyelids stretched wide in shock.

A soldier clearly more powerful than the rest stood before her. His arm, easily three times the width and twice the length of a normal man's, shook violently as engorged veins wriggled like hyperactive snakes under his skin. Nia stared at the man as his fist trembled and appeared to *shrink* back to normal human proportion.

Another soldier, a fit man in spectacles, walked toward the beastly man from behind and placed a calm hand on his shoulder.

"Thank you, Armstrong," he said.

"Anytime, sir," said Armstrong, taking a deep breath as his hand finished reverting to normal.

Nia grimaced as she slammed her palm on the floor, propelling herself off the ground, sprinting toward her assailant with fight in her eyes—

Two of the masked men immediately threw their weight on Nia and held her down upon the floor, taking hold of her arms with all their might.

She was curiously strong; they knew this. They also knew she could break free of two men or even more, given the time. They knew it was time they could not grant her.

"Get off me!" she screamed, struggling rigorously against her captors. Nia was furious, but more so, frightened. Her worst fear was coming to life.

She was captured.

The men hurriedly latched cuffs around her ankles and wrists as she twisted her body and growled, fighting to resist.

Another soldier made his way behind her and cupped his fingers under her shoulder, standing her up. He grabbed her hair and pulled it back, forcing Nia to look up. The spectacled man, apparently the leader, ambled toward her calmly.

Nia flashed teeth, her eyes rising up to meet the eyes of her enemy. "You were with Double-D today!"

"Quite right," the man replied. "You did quite a number on Mr. Marks' reputation last night, Miss Black. It was so bad, he asked our boss, Maxwell Hudson, if someone else could take over this little matter of dealing with you. I volunteered. I'm the newest member of Corp Hudson's Security. The name is Jesús Alvarez."

Nia's chest heaved with the weight of her rage. "You work for Hudson…I thought Darien said y'all was his competition or something. Why would he help you get to me?"

"This is a private matter, Miss Black, not between Hudson and Drakonis, but between Darien and myself. It just so happens that the man you affectionately call 'Double-D' is after something special and I knew how he could get it. We helped each other out. I pointed him to his prize, and he helped me obtain mine."

Nia tugged against her captors, but it was no use. With five men holding her arms and her wrists securely cuffed, she had no leverage to move.

"Mr. Alvarez, your orders?" said one soldier.

"Be careful with her. We need her alive and essentially undamaged."

"So what you want with me anyway?" Nia grunted. "Hudson wants me out of the way so bad, just put a bullet in my head and be done with it."

"If anyone were simply trying to kill you, they would have an easy time of it. You're not exactly subtle, nor hard to draw out. No, I think you'll find that you are worth far more than you realize, Miss Black. Now, it's time to go."

"Sir, shouldn't we…" a soldier began, pointing at Nia's head.

"Oh, of course," Alvarez smiled, reaching into his jacket pocket.

Expecting to see a blindfold, Nia was surprised when Alvarez instead drew a black, cylindrical object with metal claw-like prongs on its tip. The object's subtle murmur grew to an unsettling buzz and a wire of blue lightning danced between the prongs

A stun gun.

Alvarez swiftly pressed the tool into Nia's abdomen. She screamed, and then there was darkness.

...I'm going, Nia. You should come with me.

No! I'm not! I don't know why you want to go! You're all I have left...

You honestly want to stay here? He's not coming. He's dead. We're alone.

And now you're going to abandon me...?

It doesn't have to be that way. Just come with me.

...I can't. All the answers are here, and if you leave me...then we're not—

NIA OPENED HER EYES.

A steady hum and a random bump awakened her. She found herself laying on a cold metal floor, inside something in motion—possibly a van. Her body ached with every movement; she felt like she tumbled down a flight of stairs.

Nia quickly examined herself. She remained shackled at the wrists and ankles. Her clothes were not tampered with and she did not sense that her body had been violated. She felt her pendant still pressing between the fabric of her jacket and her chest. Though relieved she hadn't been taken advantage of in her unconscious state, Nia still needed answers.

The space surrounding her body on the floor was minimal, and through a small window on the wall ahead of her, she could make out the back cushions of two seats. She heard the sounds of the road and realized she was definitely in the back of a van. There were no windows save in the front, which she could barely see from the floor. Moreover, her vision was still adjusting after being unconscious for so long. She had no idea where she was or where her captors were taking her.

Two men in full tactical gear sat on either side of her, watching her, each holding cattle prods the same fashion as the one used on her by the man known as Alvarez. Nia traded glances with them as they looked down at her.

"Have a nice dream, sleeping beauty?" one laughed.

"Where…where are you taking me?" Nia struggled to speak, still stunned from the electric shock.

They ignored her.

Nia struggled to move her arms and legs. The chains made her feel stiff at the ankles and wrists—but not stiff enough.

"It's a damn shame…what a waste. A fine lady like this and we just have turn her over to the science department," one of the guards went on.

"Well, at least things should be calmer from here on out, with this psycho off the streets," said the other. "We can go back to just guarding instead of playing soldier."

"Yeah, but haven't you noticed? A lot of the guys who signed up to Corp Hudson's security detail have been disappearing. They're still on the roster, but we don't see them around."

"You know what I heard? I heard a lot of them are volunteering for a special project with R&D. They're getting paid like triple what we get for some kind of study."

"Well why didn't we get the memo? I want to move up to the special projects too!"

What are they talking about…? Nia thought. *The science department…so that's it. They must know more about me than I thought…but they didn't do the research if they think these little chains are going to hold me.*

She gritted her teeth and tensed her muscles as hard as she could, the metal cuffs grinding against the soft skin of her wrists until the shattered links made sounds like wind chimes, breaking apart like glass.

"Hey—she's free! How did she—?!" the second guard gasped as broken metal links ricocheted against the van interior.

Nia took hold of both of their left ankles.

Before the two could ready their stun guns, Nia yanked their feet. They flew backward as if they slipped on banana peels, their skulls crashing against the metal walls and seats around the area. Nia sprung to her feet and slammed her heels into their faces, blood spattering along the walls.

The van's violent shaking alerted the occupants up front.

"Hey, what's going on back there?" shouted the deep-voiced driver. "You two can't even keep one woman down?!"

"Stop the van," the calm voice of Alvarez ordered. "Quickly."

Desperate for open space, Nia turned to the doors of the van and tore them open with one swift kick. Without another thought, she leaped out as the van skidded to a halt. Nia stumbled and rolled against the hard asphalt as she crashed upon the moving road. The brilliance of the morning sun seared into her groggy eyes like fiery sand. Though her body ached and her equipment was lost, Nia's only thought was finding her way home. She found her footing and dashed away as fast as her legs would carry her, disappearing into the woods alongside the road.

The soldiers came around, pulling themselves up against the walls and seats in the back of the van. Alvarez leaped out of the passenger side of the vehicle and walked to the back of the van, his eyes widening at the sight of the broken doors.

"She escaped. How?" Alvarez roared.

All the two guards could do was groan in pain and mumble incoherently, aimlessly sifting for excuses. Alvarez looked around, across the bare road, within the lush greenery that traced a path behind the railings on either side the street, but found only a faint hint of Nia's perfume in the air. She was gone, and Alvarez grew frustrated instantly.

"What was I thinking, leaving her in the care of such incompetent guards? Armstrong, if you would."

"Yes, sir."

Armstrong climbed out of the driver's side of the van and lumbered toward the two soldiers, taking them both by the throats!

They writhed and pounded his arms with all of their might, but with each passing second, his arms grew thicker and denser; they may as well have been hitting solid steel girders. Armstrong lifted them into the air and walked toward the edge of the highway as their legs dangled about, looking over a deep hill that led into a dense forest.

"Y'all wanna know why y'all weren't called up for the big leagues?" he said to them. "This is why! Because you're fuckin' useless!"

Then he winded back and hurled both men over the hill, their screams echoing into the air and suddenly going silent, cut off by the thump of their bodies making impact several yards down.

Armstrong walked back toward Alvarez as he sighed and cleaned his glasses.

"This is quite the setback," Alvarez muttered to himself, scratching his chin. "Where did I go wrong? Did I miscalculate her recovery time by that much? Was I wrong to...?"

"Sir, you should have a look at this," Armstrong suddenly said as he looked inside the van. He lifted something from the floor of the rear of the van.

"Hmm?" Alvarez turned to him.

"Something we missed," he continued, placing the object in Alvarez hand.

He glared at it and cracked a small grin. "Interesting... I can't believe anyone still uses these things. Well, today isn't a total loss after all."

IT WAS EARLY AFTERNOON when Nia finally stumbled through the door of her home.

Charlene Wright, enjoying the early part of the day before heading off to another shift of her demanding nursing job, sat on her bed absorbed in a romance novel.

Then the crash of Nia's body slumping in the doorway broke her attention away from the intimate scene she'd been reading, and Charlene tossed the book aside, dashing downstairs. She found Nia lying on the floor in the doorway, drained of her strength.

"Nia! What happened?" Charlene bellowed. "Come here, let me help you…"

Charlene lifted Nia from the floor. Being an experienced registered nurse, hefting and carrying people for short distances was second nature for her. Charlene stretched Nia out on her own bed, with a soft blanket over her and warm pillow under her.

Nia soon came to her senses. She watched her landlord through her blurry vision, as Charlene rushed to the small washroom in the adjacent corner to prepare a hot, wet cloth in her sink.

"Did you get in some kind of trouble last night?" Charlene asked. "You didn't get raped or anything, did you?"

Nia lay in silence. What was she supposed to say? *Oh sure… 'No, Charlene, it was just a run in with the men in black from Corp Hudson trying to kill me. The usual. Then that girl would try to have me committed or something. And if I tell her I got raped or anything like that, she might try to call the cops and she'd want to be all buddy-buddy trying to counsel me and everything. No thanks. Time for another lie…*

Nia sighed and spoke. "I...I guess I gave this one guy too good of a lap dance. He got mad when I wouldn't give him my phone number, and he got kind of violent. I spent the whole night running from him. I didn't want to lead him here, you know?"

"For real? You mean to tell me you couldn't get *anyone* to help you? It must have been dozens of people out there last night!"

Not too many people go looking in the back woods, Nia thought. *I couldn't let anyone see me wandering around...end up making things worse.*

"Man, people took one look at me and probably just figured I was playing or drunk or something. They ain't pay me no mind."

"That's so wrong," Charlene grumbled. "People see bad things happening all the time and act like they don't need to take it seriously...next thing you know, somebody's dead. Let me call the cops...do you remember what the guy looked like?"

Nia flinched. "No! I mean, don't call the cops. He's just another crazy; happens all the time in my line of work."

Nia cracked a slight smile. *That's true enough.*

"Besides," she went on, "You know the cops aren't going to do anything. They'll file a report, tell me how much I deserve it for being a dancer and send me on my way."

Nia rubbed her abdomen and groaned. Her encounter from the night before left her more in pain than even she could believe. That man, Armstrong, struck her harder than anything she'd ever experienced...

"You need some aspirin or something. I didn't see anything in your medicine cabinet..." Charlene began as she stood up and slid open Nia's drawers.

"Charlene, wait...!" Nia groaned. "Don't open—!"

But it was too late. Charlene stared at the contents of Nia's drawers, and her jaw dropped in fright.

73

Charlene saw numerous pistols, automatic weapons, and boxes of bullets. Electronic devices that looked a bit like mobile phones, a bit like calculators, a bit like handheld game systems, but at the same time like nothing she'd ever seen. And money—stacks of cash still wrapped in official banding as if fresh from an armored car.

The blood drained from Charlene's face. She repeatedly glanced between Nia and the drawer with trembling eyes. Nia hung her head, waiting meekly for Charlene to start hollering.

Nia felt stupid about the menial effort she put into concealing her goods. She just never expected Charlene to go through her drawers, particularly with Bobby vouching for her.

"Nia, what's all this?" Charlene asked. "What the hell are you doing with all this stuff?"

"Well," Nia began, unsure exactly how to continue. She giggled nervously as she watched Charlene sift frantically through the items in the drawer. "Be-be careful; some of that stuff is dangerous…those guns are *loaded*, you know."

"Loaded?" Charlene immediately snatched her hands away from the drawer as if she were avoiding a bite from a vicious beast. "Nia, you're not really a dancer, are you?"

"No, I don't dance, not professionally anyway. I'm a…*different* kind of professional. That's how come I always have money."

Charlene grew curious. "What kind of professional are you then? What exactly *do* you do? You ain't no prostitute, are you?"

Nia gave her a disgusted look.

"No I'm not a prostitute, Charlene! I usually do robberies, but sometimes people ask me to blow stuff up," Nia continued.

"Blow stuff up?!" Charlene gasped. "Like…what happened to those people when that oil tanker blew up? I heard about that on the news. Was that you?"

Nia stopped. That was enough honesty.

"Um—no! I don't mess with innocent people…I ain't have nothing to do with that. There *are* other people out there like me, you know. Anyway, Bobby and Marc know about it. Sometimes, I'd use them as middlemen between me and my clients, you know, to make sure they're on the level before they see me. They're probably the only people I trust, well, them and one other person."

"Ain't this a bitch…?" mumbled Charlene, pondering what she heard. "No wonder you don't want me to call the cops!"

"Now Charlene, don't be getting any ideas!" Nia pleaded. "I mean, I bought you and Bobby that HDTV and everything…"

"Damn, Nia, can *I* be down?!"

"Wait, what?"

"I mean, I took shop class in school! I know how to hook up all that electronic stuff! You're bringing home like ten G's a week, aren't you? You got more money in this drawer than I make in a year at that damn nursing home. If I'd known about that, I wouldn't have needed to bum money off my parents to fix up this dump! We could be living in a nice new crib in the suburbs or something…"

Nia groaned. "Uh-uh. The last thing I want to be doing is big ballin' and shot callin'. Trust me; you don't want me drawing attention just because I got a little money. That's a good way to get yourself caught, shot at, robbed…heck, at least audited by the IRS."

Then Nia shook her head.

"…Wait a minute, what you mean, 'can you be down?' The stuff I do is dangerous, and, trust me; you are not equipped for my line of work!"

"So, what you saying?" Charlene asked rhetorically.

"I'm saying *no*. I don't want to have your death on my conscience. It's not a game out there, Charlene. Bullets fly. People die. And there are people out there looking for me. I keep it a secret so that none of those bullets and none of those people come in *your* direction, you know what I'm saying? So no, you cannot be 'down'."

"Oh, so it's like *that*?" Charlene changed attitude quickly. "Because, you know, I *could* call the cops. I think there's a reward out there for you. What is it, like fifty G's or something like that? That's like half my mortgage note…"

Nia's face tightened. "Charlene. Do you want to play this game with me? I don't think you know who you're f—"

Suddenly, both women heard a key grooving through the front door lock.

Bobby entered Nia's room, holding his saxophone case and a bouquet of red and pink roses.

"Um, here you go, baby," he said as he handed the flowers to Charlene. Then he noticed Nia's open drawer and turned back to Charlene, nearly dropping his sax, his heart rate doubling when Charlene's furious eyes met his.

"Aw, damn!"

"That's right, boo," Charlene snapped, the expensive roses dropping to the floor. "Where do you get off not telling me what your 'cousin' does? You got the biggest crook in the city staying in my house…"

Oh, now that I told her no, I'm a crook. But when she thought she could be down, we were best friends for a minute. She is so full of it, Nia thought.

"Look, what does it matter what Nia does for a living? She always has the rent. Isn't that the main thing?" Bobby spoke calmly, trying to get Charlene to calm down. "Nobody knows who Nia is around here. She never brought any trouble to our front door. We ain't had a utility shut off in a good long while because of her. The club is bumping because I can focus now without having to worry about the house so much, because of Nia's money. She's helping us out and we're doing all right. So what are you so worried about?"

"I'm just a little curious about what else you're not telling me, Bobby," Charlene responded.

"Oh, here *you* go," Bobby sighed with a heavy, frustrated breath. "This again. Look, if you don't trust me, why are you still with me? If I'm so bad, why don't you just put me out? Huh?!"

"Because I love you, Bobby!" Charlene cried. "But you don't care! We barely spend any time together. You're always looking for a reason to be at that club! Even when it's closed! I thought you and I would spend more time together when your friend Marc took the club over, but if anything, it's less! Why? What did I do that was so wrong to you?! Why don't you like being around me?!"

Nia suddenly sat up. She didn't want to hear this. "I think y'all need to take that upstairs. Can I get some sleep?"

"What the hell are you talking about?!'" Bobby yelled, louder than ever. "I stay buying you things! Your clothes, your jewelry, everything, that's all me, trying to appreciate my girl! But the way you act—it's hard to be faithful when you get like this...jealous of every girl that even glances at me...but I'm there! I'm always there! You the one working all those hours at the old folks' home, doing all that overtime... or are you? Maybe you're the one doing the cheating! Is that it? Are you trying to get rid of me? Is that why you keep accusing me? Who is it? Is it Silk, from the club? He's always talking about you anyway."

"Bobby, you know it ain't like that!" Charlene wept.

Nia had to look away and bury her face in her pillow. It was all she could do to keep from laughing out loud. Bobby had flipped the situation on Charlene as only a true player could.

"Yo, can you two please discuss that somewhere else?" Nia stammered; her voice muffled.

"Nia, you want me to call your boyfriend?" Charlene suddenly said to her.

"Oh! No, he, he um, went away for the week with his aunt and uncle. He's hiding from his brother again. I'm on my own right now. I'll be all right. You two need to talk, and I need to sleep, so…"

"All right," Charlene said, wiping away her tears. She left Nia's room and ran upstairs, the house quivering with the sounds and vibrations of stomps of anger as her boots slammed upon the wooden steps.

"Charlene, hold up," Bobby muttered.

Nia turned to him, whispering. "Why do you even continue to put up with her, Bobby? You don't need her. Let's just—!"

Bobby interrupted her. "Let me handle my business. I'll talk to you in a minute. Lay your behind down and get some sleep. I'll be back so you can tell me what happened, all right?"

Bobby slowly closed Nia's door. She heard him leap up the stairs, and Nia was alone in her room at last. *Damn…that's twice I was almost caught. I'm slipping. Man, I'm glad Bobby came in when he did. Charlene might have wanted to know just what did happen to me—her knowing I'm not a dancer means that story I told her about last night was straight bullshit, and if she ever figures that out…oh well…*

Soon, Nia's thoughts became incomprehensible even to herself as she passed out on her bed.

Bobby slowly stepped into the bedroom. He saw Charlene sitting silent upon their bed, facing out of their room's lone window with her arms folded. Bobby sat next to her and put his arm around her.

"Baby, I'm sorry," Bobby mumbled in his deepest voice. "I just…lose control sometimes."

Charlene relaxed her arms and leaned into Bobby's chest. "Why do she have to live here anyway? If she makes so much money she should just get a place of her own…"

"Nia needs a safe place," Bobby said. "If the wrong people found out about her, she'd be in trouble. So, I'm helping her out, and she helps us out.

You should know there ain't nothing that could ever come between you and me."

"I—I believe you," Charlene said. "And I would never step out on you, Bobby. You know that, don't you?"

"Yeah," Bobby said. "Two star-crossed lovers, just like your mom said when she saw us together for the first time."

Charlene reached out and pulled down the window shade. She turned back to Bobby.

"Do me a favor?" Charlene said.

"Anything."

"I know I've been working a lot of double shifts and we haven't had a chance to be together in a while," Charlene continued. "I...I was scared that you might look somewhere else to...get what you need. But I'm home now, and you're home now..."

Bobby, flashing a small smile, stood from his spot and opened the nearby dresser, pulling out a compact disc of music he composed himself. Sliding it within a three-disc CD-changer that sat atop the dresser, soft tunes from his saxophone filled the air. Bobby stepped back toward his girlfriend and tugged the bottom of her shirt from her waistline, lifting it off. Charlene leaned back upon her palms as Bobby struggled with the hooks on her front-locking bra.

"Poor baby," Charlene snickered. "Has it been that long? You forgot how to open a bra?"

Bobby had grown so accustomed to slipping Nia's sport bras and halter tops off that he nearly forgot how to manipulate the hooks of Charlene's undergarments.

Charlene sighed. "Damn, boy. I'll do it."

With a simple move, Charlene unhooked and opened her brassiere. Immediately, Bobby took hold of her smallish breasts, sliding his lips upon her left one. Charlene whimpered and slowly laid back as Bobby slid his hand down across her abdomen, guiding his fingers into her thong. As Bobby began to rub within and around her warmth, Charlene began to breathe softly and rapidly, enthralled with his passionate touch.

Bobby kneeled in front of Charlene, who was still lying on her back, breathing heavily. He dragged her pants and her underwear off before stroking between her legs with his tongue. She trembled and yelped in pleasure, her eyes tightly closed while Bobby pleased her in his trademark fashion.

Some time passed before Charlene gathered up the concentration to speak, her strength fading from Bobby's exceptional technique.

"Bobby," Charlene mumbled, fainting. "Come on."

Bobby, remaining silent, stood and cracked a smile as he dragged his own pants off. He rested his palms upon her rear, lifting her middle to meet his as he slid inside of her, with Charlene's legs resting on his shoulders and her back on the bed. He climbed on the bed and rested on his knees, moving his groin back and forth as Charlene began to gasp rhythmically. Charlene, her teary eyes tightly closed and her fingernails tearing the sheets, gasped loudly with rapid exhales of pleasure as her entire body vibrated. Nothing felt better to her than having Bobby's love inside of her, and she was not ashamed to show it.

The entire room began to rock. Bobby was feeling so invigorated he pressed harder and faster, Charlene's soft whimpers growing into loud, high-pitched screams in an instant. The shaking in the room quivered the walls and eventually caused the CD player to tumble from the dresser top to the floor, cutting the music as it shattered into pieces.

Charlene wriggled free of Bobby's embrace and glanced at the wreckage on the floor.

"Damn, Bobby, ain't that the second time you did that?" Charlene laughed.

Bobby looked upon Charlene, and even with her sleepy eyes and mangled hair, he couldn't help but get lost in her lovely smile and hearty laugh as he remembered why he hooked up with Charlene to begin with.

Charlene…Nia…damn, what am I doing?

FOUR MEN AND A WOMAN sat at desks inside a small, square room with fluorescent lights on the ceiling. It was a classroom, or rather a training room for Corp Hudson's security personnel.

The first was a muscular beast of a man who barely fit in his midnight blue business suit. He squeezed into the small space between his chair and desk with a sigh.

The woman was dark skinned and muscular as well, though still the smallest person in the room. She had long braids that fell past her shoulders.

The third was a Caucasian man with long fiery-red hair in a mullet style. He sat tapping his foot and his No.2 pencil on the desk as if impatient.

The fourth was another Caucasian man with short brown hair and a five o'clock shadow. He twirled his pencil in his fingertips, looking simply bored.

The fifth was a Latino man with curly hair, wearing spectacles. He sat as still as a statue, as if time had stopped for him while he awaited further instructions.

Finally, a sixth man, the second African-American, entered the room, wearing the same midnight blue business suit as the others and dark sunglasses. He stroked his low haircut, removed his glasses and stood in front of the room.

"Thank you for coming, everyone," said Vincent Marks. "I know all of us have things to do so I'll keep this brief. After all, Corp Hudson's security department has better things to do than sit in this training room babbling all night. But we have to be clear as to what our next course of action is regarding *Target Omega*."

"You mean the little girl that you seem to be incapable of keeping a grip on?" said the brown-haired man. "Funny. I've seen the surveillance photos. I can't imagine how anyone could slip their grip on a girl with an ass like that."

"That's quite enough, Casey," Vincent suddenly said. "See, that's exactly why I don't send you after her. As good as you are, you've got a problem where you think more with your dick than with your head."

"You're one to talk," Casey snapped back. "I'm not the one who used to fuck her. Isn't the whole reason she got away because *you* couldn't bear to put a bullet in her back? I guess I can't blame you. That rear end of hers is kind of mesmerizing."

"Damn, Billy!" said the woman. "Don't you even care that there's a woman present?"

"Not really, Cherie," Billy sighed. "...unless you plan on getting undressed and dancing on the table or something."

"You're a sick, twisted—"

"Come on. You're the one who decided to accept the promotion and become one of Corp Hudson's security heads, knowing good and well you'd be the only woman in the group. I'm damn sure not going to sugarcoat my words for your sake. I don't give a damn about your sensitive femininity. You want to be in the boy's club? Be prepared to listen to men talk like men."

Cherie rolled her eyes as the muscular man next to her spoke up.

"Vince, don't we know where *Target Omega* hangs out? Why don't we just go there again and strong-arm some of her buddies into telling us where she lives?"

"We've tried that before, Don," Vincent said. "Nia Black doesn't trust people easily. The one person she did seem to trust didn't even know that much about her. He died the other night thanks to that...project that the big man ordered me to bring along."

"Yeah, Carl," said the red-haired man. "Shame what happened to that guy, but hey, it did open the way for Jesús to get promoted, didn't it? But after what Carl went through in the lab, for him to go out the way he did is just sad. Let the lab boost me up some kind of way; I guarantee I won't go down that easily."

"You're crazy, Jason!" Billy Casey shouted. "You mean you'd actually let R&D run their weaponizing experiments on you?"

"Why not?" Jason retorted. "I mean, hey, if it means I become a better asset to the Corp, why not get some 'upgrades' added to my body? This is my career, after all—might as well devote my life to it."

"I hear that," said Don, the big man.

"Seriously, Jason?" Cherie spoke up. "I mean, give up your humanity and become a weapon?"

"People!" Vincent shouted. "We're getting off the subject. Alvarez, you're pretty quiet over there. Give your report on how the operation went last night."

"We don't need to hear the new guy's report," Billy Casey grumbled. "Since Nia Black isn't in our custody, we can safely assume he blew it. Am I right, Jesús?"

Jesús Alvarez took a breath, slid his glasses from his face, cleaned them with a cloth, replaced them, and sighed again.

"Not entirely."

The five others in the room gasped.

"It is true that Miss Black momentarily escaped my grasp. I'm not one to make excuses, but relying on the security guards for a task like that was my biggest mistake. However, this is far from a loss."

"What are you getting at, Jesús?" Vincent said. "You've got something on Nia—on *Target Omega*?"

Alvarez smiled. "I understand that I've yet to prove myself worthy of this exclusive club. Allow me the pleasure of continuing to pursue Nia Black my own way. It is probably for the best that Mr. Hudson does not know of what has happened before, lest his…suggestions…hinder our operations again. Mr. Hudson is a powerful, shrewd businessman, but he needs to leave the matters of security to those whom he appointed to the task."

Billy Casey laughed. "So in other words, you screwed up, you blame your men for it instead of taking responsibility like a real leader should, and then you expect Vincent to go over the big man's head and trust you to get the job done, *after* you already messed up once, without telling anybody what you plan to do? You've got to be kidding."

"Fine, Jesús," Vincent suddenly said. "You got it."

"What?!" Billy growled. "Come on, Vincent. You know it's time to send me! It's only logical! I'm the best there is! If not me, then you take the mission back. Anybody but the rookie!"

"You heard what I said," Vincent snapped back. "It's clear that I'm too emotionally involved with the situation. Alvarez, on the other hand, has better control of his emotions than anyone else in this room. That's an important trait when dealing with Nia. Not to mention; he came damn close to capturing her…closer than the cops ever have, closer than I ever did. I'm more comfortable with giving him another go at it than with trusting a loose cannon like you, Billy."

"Damn," Jason jeered. "*Owned.*"

"Shut the hell up, Jason!" Billy growled.

"Everyone else: standard operation," ordered Vincent. "Jason, Don and Cherie, you three continue to serve as executive bodyguards. Billy, you'll be on standby in case Jesús needs any help."

"I appreciate that, Mr. Marks, but Billy Casey's assistance will hardly be necessary," Alvarez said with a smile. "Now, there isn't a moment to lose. My advantage is time-sensitive, so I must get to work. By your leave…"

Jesús Alvarez lifted himself from his seat and walked out of the room. Billy Casey watched him as he left, his face tightening with indignation.

Who in the hell do you think you are?

NIA STOOD IN HER SHOWER, her head tilted toward the powerful streams of hot water that cascaded over her body. The heated water and steam brought blessed relief to her tired, aching muscles after her run-in with Corp Hudson's hunters the other night. It was the first time pain lingered in her body for more than a few minutes after an encounter; an unusual feeling for her.

Her washroom door was wide open, filling her entire room with a thin blanket of warm mist. Nia turned, looked throughout the room behind her, and sighed. Her patience wore thin, and she reached out for the knobs that controlled the water. But Nia stopped a second before she could turn off the shower when a familiar pair of muscular arms suddenly wrapped around her body.

"Hey!—oh, Bobby. About time," Nia whispered.

"Who did you think it was? I'm so glad Charlene works the three-to-eleven schedule now," Bobby replied as he pulled his naked body into the shower and wrapped his arms around her torso.

She hung her head and outstretched her arms, planting her palms against a wall of the shower as she pressed her rear against Bobby's groin. Bobby stroked her with a puff saturated in soap and washed down her body, massaging every inch of her.

"Bobby, I think I'm losing it," Nia said, her body trembling as Bobby's fingers traced a path between her thighs.

"What do you mean, girl?" Bobby said back, grinning. He was looking forward to this appointment all day, eager to have his hands on Nia's body yet again. Still, he could tell Nia needed a friend as well as a lover.

"I was captured the other night by some secret agents—I never came that close before...they had me chained up and—ooh! Do that again..."

"All right. Don't even worry about it," Bobby replied. "You know how good you are. Maybe I've been treating you too good...you're getting lazy. You know what you need to do? You need to go mess up that Darien character for setting you up like that. That'll help you get your edge back!"

"I forgot all about—damn, Bobby, who taught you how to do that..." Nia groaned, her knees buckling under Bobby's touch as she leaned backwards upon his chest, sliding her back up and down across his pectorals.

"Yeah...just go out there, load up your guns and bust a cap in his ass," Bobby said. "You keep letting people get over on you like this and your rep's going to go down the drain."

"You say it like it's so easy," Nia sighed. "It's one thing to put the hurt on people, but...Darien Drakonis is big time. He got me good. But I got out of it. I'll worry about him later. Right now, I'm going to stick to Hudson. Double-D can wait."

Bobby's palms slowly slid across her abdomen, grazing up and down between her thighs and her belly. Nia pressed her own palms atop Bobby's as she raised her head, reveling in his grasp.

Bobby stroked and gently twisted her nipples with his fingertips.

Nia moaned. "Yeah, right there. Some big-ass soldier hit me so hard I still feel it; and then some more of them jumped on my back and tackled me on the floor...my chest was sore all day. Should have shot all their punk asses."

"That's why you have so many enemies," Bobby went on as he continued to stroke and massage Nia's body. "You're always letting them live. They want you dead or alive anyway, you might as well put some people out of *your* misery."

"Maybe," Nia mumbled, groaning again as her eyes closed. She was half listening and half swooning from Bobby's seductive caress.

"I got a present for you," Bobby snickered.

"Ooh, gimme, gimme," Nia stammered, slowly and playfully.

Bobby slowly slid in front of Nia, kneeled upon the floor of the shower and pressed his face between her thighs, squeezing her butt cheeks as the steamy water rained all over him. He extended and shifted his tongue across and along.

Nia trembled gently at first. Then Bobby went faster. His tongue went left and right, inside and out; every movement of his followed by a shake of Nia's middle. She pressed her palms against the walls of the shower in an attempt to support her collapsing body as her gasps of pleasure grew.

Moaning.

Howling.

Screaming.

Nia threw her head back and exhaled sharply when Bobby finally stopped. Bobby stood, kissed her on the cheek and smiled.

"You all right now?" Bobby chuckled.

"Better," Nia whispered, writhing within the hot rain of the shower, coyly touching her lips with her index finger. "Want me to do something for you?"

"You don't have to," Bobby replied. "I know you're tired."

"I'm not that tired. I want to."

Nia slowly stood upright, faced Bobby and pressed her palms upon his trunk, sliding across his undulating, glistening muscles as she guided herself down to her knees. She looked up at his smiling face as the shower water rained across his chest, dripping upon her as she lowered her head again. She grasped his hips and pulled them toward her widening lips as her tongue rolled out. She slowly ran her tongue along the underside of Bobby's manhood, circling the head, kissing the sides and licking the tip smoothly before finally taking him into her mouth.

Bobby breathed hard, his abdomen stiffened, his knees buckled and his toes curled. She thought, he probably never thought he'd see the day when Nia would please *him* this way. The sight of her black-topped head moving back and forth down there must have been driving him wild. The feel of his erection surrounded on all sides by the warmth of Nia's mouth and her tongue slithering around it like a serpent coiling around a branch was an experience Nia would make sure he'd never forget.

Bobby's own grunts of pleasure grew louder and filled the air as he slapped the tiled walls of the shower with his palms. His entire body tingled with every subtle motion of Nia's tongue as he gasped her name repeatedly, clawing at her waterlogged hair. Nia breathed a slight chuckle and continued to pleasure him for what felt like an eternity until he roared in ecstasy.

Begging her to stop, he reached down and grasped Nia under her arms.

"Baby, you want me to stop?" Nia said with a pout. "I'm not making you happy?"

"Nah, it's just…you know I'm playing at the club tonight. I don't want to be too worn out. But tell you what…why don't you get out of the shower and lay on the bed?"

"What for?" Nia wondered.

"I'm going to help you relax, that's all."

Nia did as she was told, stepping out of the shower, taking a towel along with her as she left the washroom and approached her bed. Bobby turned off the water, dried himself off and wrapped another towel around his waist.

Nia lay prone on her bed, water still beading on her skin as she folded her arms under her head and looked toward Bobby with half-open eyes. He sat next to her, rubbed his palms together, and pressed his fingertips to her calves.

"What the…oh! Oh, wow," Nia gasped.

"You're tense as hell, baby," Bobby said. "Just chill. I took a couple of massage classes back in the day. A friend of mine convinced me it was a good way to get girls."

"Hmm…" Nia moaned as Bobby made his way up her thighs. "I think I can vouch for that."

Bobby gently rubbed his fingers across Nia's body, massaging her legs, her hips and butt, her lower and upper back, her shoulders, and back again. For taking massage classes 'a while back', he was surprisingly talented. Nia lay there feeling like her body was melting into the bed.

Then she started snoring.

Bobby smiled, thinking about her as he ran a finger through her drenched, stringy hair. Unconscious and naked, Nia was completely at ease with him; her guard was down completely. She had the utmost trust in him.

Bobby realized Nia was growing much closer to him than he'd anticipated—dangerously close.

Damn, this ain't right… Bobby thought.

Suddenly, Nia's telephone rang. Startled, Bobby quickly snatched the receiver from the hook, before the shrill chime of the phone could ring again and awaken Nia.

"Hello?" said Bobby.

"Yes, I'm looking for Charlene Wright?" the voice on the receiver answered.

"I'm her fiancée. What you want?"

"Glad to hear it."

The line suddenly clicked.

"People need to stop playing on the phone," he sighed as he replaced the handset on the receiver.

"Who was that?" Nia mumbled with a yawn.

"I don't know," Bobby said. "They hung up. Sorry; I ain't want to wake you."

"Don't worry about it. I heard it ring. Who did they ask for?"

"Charlene. Don't worry; it was probably somebody from the club playing a joke. They always do that when my birthday starts coming up—what, did you think it was for you?"

"It might have been my friend, he's the only one I know that's got the house number, and he knows not to ask for me directly on the phone just in case someone's tapping the line," Nia said as she lifted herself from the bed. "Speaking of, I need to go holler at him. Let me get dressed."

Bobby gazed at Nia's physique as she climbed off the bed and crossed the room. He never grew tired of seeing Nia's perfect body naked.

"Must you?"

"Yeah," Nia retorted, bending over and reaching inside of her drawers. Bobby grew rigid with excitement as he watched her bare body in motion.

"At least let me get a picture," Bobby smiled.

"What?"

"Let me get a photo of you naked," Bobby repeated.

"...You're crazy. You've seen me enough times. What you need a picture for?"

"Come on," Bobby urged. "I want something to look at when you're not around, you know, to remember you by. You have a camera in your drawer, don't you?"

Nia sighed. Bobby could be persistent at times. She pointed to her top drawer before throwing herself on the bed. She rested her weight upon her arms, leaned back and crossed her legs.

"Hurry up. I'm getting cold."

"That's what's up!" Bobby cheered as he grabbed the digital camera. He pressed the shutter repeatedly as Nia moved about, selecting different poses for each shot. She would cross and spread her legs, lie on her belly and raise her butt, and maneuver her tongue in and out of her mouth seductively.

Bobby simply kept pressing the shutter until Nia got bored, stood up and snatched the camera from him.

"Now, *you* get on the bed," she said, gently shoving Bobby in the chest and snatching his towel away at the same time. He flopped on the mattress on his butt.

"It's my turn."

Nia grabbed the camera and started snapping pictures, and suddenly the blushing Bobby became rowdy. He lunged toward Nia, wrapping one arm around her waist while reaching for the camera, while Nia continued to flash picture after poorly aligned picture. The two played about, wrestling for control of the camera, bumping against the walls and crashing upon the bed, both laughing hysterically all the while.

Later, Nia and Bobby dressed.

"So where you off to again?" asked Bobby, watching as Nia repaired her saturated hair with her dryer and comb.

"Like I said, I'm going to meet my friend. I need to get some information," said Nia.

"Oh, right, right. Say hi to the old chink for me."

"Damn, Bobby, have some respect," Nia groaned. "First of all, he isn't even from China. I mean, that was real ignorant of you—the man's like my father."

Bobby suddenly looked down, embarrassed. "My bad…listen; I'll let you know when the show starts at the Jazz Hall. Those record producers I told you about—they're coming through tonight. I'm trying out some new songs, some stuff I hooked up while I was thinking about you."

"That's what's up," Nia responded with a smile. "Make sure you page me, all right? I want to be right there when you tell them, 'This fine sister right here was my inspiration.'"

"Where is that pager, anyway?" Bobby chuckled.

"In my black leather jacket, like always. Don't worry. You act like that thing is so valuable. I mean, you're a big jazz musician and that's the most expensive thing you ever bought me."

"Hey, you're the one with all the money!"

"I'm serious, Bobby," Nia said with a sigh. "You know, you could try treating me like your girl sometimes."

Bobby fell quiet and scratched his head. Nia shrugged her shoulders, turned and grabbed her jacket.

"You better get going yourself," she went on. "You never know, Charlene might just come home early."

"You worry too much."

Nia showed Bobby out of her room, kissing him goodbye. "Oh yeah, make sure you leave the memory stick in my room. We wouldn't want what's-her-face finding those pictures."

"Right."

NIA SPED ALONG the streetlamp-lit roadways on her beloved motorcycle. She was relieved that she opted to leave it home the night she ventured out to break into the Hallegan building.

She drove toward the southeast section of the city, pulling into the wide open doors of a seemingly abandoned storehouse in the district. She parked her bike in front of a single desk that sat dead center in the building's main room. On the desk sat a laptop computer brimming with life. Its subtle glow illuminated the creases in the withered face of an older, Oriental man wearing a T-shirt under dust-ridden overalls. He greeted Nia with a smile, bringing life to his thin face as he sat at the desk.

"It has been a while," he said calmly.

"What's up, Kim?" Nia smiled. She was pleased to see her former caretaker and trainer, and current mentor and informant, in good health.

"I have looked into the matter as you requested, my dear. Would you like to hear it?"

Nia snorted. "What do you think? I came all this way just to say hi?"

"Well, one never knows with you," Kim laughed. "You are as sharp-tongued as ever."

"There are things you didn't tell me before, Kim," Nia continued. "I want to know. I'm old enough to handle it."

"Then I will get right to the crux of the matter," Kim sighed, taking a deep breath. "This is about Corp Hudson, correct?"

"Yeah," Nia replied. "At first I thought they were just trying to kill me. They had me cold the other night, when I broke into Hallegan. Their guys could have put a bullet in my head right then and there, but they didn't. The guy said something about me being 'valuable'. I don't get it."

"It is not difficult to decipher," said Kim. "It is clear Corp Hudson knows full well who you are and what you can do, and they view you as a threat. They would rather control you than kill you."

"But that's what I don't get," Nia said. "Yeah, I'm stronger, faster and have better reflexes and senses than most *regular* people, but I fought guys the last couple of days that were way beyond me. One guy had a damn mini-gun for an arm and didn't feel pain, mostly. Another guy could make himself bigger if he wanted. I couldn't even take that second guy. What do they need little ol' me for?"

"Yet, here you are, Nia," Kim said. "You clashed with both of them, and you remain alive and free. As powerful as those opponents seem to have been, clearly, you have something greater, and I have an idea as to what. To put it simply, you are *naturally* gifted."

Nia sighed. "You and I both know there ain't *nothing* natural about a girl who can see, hear and move like I can…a girl who can leap to the top of a roof with high heels on…who can jump across skyscrapers like some—"

"Corp Hudson's superhuman assets all have one thing in common; their abilities were granted to them somehow," Kim interrupted. "Their bodies have been outfitted with technology, or altered biologically to make them into weapons. These approaches make them powerful, but they are not without flaws. You are different. Everything you do, while it may seem remarkable to most people, is second nature to you; no training, no additives, no re-application required. You are intuitively more powerful than any human being, or even any *super*human, any Exceptional, will ever be. This is what sets you apart. And I would guess that this is what Corp Hudson seeks to understand, and control."

"Well, at least I know that I matter to them. Maybe I can use the fact that they don't want to kill me to my advantage or something."

Nia turned back toward her bike, then stopped.

"Anything on that other matter I asked you about?"

Kim shook his head. "I'm afraid not."

Nia exhaled. "…I'm sorry. I know you said you would tell me the moment you learned anything about him, and I keep bugging you about it."

"Do not apologize," Kim sighed. "It is only natural that you would want to know what has become of your father. It was easy to keep tabs on his world-spanning exploits as a mercenary, but the fact that he disappeared completely off the grid a year ago…that is unsettling."

"I don't even know why I care," Nia grumbled. "The man left us when we were only little kids. Left us to fend for ourselves while he went off to be a soldier of fortune or whatever, and I guess he got his selfish ass killed, and what does he leave me? Nothing. Not even a damn note."

Kim watched as Nia repressed sorrow and wiped away tears. This happened often. He knew Nia had to put on a display of strength in front of others, but times would come where Nia needed to release all the emotions she so often held inside. That was why she would visit him, even if she were not on a mission, even if she weren't looking for information. Kim was the closest thing Nia had to a relative, a listener—a true confidant.

Nia forced her sadness back in the recesses of her mind.

"Thanks, Kim," Nia sniffed. "I need to go—oh shoot! What time is it?"

Kim glanced at the corner of his computer monitor. "It is about eleven…are you in a rush?"

"A friend of mine was supposed to page me; he probably did while I was riding on my bike. I wouldn't have been able to hear it over the engine…I don't think."

Nia reached into the inside pocket of her jacket, tunneling around the lint and the barrel of one of her pistols. She moved gently at first, taking care not to drop her guns. Then her hands moved faster, violently sifting through

97

every orifice of her clothes, patting her hands around every inch of her clothing in vain.

"I could have sworn it was in my jacket pocket…I must have dropped it when…oh no…that prank call—*oh shit*."

"What? What is the matter?"

"I have to go, Kim—I'm sorry!"

Nia dashed to her motorcycle and turned over the engine. She sped away as fast as she could.

CHARLENE UNLOCKED THE DOOR to her home and stepped inside. With a sigh, she dropped her purse and jacket to the floor, relieved that another eight-hour grind in the elderly rest home was over. She was looking forward to a steamy shower, cold champagne, and a hot night of passion with her man, with no plans to let a broken music player distract them this time. Charlene flipped the nearest switch, activating the hall light, noticing something as she passed Nia's room on the base level.

Damn, Nia must have left in a rush. She never leaves her door open. Oh well, I ain't even messing with it, a bomb might go off or something, Charlene thought. *I would call the cops, but like Bobby said, she is bringing in the paper. I guess I just gotta put up with it for now. But when Bobby gets that record deal, her ass is* out!

She scaled the flight of stairs that led to the bedroom that she and Bobby shared, her mind chaotic with plans of giving her boyfriend a full night of pleasure; she was looking forward to coming home throughout her entire workday.

Then she remembered: *Oh damn, Bobby's at the club tonight, isn't he? Hmm… maybe I should go and surprise him!*

As Charlene approached the bedroom, she noticed a small slit of light peering through the crack between the door and its frame. She walked into the room and saw their computer, sitting on a desk near the back of the room and running, the only thing providing light in the otherwise pitch-black room. A screen saver displaying the time bouncing around in 3D against a black background played on the screen.

"I keep telling Bobby to turn off the computer when he's done with it," Charlene said to herself, approaching it. "Ain't no sense in running the thing if we're not doing anything with it. Electricity ain't free…"

With plans to shut the machine down, Charlene leaned upon the desk and took hold of the optical mouse. When the screen saver disappeared, Charlene saw a slideshow playing on the screen, transitioning between a series of digital photos reading from a memory stick protruding from the computer's card reader.

And when she took in what she was seeing, Charlene's eyes went wide, her heart pounded and her jaw dropped.

The photos flashing on the screen were poorly aligned photos of Nia and Bobby, completely *nude* in every pose imaginable and a few that were entirely unbelievable. Bobby's hands all over her body. Nia's hands all over his body. The two looking as happy as could be.

Charlene shook in rage and disgust as she gazed at the screen, watching the lewd pictures fade in and out across the display repeatedly, finally seeing concrete evidence of what she suspected all along.

Her heart palpitated furiously, her eyes moist. Charlene didn't even notice her bedroom door creaking shut, and a man emerging from the shadow behind it, a stun gun firm in hand, a small grin on his face.

The Jazz Hall was crowded and chaotic that evening, as Marc made it well known, via flyers and radio commercials, that Bobby Styles was finally premiering a new set of music. Bobby anxiously paced about in the backstage area, frequently polishing his saxophone for smudges that didn't exist. As people randomly whizzed back and forth throughout the club, Bobby's heart skipped a beat in vain a dozen or so times when he thought Nia finally arrived.

A friend approached him with a laugh.

"Hey, the record company guys ain't here to see how shiny your sax is. What are you so nervous about, Bob?" said the poet who often performed spoken word in the club. "Your music is tight. The record company reps wouldn't even be here if it wasn't."

"It's not that…Nia's supposed to be here," Bobby replied. "This new set; it's my gift to her."

Marc approached.

"So, you're finally ready to stop playing both of them and pick one?" Marc uttered. "You like Nia like that, huh?"

"About time he made a decision," added Silk. "We all knew it'd be that thick ass shorty."

"Speaking of," Bobby said, "Where the hell is she? I paged her like an hour ago."

"You still got that girl still using that old-ass pager?" Silk laughed. "What, you *trying* to get caught? Don't you know that if Charlene got her hands on that pager, she would see every number in it, and ninety-nine percent of them would be yours?"

"So what?" Bobby griped. "That doesn't mean anything…"

"It means Charlene would know good and well most of Nia's phone calls are coming from *you* and she would know about all your secret get-togethers," Silk went on. "You're too soft, Bobby. You can't have two girls and do right by both of them. See, what a real player would do is buy his side shorty a cell phone just for her, so nobody has to know about when you two communicate."

"Man, you know what…" Bobby began, "You're right! I can't believe I ain't think of that! She's been asking me to get her something too. I'm going to get her a phone tomorrow."

"Not a bad idea," Marc interjected. "I hope it isn't too late, though."

Bobby looked inquisitively at Marc as he peered out from behind the stage, watching as the usual large crowd of stylish and sharp-dressed patrons made their way into the bar and dining areas of the club, taking seats at the various barstools and tables.

"Looks like it's going to be another jumping night at the Jazz Hall," he muttered.

Bobby looked longingly at Marc, and then turned to Silk.

"Do me a favor and call my crib, see if Nia's there," Bobby said.

Silk shrugged, walking away. "Everybody thinks I'm their errand boy. Whatever. Be back."

Marc took a breath, watching as the club's bouncers led patrons into the club and ushers guided them to various tables. He looked skyward, and smiled gently.

"What's on your mind, Bobby?"

"You know what's going down tonight, right? The producers and everything," Bobby went on.

"Yeah…"

"Yeah, well, I was thinking. If everything goes smoothly tonight, you know; if I get a contract…"

Marc turned and stared at Bobby.

"…I want to buy back my piece of the club."

Marc gently closed his eyes and nodded. "Uh-huh. What's wrong? You don't like the way I'm running things?"

"It ain't that, man," Bobby stammered. "It's just, you know, it's *my* club…I mean, I'm grateful you helped me keep it open when times were tough, but if this record deal goes through, I'm definitely going to be able to pull my own weight, you know what I mean? I mean, I could…I could *blow up* from this! I could end up opening a chain of Jazz Halls; you know what I'm saying? I mean, I'll be more than happy to keep you on as the manager and everything…"

Marc chuckled. "Don't get ahead of yourself, man. Just go out there and handle your business. Now ain't the time to get into all that. You want to be nervous and thinking about this club when you need to be pouring your heart and soul into that sax for them folks out there?"

"Yeah, but…"

"You never know what can happen," Marc continued. "You need to worry about right now. We can discuss the future later, when things are quieter."

Bobby sighed. "You're right. But we *are* going to talk about this."

Marc grinned. "Of course. Now—"

"Yo, Bobby!" Silk's voice suddenly called out, breaking through their conversation. "There are some people here that want to talk to you!"

Bobby glanced in the direction of Silk's voice, then back to Marc. "We're going to talk about this when I'm done with the show, right?"

"Okay, Bob. After the show."

Bobby set his saxophone on a chair and dashed off, toward the front doors of the nightclub. Three men clad in blue suits awaited him.

"Mr. Styles, can we talk to you for a minute?" spoke the man in the middle. "Let's step outside. It's too noisy in here…we need to discuss something important."

Bobby followed as the three stepped out of the building. "You guys must be from the record company."

Nia pulled up across the street from the Jazz Hall's doors. She turned toward the door and gasped; the sparkles of glistening sequined dresses and flickering rims of expensive luxury cars that normally littered the outside of the club were gone, replaced by the all-too-familiar and foreboding red and blue lights of police sirens.

Nia stealthily concealed herself in the shadows of a nearby alley, hiding from the multitude of cops standing around the doors. She focused her eyes and ears on four people she saw standing near the club's doors. One was a police officer, another was Silk, the third was Marc, and the fourth was one of the Jazz Hall's bouncers.

No sign of Bobby.

She was able to clarify the words even over the random jumble of sounds; the running motors, the gossip and the whining of departing customers and would-be customers, the banter of police and the moan of the night. Her eyes grew irritated as she incessantly wiped away tears, fearing the worst. She finally decided to press her cycling goggles over her eyes and focus on the conversation across the street.

"...told you, these guys said they wanted to see Bobby. Next thing I knew, he was gone," said the bouncer.

"Yeah, they even left a note, it's not addressed to anyone, but it says—!" Silk began.

Another cop approached the scene and stuck his palm in front of Silk's face, compelling him to stop talking. The cop addressed his partner, whispering. Then the police turned to Silk and Marc.

"Uh, there's not much we can do right now. Come down to the station and file a report after your friend's been missing for more than 24 hours. Have a good night."

"What the hell?" Silk gasped. "Y'all supposed to be the cops! My friend was kidnapped by some goons and y'all just gonna leave? It wasn't even that long ago! Y'all might be able to track them down! Use the traffic cams or something!"

"Look, he probably just went for a smoke or something," the officer went on. "Just give him a couple of hours and he'll probably be back. Let's go, guys."

"Bobby doesn't smoke, you jackasses! And besides, why the hell would he walk off somewhere when he's supposed to be performing tonight? This is foul, and y'all know it!"

Suddenly, Marc touched Silk on the shoulder, nudging his head in the direction of the alley across the street and the bike parked there. Silk appeared to recognize it.

"You know what? Never mind. Get lost then, you useless…" the poet hissed as the cop cars drove off one by one. Nia carefully made sure all the cops departed, listening to ensure their cars were long gone. When the venue was finally clear, she rushed across the street and ran up to Marc and Silk.

"What happened?" cried Nia.

"Some men in suits took Bobby! You know anything about this?"

Nia looked down. "Damn."

"Hey, you better not have gotten Bobby in no kind of trouble," Silk growled. "I know you're into some shady stuff, but you promised us you wouldn't bring that mess to the club! Now look at what happened after you went wild the other night. This has that damn corporation written all over it, doesn't it? They came after Bobby to get to you, didn't they?!"

"Chill out, Silk," Marc intruded. "Whatever happened, I'm sure it's not Nia's fault."

"Look," Nia asked Silk, "What were you saying about a note?"

"How'd you hear…? Never mind. Yeah, they left some kind of note. I think it's for you."

Silk handed an envelope to Nia. She withdrew the contents and examined the typed print on a sheet of paper.

THE RILEY WAREHOUSE, JUST OFF OF ROUTE 23. COME ALONE. THEY WON'T BE HARMED, PROVIDED YOU COME A.S.A.P.

P.S.: NICE PICTURES.

Nia groaned. *Fuck. The pictures...I guess it's all out in the open now...Charlene must be pissed off...probably doesn't even want to be rescued—at least not by me.*

"The hell with it," she grunted, turning back toward her bike. Marc suddenly grabbed her shoulder.

"Where are you going?" he asked.

"Away from here," Nia said back. "I'm not walking into that trap."

"So you just gonna abandon Bobby and Charlene?"

Nia clenched her fists. "Look, they're not after Bobby, they're after me. If I get my ass out of this city, they'll be just fine. Hudson's goons will let them go. They won't have no reason to hold them!"

"You sure about that?"

Nia fought back tears. "It ain't my problem what happens to them!"

Marc stood before her, running his hand through Nia's hair. He pulled out his handkerchief and blotted Nia's moist eyes. She snatched it and used it herself.

"It sounds like Bobby and Charlene could use your help, Nia. You gonna abandon the only people who were there for you when no one else would help you out? You gonna leave them in the hands of Corp Hudson? You know the big man practically *owns* this town. The police won't help them. If Bobby and Charlene disappear for good, you better believe it's going to end up looking like an accident."

"What; what do you mean?" Nia wondered, trembling with worry she fought in vain to conceal. "Why would they even *go* that far?"

"You saw what happened to Charlie that night. These ain't cops you're dealing with. Corp Hudson wants you *bad*. They're going to do whatever it takes to get you to fall in line. If it takes killing Bobby and Charlene to get your attention, they'll do it and no one who matters will know the difference. If that don't work, well, they do know about how much you like this place, thanks to your boy Charlie. They'll just come here and find someone else to use against you. They might come pick *me* up tomorrow."

Nia pressed her fingers to the bridge of her nose in frustration.

"Remember what we talked about the other day?" Marc said. "I thought you said you didn't want innocents getting hurt because of you anymore. Ain't that what you said? Well, Bobby and Charlene are innocent, and they got snatched because of you. Now, if you were lying to me, and you don't give a damn about anyone but yourself, fine. Go. Just don't show your face around here again."

Nia trembled.

"But," Marc went on, "...if you're ready to *woman-up* and deal with this, you need to go wherever they're telling you to go, and you need to go *now*."

Nia groaned. It pissed her off, but she knew Marc was right. She couldn't stand the thought of leaving Bobby to whatever Corp Hudson's men were planning to do to him.

"But..." Nia began.

"You still making excuses?" Marc growled.

"No, it's just...I don't have any weapons. All I have is my Baby Eagles. I don't have enough equipment to go up against no army. I don't have time to go to my other contacts. I don't know how many of them—"

Marc sighed. "Oh, is that all? Come on with me."

Nia gave him a bewildered look.

She followed Marc into the Jazz Hall. The two walked through the vacant ballroom area, winding their way past the tables. Marc led Nia to a door in an alcove behind the bar; a door that until that moment was closed and securely locked. Marc drew three separate keys and unlocked the padlock, deadbolt and latch that sealed the door and it creaked open. He gestured for Nia to enter; she did.

She gasped when she looked inside.

It was a room of wooden walls and floors, with makeshift shelves built along the perimeter. On one side were stacked a variety of liquor bottles and filled kegs, but the other side was what Nia transfixed her gaze upon.

She saw guns, and lots of them. Revolvers, semi-automatics, fully-automatics, grenade launchers, scope-mounted rifles, explosives, grenades...

Nia finally found words. "Marc...what the hell?!"

Marc smiled. "Don't look so surprised, sweetheart. Why do you think the hoods in this town like to hang out here? You think they come for the music and the booze?"

Nia shook her head. "I never figured you for a gun runner."

"This club was a big ol' money pit," Marc explained. "When I took over, Bobby never asked where I got the money from. It's probably better he doesn't know. I spiced this place up, and now, I don't need to sell this merchandise. But a lot of my old clients, and a couple of new ones, keep coming by with money, so what you expect me to do? Tell them 'no'?"

"How much?" Nia mumbled.

"Ain't no time for that, Nia. Just let me know what you need," Marc said. "I'll start a tab for you. You are my favorite customer, after all, and Bobby's my friend too."

NIA QUICKLY BUT METICULOUSLY sifted through Marc's arsenal, after sliding a coat with several pockets and compartments over her shoulders, designed to hold gun magazines. Nia was planning to carry a lot of ammo.

Fastening a thick leather belt around her hips, she was able to secure two AK-47 machine guns to straps designed for them. Around her shoulders, she secured two more straps for a pair of powerful sawn-off shotguns, modified specifically to have an increased fire rate and extreme stopping power. She snatched a pair of hand grenades from the shelf and affixed them to the coat as well.

After loading her main weapons, the chrome-plated Baby Eagle handguns that served her so well, so often, Nia filled all remaining pocket space with ammunition before turning about and leaving the room.

She stormed past Marc and Silk, where her bike sat waiting near a curb, the engine humming.

"Good luck," Marc said.

Nia nodded and faced the road. The roar of her motorcycle engine filled the air and roared away.

Nia sped toward an expressway, heading south, toward the location as ordered by Alvarez. Her bike leapt upon an on-ramp and soared across the open three-lane road, overtaking many cars and trucks with its incredible speed.

If anything happened to Bobby, I swear... she thought.

Dazzling white light suddenly surrounded her—the high beams of a black van that pulled up her behind her motorcycle.

The passenger-side window of the van slid down and the figure of a muscular man dressed in black leaned halfway out. Tightly gripped in his hands was a high-powered submachine gun.

Nia glanced back and gasped.

Machine gun fire tore through the air, bullets screaming directly at her.

Nia quickly swerved to the side as the shots ripped through the asphalt of the highway.

The van swerved toward Nia's bike in an attempt to crash, but Nia reacted quickly, leaning hard on her side and turning away. Screaming horns of passing vehicles blared by as other drivers spun out of control at the sight and sound of the gunfire. Nia's bike and the van zoomed away from the rest of traffic, narrowly escaping a vicious pileup of multiple cars crashing.

These guys don't give a damn who gets hurt, huh? Nia thought angrily. *No more holding back.*

Nia slowed down, positioning herself behind the van.

"She's behind us!" said a voice.

"Open the hatch!" another voice shouted. "Bust her right in the face!"

Nia increased her speed and began to control her bike with a single hand, her other one reaching within her coat. She clutched the handle of a machine gun, her finger grazing the trigger.

Nia stopped to think. Was she going to do this? Would she —

Bobby's words echoed in her mind.

"...you need to put some of them out of your misery..."

Nia jerked her head to the side as machine gun fire whizzed past her head.

Back to reality.

She had no choice.

She drew one of her AK-47s and aimed it at the back of the van, listening carefully. She heard a click, and she knew the back doors of the van were unlocked. As soon as the doors flew aside, Nia pulled the trigger.

Rapid-fire bullets made a soldier dance in place, blood soaring past in the wind.

Her heart thundered in her chest. She'd carried guns for years, but for the first time in her life, Nia killed a man with one.

It didn't feel as strange as she'd expected it would.

"Johnson!" screamed a voice while the body slammed on the van's floor and slumped out. His body crashed and rolled on the street, the wheels of passing vehicles crushing the corpse with a sickening rumble.

Nia tightened her grip on her bike's handles and sped up, swerving until she placed herself back in front of the van, to get a good look at the occupants. Like the men in the Hallegan Building, they wore black spandex outfits under body armor with full tactical gear, and ski masks hid their faces.

Nia shoved her machine gun back into her jacket, reaching for another weapon.

The van sped up, bumping into the back tire of Nia's bike. Her vehicle began to wobble back and forth, but Nia stiffened her muscles and held onto the handlebars with all her might, forcing the bike back under her control.

Nia yanked a grenade from her coat, flicked the pin off with her thumb and raised it in the air. Without hesitation, she hurled it at the van.

The driver gasped in horror as the round object struck the front grate of the van, and instantly exploded.

The blast forced Nia to lean forward, a fireball of orange and white erupting behind her with a thunderous boom.

She breathed a sigh of relief and looked back again…in shock.

The van slashed through a plume of smoke and flame, continuing to speed toward her; its frame damaged and smoking, but intact.

111

Nia twisted around, aiming behind her as her motorcycle steadily kept ahead of the van, an invisible bridge of distance maintained between the two vehicles as they sped along the road. She drew her AK-47 again, firing directly at the windshield. Nia was astounded when her bullets didn't even dent. The rounds bounced off the window like dust in the air.

The driver stared at Nia and nodded cockily, his cheeks stretching the sides of his mask and betraying his confident grin. The vehicle was designed for combat. They knew what they were up against, and they came prepared.

Then Nia noticed something… the grate that protected the van's engine fell away and clattered onto the road. It must have been dislodged by the grenade's blast.

Nia put away the AK-47 and drew a shotgun, and lost no time pulling the trigger.

The blast from her shotgun tore a large hole in the van's engine. A plume of smoke quickly rose, pulled by the drift. The smoke covered the front of the van like a billowy blanket.

"Damn it!" the driver yelled. "I can't see!"

The van swerved back and forth as if in the hands of a drunk. Frightened drivers zooming by in the opposite direction frantically steered away from it. The other men in the van followed their instincts and leaped out, rolling and tumbling on the road.

Nia forced all of her weight on her handlebars and pressed the brake, which forced the rear wheel of her bike to lift from the ground, performing a *stoppie*. Balancing forward, she skidded ahead, her elevated rear wheel narrowly missed by the careening van behind her.

The van tore through the restraining gate on the highway and tumbled down a massive hill, sinking into the river.

The remaining soldiers pulled handguns, but suddenly realized the folly of wearing all black on the highway in the dead of the night. Horns blared and blinding headlights whipped about as the other cars flew by, forcing the men to ignore their target and concentrate on their own survival.

Nia Black sped away.

She eventually pulled up to the warehouse and turned off her bike's ignition, laying it on its side within the dying reeds. She observed the scene.

The building was old and dilapidated, its wooden planks peeling from the foundation and had several windows cracked or broken, the once colorful 'Riley Distributing' logo faded and weathered with age.

Despite the desolation however, the area was akin to a lively military base. Nia could make out black-uniformed men, armed with pistols and assault rifles, pacing back and forth within the building. Several vans like the vehicle Nia dealt with on the highway sat at rest around the building. From the number of vans parked, Nia guessed there were at least two dozen soldiers waiting for her.

She slid shells inside of her shotguns, attached fresh magazines to her AK-47s, and slammed new clips inside of her pistols before slowly stepping up to the warehouse's large double doors.

Nia stopped in her tracks when brilliant beams of light suddenly shined on her, the intense glare stunning her vision for an instant. Mounted strobe lights sat on top of the building, manned by guards. A booming voice, amplified by a public address system, filled the air.

"NIA BLACK!"

"What the—who are you?"

"YOU KNOW ME, BABY," the voice continued. "WE MET THE OTHER NIGHT IN THE HALLEGAN BUILDING! NAME'S ARMSTRONG! IT'S GOOD TO SEE YOU AGAIN. NOW, LET'S GET STRAIGHT TO THE POINT, ALL RIGHT? DROP YOUR SHIT, PUT YOUR HANDS UP, AND COME INSIDE, OR YOUR FRIENDS ARE DEAD!"

"Where the hell's your boss?!" Nia screamed. "Where the fuck is Alvarez?"

"Bitch, I am the boss!" Armstrong bellowed. "I'm running this operation! If you think I'm playing with you… yo, bring her over here!"

Nia heard the sounds of a scuffle echoing over the PA system. She made out Charlene's yelps.

"GET OFF ME! GET OFF MY HAIR!"

"SHUT THE FUCK UP!"

Then the sound of bone smacking flesh echoed and Nia flinched as the thump of a body hitting the ground echoed in the air.

"LIKE I SAID, THIS IS ALL MY CALL. I WILL SNAP THIS SKINNY BITCH LIKE A TWIG IF YOU DON'T DO WHAT I TELL YOU, RIGHT NOW! YOU KNOW WHAT I CAN DO!"

Nia stopped to think. She thought about Bobby, all those nights of passion she shared with him. She always worried it would be temporary, and wondered if she would eventually have to uproot, or risk her dangerous lifestyle becoming a threat to the fragile peace that he and Charlene enjoyed, despite her strong feelings toward Bobby.

But it was far too late to worry about that. Nia cared for Bobby, and he loved Charlene, so she couldn't allow anything to happen to either of them.

"Let Bobby and Charlene go now!" Nia demanded. "You want me, right? Fine, let them ride away on my motorcycle. Then I can't get away! But if you hurt them, I will be out of here so fast…"

"DROP YOUR GUNS FIRST. NO GAMES!"

Nia watched as the warehouse doors opened. Soldiers emerged, leading Bobby and Charlene out, both with the barrels of assault rifles pressed into their backs.

Nia looked at them and saw the anguish in their eyes; Bobby's sorrow and dread, his secret exposed; and Charlene, whose bruised face only made the bitter rage emanating from her more apparent as she glared at her hated rival.

Armed soldiers nudged Bobby and Charlene in the direction of Nia's bike as Armstrong approached Nia.

"Throw your weapons away. Do it now!" said Armstrong as he aimed his weapon at Nia's head.

Staring down the barrel of his rifle, Nia tossed her shotguns and her AK-47s into the grassy field.

Armstrong turned his weapon toward Bobby and Charlene. "You know, we might as well ventilate these two right now. Why wait?" Armstrong muttered, his finger twitching on his Magnum's trigger. "There ain't no other witnesses out here, so it doesn't even need to look like an accident. They just got murdered out on the streets one sad night and buried in a field; that's what the news can say."

"I've got no problem with that," replied one of the soldiers. "Already got our contact at the newspaper on speed dial."

"'Kill the civilians'?" Charlene gasped. "Hey wait, that's…no…NO!"

The soldiers cocked and leveled their weapons.

NIA TURNED TOWARD BOBBY AND CHARLENE.

"Get down."

"Nia…what…?" Bobby stammered.

"Now!" Nia hollered as she reached inside her jacket.

Bobby immediately threw his arm around Charlene, dragging them both to the ground.

Armstrong's lips parted; he started to say something, then a red blast popped from his forehead as three bangs echoed in the air. His accomplices tumbled to the ground after him, their heads sputtering blood.

Nia lowered her smoking Baby Eagle.

Charlene suddenly squealed, her body jittering uncontrollably as the soldiers fell to the ground dead. "H-h-how…you…you killed…"

"Damn, ain't you ever seen a person get shot before?"

"N-not in *real life!!*" Charlene cried. "You…you're crazy! You're…you lost your mind or something!"

Nia sheathed her weapons, rushed over to her motorcycle and lifted it back up.

"Charlene, what, I wasn't *supposed* to kill them? You think they were playing? This shit is *real!* It was us or them! Now, get your asses on this bike!"

"What the hell is going on, Nia?" Bobby said. He tried to calm Charlene by grabbing her shoulders. "Who are these guys? What they want with you?"

"I don't care who the hell they are!" Charlene snapped, thrashing about and forcing Bobby off her. "Just get me the *fuck* out of here!"

"Just get on the bike and get out of here! I'm going to make sure they don't bother any of us anymore," said Nia.

Charlene followed Bobby as he climbed on Nia's bike. Charlene reluctantly wrapped her arms around Bobby's waist as he started the ignition. She was still shuddering at the sight of the deaths. But Nia could tell Charlene hadn't forgotten about her rage toward them. Charlene looked disgusted that she had to rely on them for her safety, the revolting pair that betrayed her so mercilessly.

"Charlene..." Nia shouted out.

Charlene slowly turned to Nia.

"What?"

"...I'm sorry."

Silence followed. Charlene looked at Bobby, then back at Nia.

"Go, Bobby."

The motorcycle roared away, wobbling back and forth. Nia hollered.

"Don't crash my ride, Bobby! Damn, do you even know how to drive?"

Nia turned back toward the building as the bike shrank in the distance. More soldiers poured out of the facility, including the men who'd been manning the strobe lights before. They were off now, the area illuminated only by moonlight. The men leveled their weapons and stood in formation before her.

"Kill her! Kill her now!"

Nia wasted no time. She whipped out her AK-47s and their thunderous chatter crackled the air, while she leapt out of the way of their gunfire, swirling her body in the air like a gymnast.

Shredded bodies collapsed in heaps under Nia's gunfire, showering the air in crimson rain. Nia began to grin. She thought she'd have trouble killing her assailants, but after what they put her and her friends through, Nia felt no remorse.

She instinctively listened for the sound of their fingers touching the triggers, the sound of the mechanisms moving bullets into the chambers and the hammers igniting the gunpowder, and her body moved out of the line of fire almost automatically.

Nia continued to blast away at every attacker that crossed her path, her arms extended, and her fingers locked on the triggers. She sidestepped every shot that flew her way and answered the shooters with bullets, their heads cracking like coconuts, their bodies bursting into blood-soaked lumps.

Where is he?! Nia thought. *Where is that Alvarez dude? I could have sworn he was running the show. But nobody's giving orders now that that Armstrong guy is down. I just don't see his big dumb ass pulling off nothin' like this. Something's not right.*

The rattling sound of the AK-47s changed to a rapid clicking, and Nia tossed the empty guns aside as she stepped closer to the building.

Bullets rang out and struck the ground where Nia was standing an instant after she leaped backwards out of the way. Six more agents, trying to ambush Nia, leaped from behind the doors of the warehouse and landed in front of her.

Nia pulled out her shotguns and fired one shot from both guns simultaneously, knocking away all six soldiers with a thundering boom, their perforated bodies flailing in all directions away from Nia like bloodstained rag dolls. The recoil from both guns discharging at the same time was so powerful that it forced Nia to take a step backward.

Is that all of them? Nia thought. She turned around to make sure and—

WHOOSH!

She sidestepped just in time to avoid a *massive* fist, dodging a punch that nearly took her head clean off.

Nia faced her attacker, and her jaw dropped.

The man called Armstrong stood before her, but he looked different. His torso had *tripled* in size and his muscle mass made his head look comically small. His pupils shrank and his eyes were almost full-on white. He looked like a demon.

Her eyes met his fierce glare as blood trailed from the bullet dent in his forehead, tracing a path down and across his round nose. The bullet itself sat imbedded in muscle mass *pulsating* from his skull, barely penetrating his flesh and bone.

Armstrong growled like a beast as he leveled his gigantic fists, his monstrous shadow looming over Nia like a towering tree in the moonlight.

"Oh my God…" Nia mumbled.

She realized that Armstrong wasn't just a heavy hitter, as she thought after her initial encounter with him in the Hallegan Building. She hadn't imagined his hand growing and shrinking before—there was something different about him…something *corrupt* about his body.

Armstrong reached out for Nia.

Nia raised her shotguns and pulled the triggers just as Armstrong covered the barrels with his hand. The discharge sounded like a muffled explosion.

Blood shot out like spikes from Armstrong's clutched fist. He tightly gripped the barrels of Nia's cannons within his left palm, the length of the weapons held between his fingers.

Blood dripped across the bottom of his wrist. He flashed teeth and swung his arm skyward, yanking the guns out of Nia's grasp. The shotguns swirled into the starry sky and vanished.

Armstrong immediately threw a punch at Nia, his massive fist trembling the ground as it slammed into the surface. Nia barely dodged.

She rolled on the ground and retrieved her remaining grenade. In a split second, she flicked off the pin and hurled it at Armstrong.

He caught it, and it detonated in his hand like fireworks, the force completely suppressed by his grip. He wagged his fingers as if he touched a steaming pot on a stove, and then growled, leaning toward Nia.

Nia's eyes bulged.

The small woman darted forward and shot her foot towards his crotch—

Armstrong grasped her foot in his right hand. Apparently, he was as fast as he was strong.

Armstrong swung his right arm skyward, hurling Nia into the air.

Reacting quickly, Nia outstretched a Baby Eagle in midair and sent bullets booming toward him as she soared back down to earth. The shots met their mark, blood shooting up like small volcanic eruptions on his shoulders and chest, but Armstrong did not so much as flinch.

He met Nia's falling frame with a shot from his left hand, sending her stumbling into the reeds.

Nia kept a firm grip on her pistol as she crashed into the ground. She watched Armstrong rush toward her, his hideous, elongated arms flailing in the air as his boots thumped in the earth. Nia jumped to her feet and opened fire, bullet holes bursting in Armstrong's flesh as he continued to swing at her.

Armstrong's fists swung past Nia's head with a *whoosh*, cutting the air as she ducked. Nia rolled behind him, narrowly avoiding a double-arm strike that left a crater in the ground and an echo in the air. She emptied her chamber into his back, blood splattering everywhere. He wheeled around like a top, his left fist smashing into Nia's head like a wrecking ball. Nia whirled away from him headfirst and crashed into the ground again.

Nia slowly hefted herself by her arms, groaning, breathing hard. She was dazed. Blood dribbled from her mouth. She saw stars and clawed the earth; her head throbbing in pain as Armstrong's roaring shook the air.

She'd never felt this way before…so overpowered, so inferior.

He'd only struck her twice, but the force of his blows left her feeling like she'd been fighting for hours…and losing.

The blood-coated man-beast slowly turned and lumbered toward her as Nia lifted her pistol again…and with a pull of the trigger and the strident click that followed, she realized in horror that her chances went from slim to none.

No more bullets.

Armstrong took another step toward Nia. Then another.

He wrapped his hand around Nia's belly, gripping her entire torso with only his right hand; snatching her from the ground like a toy, and started to squeeze.

Nia felt unbelievable pressure squeezing the life out of her like a wrench tightening around her body.

She couldn't even summon the breath to scream in agony. She felt her body weakening, her heart rate slowing, her consciousness waning.

Blood rushed to her skull, her fingertips, her toes, as if being forced out like toothpaste. She felt dizzy. She opened her mouth; an incoherent, barely audible moan squeaked.

She was blacking out.

Armstrong raised his left fist, easily five times the size of Nia's head, preparing to smash her face in with all his might.

He roared like a conquering lion, as his muscles tensed and tightened. He held Nia high in the air, silhouetted against the moonlight, readying his final punch.

Then something happened.

Nia's pupils dilated. As if a switch turned off in her mind, her expression changed from fearful, to blank. Her face tightened. Her eyes glazed over with the hue of the night.

Armstrong squeezed with all his might, but he felt his grip slipping. His fingers lurched apart, a trembling in his palm weakening his hold.

Nia found immeasurable strength and resisted his grip, forcing his hand apart.

She outstretched her arms, blasting Armstrong's hand wide open! His fingers broke away from Nia's outstretched body, his bones snapping.

Nia landed on the ground, her weight making an impact crater in the earth. Armstrong stumbled back, holding his hand, stroking his fractured fingers. Her muscles tensed and bulged, her teeth clenched and her fists closed, she stared at Armstrong, breathing hard.

Armstrong rushed toward her, his fists high in the air. Nia stood still and watched him grow larger and larger in front of her, watched as the earth shook under him from every thunderous step, watched as he barreled his fists upon her small frame like toppling pillars.

Nia instantly outstretched her palms high above her—

And *caught* his fists.

The impact passed through Nia like a shockwave, sending a plume of dust rising from the earth around them in a ring, but she didn't even quiver.

Armstrong stood thunderstruck, gazing at Nia in total disbelief.

She just glared back with eerily calm eyes.

Nia grasped Armstrong's massive fingers like rungs on a ladder and pulled him down, his fists impacting the earth with a deafening BOOM.

Armstrong could only watch helplessly as Nia clawed his fingers with her own, her fingernails digging into his flesh like talons. She vaulted forward from his hands and shot toward his head like a magnum load, her knees crashing into his face. His eyes rolled to the back of his head and he fell on his back, blood pouring out of his ears and nose.

Nia landed behind her enemy in a roll, collected herself and took a breath.

She blinked rapidly. Life returned to her eyes, and her muscles settled.

She turned and spotted at the body of Armstrong, his blank eyes staring at her upside down.

She trembled.

Did I do that?

Then Nia looked up at the warehouse and saw the man known as Alvarez in the doorway, staring at her.

"Found your punk-ass..." she muttered.

Alvarez quickly raised his pistol. Nia looked around on the ground and saw her guns, remembering that the chambers empty. Her heart started pounding.

Then she felt the air grow dense behind her.

A gunshot rang out.

Nia scrambled around and saw a bloody eruption in the chest of Jackson as he tumbled backward, a hole in his heart putting him down for good.

Alvarez lowered his gun and sheathed it, turned around and walked into the warehouse.

"What the..." Nia began. *He...he saved me. He saved my life.*

Nia took heavy breaths, ingesting as much oxygen as her lungs would allow. Her body would eventually feel normal again, but she had no time to waste recovering.

No more soldiers.

Bobby and Charlene were long gone, safe.

There were no more distractions left.

And Alvarez was finally there.

Nia Black ran into the warehouse, with gray walls and grimy floors littered with wooden crates blackened by age and dust. Illuminated only by the dull yellow lights hanging from the ceiling, the derelict building's atmosphere was heavy with the smell of gun smoke. Nia looked up and saw the man known as Alvarez standing with his legs parted and his hands clasped behind his back on a catwalk that lined the upper region of the building.

Nia stopped running and walked slowly, sliding fresh magazines into her Baby Eagle pistols. Nia glared at her enemy. Their eyes met at that moment, the air dead quiet.

"Tell me!" Nia growled. "Why are you doing this?! Why are you messing with me?!"

"I know more about you than you could possibly imagine, Miss Black. I have the answers you are looking for, the direction you seek."

Screw the answers, she thought.

Nia raised her guns and opened fire.

What happened next actually *scared* her.

Alvarez became a blur. He zipped away in an instant, Nia's shots cracking the wall.

Nia glanced up and the glare of Alvarez's spectacles glinted in her eyes as he somersaulted over her, as if frozen in time for an instant, their faces almost close enough to kiss.

Nia stuck her gun skyward and shot through the air but hit nothing but the warehouse's ceiling. Then she froze in place as a metal object touched the back of her head.

Alvarez was *behind* her, the barrel of his black Desert Eagle burrowing into her pitch-black hair and pressing against her skull.

She instantly spun around on her heel, knocking away Alvarez's gun with her right hand and squeezing off with her left, an instant before Alvarez pulled his own trigger and sent a bullet screaming into the ground. The bangs of Nia's gunfire played in the air like a thunderstorm. Alvarez swirled away, bullets slashing between his locks of hair and striking the walls.

Alvarez stooped low, the sole of his boot squeaking against the stone floor. He stuck his gun out and pressed it between Nia's breasts.

His smile dropped though, as he glanced upward and saw Nia's own pistol was pressing into his forehead.

"Nicely done, Miss Black," Alvarez muttered. "Your look says it all. You can see I am more than what I seem. But compared to what you're *truly* capable of, I'm no better than those regular soldiers you killed. You got a taste of that when you broke free of Armstrong earlier."

"Huh?"

"Regarding him, it's rather sad that you went with such a simple attack strategy without thinking; you should have known he would burn through his enhancement eventually. Had you simply avoided him for a while, he would have lost the ability to maintain his mutation, and you could have defeated him painlessly. But I suppose it isn't your fault. Clearly, you were trained by someone who didn't know how to compensate for your...unique gifts."

Alvarez withdrew his gun and sheathed it. He leveled his shoulders and smiled again.

"What the hell are you talking about?!" growled Nia.

"I've tested you enough. Now that all those bothersome soldiers are dead, we can get down to business."

Nia was completely dumbfounded.

"I understand your confusion, Miss Black," said Jesús Alvarez. "Things are not quite as they seem. I tried to keep Corp Hudson out of it...tried to handle things my way, but apparently, they don't trust me. Of course, that's not without just cause."

Nia looked around, gazed at all the dead soldiers that she'd put down, and the hulking beast of a man known as Armstrong, the man Alvarez finished off with his own gun. She didn't know what to think.

"All right...so what's your deal?"

"In simple terms, I am not exactly a loyal associate of Corp Hudson. I work for someone else; someone who wants to keep you out of harm's way. It's my job to ensure your safety."

"Oh, you mean by sending your men after me in the Hallegan building? That's what you mean by keeping me safe?"

"That was...before," Alvarez explained. "Initially, my plan was to capture you, then get you out of the city. Once we were far enough outside the city, I would have eliminated Armstrong and the soldiers guarding you, and we would have gone from there. However, you proved stronger and more tenacious than I expected; you recovered more quickly than I thought you would, and you escaped. This complicated things."

"So you needed to kidnap my friends to draw me back out," Nia muttered. "Right?"

"That was not my game," Alvarez explained. "I would never stoop to such levels. But because of my failure to bring you in the first time, I suppose Vincent and the others decided to keep me out of the loop. By the time I realized what was going on, it was already too late. Your friends were kidnapped and I found myself playing catch-up."

"Whatever. That Jackson dude wasn't smart enough to pull something like this off. He wasn't no different than that other psycho y'all set loose outside the Jazz Hall the other night…just a trigger-happy killer who liked to see people suffer. Ain't no way that guy was in any kind of leadership position."

"Those who choose to be weaponized by Corp Hudson's R&D come from the top ranks of the Corp's security detail, Miss Black," Alvarez went on. "Carl Jenkins, the man we called 'Gunner', was no different. In fact, the reason I stand here before you today is because you defeated Gunner so effectively. He was…removed, and I was promoted to his position."

"So you're just another one," Nia said. "You're the next in a long line of guinea pigs."

"Well, not exactly. What I can…what *we* can do has nothing to do with Corp Hudson's current experiments. Gunner and Armstrong shared a common flaw. Once they gave into their desire for violence, they lost control over their emotions and only saw bloodlust. This is a common problem with those who volunteered for Hudson's experiments. This is the reason Hudson wants you so badly."

"Huh?"

"Corp Hudson has been trying to perfect the human condition for many years now. He approached a glimmer of success when he developed a formula called *Hercules*, a human performance enhancement additive that was intended to alter a human's physiology at the base. It would redefine what the human body was capable of at the cellular level. Hudson contracted young soldiers, mercenaries and hired guns for trials, but the formula only worked on one percent of the test subjects, and even among them, only one person maintained self-control after receiving it. That person's name was *Alexander Black*."

Nia gasped.

"Yes, that's right," Alvarez nodded. "Your father, Alexander Black, was the sole test subject capable of enduring the effects of *Hercules*. All the other subjects either lost their minds or their bodies rejected it, resulting in painful symptoms that ultimately resulted in death. Only Alexander Black managed to survive, and thrive, with the power of *Hercules* coursing through his veins."

"Yeah, well, I figured my dad had something special going through him," Nia said. "That's why I was born the way I was. So what?"

"Alexander Black reveled in the fact that he was 'special' this way. While Hudson kept experimenting, Alexander was not interested in seeing more people like him—he couldn't bear the possibility that someone *more* compatible with the formula, someone *better* than him might come along. He recognized quickly that becoming the world's finest physical specimen had its perks. He destroyed the facility in which *Hercules* was created because he wanted to remain the only one."

Nia rolled her eyes. "Get to the point. I ain't come here for a lecture."

"The point, Miss Black," Alvarez sighed, "Is that Hudson lost Alexander Black, and with him, any hope of resurrecting *Hercules*. All Hudson has left is the data and records. Black disappeared; went into hiding. That's why he abandoned you as a child; did you know that?"

Nia flinched.

"Your father left his family to draw Hudson away," Alvarez continued. "But you were conceived *after* Alexander Black was enhanced with *Hercules*…so you inherited his abilities—naturally. Hudson is after you because wants to know the extent of your abilities, and harness the results for his projects. It's that simple."

"And you're telling me all this because…?"

"Because I'm a double agent," Alvarez went on. "My job was to get inside of Corp Hudson and learn their secrets. I worked my way to the top of their security detail, learning everything I could about what goes on inside the organization. My superiors want to take control of Corp Hudson's resources. We believe they're engaging in illegal and unethical activities, but we can't prove it. There's something I need to get, and I need your help."

"My help?" Nia gasped. "You think I'm going to work with *you*?"

"We both stand to gain," Alvarez explained. "You will help bring down Corp Hudson, and I will complete my mission. You will never have to worry about them coming after you again. You'll be free to live your life without having to watch your back, Miss Black. Think of it. This is why I went through all this trouble…I need you."

"You got some kind of…credentials or something? Like a badge?" Nia mumbled, circling her hands in wonder. "Because for all I know, you could just be trying to play me."

"Miss Black, there's no time," Alvarez said. "I need you to come with me, now."

"Oh, yeah right!" Nia squealed. "I guess since you couldn't *capture* me or get your big, ugly-ass friend to *beat* me, you figured you'd *ask* me to be your prisoner?! Catch more flies with honey, huh? Well, hate to burst your bubble, but I ain't no—"

"It's not like that at all. As I told you, it's my job to get you out and keep you safe from harm."

"Prove it," Nia said. "Prove to me that this just ain't some game. You were there when I got the job from Darien Drakonis. You're the one who cattle-prodded me. I've got no reason to trust you."

"Perhaps not…" Alvarez sighed.

Then Nia looked at his spectacles, noticing a glare reflecting off their metallic frames. She spun around and saw several cars speeding toward the warehouse in the distance.

"They arrived more swiftly than I anticipated," Alvarez muttered. "It's Hudson's men. He must have tried to contact Armstrong. With him dead, Marks would most likely have sent the next agent in line... What will you do, Miss Black?"

"What? What you mean 'what will I do'? You know what I'm gonna do. I'm going to take my Babies and—"

"And what?" Alvarez stopped her. "You'll be hopelessly outnumbered. You're tired from battle. And I doubt you have enough ammunition left to deal with everyone who's coming."

"Then you help me fight them. That'll prove that you're on my side."

"I can't do that. I need to maintain my cover."

Nia rolled her eyes. "Whatever. Then I'll get away like I always do."

"How? What do you plan to drive? Can you outrun a car?"

Nia grimaced. She remembered that Bobby and Charlene were long gone on her bike. She didn't think that part through.

"What, you got a better idea?"

"As a matter of fact..."

Alvarez guided Nia's glance to a blue coupe parked at the side of the warehouse.

"How do you think I got here? Get in the car. They haven't seen us yet. We can get away before they realize what's happened."

Nia paused, looking back and forth. Had she not given her bike to Bobby, she wouldn't have this problem. But Alvarez was right. There was no telling how many people were coming, and all she had left were her spare clips, some of which she already expended fighting Alvarez earlier. She hadn't fully recovered from the fight with Armstrong, and she had no desire to do any more fighting that night.

Nia exhaled sharply. "Let's go."

The two rushed to his coupe and quickly drove away.

Several SUVs pulled up to the warehouse, and men in full tactical gear climbed out. Afterward, one more man with brown hair tied into a ponytail appeared along with the rest, wearing a black suit.

"Mr. Casey," said one of the soldiers. "This is the place. We've got men down here… a lot of them."

Casey walked about and looked at the bodies.

"So this is what happens when we leave Alvarez in charge…"

"We don't know if it was Alvarez's fault, sir," said the soldier.

Casey chuckled. "It was Alvarez's job to take down Nia Black, wasn't it? We tracked her here, and this is where Armstrong's detail went. She's not here, he's not here, and a bunch of our men are lying in the dirt. Something happened… something bad."

Then one soldier nearly tripped over a large body in the earth.

"Sir!" he said. "It's number 623…Armstrong! He's dead!"

"What?" Casey gasped, rushing toward the soldier. He stopped and looked down as more soldiers rolled Armstrong's body over—it took several men to do it. Billy spotted the gaping chasm in his chest, a hole where his pulsating heart used to be.

"Investigate the site. Search everywhere. I want to know everything," Casey said.

"Everything, sir?"

"I said everything. Shell casings. Blood samples. Forensics. I expect you people to be able to tell me exactly how many blades of grass are out here and how many of them are brown. I want to know exactly what happened out here and I want to know now."

THE BLUE COUPE SPED through the night as it passed away to sunrise, leaves rustling under the wheels as it sped across the vacant, forest-lined roads. Nia Black sat in the passenger seat, the chair in full recline as she stretched out and fought sleep. She refused to let her guard down for an instant, even though lethargy was beginning to overwhelm her.

She glanced at Alvarez, observing the way he steered the car. His presence was the epitome of tedium with his unwavering stare, perfectly rigid reflexes and meticulously controlled breathing, the perfect soldier.

For a brief moment, he broke the monotony. He took off his glasses and rubbed his eyes briefly, then quickly replaced them.

Hmm…he's actually kind of cute without those glasses on, Nia thought, staring at his sharp profile. He shot a glance at her and she quickly looked away.

She sat quietly, unloading and reloading her weapons repeatedly in a vain attempt to ease her boredom. The inside of Alvarez's car reeked stale of gunpowder and cigarettes, and the hard leather seat had her rear growing numb from sitting far too long.

Then she couldn't take it anymore. She needed some sound in the air.

"Tell me something."

"What?" Alvarez responded to her.

"…I don't know, anything," Nia grumbled. "I mean, talk. I'm bored. Tell me what you want with me. What are you trying to get from Hudson?"

"I can't be sure exactly what it is, but we need evidence of Hudson's performance enhancement experiments. His human trials were never approved by the government," said Alvarez. "The key is something only Hudson himself, or his scientists, would have access to. We need to get to him, detain him, and get him to talk."

"You mean to tell me you spent all that time working for Hudson and you never got the chance to interrogate him yourself, bug his office or nothing?"

"Hudson is far too well-guarded, and far too secretive, to allow even his highest-ranking officers to access him easily. But we'll have our shot. Even a man as powerful as Hudson can't have his subordinates do everything."

"What do you mean?"

"He's meeting with Ivan Worthington, the head of a construction firm, to discuss groundbreaking and manufacturing of a new research facility downtown. Worthington is an old-school businessman—he doesn't want to deal with liaisons or representatives, he doesn't believe in making decisions by email and he doesn't have a Blackberry. He's only going to begin negotiations by shaking the hand of the man in charge...only then does he even consider signing on the dotted line."

"So Hudson's going to have to go out to meet this guy personally," Nia ascertained. "When?"

"Two days from now," Alvarez answered. "9:00 AM. Bright and early."

"Damn, two days..." Nia sighed.

Alvarez shrugged. "It's all I've got. You need to do is get there and be done before he has a chance to summon the security team. If it comes down to it, you know how to get away from them, and I'll create a diversion to make it easier. You stop him and I'll do the rest."

The coupe came to a stop on a crowded downtown street. Alvarez reached across Nia's lap and opened the passenger side door.

Nia shot a glance outside the car, and then back at Alvarez. She saw he was holding her pager in his open palm.

"I'll contact you when the location is definite. Once we have him, you'll be free."

Nia hesitated for a moment, then snatched the pager, and climbed out of the car. She quickly walked down the crowded sidewalk as the coupe sped off.

Nia looked at the pager in her hand. Every ounce of her being wanted to slam it on the concrete and shatter it into pieces. It was how the bad guys tracked her down in the first place, after all.

But what if Alvarez was telling the truth? Never mind whether he was trustworthy or not. If there was any chance Nia had of getting Hudson and his corporation out of her life, bringing them down once and for all because of what happened to her family, Alvarez was the key. Even if he were only planning to use her for his own ends, even if he were an enemy, it was the closest Nia ever came to having an inside track with Corp Hudson since she stopped dating Vincent Marks.

She shoved the pager into her pocket.

Nia strolled past a gang of girls and guys not far from her age; laughing, playing, gossiping, and talking about how they intended to spend their weekends. Catching wind of their conversation, Nia found herself growing envious.

They sure look like they're having a good time... She thought. *Must be nice to be able to chill like that. I mean, I love running and gunning, but I sometimes wish I didn't always have to watch my back. It must be great not to have a care in the world...or at least to have nothing to fear from the law.*

Finally, Nia came across a pay phone. She dialed the number that was foremost in her memory, a number she'd been itching to dial for hours. Soon, the charges were accepted and she was in conversation.

"Sorry about calling collect," Nia said.

"*Are you all right?!*" the voice on the other end shouted. "*What happened? Is everything cool?*"

"Everything's fine," Nia whispered, relieved. She was glad Bobby answered and not Charlene, and it was evident in her voice. "How's my baby?"

"I'm all right, we're both all right."

Nia groaned. "I was talking about my other baby, Bobby."

Bobby sucked his teeth. *"Oh…the bike. It's cool too. I got it parked out front. That thing's got some serious torque! I don't know how the hell you handle that thing; I damn near lost control a couple of times. Oh yeah, Charlene has me sitting in your room— your old room—waiting for you to get back."*

"She didn't toss you right out?" Nia gasped.

"She wanted me to make sure you came back and got your stuff. She didn't want any of it being connected to us by the police or anything like that."

"She called the police?"

"I had to convince her not to. She was going to get them to confiscate all your stuff, but I told her not to mess with you like that…she was pissed but she let it go."

"Was everything there? Was the place ransacked?"

"No, everything was cool…nothing was missing from what I could tell. Except money. I'm guessing Charlene took it—she didn't say anything to me."

"You mean to tell me that bitch stole my—you know what, forget it. It wasn't all that much anyway."

"Can you blame her?" Bobby chuckled nervously. *"I mean, come on, after last night, she deserves something…"*

"I'm sorry, Bobby…" Nia sighed. "I came and messed your life all up."

"Look…let's talk about that later. Are you coming back here? What's going on with those dudes that kidnapped us?"

"I'll tell you everything, but I need my wheels back," Nia answered. "Drive it to this address I'm about to give you, all right? I want you to meet somebody. Bring the bike, and all of my stuff that you can fit in your sports bag."

"All right," Bobby said. *"Look, I gotta go."*

135

Footsteps echoed behind Bobby, from outside of Nia's bedroom. Bobby hung up the phone as Charlene walked in, finding him seated upon Nia's bed, which was stripped of sheets and pillows. Only one night ago, he sat in the same spot, with Nia laying nude in his arms. He remembered answering the cryptic phone call from Jesús Alvarez, just before the two took the photos that exposed the truth of their relationship.

"Who was that?" asked Charlene. "Was that that bitch Nia? You told her to get her ass back here and get her shit, right?"

"Um, nah, it wasn't her...wrong number," Bobby replied.

"You were talking for a minute for it to be a wrong number," Charlene added. "You still lying to me, ain't you? Damn it, Bobby..."

Bobby thought quickly. "Look, some fool was asking directions to the stadium. He thought he was calling a friend and got me instead, so I just gave up the goods."

"Oh," Charlene said. "Whatever. Just hurry up and pack that junk up. And be careful...a bomb might go off or something."

Bobby stood. "Look, I need to run to the club for a minute...let the peoples know we're all right."

"You can't just call Marc and let him know?"

"I think it'd be better if they see I'm in one piece, you know what I'm saying?" Bobby retorted.

He had an answer for everything.

Charlene walked away, back toward the stairs leading to their room.

"Just hurry back."

Bobby drove across town in his jeep, barely able to concentrate on the road as he thought about his situation. After the second near-miss accident at an intersection, he knew he had to find clarity of thought as curses and horns blared in his ears. But Bobby knew that he wouldn't be able to focus on his situation until he tied up all the loose ends, no matter how minor.

He arrived at the Jazz Hall. As per usual in the sunlight hours, no one was present at the hall except for the one person Bobby needed to see: Marc. Bobby drew his key and entered the building.

The club's bartender and owner was present as usual, but instead of his routine cleaning and organizing the bar, he was on the phone. Bobby crept inside of the club and patiently waited for Marc to notice his presence.

Marc finally looked up and saw Bobby. He nearly dropped the phone in surprise.

"Look, I'll contact you again later…yeah, later. You know me, pleasure before business," Marc said, and hung up the phone.

"You ain't have to hang up for me," Bobby sighed.

Marc charged over to Bobby and embraced him.

"You're all right! Man, I'm glad to see you! You okay, man? You ain't hurt, right?"

Bobby shrugged. "I'm good; me and Charlene, we're both all right. I don't know what it was all about, but Nia came to get us."

"Good," Marc smiled. "That's my girl. Let her know I'm proud of her."

"I'll do that," Bobby agreed.

Marc looked sorrowful. "Look, Bobby, the record producers…"

"I know," Bobby sighed. "They came through and I didn't show. I guess I can write off that little opportunity…I ain't never getting my club back…"

Marc grinned. "Hey, man, whatever happens, the Jazz Hall will always be your joint. I'm just here supporting everything you do. Besides, those guys heard about the kidnapping and everything. I know you're kind of off your rocker about being snatched by secret agents and what not, but this might actually have done you some good."

Bobby was dumbfounded. "Huh?"

"Think about it, man," Marc went on. "What do all these rappers and hip-hop artists go around talking about? How they get mistreated by the law, how they be busting caps and all that mess? You got the real scoop. You were falsely detained, man! You know it and everybody who was here last night knows it. So you're now a smooth jazz musician with real street rep. Those record producers are coming back in a week to hear what you got. You're the man, Bobby!"

Bobby's lips formed a slow smile. "Huh. Look man, I gotta go, but I'll talk to you later on, all right?"

"Sure, man," Marc smiled as Bobby started toward the door. "Take care. And tell Nia to call me!"

EVENING FELL. Nia waited impatiently inside of Kim's warehouse.

"He is taking forever," Nia groaned.

Her accomplice, Kim, was more relaxed, as always.

"Give him time, my dear. You are not the only one with problems to deal with."

Nia folded her arms. "It's probably that bony-behind Charlene, asking him a million questions as usual."

"Envy does not suit a person of your upbringing, Nia," Kim sighed. "You have spent too much time in those nightclubs. You forget your honorable teachings more and more by the day."

Within moments, the familiar roar of a sport bike sounded in the distance and grew progressively louder. Nia's frown turned upside-down immediately.

"That's him!" Nia cheered, trotting toward the door.

Kim quickly called out, "Foolish girl! Wait for a moment, it may be a trap. Ready yourself. Remember your training."

"Whatever, old man," Nia said with a chuckle. "The only training I need to remember is how to pull the trigger…as long as I got these babies, can't nobody stop me."

"Only a fool entrusts their life to a weapon, Nia," Kim warned. "You need not rely on mere guns if you are one with your surroundings."

Nia sighed and rolled her eyes. "Yeah, all right. Look, I can see from here…Bobby came just like I asked, and he's all alone. See? You worry too much, K."

Outside of the warehouse, Bobby, wearing Nia's riding goggles, leaped off Nia's silver sport bike, lugging along a large duffel bag. He smiled slightly when he laid eyes on Nia's bouncy body approaching him. Bobby carefully set the bag down, leaned his saxophone against it, and embraced Nia when she got close enough. Nia leaped into his chest, wrapping her arms around his neck and kissing him, her legs flailing in the air.

"I was missing you, baby," said Nia between pecks as she pulled the goggles off his head and nestled them in her hair.

"Yeah…" Bobby muttered, staring into space. "I was worried about you, too."

Nia stopped kissing him and dropped to the ground.

She sensed something different about him. As her chest pressed against his, she felt his heart rate quicken, as if he dreaded having her close to him.

Something's the matter, Nia thought. *He must be real shook up about that whole kidnapping thing, especially since it only happened because he's cool with me. But still, I figured he'd be a little happier to see that I was all right? If for no other reason than because we're friends? We* are *still friends, aren't we?*

Bobby looked ahead for anything he could use to change the subject and caught sight of the overalls-wearing Oriental gentleman inside the building.

"…So who's this? Is this the guy you wanted me to meet?"

"Yeah," Nia answered. "Kim, Bobby. Bobby, Kim."

"So this is the legendary musician Nia is always talking about," Kim smiled. "I have heard much about you, young man."

Bobby grinned nervously. "I don't know about 'legendary'…but thanks. Nia's always talking about you being like her father."

"That sounds about right," Kim responded with a nod.

Nia spoke up. "So how's Marc doing?"

"You should have seen him," Bobby went on. "As soon as I got back at the club, he smiled like he saw his newborn child for the first time or something! He told me to tell you he was real proud of you. He wants you to call him sometime."

"Will do," Nia smiled. "But pleasure before business."

"So Nia," Kim suddenly spoke. "Regale us. What happened last night?

"Yeah," Bobby interjected. "How did you get away? I know you got guns and you can shoot and all, but that was like twenty armed soldiers against one little midget girl…"

"I'm not *that* damn short!" Nia snapped. "But I took your advice. I decided to use the gifts I got from my dad to start putting the bad guys out of *our* misery."

"So they're not going to bother us anymore? Life goes on, and all that? Charlene and I are safe and sound?"

"Yeah…" Nia's voice trailed off. " much. Anyway, you'll have to excuse me for a minute. I've been wearing this same get-up since last night and I need to freshen up. Is the washroom in the back clean, Kim? Is the water running?"

"It is as clean as the bathroom in any derelict warehouse, my dear, and the water runs fine," Kim answered.

"Good. I'll be back. You boys play nice," Nia smiled, lifting the black bag and trotting toward the back.

Kim rested himself at his desk in the center of the room, looked back, listening as Nia's footsteps trailed off until they were silent, and he then turned to Bobby, who sat upon a nearby wooden crate after sweeping away the dust.

"This town's full of some crazy folks," Bobby sighed, "But man, she's the cream of the crop."

"She is in love with you, you know," Kim suddenly said.

"What?" Bobby bellowed. "No, not Nia. She doesn't feel that way about anybody. She won't let herself get too attached to anyone. She'd never let anyone in."

"Do you truly believe that? What do you think keeps her going?" Kim continued. "She puts her life on the line night after night. What do you think truly drives her to make sure she is not caught, no matter what?"

"What…me?"

"She cannot bear the thought of being torn away from you. She was so sad, the night she spent in her enemies' clutches, in the van with those other agents and nowhere near you. When she told me about it, every other sentence was Bobby this, Bobby that. 'I missed Bobby…all I kept thinking about was Bobby…'"

Bobby blushed. "She told you about the setup at the Hallegan Building? I thought I was the only one she talked to about stuff like that."

Kim smiled. "She tells me everything."

Bobby lowered his head with a heavy exhale. Something was definitely weighing heavily on his mind. Kim spoke again.

"Bobby Styles, let me inform you of something you may not have considered," said Kim. "She did not need you to come here."

"What? That don't make sense. She asked me—"

Kim smiled and stared into Bobby's face as his voice trailed. "Do you believe Nia *needed* you to bring her that bike or her clothes? Do you not think she could have retrieved it herself without you knowing a thing? Or that she simply could have abandoned it all and bought what she needed from elsewhere? But if she had, she would not have *you* here, all to herself."

Kim rested his head on his knuckles. Bobby exhaled again, and their eyes met.

"What about you, young man?" Kim asked. "How is it that you feel about the matter?"

Bobby took a deep breath. "To tell you the truth, I don't—"

Nia suddenly trotted from the back of the warehouse, clad in a half-top and denim miniskirt, along with her biker gloves, heeled boots and tinted glasses. Her stride was brisk as she switched her way toward the entryway of the warehouse. With a bright and cheerful grin, she pounced up to Bobby and pressed her lips upon his cheek.

"Thank you, baby," said Nia.

"For...for what?"

"You packed my hair stuff...my brush, my curling iron and everything!" Nia explained. "That's why you're my favorite person. You're so thoughtful."

"Well," Bobby scratched his head nervously. "I know how much it means to you to have your hair tight."

Nia smiled at Bobby, and then turned to Kim.

"I already know what you're going to say," Nia sighed. "After everything that's happened, it's time to cut and run, right?"

Kim gave Nia an accommodating glance, his eyebrows going up.

"Well, I can't. I still have stuff to do."

"'Cut and run'?" Bobby interjected. "What are you talking about?"

Nia took a breath and turned to Bobby. "See, thing is, we found out the other day that those guys, you know...Corp Hudson's people...they're after me."

Bobby scoffed. "I could have told you that. I *was* at the Jazz Hall that night, you know."

Nia shook her head. "That's not what I meant. They're not just trying to arrest me or collect a bounty. They want to use me for something...study me or something like that. And old man Kim here thinks I need to be getting out of this city, like that's going to help."

Bobby turned to Kim with a grin. "You ought to know better than that. Nia's not the type to run away from anything."

"And besides," Nia added. "Ain't like I can run from them anyway! I mean, they found my house when I was a kid and got to Mom… Hiding don't work. No, what I gotta do is take Hudson down…cut off the head and the body dies."

Kim sighed. "Still so stubborn."

"Stop worrying," Nia grinned. "This is *me* we're talking about here. They ain't got nothing for me. I mean, if you'd seen that *thing* I dealt with last night, you'd be convinced too—they can't beat me!"

"What 'thing'?!" Bobby interrupted. "I thought it was just soldiers."

Nia swallowed. She'd opened up a can of worms. She'd forgotten that Bobby and Charlene escaped *before* she fought Armstrong's enhanced form.

"Well, see, they had this thing… this monster. Bullets weren't even slowing the dude down. But, I beat it!"

"Oh yeah?" Bobby stammered. "How?"

"Um…I was just stronger, I guess."

"You think they've got…more like that 'thing'? Or like the dude from the other night, with the gun for an arm?"

Nia looked into his eyes. *Damn—here I go. Bobby must be scared out of his mind right now after what happened the other night. I keep forgetting he's not like me.*

"Now don't you worry," Nia smiled. "I'll keep looking out for you, Bobby!"

Bobby's attitude changed. His eyebrows furrowed and his fists closed. He was suddenly a man facing a challenge to his manhood.

"I don't need you to be 'looking out' for me, Nia. I can take care of myself."

"Chill," Nia laughed. "We can't all be fearsome like me. You just keep worrying about that sweet music you play…for the club, and for me…and let me handle the light work. I mean, after beating that thing last night and the dude with the gun-arm, I know those guys ain't got nothing for me. As soon as my client gets back to me, it's back to business."

"Client?" Bobby wondered.

Nia nodded. "Yeah, I got, um, a new job."

He gasped. "That was fast! Is it somebody we know?"

"Bobby, not all my clients meet me at the Jazz Hall, okay?"

"Oh…so who is it? I know it ain't Drakonis again, is it? You ain't learned your lesson from the last time?"

"No, it's somebody else, somebody you don't know."

"Huh. I thought I knew all of your clients," Bobby muttered.

"Well, you don't!"

Kim interjected. "And what do you plan to do in the meantime, Nia?"

"I'm just going to chill for a minute," she answered, grateful for Kim's timing. "Practice the kickboxing; get my plans in order; wait until I hear from my client."

"And just where do you plan to do this 'chilling'?" asked Kim. "Surely you do not plan to stay here?"

"Why not?" Nia shouted. "You stay here!"

"I am a quiet old man who tinkers with machines and does not draw attention to himself. You on the other hand are loud and dangerous. It would not look good for you and I to be seen together here."

"But I can't stay with Bobby anymore; Charlene damn sure ain't having that," Nia mumbled. "I don't have any options. There's no way somebody like me can just walk up into an apartment building and apply for a lease."

Bobby spoke. "I know somebody running some apartments down in the waterfront. He doesn't do the background check as long as you've got the money, and as long as you got someone to put in a good word. Since he's a friend of mine, we should be able to hook you right up."

"For real?" Nia cheered. "That's what's up!"

"Just make sure you got enough cash to make my man keep his mouth shut and you should be all right," Bobby went on. "I was thinking about telling you about his place sooner, but...you know...I was kind of enjoying your company at the crib."

"I'll just bet you were," Nia giggled. Then she reached into a pocket and drew a clip of money. "Does this look like enough cash for your man to keep his mouth shut?"

"Damn, is that real?!" Bobby gasped in awe. He had never laid eyes on so much money at once before.

Nia pulled some money from the clip and handed it to him. "I know you lost out last night, so here...from me to you, as an apology."

Bobby accepted the money without another thought. "Thanks. I lost big when those people snatched me...they messed up my biggest gig of the year."

"I hope that kind of makes up for it," Nia said apologetically.

She actually expected Bobby to refuse the money.

"Well, I don't know if I'm going to get that record deal now or not, but what the hell...you ready to go?" Bobby continued, stuffing the cash in his pocket. "Gallagher's not a night person...we need to get on the ball if we're going to catch him before he turns in. Let's go back to my spot so you can get the rest of your stuff first. We can load it in my jeep after you drive me back home. Charlene is at work, so we shouldn't have any problems if we go now."

As Nia and Bobby turned toward the building entrance, Kim called out to her.

"Nia!"

Nia turned to him. "Hmm?"

"Guard yourself."

Nia and Bobby climbed on her silver sport bike, Bobby clutching Nia's sides as she started the ignition.

"You know me, I'm always careful!" she assured her mentor.

Nia and Bobby sped off, the motorcycle roaring into the dark and starry horizon. Kim shook his head, watching them until they were out of sight. He sealed the doors of the warehouse and retired for the evening, the quiet of his peaceful domain returning once more.

BOBBY AND NIA pulled up to the house that Nia once called home. Bobby jumped off the bike before Nia even turned it off, rushing directly for the door.

"Bobby…" Nia muttered as she stepped up behind him. "How long until Charlene gets home?"

Bobby groaned. "Not long enough."

He immediately charged into the house and turned to the first door on the left, Nia's door. The drawers were empty: as suspected, someone, presumably Hudson's men, had searched the house and confiscated all of her weaponry, along with what money she'd stashed there. Her clothing and other personal items remained. Bobby and Charlene took the time to load Nia's things into large plastic bags earlier. Her bed was dismantled and ready for transport.

"She was just waiting for you to come back for your things," Bobby added. "Come on; let's get this stuff into the back of my jeep."

Nia looked down as he bolted back and forth past her.

He must be tired…maybe he just wants to hurry up and get me out of here before Charlene gets back. Yeah. He doesn't need any more drama.

"What you waiting on? Come on!"

Soon, the loading was complete. Bobby climbed into his vehicle and started the ignition.

"Just follow me on your bike," Bobby said. "Won't take but twenty minutes to get to Gallagher's on the expressway."

Soon, Nia was riding on her motorcycle, following Bobby's jeep. It reminded her of the time when he'd first brought her to his house; though only a year had passed since then, Nia felt nostalgic.

Nia pulled up beside Bobby's jeep so she could see his face. He was smiling when he turned his head quickly to return the look. She couldn't figure out why he seemed so elated, now that they were away from the house.

Is he actually happy to see me moving out?

Soon they arrived, parking in front of a small row of buildings that made up a residential area just off the coast of the bay. Bobby leaped from his jeep and locked it up.

"The first building..." Bobby said. "This is it."

"This *shack*?" Nia griped. "As much money as I got..."

"Hey, if this ain't up to your demanding standards, feel free to look somewhere else," Bobby snapped back. "Ungrateful ass..."

Nia trotted up to Bobby and clutched his arm, resting her head on his shoulder. "Baby, I'm sorry. But why are you so stressed?"

"Look, I'm just...dealing with a lot right now," he responded, raising his head to the sky with a heavy exhale. "I need to relax, I know. Everything's cool right now, right? Charlene and I aren't in any more danger, are we?"

"I already told you, no," Nia said, her hands slowly sliding down until she no longer held his arm. "What, you don't believe me?"

Bobby exhaled. "Well, come on; let's get you a place to live. You'll love it down here. You got the beach right there, and it's real quiet so I doubt anybody will come here looking for you."

"Yeah, and it's not that far from Charlene's house, so I'll be close to you, too!" Nia cheered.

Bobby immediately stormed ahead of her and entered the building, shaking his head.

What? Nia thought. *What did I say?*

Nia caught up and followed Bobby inside. The building's wooden construction did little to stifle the sounds of the outside. Nia liked that. Since they arrived, the soothing sound of the moving waters relaxed her, especially in the presence of a man she found most attractive. The air was much fresher than that of the inner city as well. And being able to hear what was going on outside with ease would make it easier for her to react in the event of danger.

The building and the surroundings had a certain flavor, a cozy, undemanding essence that made Nia actually look forward to staying there. She preferred a simple place to disappear to when her missions were over, and while it lacked some of the benefits of staying with Bobby and Charlene, the soothing atmosphere and fresh air made up for it.

At the front desk sat a chubby and balding man wearing a red flannel shirt that was a bit too small. He smelled of trout and sand but when he laid eyes on her and Bobby and when his rosy smile lifted his hefty cheeks, Nia actually felt the place was even more inviting.

"Bobby!" grumbled the man in a raspy voice. "Long time no see, buddy boy!"

"Gallagher, you still up, man?" Bobby chuckled, clasping the man's palm in friendship. He then turned to Nia. "This is Gallagher, a good friend of my mom's. He took me and my mother in when I was a little kid, after my dad ditched us, even though she couldn't afford it. He let us stay here until my mom could get back on her feet. I promised him that I'd pay him back any way I could when I could, so I always donate to his little building and help him find good tenants."

"Damn, Bob, you've got some crazy connections in this town!" Nia laughed.

"All comes from doing right by people," Bobby sighed. "That's all I do."

"Doing right, huh?" Nia muttered. *Trying to tell me something?*

"So is this that mystery woman you're so in love with, Bob?" Gallagher grunted. "Finally introducing me to the lady of your dreams? You've been hiding her from me for so long…"

Bobby stammered. "Well—"

Nia immediately stepped forth and reached out to shake the man's hand.

"What's up? I'm Nia."

"'Nia'?" Gallagher coughed. "I thought the gal's name was Charlie or something, Bobby…"

Bobby cleared his throat as Nia stepped back, twisting nervously.

"Gallagher," Bobby spoke, "My friend here needs a place. Can you hook her up?"

"For a friend of yours, no problem!" Gallagher responded. "Just so happens an efficiency just got freed up recently. Is she, you know, reliable?"

Nia grunted. "Excuse me, I'm standing right here. Trust me; you'll get your rent money on time. Early if you want."

"Oh, okay, little lady, excuse me," Gallagher laughed. "We're going to get along just fine, I can tell. So when do you want to move in?"

"How's tonight sound?" Nia spoke again.

"It's going to cost you…" Gallagher said. "You know, first month, last month, security, all that jazz."

Nia filed out a mass of hundred-dollar bills and glared upon Gallagher with her most charming, pouting look.

"Uh, is this enough?" she said whimsically.

"Well! This'll do just fine," Gallagher gasped, snatching the money. "Just what do you do for a living, girlie?"

"I'm a dancer," Nia lied. "Look at me; don't I look like I'd make a lot of money dancing? I work way uptown…need to live as far away from there as possible, you know? I can't have fiends knowing where I live."

Gallagher scratched his rough chin. "I guess I can understand why you'd want to live somewhere inconspicuous. You seem nice enough, and your money's good. So you've got yourself a deal. Here's the key. Room 2-C, the first door on the right hand side when you get to the second floor."

Nia turned to Bobby. "Well? Are you going to help me move my stuff in?"

"What you mean?" Bobby said. "You're strong enough to—!"

Nia scowled.

"Go on, Bob," Gallagher interrupted. "Be a gentleman! Help the lady out!"

Bobby sighed. "Yeah. All right. Let's get the bed first."

Bobby and Nia spent a few hours moving and arranging her things into the room. The bags of clothes sat on the floor along with the suitcase filled with her weapons and equipment.

Under closer examination, Nia felt the modest room held some promise. It was a square with three doors, one leading to a closet, one leading to the bathroom and one leading out. On the eastern side of the room was a small opening leading to an even more humble kitchen. Heating came from a central unit through ventilation ducts and gave the room a comfortable atmosphere without drying out the air.

Less the kitchen, it was a bit smaller than the room she rented in Charlene's house, but for the reduced rent she would be paying, Nia thought it was worth it. A single window opposite to the door allowed Nia to view the outer front of the building, and the rear of the structure faced the waters, so it was unlikely anyone would be able to approach her without her noticing. Though a simple place, it was quiet, secluded and cozy.

Bobby and Nia reconstructed the bed and positioned it near the window before laying sheets upon it. Nia sat upon the mattress and crossed her legs as Bobby wiped his brow and turned to the door.

"Thank you, baby," Nia smiled.

"We both know you didn't need my help with this stuff," Bobby said back. "You're probably *way* stronger than me. So what's up?"

"You're right, Bobby," Nia replied. "It wasn't about the extra pair of arms or you doing the heavy lifting for me or anything like that. It was the principle of you helping your girl out."

"See, Nia, that's just it," Bobby groaned. "You're not…"

"Shush. Never mind that right now," Nia said as she stood and wrapped her arms around Bobby's waist, pulling him as she stepped backwards toward the bed. "I'm not going to let you go until you properly thank me for saving you. I'll use force if I have to."

Bobby could not help but to laugh. "Girl, you got problems."

With a wily grin, Nia took hold of Bobby's belt and instantly swung him around, slinging him until he flopped on her bed!

"What are you doing?!" Bobby gasped, leaning on his elbows.

"Don't you think you should give me a housewarming present?" Nia wondered, leaning on the bed over Bobby, holding herself up with her arms, bouncing her hips left and right. His eyes followed her hips, and then Bobby shook his head and tried to clear his head.

"Nia…, I need to get out of here. Charlene is—"

"Not yet," Nia said. "If I told you once, I told you a thousand times; I get real hot and bothered after running and gunning. You gonna keep me waiting another day?"

Bobby threw his head back and silenced. Nia was there, parading that perfect body of hers before him as he lay back, and she would not let him go. He could not resist forming images in his mind of her curvaceous naked form once again riding atop him and grew excited at the idea of touching her, kissing her, pleasing her once more. The whole time they were together, from the time they left Kim's place until they reached the apartment building, Bobby tried to make Nia lose interest by being cold and insensitive toward her. It clearly didn't work.

Bobby made a decision. He would do it once more. But it was going to be different this time.

"The hell with it..." Bobby stammered, undoing his belt buckle.

"...What did you say?!" Nia gasped, incensed by his tone. "You act like this is some kind of chore. If you don't want me, never mind."

Bobby's heart jumped. "What—?! I...I ain't mean it like that!"

Nia tightly folded her arms and twisted away from him, her frustration seething like a blazing furnace.

Bobby was excited now, and refused to leave before satiating himself. He immediately sat up and grasped her hips, stroking her belly with his thumbs as his tone softened. He knew he had to say whatever it took to get Nia to open back up.

"I'm sorry," Bobby said, as he looked up at her. "I'm stressed. I'm so sorry."

"I know you're stressed, Bobby," Nia cried, returning the look. "I'm stressed too. We're here alone together and you're acting like I got fat and nasty all of the sudden, like you can't stand the sight of me."

Bobby pulled Nia's belly to his lips and began to kiss her there. Nia tripped over to him, rolling her eyes and pouting as he dragged her close.

"Girl, ain't nothing I love more than your body," Bobby whispered, kissing her some more as he eased her skirt down with his thumbs. Nia finally stopped resisting her smile when her skirt fell around her ankles and Bobby's teeth grasped the top edge of her panties.

"My baby looks like he's hungry..." Nia whispered. She kicked off her skirt and dropped it to the floor before kneeling upon the bed and resting her rear on Bobby's lap. Bobby's fingers slid upward across her sides, digging underneath her top as she raised her arms. Bobby pushed the top past Nia's shoulders, freeing her breasts as Nia took hold of the shirt and pulled it off.

154

He slid his mouth over her left breast and circled her nipple with his tongue. Nia whimpered as Bobby's tongue continued to gradually roll and swirl about her breast. He alternated from her left breast to her right and Nia enjoyed every second his warm touch oozed over her. Bobby wrapped his strapping arms around Nia's waist, this time swinging her around and laying her flat on her back upon the bed. He immediately pulled off her panties and traced a line of tongue kisses from under her chin to between her thighs, where he stopped and pulled away.

No oral pleasure.

Nia was confused, but she didn't mention it. She was certain Bobby loved to provide it for her, yet for the first time since their relationship began, Bobby didn't do it. He only continued to kiss her around her thighs, with only his breath caressing her. She groaned excitedly and trembled, anticipating when Bobby would cease with the foreplay and give her what she wanted.

But Bobby never drew his tongue. He stood to his feet and stripped down. He donned his condom and immediately thrust inside of her, taking Nia by surprise.

"Ooh!" Nia gasped. "Go ahead...rough rider!"

Bobby, still silent, hurriedly and rhythmically probed Nia as he moved his groin back and forth. Nia stared at her lover and saw he was looking skyward, as if ashamed to look upon her.

Nia raised her legs to wrap them around his back, but Bobby arched his spine and Nia's short legs couldn't reach. They fell to the floor, her feet slapping the wood planks.

Then it hit Nia. She looked upon him as his breaths echoed from his pursed lips in perfect rhythm with her body rocking back and forth, almost in a mechanical way.

Bobby wasn't making love to her.

He was just *fucking* her.

Nia sensed the difference even in her ecstatic stupor. The feeling was different. It was more…typical. No emotional connection, no embracing, no passionate gaze shared. Just penetration.

Nia wondered for once who Bobby was actually trying to please. Did he care at all how she felt?

Soon, Bobby seemed fatigued and pulled out of her, his head hanging. Nia, her body trembling, could only lie back and glance at him with half-closed eyes. Then, as if he suddenly got a second wind, Bobby quickly reached out and grabbed Nia by the arms, pulling her up to her feet.

"Huh?" Nia wondered, her wobbling legs barely able to support her as she stood naked before him.

He grabbed her shoulder and pulled, silently compelling her to turn her back to him. He pushed his palm into her shoulders and eased her into a kneeling position, her butt high in the air.

Nia shut her eyes and smiled uncontrollably as she spaced her thighs, waiting feverishly for Bobby to make his way inside of her.

Bobby *slammed* into her with brute force.

"Ouch!" Nia yelped.

"You mean to tell me you can't take it?" Bobby suddenly grunted as he grasped her hips, supporting himself as he forcefully rifled in and out of her. "Supposed to be all strong and shit…"

"I—I can take it!" Nia shouted as if in competition. "Go ahead! Do what you gotta do, rough rider!"

Bobby rapidly pounded her from behind with all the strength he could summon, slapping Nia's butt so hard, the sound of the smack echoed. Nia screamed in a mix of pleasure and pain as he took hold of her mangled hair, yanking her head back and thrusting inside her like a piston.

Nia growled like a lion in combat. She spread her legs wider and raised her butt, leaning forward until her cheek pressed against the mattress.

She moaned loudly, closed her moistening eyes and clawed the bedspreads, pleasure rippling through her every nerve.

Bobby leaned forward, pressing even deeper inside. Both of them roared louder and more bestial. The bed began to quiver with their force and eventually the entire room was shaking with a cadenced banging, all the furniture rocking from their weight and force.

Bobby roared, "Yeah! You like that, *bitch*?"

"W-what?!" Nia stammered.

"Shut the hell up!" Bobby clawed the soft flesh of her butt as he continued to thrust and groan. "You ain't nothing but a ho anyway...get *fucked!* That's all you're good for..."

Nia suddenly pushed herself away and rolled over, making Bobby withdraw from her.

"Who you think you're talking to like that?"

Bobby lunged forward and threw himself on top of Nia, grasping her pendant in his fingers.

"Take this off! I told you I was sick of this damn thing scratching me up!"

Swiftly he yanked the pendant from around Nia's neck, breaking the chain and casting it away.

Nia shuddered, her eyes following the necklace as its pieces drifted to the floor.

"Bobby! That's my mother's—!"

"I told you to *shut up!*" he roared. "You want this so bad, you're gonna get it...*raw!*"

Bobby snatched off his condom and leaned toward Nia, then all movement ceased.

Nia stared daggers at Bobby, pressing her feet into his chest. The muscles of her calves tensed.

"Bastard..."

Nia thrust her legs outward and Bobby soared backward!

He flew across the room, his arms and legs flailing helplessly until he crashed into the wall near the front door and tumbled to the floor like a rag doll.

Nia leaped to her feet. "Bobby…what the…what the hell was that?!"

Bobby grumbled as he looked at the naked woman standing over him with clutched fists, rage in his eyes. But his rage turned to shock as his eyes rolled down to Nia's thighs and calves. The muscles had hardened and thickened to twice the size they normally were, as if the legs of a much larger, more muscular woman were attached to Nia's diminutive body. Then, the muscles and veins pulsated and trembled under her skin until her legs shrank and returned to normal.

Nia herself finally noticed it, and gazed at her legs with bulging eyes. *Is that…what happened to my body when…*

Bobby moaned as he pulled himself up by the door handle.

"What the fuck *are you?*"

"I…" Nia stammered, then shook her head.

"Fucking *whore*…that's what you are…fucking science freak monster *whore*…"

"What did you say?!"

"What the hell was I thinking…" Bobby muttered, fishing for his clothes. "Wasting my time with a freak-of-nature skank like you when I got a real woman at home…"

"What…?" Nia cried.

"Look. You got your shit and you got your crib. So do me a favor. Do me *and* Charlene a favor. Stay the hell away from us, Nia. Just…just stay the hell out of my life, all right? We're through."

Nia flopped backward on the bed. Her body trembled with a cold that had nothing to do with the temperature.

Bobby's face hardened and he turned away from Nia. He looked as if he were disgusted with her.

Nia crossed her arms over her breasts and squeezed her thighs together as if suddenly ashamed. She finally realized the heartrending truth; what she should have known from the start.

Bobby made every effort to preserve his relationship with Charlene *and* sleep with Nia. Have his cake and eat it too.

But no matter how things turned out, he would *never* let Charlene go.

Charlene was the woman he loved. Nia was just the shorty he *fucked* on the side.

That's all Nia ever was to him.

Bobby rambled on. "I don't see what you're so upset about. It is what it is. We *fucked*. That's all it was, wasn't it?"

Nia sobbed, yanking a sheet from the bed and covering herself. "You don't know a damn thing. All like, 'Not Nia. Nia doesn't feel that way about anybody.'"

"You...you heard—?" Bobby gasped, turning back around.

"Heightened senses..." Nia interrupted. "Apparently that's one of my gifts. I hear *real* good. Yeah, I heard everything Kim said to you and everything you tried to say back. All you ever care about is getting the most ass."

"It ain't just about sex, Nia!" Bobby hollered. "Charlene and I have something special together. Something real. Not just late night fuck sessions."

"So do you always creep around on somebody that you got something 'real' with?! Is that your thing? That's just how you do?" Nia snapped. "You already lost Charlene, so why—"

"That's where you're wrong," Bobby interrupted. "She and I talked just before I came out to see you. She forgave me for cheating on her. We're still together."

And Nia finally understood his drastic change in behavior. Charlene took him back. In Charlene's shoes, Nia would never have done it...and then it hit her.

Maybe that's what love really was.

"Yeah," Bobby went on. "And I promised her I'd never let it happen again. But you just couldn't let me get away clean, could you?!"

"Oh, yeah right!" Nia sobbed. "Like I forced you to run your little dick up in me! I can't believe myself...I thought you were something special...I thought you were the *shit*! You're just as dirty as any other raggedy-ass, fake-ass player out there. You know what, Charlene's stupid ass deserves to be with a cheating-ass piece of shit like you. Get the hell out of my apartment!"

"Gladly."

Bobby quickly turned toward the door. She looked away as he left, curling up in the sheet, shaking with grief. Bobby lingered for a moment before he ultimately left the room and closed the door.

Bobby darted downstairs where Gallagher still sat at the lobby desk.

"What in the hell was all that ruckus?! I can't have all that—"

"Chill, Gallagher," Bobby muttered, slowing down as he walked toward the entrance. "It won't happen again."

"...I'll take your word for it, Bob," Gallagher shouted as he left. "Hey, don't be a stranger, all right? We haven't been fishing in ages!"

"I won't. Peace, Gallagher," Bobby's voice shouted from outside as he started his jeep.

Soon, he was driving away, and exhaled a sigh of relief. *I knew she was some kind of monster... I think I'm lucky to be alive...all this time I was fucking around with somebody that ain't even* human...

An hour passed. Gallagher lifted his large frame from his seat, shut off his television and headed toward his own room on the first floor to retire for the night. As he turned toward the hall leading to his domain, a breeze glanced across him from behind, and he flinched.

"What in the river's name..." Gallagher mumbled to himself as he turned and saw the building's front door, wide open. Outside of the building, he saw a silver motorcycle already speeding away, a plume of dust and smoke rising like a typhoon in the wake.

"That...that couldn't have been—I'm getting too old for this."

Nia's sport bike exceeded the speed limit. The roar of its engine could be heard miles away.

As she bolted through the late night under the orange street lamps that lined and illuminated the near-empty road, Nia could only think about her hunger for support. She felt a sense of abandonment she hadn't experienced since she was younger. She cared nothing about whether she just compromised her hideout or if she'd run into any sort of conflict. She needed to talk to someone again.

But this time she couldn't see Marc. She couldn't bear to go anywhere near the Jazz Hall, where she first met Bobby. With night having fallen, the club would be packed as usual. She did not want all of the Jazz Hall's regulars in her business. She only had one choice. Nia needed to see the one person left whom she could rely on.

She pulled up to Kim's warehouse and found the lights were on, unusual for the time of night; he was usually asleep by that time.

As soon as she stopped, she saw Kim, standing in front of the building, waiting with his hands clasped behind his back.

Kim was *expecting* her.

Nia climbed off the motorcycle and sauntered toward Kim, staggering with little energy in her steps.

Their eyes met. Immediately Kim stepped forth and wrapped his arms around Nia, stroking her back as she fell into his embrace and buried her face in his chest, letting go of her tears at last.

...They said they knew Mom. They're good people, Nia. They said they would teach us about ourselves, give us good jobs, and even train us.

You don't know that, Tia! Just because the headmistress said that doesn't mean...

Anything's better than being here. We've spent our whole childhood in this house. All the other kids are scared of us. No one's ever going to adopt us. We have to get out of here!

Those people gave us the choice. They said we can stay or we can go...I'm staying. That's the only way we can find out the truth...it all happened here, in this city...don't you care?

You still believe he's coming back, don't you? You still believe dad's coming back...he's not going to get us out of here. He can't. He's dead. No one wants us. Only them. Only the Phoenix Group. I want you to come with me. I need you to.

Don't leave me, Tia...please. I meant what I said. If you leave...

If you're stupid enough to believe anyone besides the Phoenix cares about us, then I don't want you for a sister anyway. So say what you want.

Tia!

… I'm leaving. I can't take this anymore. I want to have a life. I'm done with this orphanage and I'm done with you, *Nia.*

THE MORNING SUN ROSE.

Inside a room deep within the warehouse, the sun shined through a window and beamed across Nia's body as she rolled away from the light. As the heat of the concentrated sunlight began to sear her skin, Nia finally forced herself awake.

She had managed to cry herself to sleep the night before; incessant rubbing left her eyes reddened and irritated. Her head throbbed with a stress headache. Bobby. He still weighed on her mind.

She wanted nothing more than to lie down all day, but the sun, lancing across her skin like a laser, would not allow it. Wearing only a camisole and panties, Nia lifted herself from Kim's cot in the back of the warehouse. As soon as she sat up and looked ahead, she saw Kim standing over her.

"Nia Black."

Nia rubbed her head. "That's me…"

"On your feet!"

Nia grumbled. "Kim, what's up with you? Why you all up in my face this morning? I'm not even dressed! What time is it?"

"You are a warrior, Nia Black. You cannot dwell on what has happened in your personal life. On your feet."

"Five more minutes."

Kim grunted in disgust.

"On! Your! Feet!"

Though he did not condone Nia's dangerous lifestyle, Kim understood why she deemed it necessary. As such, it was up to him to make sure his protégé remained strong and focused when a mission was at hand.

"You must harden your body and mind. We will practice right now!"

"*Now*?!" Nia gasped, sitting up. "Come on man, Kim…you know I'm not up to that right now. Besides, if anything comes my way, my guns will take care of it."

Kim grumbled in another language before raising his knee. He quickly shot out his foot, slamming his heel into Nia's chest! She shot backward like a toppled chair and crashed back on the cot.

"What the hell, man?!"

"Did your gun protect you from that? Will it prevail the next time you are caught empty handed? On your feet!"

Nia finally obeyed and got up. After sweeping Kim's dusty footprint from her top, she immediately took her innate kickboxing fighting stance, with her fists forward, and her elbows and knees flexed.

"No you did *not* just kick me! You're going to get it!"

Kim wrapped his toe within a pair of shorts of Nia's that sat on the floor. He gripped them between his toes, pressing the fabric against the base of his sandal. He snapped his leg in the air and tossed the shorts toward Nia with his foot.

Nia snatched the shorts out of the air.

Kim pressed his foot back to the floor, turned and stepped out of the room. She dragged her shorts up around her hips and ran after him.

They met in the center of the wide-open entryway of the warehouse. Kim dragged his desk out of the way to make space.

"You must not let the softness of your heart grow contagious, dulling your fighting spirit."

"I don't have a soft heart!"

"You spent all night crying like a baby…crying over a man-child. Show me you are tougher than that. Show me you are still a warrior!"

Nia grunted and charged toward Kim, lunging forth with her knee. Kim parried, shoving her aside and Nia stumbled.

"For all of your so-called power, you are slow and predictable!" Kim went on. "You wish to overcome your enemies? How will you do it, with tears? What will happen when your guns run out of bullets? Will you run? Will you hide? Will you cry or will you fight, crybaby?"

"I *ain't* no crybaby!" Nia cried, throwing elbow punches, knee strikes and flailing kicks at her mentor, all of which he blocked.

"Pathetic!" Kim griped. "Have I taught you nothing? Clear your mind! Focus on the objective!"

Nia breathed hard and stared into Kim's small eyes. She wasn't getting anywhere being angry or feeling sorry for herself, she realized.

For the first time in a long time, Nia started to listen to Kim. Heeding her mentor's words, she stopped thinking about what had happened. She emptied her thoughts, found focus.

Nia took a deep breath and charged Kim again. He readied his stance.

Nia attacked, but anger no longer fueled her blows. She cleared her mind, focused on technique, not on blind fury. It felt as if every blow forced an ounce of sorrow out of her heart, siphoning in renewed fervor and determination.

The two sparred together for what seemed like hours, the pounding of their fists and feet slapping flesh and bone echoing throughout the walls of the warehouse.

Kim began to stagger under the might of Nia's attacks. Despite his far more advanced knowledge of the martial art, Kim was no match for Nia's youth or especially her superhuman strength. A final knee strike sent him stumbling to the ground, even though he had blocked it.

Nia outstretched her hand to help him up. "So, how was that?"

"Acceptable," Kim said, taking her wrist and pulling himself to his feet. "You will need a bit more practice. But next time, hopefully you can be a bit more under control."

"Man, you're just mad because I'm stronger than you," Nia chuckled.

"Strength is not the only deciding factor in a battle, Nia," Kim sighed. "Have you not figured that out by now?"

Nia smiled wide, breathing hard as she felt the euphoric joy of action flow through her—an adrenaline rush. She remembered what it was in her life that truly made her happy: action. Running and gunning, fighting, high speed chases, armed pursuers and money... Nia was looking forward to getting back into the swing of things.

What was she thinking? A relationship? Not yet. She had more important things to do—loose ends to tie up.

Nia and Kim sat on the floor, drinking bottled water.

"Whew!" Nia cheered happily. "I feel so much better! Come on, let's go again!"

"Remarkable," Kim said, blotting sweat from his forehead with a rag. "I suppose your emotional recovery is as swift as your physical recovery."

"Come on, stop the jibber-jabber! Get up and let's spar some more," Nia grinned. "I know you're not worn out already...it's too early for that!"

Kim smiled. "You are just like your father. Just like him."

"What do you mean?"

"He was so excited about learning the arts. The close-quarters combat techniques he'd learned in military training were efficient, but he was quite impressed with the sheer power of the strikes in Muay Thai."

"You and my father worked together for a long time, right?"

"I trained many young initiates," Kim explained. "But your father was different. He was one of my greatest pupils. He didn't just want to be combat-ready; he wanted to *master* the art. The last thing on his mind was pulling out a gun."

"Here *you* go," Nia sighed. "The streets today ain't like in karate movies. Nobody fights anymore; it's all about who has the fastest draw and the smallest conscience. I could be the best martial artist in the world and it won't mean a damn if somebody's shooting at me from across the street. At least with my hammer I'd have a chance to bust him first."

"And as you throw bullets, so more will be thrown back at you," Kim went on. "The cycle will never end, until the day they find their mark."

"That day ain't ever going to come," Nia hissed. "I can *dodge* bullets. Heck, I can probably take a couple. I mean, I took a damn hard beating from that Armstrong guy and I'm still here, bruises healed and everything."

"And how long do you think it will last? Look at me, Nia. I am more than twice your age. I have more years behind me than ahead of me."

"Look, stop it, all right?" Nia muttered. "I told you—"

"Listen!" Kim snapped. "You may heal faster than many, you may possess sharper reflexes than most, and you may possess great strength, but all of us age. You will slow down. And someone will take advantage of you when you are vulnerable, someone so eager to take you down that they will wait months...*years* for their opportunity if necessary. You have been captured before; you have been at the mercy of your enemies, only days ago. You are lucky to be here, now...please consider that. You will always be a target as long as you are living as you are, using your gifts selfishly."

"So what are you saying, Kim?" Nia growled. "Run away? Go off to fight some hopeless revolutionary war like my dad did, because these so-called 'gifts' are meant for some greater purpose? Please."

"At least your father made a noble choice..."

"Yeah, and he left his family to die for it!" Nia roared. "I will *never* be like him, you hear me? The one thing I learned from him is that it's better to be free, even if it means being selfish. Fuck honor! Fuck noble! And *fuck him*!"

Nia suddenly heard a muted beeping sound. She raced back to the cot she'd slept on and unearthed her pager from a pile of clothes, the beeping growing louder once it was exposed.

She ran back into the main room and picked up Kim's touch-tone phone, dialing the number on the face.

"Hello? Is this Alvarez?"

"Miss Black. You need to head downtown. Hudson has moved up his meeting. You have to strike now."

THE SUN GLISTENED over the city, the reflected light from the office building windows glazing the skyline with pale beams of yellow light. Few cars occupied the streets so early in the morning. One, a black sedan, sped across the roadways skirting dangerously close to the speed limit, weaving around the scant traffic and slashing through intersections a split second before yellow lights turned red.

The car came to a stop in front of a construction site in the center of a wide-open, grassy field along a parkway a fair distance from office buildings. The site was little more than a series of stone markers designating where a building was to be raised, with girders sitting in a pyramid pile off to the side. Vacant cranes and bulldozers sat waiting to be put to use.

An executive climbed out of the back seat of the four-door sedan; extremely tall, with a goatee on his hard, chiseled face, wearing opaque sunglasses. A second man climbed out of the front door on the passenger side, with a thick beard and a portly build. A slender woman emerged from the driver's seat.

"Here we are, Mr. Hudson," said the man who'd sat up front. "As you can see, the equipment is being prepared. We've already got a crew lined up. They should be here by the middle of the day to begin working."

"Good," said the large executive.

Hudson stood at a soaring height, his powerful muscles bulging under his custom-tailored suit to the point of appearing unnatural. His cold, stony face was like a statue that came to life, but only when there was something vital to impart. Hudson was a quiet man, a recluse, neither power-drunk nor boisterous, but the quintessential disciplinarian and commander-in-chief. When he spoke, people listened, even if they had the utmost contempt for him. Always wearing the finest wardrobe and accessories, working out of an office the size of a banquet hall, living in the penthouse of the city's tallest building, Hudson was the kind of man who seemed to be able to move mountains with just a stroke of the pen.

"I need this to go forward quickly, Mr. Worthington. You could have simply sent pictures of this to me through email."

"But there's nothing like seeing your pet project face to face in its infancy, Hudson," Worthington rambled. "Smell that fresh air; let that concrete dust flow into your nostrils... get a sense of what it's going to be like when my guys are up here bringing your vision to life."

"I have no time for such trivialities. If it's a matter of trust..."

"This meeting just makes sure you and I are on the same page. You can see it with your own eyes," Worthington nodded. "Now, I trust all the zoning issues have been cleared up?"

"Of course they have," Hudson retorted quickly. "This meeting would not be happening if there were a shred of doubt that this endeavor would go forward."

"I'd heard stories about the former Councilman, Washington, trying to put a stop to these plans...something about you having too much influence over local businesses and job opportunities or something."

"Yes, he was an annoyance for a while, but he chose the wrong time to cross me," said Hudson. "He was primed for re-election, and he underestimated the power of my influence. I had some trumped up charges brought to light by the local media, and now, Washington is nothing. Let's begin our final inspection...I have other pressing business to—"

"Sir!" the woman called out to Hudson.

"What is it, Rachel?"

"Something's coming our way...fast!"

All three individuals turned their attention to the road, the deep grumble of an engine growing ever louder.

Like a shooting star, a sparkling silver sport bike shimmering under the morning sun sped in their direction. As if accessorizing to match the vehicle, the woman riding the bike wore a shiny white cat suit, two belts resting across her hips in an X-pattern with a diamond-shaped buckle holding them together. Two individual handguns dangled aside her hips on each side. The two higher guns were small and sleek semi-automatics; the two lower ones were a pair of massive revolvers.

"One of your mistresses, Max?" Worthington laughed. "I always try to avoid the ones who know how to handle a piece. Never know if they'll snap if you cut 'em off…"

"Get back in the car," Hudson said, taking his own advice. Ivan Worthington and Rachel Jones followed suit. "Rachel, drive."

The black sedan's engine turned over and the car skidded back onto the road. But the sedan barely traveled a city block before the much-faster biker caught up. She drove alongside it, glaring at the car's windows through her goggles.

Hudson, sitting in the seat furthest to the back, turned and faced the biker.

"Yeah!" Nia Black screamed. "Remember me?"

Hudson nodded slowly.

"Oh, you're not worried at all, huh? Well maybe this'll give you a little pick-me-up."

Nia snatched one of her Baby Eagles and aimed it at the window, still staring Hudson in the face. He didn't flinch, didn't look at the gun—he barely reacted at all.

Nia pulled the trigger to thunderous effect. But the telltale screech of her bullet as it glanced off the window—where it otherwise would have gone right through and found its mark between Hudson's eyes—reminded her of how well protected Maxwell Hudson was.

Damn...is every car they have bulletproof? Nia thought. *Hmm...I bet those tires ain't.*

As the sedan and the bike sped into a curve in the road, Nia looked around. She realized the sedan was circling the grassy field where Hudson's meeting had taken place.

The hell? What are they doing? What is he gonna do, make his driver spin them around the block until one of us runs out of—

Then Nia's heart hammered in her chest.

She started hearing more engines.

A *lot* of them.

Jeeps dashed on the scene from every surrounding intersection, with turrets mounted on the rooftops, men in full tactical gear at the controls.

Dammit! Nia thought. *I took too long! All he had to do was make a phone call and his goons are on tap! I should have gotten here sooner!*

Nia shoved her small handgun back into its holster and reached for a larger one.

Screw it...I'll take them all down today. I'm not running away anymore. This is the last time...

Nia aimed her revolver at the closest opposing vehicle and pulled the trigger. The shot smashed into the jeep, sending the vehicle somersaulting forward with a concussive blast, with such impact that flanking vehicles had to swerve out of the way as the flaming wreck tumbled upside-down on the street.

The smaller guns Nia held were her Baby Eagle pistols, the guns she'd relied upon more than any other. But the second pair were a set of specially modified Taurus Raging Judge 28-gauge revolvers, chambered to fire explosive shells. She bought them from a gunrunner with the understanding that sometimes splash damage and explosive impact was more effective than simple bullets in a large-scale combat setting.

She had them in her possession for quite a while but never planned to use them, since her *modus operandi* was to get away from her enemies, not fight them.

Things were different today, just as they were different when Nia rushed out to rescue Bobby. She'd have brought the cannons along then if she had the time to go to Kim's place to pick them up. She could never have risked leaving guns that lethal where Charlene could have stumbled upon them. Fortunately, Marc's supply made a decent substitute at the time.

This time, she was fully prepared.

She whipped the bike around and fired again and again. Every time she pulled the trigger, a shot would send one of the attacking jeeps sailing into the air in a burst of flame and smoke.

Two more jeeps darted toward Nia from both sides, picking up speed.

Nia took both hands off of her handlebars and outstretched both arms, a hand cannon in each fist. She fired the Judges simultaneously, the explosive blasts jerking them away in burning heaps.

Nia glanced ahead and saw another jeep speeding directly for her. She didn't have time to put the guns away and take hold of the handlebars again.

So she put a foot up on the seat of her bike and pushed herself skyward, her bike skidding into the jeep head-on. It smashed into the vehicle and exploded, but the armored vehicle was unscathed...

Until Nia, in midair, aimed her cannons at the jeep under her and opened fire. The resulting explosion produced a shockwave that sent Nia sailing backward through the air. She somersaulted and landed gracefully in the grass.

Nia spun around and took in the sight of the flaming piles that used to be her opponents' vehicles. She counted and saw that the number of jeeps still on the road outnumbered the ones that were down and out. They still circled her, still loaded with soldiers out for her blood....

She took a deep breath. She wasn't playing, but neither were they. They came out in force.

Nia flipped open the exhausted cylinders on her Judges and reached in her pockets for speed loaders. She couldn't find them. She looked several feet ahead and found her spare rounds on the grass. They must have fallen out when she jumped, she thought. She started to dash for them, then a jeep screeched to a halt right in front of Nia.

More jeeps drove off the road and skidded to a halt around her, forming a wide circle of vehicles and flames. Nia was surrounded.

Hudson's sedan parked outside of the makeshift ring, and Maxwell Hudson himself emerged from the car. Rachel Jones and Ivan Worthington glared inquisitively from the safety of the sedan's bulletproof frame.

Nia Black tossed away the Raging Judges and snatched her Baby Eagle pistols from their holsters. She aimed her guns at Hudson.

The air chattered with the endless sound of rifles being leveled and aimed at Nia. Hudson waved his hands, and the soldiers remained still, but held their aim.

"Where is he?!" Nia screamed at Hudson, paying the soldiers no heed.

"Who?"

"You know damn well who I'm talking about! My father! Alexander Black! What did you do with him?!"

"I would love to find your father as much as you would, Miss Black," Hudson muttered. "He has cost me a great deal. But I am prepared to cut my losses. Given the turn of events, I've found a way to make up for it. Finally."

Nia grew furious and her fingers grazed the triggers. "You're lying…I'll—!"

Suddenly her reflexes reacted. She sensed danger. She swerved to the side, sensing an attack from behind…

THUMP!

Nia felt a piercing sensation in her butt. She looked at her backside and saw a dart piercing through her pants and her flesh.

"The…the hell…?"

She didn't swerve far enough. Her attacker *led her into the shot!*

Hudson smiled. "You'll make a fine substitute for your father, *Target Omega.*"

Suddenly, Nia's pistols felt heavy…so heavy that she couldn't keep her arms raised. Her grasp on the guns loosened, her fingers unable to summon enough strength to keep a firm grip. Her arms went limp and the twin Baby Eagle pistols slipped from her grasp, pounding into the grass as she began to stumble. Her legs followed suit, starting to feel like wet noodles, unable to support her weight.

Nia didn't get it. She could dodge bullets. Her superhuman reflexes were so honed she could tell when an assailant was about to shoot. She had an almost clairvoyant ability to predict and evade incoming fire.

But whoever shot her with the tranquilizer dart that stuck out of her butt cheek did so with such precision that her attempt to dodge it only led her right in the line of fire. The shooter even had the good sense to aim at the largest and fleshiest mass of muscle on her body—the easiest and most effective part to hit. That took more than a good shooter. It took someone who would have known precisely how to target someone with her reflexes. Someone who *knew* her abilities, like—

Nia looked ahead, her vision blurring as she teetered back and forth. A man holding a long scope-mounted rifle rushed across the distant street and ran toward her.

He was barely close enough to look in the eyes when Nia's legs seemed to drop right out from under her and she crashed on the grass. But before she did, the glare of his spectacles flickered in her eyes and provided her an instant of clarity.

"Hey—!" Nia started to yell his name, but even the strength to give voice to her breath failed before she blacked out.

A MANMADE ISLAND sat offshore in the center of the bay, visible from the city's waterfront, barred from visitors. Dead center on this island, rising above the jungle landscape was a research facility that spent the better part of the last two decades in a derelict state, dark and defunct.

Only a year ago, the facility came back to life, with ferries traveling to and from the island in the midnight hours. No one outside looking in knew what took place there. Only high-level employees of Corp Hudson, and those they choose to approve, could access the island and the facility upon it.

Inside the facility were winding corridors that led to dozens of testing chambers and server-filled computer labs. White coat-wearing technicians milled throughout the base and passed through the halls with memory cards and clipboards and PDAs in their hands, discussing experiments, hypotheses and research results with one another.

Two individuals walked along a corridor approaching a hall of examination rooms. One was a Puerto Rican man in glasses and combat gear; the other was a voluptuous blonde woman, also wearing eyeglasses, as well as a lab coat, a blouse and pleated khaki skirt.

"Thank you, thank you," the woman cheered. "I always figured *somebody* in the security detail was worth the big paychecks we hand out."

"I was just doing my job, Dr. Romedrux," said Jesús Alvarez. "You wanted Nia Black alive and unharmed. Most of Hudson's security staff would just as soon put a bullet in her head as look at her, but I know when a situation calls for delicacy."

"You played that poor girl like a fiddle too," Romedrux laughed. "But hey, whatever it took to get her here. I'm so glad. I can't wait until she wakes up."

Alvarez stopped in his tracks. "What? Why would you want her to wake up?"

She sucked her teeth. "Because—!"

Then the vocals from a well-known pop song echoed from tinny speakers and interrupted the scientist. Chelsea Romedrux lifted her smart phone from her belt, glanced at the screen and hurriedly pressed the 'Talk' button.

"Mr. Hudson! How are you? Are you hurt?"

The guttural voice of Maxwell Hudson echoed through the phone. *"I'm well, Doctor Romedrux. Let's not lose time. What did the initial analysis show?"*

"We ran blood tests, but there was nothing out of the ordinary," the woman responded. "I guess *Hercules* was made too well after all. It just looks like ordinary Type O positive to me."

"It's more than that. She was not born with her superhuman strength through some twist of fate. With Target Alpha lost, this woman is the only means I have to figure out how to resurrect the formula."

"Maybe we need to go deeper," Dr. Romedrux continued. "We've drawn blood, but we could try tissue tests, spinal fluid…perhaps even brain matter…"

"Are you sure that's wise?" Alvarez spoke up. "We can't risk killing her before we learn the truth…dead cells tell little tales, Doctor."

"Look, let the thinkers do the thinking, and you soldier-types just keep… soldiering," Chelsea Romedrux said with spite. "You did a good job, so just worry about keeping guard, okay? We wouldn't want what happened to my father to happen to me too, right?"

Jesús Alvarez sighed. "I assure you, you are in no danger, Doctor. Nia Black is heavily sedated, and doped up on muscle relaxants. Even if she were conscious, she wouldn't have the strength to break the shackles."

Hudson's voice filled the air again. *"I have a meeting to attend. I trust you will have favorable results for me by tomorrow, Dr. Romedrux?"*

"You can count on me, Mr. H," Chelsea smiled. "I'm looking forward to trying out every little trick in the book on this freak."

The phone line clicked. Alvarez turned to Chelsea.

"So, do you remember what we talked about?"

"Yeah, yeah," Chelsea sighed. "You want access to the storage chamber for defunct projects and applications. It's all yours. Here's the key card. You brought me what I wanted, so I'm giving you what you want."

Alvarez took the key card with a smile. "Well, I'm off."

Chelsea turned toward the examination rooms as Alvarez walked toward the elevator. He pressed a key near the elevator door and a chime sounded. The door slid open, and a man stood inside.

Alvarez froze in place and grimaced.

"Well if it isn't the man of the hour?" said the man.

Alvarez turned away.

Casey laughed. "Come on, big guy, let's let bygones be bygones. I mean, I had my doubts, but you pulled it off. You managed to get Nia Black into custody, and it only cost us…what, a couple dozen soldiers, a fleet of vehicles and a whole mess of ammunition and red tape, right? Oh yeah, and that whole kidnapping-slash-false detainment allegation with that couple that the boss needs to clean up. Yep, all of us officers need to follow your example; you're the premiere example of a smooth operator."

Alvarez sighed. For all of the facility's complexity, it only had one elevator that allowed access to all of its levels, both subterranean and above ground, and Billy Casey was on it. Alvarez eventually stepped into the elevator and stood next to Casey, facing forward. Casey pressed a key and the elevator closed.

"I had nothing to do with any kidnapping," Alvarez said. "Blame Armstrong for that."

"Speaking of," Billy went on, "You know? He was murdered that night. But when we found him, his enhancement was fully activated. It would have taken a hell of a gunshot to get through his flesh in the state it was in. We know that Nia Black doesn't generally carry—"

"What are you getting at, Casey?" Alvarez snapped. "Do you presume to know exactly what weaponry Nia Black brought with her that night? Do you presume to know whether *Target Omega* was out there at all?"

"Shell casings we found didn't match up with any weaponry we use…except for the shot that blew a hole in Armstrong's chest. That came from a high-powered, customized Desert Eagle… you know, like the one *you* use."

"I'm certainly not the only one in Corp Hudson security who carries such a gun."

"I haven't done the research, but maybe you're right," Casey shrugged. "Just a funny coincidence is all. So, tell me. How'd you do it? How did you get Nia Black to go along with you?"

"It was easy," Alvarez muttered back, without returning Casey's look. "I convinced her she'd get what she wanted. I promised her a shot at Hudson himself."

Casey scoffed. "I wish I'd have thought of that. Of course, if it were me, I would have just approached her without getting our men killed, but hey; to each his own right?"

A pause. For what seemed like an eternity, only the hum of the elevator's engine filled the air.

"I wonder what Chelsea's going to do to her. It would be a shame to just let that hot body of hers go to waste, being cut up and pricked and probed in some lab," Casey spoke again.

"Do you ever shut up?" Alvarez grunted.

"Sounds like I hit a nerve," Casey chuckled. "You care about her, don't you? You can't stand to see that young girl get turned into filling for a Petri dish, right? She's a dime, I know. But she caused a lot of trouble. She made a choice, and she's going to pay the price. That's all there is to it. But you know, there's something that's not adding up with me."

Alvarez finally turned toward Casey.

"Why didn't you inform anyone of your plan? There was no reason to keep your plans a secret from us."

"If I had told you, you would have interfered. That's how you are. You would have done something silly in an immature attempt to steal the glory. It was important to remain professional. Vincent Marks gave command of the mission to me, not you, no matter how you worship being his right hand man."

"Uh-huh," Billy shrugged. "And why are you so interested in *Hercules?*"

"What?"

"I see you've got the key card to the storage facility in the basement there," Casey went on, glancing at Alvarez's hand. "You bring *Target Omega* here, and blondie gives you access to a storage room that has nothing but defunct projects and old data stored inside of it…including the data about *Hercules.* For what? We all know Nia Black inherited the effects of *Hercules* from her coward father, and that's why Hudson wants to study her. But what's *your* angle?"

"There is other data down there, Casey," Alvarez said. "What I'm researching is none of your business."

Casey lost his temper. "You're hiding something, Alvarez! I know it! And I'm going to find out what it is! I am going to expose you for the fake you are!"

"You talk bravely while we're on security cameras, Mr. Casey," Alvarez mumbled as the elevator reached the facility's lowest level and stopped. The doors slid open, revealing a dusty, dimly lit corridor with flickering lights, their bulbs in need of replacement, a hall clearly infrequently traveled by the facility's workers, if ever.

"I would strongly suggest you stay out of my way," Jesús Alvarez grumbled. "You have a good life. Don't waste it chasing shadows. You should relax. You'll be the head of the security detail eventually. As soon as Hudson promotes Vincent Marks to something like his personal protector, you're next in line. You don't need to kiss his ass any more than you already do."

Casey watched as Alvarez disappeared down the corridor, staring fiercely until the elevator doors closed in front of him and cut off the view.

Then a jingle echoed in the air and a voice chimed over the public address system.

"Dr. Romedrux, please report to room 23-A."

The elevator ascended a single floor and the doors opened again. Chelsea Romedrux walked on, gazing at the screen of an electronic tablet in her hand, appearing oblivious to her surroundings. She glanced at Billy Casey briefly and returned her attention to the data displayed on the screen.

The elevator beeped as the doors shut.

"Hi there," said Billy. He smiled as he looked upon the woman; her green eyes glistening under the elevator lights, widened by the magnification of her glasses, her soft features and fair skin, her long, shimmering, naturally blonde hair...and her *stacked* figure.

"H-hello."

"Hey, are you crying?"

"What?" Chelsea stammered, as if shaken out of a daze. "No... I mean... I guess I am. This is totally embarrassing..."

"What's the matter?"

"This whole situation...I'm just glad it's over. I'm glad I'm about to get my revenge."

"Revenge?"

"Yeah, you know, like, vindication," Chelsea grimaced. "Absolution. Justice. All that."

Billy frowned. "I know what you meant. But I...don't know what you mean."

Chelsea chuckled nervously. "I'm sorry. I'm not myself today. That...that bitch killed my father."

"You mean Nia Black," Billy Casey surmised. "So you must be Chelsea Romedrux. The new scientist. Everyone says you're some kind of genius."

"Guilty as charged."

Billy smiled. "So, Nia killed your father? You mean Kane Romedrux? I met him a couple of times. He was a good man—sorry for your loss. Still...doesn't sound like *Target Omega's* M.O."

Chelsea's face went tight. "Well, it's true. She robbed my dad's facility and, like, for no reason, shot him in the back, twice, after she'd already got past the guards. They found his body in the river. Mr. Hudson told me all about it. He was there when it happened. That's why I'm here, you know. Mr. Hudson knew that I'm just as talented in the field as my father—heck, I'm better. This job was meant for my dad, and I was just going to be his assistant, so Mr. Hudson decided to give it to me. And my first big project is figuring out what makes that freak tick."

Billy gave her an affirmative look. "Is she in room 23-A?"

Chelsea nodded. "Mr. Hudson wants me to examine her right away. But I'm not. Not yet. She's not awake yet. The sedative Alvarez hit her with works for like four hours. They only brought her in an hour or so ago. I want her fully awake. I want her to feel every bit of what I'm going to do to her."

The elevator chimed again and the doors slid open; it reached the top floor.

Chelsea looked at Billy again. "You're…what's your name again?"

"Call me Billy," he answered.

"Well, Mr. Billy, I'm going to get myself a Slim-Fast and play some *Spades* online in my office while I wait. Wanna come?"

"Sounds fun, but I'm with security. My job here's to look out for the staff. It might be best for me to stay near the room, you know, in case she wakes up."

"No chance of that," Chelsea sighed, stepping off of the elevator. "But knock yourself out, handsome; by all means do your duty. Maybe we can talk some more another time."

Billy watched Chelsea's figure saunter away as she disappeared down the hall, heading toward her office.

"'Handsome', huh?" Billy grinned. "You ain't so bad yourself, babe. But before I give you my attention, there's something else I want to do first…"

Jesús Alvarez sauntered through the dingy underbelly of the research facility, approaching a large steel door at the end of a long hallway. He approached a card reader adjacent to the door and raised the card key Chelsea Romedrux gave him. With a swipe, the reader's red LED turned green and the steel door grinded open.

He looked on the shelves inside the dimly-lit room, taking in the sights of the file cabinets caked in dust and rusting along the edges; piles of manila jackets that hadn't been opened in years; locked safes and refrigerators with shelves stocked with forgotten, unapproved or expired organic matter.

Alvarez made a beeline for a file cabinet, snatched it open and rifled through it quickly. He dragged a folder out with the words HERCULES – NOTES scrawled upon it. Alvarez flipped through the contents of the folder until he came across an optical disc labeled HERCULES – DATA, which he promptly slid into his inside jacket pocket.

"Time to move on," he muttered to himself.

But he didn't move. Something else caught his attention. A manila folder was protruding slightly above others in a file cabinet with a peculiar name on it:

HUDSON EXPERIMENTAL X-TERMINATOR PROJECT

Alvarez opened the folder. Inside were scans, blueprints, and all kinds of esoteric text that would probably have made perfect sense to a researcher, but not to him. One thing he did recognize was a series of photos inside a section of the jacket labeled 'Candidates'.

These are... thought Alvarez. *Jason Priest. Cherie Wilson. Don Thompson. It's them...the other three members of the security team. What are they up to?*

He began reading.

"'Development of first generation SS units proceeding normally. Production halted during search for replacement R&D department head. Position filled. Project resumed, expected return to nominal production efficiency in a week. Commanding officer HEX units development halted in lieu of acquisition of *Omega*. Objective: research *Omega*'s DNA to determine how it can affect future SS and HEX weaponization development.'"

He froze in place and looked skyward.

Nia...

The bright glare of piercing halogen lights cut through the darkness as her eyelids slowly parted.

The stiff, sore and weakened Nia Black lay on a metal table in an examination room, she guessed, based on the computer terminals and monitoring equipment that circled her around the walls in the room, whose hum steadily filled the air along with the murmur of the air conditioning. No one was present. Barely visible over her lower eyelids and the curvature of her chest was a sliding door. Her limbs, restrained by cuffs attached to the surface of the table, could not summon the strength to snap her bonds. They wouldn't budge.

She wasn't wearing anything except a hospital gown and her panties. She spotted a locker in a corner of the room that she hoped contained her clothing.

Nia heard footsteps from outside and listened as the door hissed open. A man wearing a blue suit walked in. He was Caucasian, with long brown hair secured into a ponytail, and five o'clock shadow. He looked upon Nia, laid before him like a prize he'd won.

"Just as I thought," he said. "The sedative works for four hours or so on *normal* people. But we both know you're about as far as it gets from normal, right Miss Black?"

"Who the hell are you?" Nia growled.

"The name's Billy Casey, with Corp Hudson, of course," he said as he examined her. "Welcome back from dreamland. I guess I should let the good doctor know you're awake now. She's itching to find out what makes you tick."

Nia gasped.

"The real funny thing? All this is thanks to a guy who's probably just as worth looking into as you are. Yeah, that's right. I know Alvarez has something in him, just like you. How else could a newbie like him manage to capture one of our hardest targets with next to no effort?"

Casey walked around, his gaze transfixed on Nia as if he wanted to ensure he saw every inch of her body from every angle. The hospital gown did little to hide Nia's body. She knew it, and she knew this man knew it too.

"I don't have concrete proof, but after what I've seen, I'm confident in my theory. And as soon as I'm done here, I'm going to take it to my boss."

Nia frowned. "So what? Put a bullet in his head for all I care. What that got to do with you being in here with me?"

Billy licked his lips. "Yeah, about that…"

He leaned against the table and slid his hand underneath Nia's gown, grasping her inner thigh. She tried to squirm, but she could barely summon the strength to tighten her muscles.

"Having trouble? You're sedated, little girl," Billy laughed. "You're doped up on muscle relaxants…you won't be snapping the cuffs this time. You're not going anywhere."

Nia's face tightened.

"See, the thing is, the doctor's got it bad for you," Casey went on. "She wants to tear you apart. Gut you like a fish, prick you like a dartboard and drain you like a piece of fruit. When she's done with you…man, it's not going to be pretty. Not like you are now."

He suddenly pounced on the table on all fours like an animal, kneeling between Nia's legs.

"It would be a damn shame to waste the chance, you know what I mean? A girl like you is clearly used to this sort of thing anyway. So before Dr. Chelsea has her way with you… I'm going to have mine."

Nia tried to raise her voice, but her lungs were as weak as her muscles. She could only whimper.

"Don't waste your energy, you're going to need it," Billy said, taking hold of the bottom of her gown.

Billy pulled the gown up and tore it off, exposing her breasts. Goosebumps appeared on her skin.

Nia began to tremble in horror. She was in a sealed room in an unknown building that could have been anywhere in the world, and completely at the mercy of a lecherous soldier.

She felt nauseous. A cold, sick sensation flooded the pit of her stomach.

But she did all she could to keep her fear inside; keep it from showing on her face. She knew the moment her fright was evident in her eyes, it was all over. He'd have completely conquered her. He'd win.

Nia commanded her muscles to thrash about, but her body barely quivered. She was helpless.

Casey laughed.

Nia shut her eyes. Tears leaked through her tight eyelids. She could only think of all the things she'd experienced up to this point.

She thought about how easily she'd bested her opponents on the battlefield, dodging bullets, defeating soldiers with her guns and martial arts, taking out armed troopers in mobile assault vehicles. She envisioned how she overcame biologically engineered living weapons with only her skills and her confidence.

And she thought about when she'd lay under a man, as nude as the day she was born, only one night ago...how easily she'd stopped that man from forcing himself on her with just the strength in her body.

How ironic, she thought, that she would wind up like this. In the end, she was just another textbook weak and helpless woman, dominated by a man who hungered for her body and would take it by force.

As Billy Casey took it upon himself to stroke his rough palms across her breasts and abdomen, slowly making his way toward her panties, Nia knew she was kidding herself.

It *was* all over. She *was* conquered.

He *did* win.

CHELSEA ROMEDRUX'S TEAM HAD WON their fifth game of online Spades in a row. She sighed and looked at the clock display in the lower right of her monitor.

"Screw it, I'm tired of waiting," Chelsea muttered to herself. She looked across her office at a terminal with several monitors that displayed the images from the cameras placed throughout the facility.

She turned toward the monitor connected to the camera outside of the room holding Nia Black, the camera scanning the corridor outside of Room 23-A from above.

Chelsea Romedrux swallowed.

She watched Jesús Alvarez walk toward the room at a hurried pace. He jabbed a keypad on the wall and the door slid open, illumination from inside the room cutting a square pattern of light in the dim hallway. Alvarez stormed in, leaving the view of the camera.

Then another man soared backwards out of room 23-A, crashing into the wall outside as if he were pushed or thrown—Billy Casey.

As Casey scrambled to his feet, Chelsea could have sworn she caught a glimpse of his penis. But he quickly straightened his pants and stood up, and he yelled. Unfortunately, the cameras only relayed video, not audio.

Alvarez appeared on camera again, dashing through room 23-A's entryway, but he moved so fast, he looked like a smudge on the screen with motion blur all over him—until he stopped in a jolt and smashed his elbow into Billy Casey's skull. Billy crumbled back down on the floor and stopped moving. Then Alvarez pulled out his gun and pointed it at Casey's head.

Chelsea trembled with fright. Was she about to see a murder?

Then Alvarez withdrew his gun and went back into the room. Chelsea breathed a sigh of relief.

She stared in horror when a moment passed and Alvarez emerged from the room once more...with a fully conscious, and fully dressed, Nia Black following closely behind.

Then Chelsea flinched when she saw Nia kick the already-unconscious Billy Casey so hard, the man flew out of the camera's line of sight. The camera view quivered and flickered with static as if the entire area shook. Nia ran in the other direction, following Alvarez, and disappeared from view.

The show was over.

Chelsea remembered that there was roughly a ten-second lag between what the cameras displayed and what was actually happening in real-time.

Her heart pumped faster as she shot to her feet and raced out of her office.

Just before Billy Casey would have his way with Nia Black, he was stopped at the last possible moment.

Billy reached down, unbuckled his belt and exposed himself. He flashed teeth and took hold of the waistband of her panties, pulling the fabric from her, exposing her.

Then Nia's eyes shot open. She heard a whooshing sound—the sliding door.

Billy stopped moving. He winced as four fingers pressed into his shoulder like talons from behind.

"Get off of her."

Billy suddenly soared backward, crashing in the hall outside the room!

Nia whimpered and sobbed, looking around.

A man circled the table, unlatching the cuffs that bound Nia's wrists and ankles.

"I'll get you out of here," he said.

"…Jesús?"

Casey scrambled to his feet and fixed his pants. "I knew it. You're breaking her out now, huh? I knew you were a traitor!"

Alvarez bolted toward Casey in a blur. His forearm met Casey's skull with incredible force, slamming Casey's head into the wall behind him. Casey slumped to the ground and passed out.

"You piece of filth…" Alvarez grumbled. He raised his custom Desert Eagle with onyx plates on the grip, aimed at Casey's head, and pulled back the hammer.

Then Alvarez wheeled around to the sound of a body slapping against the tile floor in the room behind him. He saw Nia Black, collapsed on the floor. She tried to drag herself to her feet, but her body was still weak.

Alvarez put away his gun. He rushed to Nia's aid, taking her by the shoulders and helping her to her feet.

"It won't be long before they find out what's going on here."

Nia soon felt strength returning to her body. She quickly wrapped her arms around her bare breasts. "What…what did you do to me?"

"I am sorry," Jesús muttered. "I will explain later, I promise you. Can you walk?"

Nia slowly nodded. Alvarez left her to lean against the examination table and opened the locker in the corner of the room, where he found her clothes. He tossed them to Nia and turned his back.

"There are no cameras inside of the medical examination rooms, but plenty of cameras in the hallways. No doubt, someone has already seen what has happened here. We have to get out, now."

"No…" Nia uttered, quickly dressing up in her white leather body suit. "No! I'm not going anywhere with you! You're the reason I'm here in the first place! If I had the strength, I'd—!"

"Nia, listen to me!" Jesús screamed.

She flinched. It was the first time he'd ever addressed her by her first name.

"I need you to trust me. This is not how it was supposed to happen! I will explain everything later, when we get out of here!"

Nia stood silent.

"Trust me or not, what I've done here, now, proves I'm no friend of Corp Hudson, doesn't it? We are in the depths of the facility where *Hercules* was created…the place where it all began. We're not far from the city. There aren't any guards inside, but there are all over the perimeter of the island. We need to get moving now, before they flood the place. When Dr. Romedrux learns of this, she's sure to sound the alarm. We have to get moving. I've examined the layout of this place; I can lead you out."

"Romedrux?" Nia gasped. "Just like…"

"Chelsea Romedrux, the scientist in charge of this facility. What she wants, she tends to get. And she wants you dead. Apparently something about you killing her father?"

Nia shook her head. "Fine. Let's go. Give me my guns."

"I'm afraid I don't have them," Jesús muttered. "Had I brought them along, they would have been confiscated by the Security Soldiers. When you were captured, I managed to conceal your weapons. I locked them in my car before I boarded the ferry that transported you over here. We get to my car, you get your guns."

Nia sighed. "Okay, whatever. But after we're done here, it's going to be you and me."

Alvarez nodded and rushed off. Nia started after him, but she stopped in her tracks when she spotted the comatose Billy Casey on the floor.

194

Her heart pounded in her chest. Blood rushed to every corner of her body. Every nerve stood on end. Her muscles tensed up and bulged. She visualized every moment he had his fingers on her body, each instance like acid in her veins.

Suddenly, it was as if the muscle relaxants were never coursing through her body. She'd never felt so strong…not since the night she fought Armstrong.

Alvarez skidded to a halt and turned to face her.

"Miss Black!" Jesús roared. "There's no time!"

Nia blinked rapidly, coming to her senses. But her anger wasn't gone.

She screamed and slammed her foot into the already-unconscious Casey's chest, her overwhelming strength sending his body flying down the corridor!

He crashed into the wall at the end, his body stuck in the hole made by his own back.

Alvarez ran off. Nia turned and followed.

For a time, only the sound of snapping twigs and rustling bushes filled the air around Jesús Alvarez and Nia Black as they raced through the jungle-like environs surrounding Chelsea's facility, slapping aside branches and sidestepping around trees. Then the moan of a siren echoed from the building several yards behind them.

"Took longer than I thought," Nia muttered.

"Or perhaps we're just fast," Jesús stated. "Either way, the Security Soldiers will be on the move now."

"How far do we have to go anyway?" Nia gasped. "Why isn't there a road or something? These plants are making me itchy!"

"There is a road," Jesús retorted. "But it would be too obvious. We'd be sitting ducks out there in the open. I figured you'd have figured that out for yourself."

"Ain't no reason to be scared of them!" Nia roared. "How many times do I have to beat—"

"How many times have you defeated soldiers *without* your precious guns?" Jesús interrupted her. "The less conflict we get into here, the better. There will be plenty of time for battle."

"I don't need no damn guns..." Nia mumbled petulantly.

"Very well," Jesús said as he and Nia reached a clearing in the trees. "Tell that to them."

Six men in gold and chrome armor raced seemingly from out of nowhere and stopped before the two escapees. Their breastplates looked thick and sturdy, their gauntlets and boots an inch thicker than their forearms and shins, their helmets covering their entire faces except for their mouths and chins, and an 'H' logo was embossed upon each one.

"Corp Hudson Security Soldiers," Jesús muttered. "Hudson deploys them to protect his most important assets...things, or even *people* too valuable to entrust to the main security detail."

"Why? What's so special about them? They ain't nobody!" Nia snapped, dashing forward with plans to send one sailing to the ground with her knee. She jumped higher than a girl of her stature should have been able to jump, put more force behind the blow than a girl of her size should have—

An armored palm slammed into Nia's chest mid-flight like a battering ram! The air shot out of her lungs and she flew backward, crashed-landing on the ground, rolling in dirt and weeds.

Alvarez reached down and pulled Nia up by the arm.

Each Security Soldier took a single step forward.

"Corp Hudson analyzes soldiers from all walks of military service, determining which ones are best suited for his personal protectors, and asks them to volunteer for the procedure," Jesús explained. "Microchips are implanted into their brains that compel them to disregard all stray thought that might be a detriment to their duty...thoughts of fear, for example, or thoughts

196

that the small, attractive woman attacking them looks unassuming and unthreatening. In other words, all they care about is following their orders."

"I've had just about enough of all y'all calling me little," Nia grumbled. "And how the hell can Hudson get away with that?"

"Because he's Hudson," Alvarez said. "No one dares cross him. He's got far too many politicians and media outlets in his pocket for anyone to try to expose him."

"Craziness…" Nia shook her head and tightened her fists.

"We need to get through them to get to the ferry dock. Ready?" Jesús said.

Nia nodded.

Billy Casey slowly opened his eyes, feeling the shooting pain in his abdomen and in his head. He found his back making an impressive crater in the drywall at the end of the corridor as he tried to recollect what happened.

As he looked ahead and tried to focus his vision, he spotted the figure of a curvy, lab-coated blonde woman bouncing toward him and coming to a crouch. The clack of her high heels echoed in his head like a tap dancer on stage, and her high-pitched voice faded in and out as if her voice reverberated from within a deep cavern.

Finally, he was able to make sense of what she was saying.

"…you all right? Come on, wake up! You're not badly hurt, are you?" said Chelsea Romedrux.

Billy dragged himself out of the wall and swept dust and residue from his uniform. As he did, he coughed, and blood forced its way out of his mouth.

"My goodness…" Chelsea stammered. "You're bleeding internally…"

"I'm fine," Casey grunted. "Where are they?"

"Like, out. Duh! They have to be heading for the dock. You've got to get her back here. I don't care what you do with Alvarez."

"To hell with that. She's too much trouble. This is a waste of fucking time. Just kill her…"

Chelsea took hold of Billy's shoulders and pushed him against the wall, staring into his eyes with fierce determination.

"Look. I'm sorry if you got your little ego bruised, but we have orders. That girl is *Target Omega*. That means she is the final element in our boss' big plans. 'Waste of time'? Like, don't you get it? She *is* our time. She's totally the whole reason we have jobs. She also happens to be the bitch that killed my daddy. So, like, get off of your ass, and go get her."

"*Fuck you!*" Casey grunted, slapping her hands away. "I take orders from Vincent Marks. You put me in touch with him and—"

"Like, you take orders from Maxwell Hudson too, right?" Chelsea interrupted him.

Billy froze and silenced immediately.

"You might have fallen asleep during this part of the orientation so I'll give you a little reminder. Research and Development is, like, the biggest, most highly funded arm of Corp Hudson. And why wouldn't it be? We make the weapons, we make the armor; we make *you*. R&D is the voice of Hudson when Hudson's not around, and since that bitch killed my daddy, *I'm* the voice of R&D. One word from me and you can either be the next security chief…or the guy who cleans the boots for the grunts, Mr. Billy."

Billy Casey grimaced and clenched his fists. "Yeah, or I could make it so that not one word will ever come out of your cute little pie hole again."

"Um, hel-*lo*?" Chelsea bellowed. "You were assigned here to protect *me*, I-I-R-C. And check it out, real-time video all over the place. So, how exactly would you explain how I got whacked on *your* watch, *after* Nia Black and her little co-conspirator got away? I bet Vincent and Mr. H would *love* to hear that story."

Billy fell silent.

"Look, I'm going to level with you," Chelsea said. "I think you're really cute. A little reckless, but you've got it going on, you know? So I would love it if you and I could be buddies in this little endeavor. I need somebody I can trust to help me do the heavy lifting. Like I said, I can put a good word in with the boss to get you moving on up. And, I come bearing gifts! Have a look."

Chelsea reached toward the floor and lifted a black case, unlatched its twin locks and lifted it open. Only then did Billy remember that she was carrying it when she approached him, and set it down as he came to his senses. He first thought it might have been a first aid kit, but then he looked at the contents of the case, and his eyes went wide.

"You should have some fun with this," said Chelsea.

It was a huge handgun; a revolver with large chambers and two barrels that looked like a double-barreled shotgun tilted vertically. Casey wondered how a woman like Chelsea even managed to carry it to him.

"It's something R&D's been working on for a while. I don't have a name for it yet, but it should come in handy in case you need to take down a hard target…like Alvarez."

"And how am I supposed to catch up with them?" Billy grumbled. "What if they got away by now?"

"Go to the garage and tell the grease monkeys that Dr. Chelsea said you can take the 'JTB-36'. It's a cool toy that they designed before I started working here…you get to give it the field test. Just make sure you read page 53 of the manual. That and the gun will be all you'll need, okay?"

Billy Casey nodded and accepted the weapon. He forced himself to his feet. Chelsea spoke one more time, standing with her hands on her hips.

"Bring that shrew back for me, and you can have anything you want…" Chelsea said.

She shifted her chin skyward and stuck her chest out as she parted her lab coat at her sides, putting her figure on display.

"…Anything."

Casey stopped in his tracks and turned to face her. He looked Dr. Romedrux up and down, like a scanner tracing every curve of her form.

She nodded with a devious look.

And with that, newfound determination fueled Billy's steps and he stormed off with energy he never knew he had.

Nia Black charged toward the Security Soldiers with fight in her eyes. She ducked a punch and tangled the arm that threw it within her own. She dragged the Soldier's arm down while shooting her knee up. A blood-curdling crack followed as his forearm was split across the middle. Nia threw a final roundhouse kick that sent the trembling Soldier soaring out of her sight.

Before she knew it, a blow struck her in the back with the force of a lightning bolt. Every nerve trembled as a jolt of electricity traveled through her, but Nia quickly recovered. She winced and rolled on the ground, glancing at the Soldier who snuck her from behind with an electrified rod protruding from his gauntlet.

"I see you guys shop at the same store as those punks at Romedrux Labs did," Nia chuckled. "And you'll go down just as easily, too."

Alvarez fought two Soldiers at once, keeping them at bay with far-reaching glancing blows and shooting kicks.

"It has been a while since I've done this," Jesús muttered as he caught one Soldier's arm, twisted his wrist and sent his opponent swirling to the ground. Before his other opponent could react, Alvarez shot his elbow backward, cracking the dense armor and sending the second Soldier stumbling back. The sentinel reset his stance, pressed a button on his gauntlet and produced an electrical rod. Raising it to the sky, the Soldier charged toward Alvarez—

And tumbled to the ground face first as Nia slammed her knees into his helmet-covered skull from behind. She pressed her palms to the ground, raising her legs skyward, and brought her knees together again, barreling her weight into the grounded Soldier and pressing his face into the dirt, leaving a deep impression. He did not move after that.

Nia climbed to her feet and swept the dirt from her body suit.

"What the hell was taking you so long?"

Alvarez slammed his fist into the head of the Soldier he'd thrown to the ground, cracking his helmet and knocking him out. Alvarez then looked around and saw that Nia had managed to incapacitate the remaining five Security Soldiers, including Alvarez's second opponent. Their comatose bodies lay in the dirt and branches, broken trees and mangled bushes strewn about.

"I'd gotten dirt on my glasses," Jesús mumbled, taking his spectacles off and cleaning them with a smooth, lint-free cloth.

"So, I guess Hudson's security team has specialists and what not," said Nia.

"What do you mean?"

"Some of y'all are good at fighting, and others are good at…other stuff. You're clearly one of the other guys."

Alvarez could only chuckle as they took off running toward the dock. "Well, you're right. I'm a sharpshooter. Staying out of direct assault operations was the best way to keep my enhanced strength hidden from the Corp's watchful eye. After all, it would only be natural that a man who specializes in marksmanship would have good eyesight and remarkable accuracy."

"And yet…you wear glasses…"

"Glasses with specialized lenses, designed to automatically adjust to varying levels of brightness," Jesús explained. "I don't need them to *see*, per se, but in certain situations, they do come in handy. When you have heightened senses, there is a tradeoff; we also become more sensitive to extremes. Something you'll learn in time…"

The two skidded to a halt at the dock, where a speedboat sat waiting. Two guards were present, but Nia Black and Jesús Alvarez made short work of them, and in moments, they were cutting across the water, headed back toward the mainland.

"It won't be long," Jesús said. "My car is parked at the dock on the mainland. We'll get away and decide our next move then."

"So why not just take this boat and go somewhere else, somewhere way off the coast?" Nia wondered.

"Do you want your guns back?"

"Hell yeah! My bullets got mister 'fondle-the-hot-black-girl-while-she's-strapped-down' perverted-ass *motherfucker's* name written all over them."

"And I'm sure you want to keep your friends safe, right?"

"Friends? What friends? You mean Bobby? Please," Nia scoffed.

"Hudson's corporate tower is on the mainland…still want to take him out?"

Nia folded her arms.

"We're not done, Miss Black," Jesús said. "Soon, everything will be made clear. But we still have a bit of work to do."

Nia turned at the faint sound of a second motor, piercing through the roar of their speedboat's engine as it slashed through the waters. She looked behind them and saw a small object speeding in their direction.

"Is that who I think it is?" Nia gasped.

"If you think that's Billy Casey," Jesús grumbled, "Then, yes."

Nia Black and Jesús Alvarez glared back, catching sight of their pursuer. Roaring across the water, cutting a massive wake that left walls of water spreading away from his sides at three times his height, Billy Casey drove a specialized vehicle that looked like a sleek combination of jet ski and hovercraft. Propellers mounted on its back provided the propulsion, encased in round structures that looked like tires, stacked similarly to the insignia of the Olympics without the center ring. The vehicle sped through the water like a torpedo, Billy Casey tightly grasping and twisting its handlebars almost as if he were operating a motorcycle.

"Interesting vehicle," Jesús muttered. "Fast, too."

"His stupid ass…" Nia chuckled. "We're almost to the dock. What's he going to do when we park and go to the car…get off his mutant jet bike and chase after us on foot? I say we just wait for him and kick his ass."

"Billy Casey is a lot of things," Jesús muttered, "But a fool is not one of them. He must have a reason—"

Then a thundering boom echoed and the speedboat shook! Alvarez glanced and saw a hole in the hull on the starboard side. He looked back and saw Billy Casey brandishing a large, double-barreled revolver, aiming it in their direction while holding the handlebars with his off-hand.

"Ah," Jesús sighed. "I suppose he means to do us in before we get to the dock."

Nia squealed. "I need my guns! I got half a mind to jump off this death trap, swim over there and—!"

"…Be completely at his mercy," Jesús stopped her. "You still have a lot to learn. As you said, we're nearly to the dock. Soon he won't be a factor."

Nia rolled her eyes. "Do they pay you people enough to be this determined?"

"Not usually. I suspect there's something else driving him. He's always been… ambitious."

"Well after that shit he tried back in the laboratory, I'll be happy to oblige him if he wants to get himself killed," Nia grimaced. "Just get me to my guns."

"Hopefully I can do that…" Jesús resolved, tightening his grip on the speedboat's controls.

"Don't say 'hopefully'!" Nia snapped. "You *will.* Let's pull this off, get rid of this pest and get back to business. Hudson's still gotta go down, right?"

"Yes, of course."

Then a second shot rocked the boat! Alvarez looked back and saw a gaping chasm in the hull, and fluid leaking out.

Fuel.

"Well..." he muttered. "This is becoming a more interesting day by the minute. I hope you can swim, Miss Black."

"I just said I—what?!"

Billy Casey fired again.

Alvarez let go of the speedboat's controls and sprang into the air, yanking Nia by the torso as he did so.

The boat erupted in orange flame and black smoke with a deafening BOOM!

As singed wood and metal and plastic and glass fragments crashed into the water, splashing everywhere, Casey raised the cannon and slid a new round of shells into its chamber.

"Hope I didn't mess her up too bad," he muttered to himself. "The doc said alive... she didn't say unharmed."

Casey stopped his watercraft, released the controls and knelt toward the water, trying to see below the surface as he bobbed up and down.

"Hey, Miss Black!" yelled Casey. "I know you're alive, and I know you can hear me! I also know you're unarmed! You'd have shot at me if you could! You've got nothing going for yourself right now! You might as well come up! Alvarez can't help you now, but maybe the doc and I will go easy on you!"

Alvarez, floating about immersed in water, looked around and saw Nia Black drifting further into the depths beneath him, eyes shut, nonresponsive. He swam down to her, took hold of her cheeks and aligned her face with his.

Nia's eyes slowly opened as she felt pressure in her head. Her eyes bulged when she realized that Jesús Alvarez was pressing his mouth to hers, breathing hard.

She wrapped her arms around his neck and closed her eyes.

BILLY CASEY grew frustrated.

He'd been floating around the water on the specialized JTB-36 for several minutes after blasting the speedboat carrying Jesús Alvarez and Nia Black to bits. He saw their bodies flail into the water an instant before the boat blew, so he was certain they were alive. But he scanned the surface of the water looking for any evidence of a breach around him, circling like a lighthouse beacon, to no avail. He was certain his enemies would try to pop up and try to take him by surprise; after all, he was their lone pursuer, and a deadly one at that, so he thought, and even they had to come up for air eventually. But the density of the water would slow even them down; after all, enhanced or not, they weren't fish.

Casey had it all planned out. The slightest quiver in the water, and he'd send a thunderous blast from his revolver into the depths in kind. He figured, they're superhuman; they can take a shot or two. Dr. Chelsea wouldn't mind if Nia Black has a couple of nicks on her, he thought. But for Alvarez, Casey would fire considerably more shots.

It hadn't occurred to the self-centered man that taking him out was the furthest thing from either of their minds, at least for the time being.

That was, until he shot a quick glance at the dock far away from him, and saw two figures: a tall man in a dingy uniform and a short, curvy woman wearing a white leather cat suit, dragging themselves out of the water and pulling themselves up on the wooden surface of the nearby dock connected to the mainland.

He flashed teeth and cursed, aimed his pistol forward, and fired. The shot tore through a piece of the dock, sending wood fibers flailing in the air inches from Nia's feet. They looked in his direction and sprinted off, running toward the parking lot well away from the docks.

Nia glared at Jesús Alvarez as the two ran together.

"Why did you do that?" Nia asked.

"What?" Jesús exhaled in response.

"You know…underwater…that. Why?"

The two rushed to a car sitting in the parking lot, a convertible. Alvarez fished out keys, leaped over the driver's side door and started the car. Nia Black leaped over the passenger's side door and flopped into the seat next to him. Alvarez shifted the gears and floored the gas pedal, his tires screeching against the asphalt as a plume of smoke billowed behind them.

"Slow down!" Nia shouted. "Where are my guns?"

"Glove compartment," Jesús said.

Nia froze briefly, then opened the glove compartment as Alvarez said. She lowered the door and found her chrome-plated Magnum Research .40 caliber Baby Eagle pistols sitting there, waiting. She smiled as if she'd won the lottery as she checked and found their clips were fully loaded, then immediately straightened her face out, remembering her train of thought.

"Answer me," Nia growled. "Why did you—?"

"You mean, give you mouth-to-mouth?" Jesús suddenly said. "It looked like you were unconscious. I thought you may not have had time to take in any air when we jumped from the boat."

Nia looked down. "Oh. Well, I…I did. I was all right. But thanks anyway."

"You're welcome, Nia."

Nia looked toward the water and shot a glance at Billy Casey. "Stop the car. I want to take his punk ass out."

"Forget it. We'll have more time for that later. There's something I have to tell you. But now's not the time. For now we get out of sight."

Nia sucked her teeth. "You're pissing me off, you know."

Billy Casey grimaced. His eyes narrowed as he started the engine of the JTB-36.

"Page 53 of the manual..." he muttered to himself. "Right."

Steering the vehicle in a circular path through the water, Billy built up momentum and sped toward the dock. The vehicle soon slashed through the waves with such velocity, it was almost as if it weren't touching the water at all.

Casey drove across the water, moving almost side-by-side with Alvarez's convertible on the street. As the two vehicles soared forward, one on asphalt and the other on water, Billy Casey made eye contact with Nia, and looked sternly at her as she smiled cheerily and blew him a kiss in jest.

Billy flipped up a small latch on the controls of his vehicle, exposing a red button. He pressed his thumb into the button and the propellers of the JTB-36 suddenly quivered violently, spinning at nearly thrice the velocity.

He pulled back on the handlebars as the vehicle *leaped from the water!*

Nia and Alvarez looked skyward. Billy's vehicle was suddenly so high in the air that it blocked the sun before their eyes.

The propellers stopped spinning and they rotated sideways, sliding along tracks on either side of the vehicle's chassis as it as it sailed through the air. The propellers aligned parallel with the length of the vehicle, locking together on either end, until the four propellers transformed into *two tires*, one in front, the other in back.

Billy Casey's jet ski had become a motorcycle!

"'JTB'..." muttered Billy. "What, 'jet ski-to-bike'?! So lame."

The vehicle landed on the road behind the convertible and its engine buzzed with life, Casey suddenly speeding behind them on wheels!

"Well, I'll be damned..." Nia raised her pistols. "Corp Hudson's got some banging toys. But that's all it is—a toy. It's on now because I'm strapped and ready to—!"

"Nia…" Jesús interrupted her. Nia knew why, too.

No sooner did they look back at the pursuing Billy Casey, Nia and Alvarez picked up more grumbling sounds coming from the distance; more engines.

A group of bikers joined Billy Casey from an intersection, aligning with him in a V-shaped formation, their engines growling like a pack of wolves. Each biker wore full tactical gear and carried TEC-9 machine pistols.

Billy Casey, riding behind the other four, barked orders.

"Shoot to kill!"

The chase led to a highway; a wide strip of road with three lanes on each side, a thick forest on one side of the road, the river on the other.

Each biker raised his weapon and opened fire on the car, the deafening chatter of their high-powered bullets screaming in the air. Nia kneeled in the passenger seat of the drop-top and fired back. Alvarez weaved the car through the highway traffic, his tires screeching against the asphalt as enemy bullets ripped up pieces of the road around them.

One rider pulled up alongside the car, aiming his gun directly at Nia. She lost no time whipping her guns around and yanking the triggers, her bullets like battering rams slamming into his chest. The soldier's body flipped backward in a forced somersault, his head crashing first on the street. His neck cracked as his body bounced and tumbled away. The motorcycle flipped over and skidded backward, crashing into a car as the other four SPI bikers veered away from it.

Nia glared at Billy Casey afterward, and when their eyes met, she could tell Casey had just learned something new about his target. She knew when to cease the fun and games. She knew how to be serious.

Casey's eyes followed the body of his man as it tumbled past him. He lowered his speed and distanced himself from the other three bikers. Though he knew what happened to Alvarez's unit at the warehouse, as well as the security forces that attacked her at the Worthington site, he didn't expect to see Nia kill an enemy that swiftly, without hesitation.

But he also remembered that Nia Black would do her best to avoid harming innocent people.

"Surround them!" he ordered. "I have the rear! Two take the sides! One head up front! We're lighter than they are, so you should have no problem keeping up! Make a ring around them and tear them apart from all sides! Use the passing drivers as shields and take your shots when you can!"

As ordered, the other three bikes spread out and positioned themselves around the sports car, swerving around the passing vehicles zooming by as they closed in on Nia and Alvarez.

Alvarez released the gas as the bikers sped ahead, intending to evade them by slowing down, but they were on to his plans. The rider on the left also slowed and lined up with the car again, opening fire at once. Nia and Alvarez ducked in their seats, scarcely avoiding the bullets that flew over their heads and left spider web cracks in the front windshield. Nia returned gunshots but the biker was already out of the way.

Nia turned to Jesús and yelled, "They're on both sides of us. You know what to do!"

Alvarez nodded as Nia crouched in her seat. He tightly grasped the steering wheel, flashed teeth and turned hard to the left, slamming into the biker on the left of the car. Alvarez repeated the action to take out the biker on the right. Both lost control of their bikes and skidded from the road, capsizing on their sides and skidding away.

Nia sighed. "I'm sorry...that must have been murder on your paint job."

"Just worry about taking care of that one in front of us."

The soldier driving in front of them fired backward, his rapid-fire bullets ripping through the windshield, showering glass in all directions.

Nia instantly stood in her seat, pressed her foot on the dashboard to steady herself and stuck out her arms, her dual pistol rounds tearing through the biker and his vehicle. His bike fell and spun on the road as Alvarez floored the gas and shot past, knocking the motorcycle aside. The spinning wreck grinded on the street, a pinwheel of sparks shooting skyward. It crashed into a guardrail and erupted in an orange cloud of flame.

"Yes!" Nia shouted. "That's all of them—ah!"

Blood spattered on the passenger seat of Alvarez's car after a gunshot; Nia's blood. Billy's attack grazed her across the edge of her left shoulder, leaving a burning gash.

"It's a good thing Casey isn't like us," Jesús said, glancing at her. "If his aim were better he might have killed you."

"I'm fine, thanks for asking!" Nia screamed. "I forgot about that punk-ass. If I was a hundred percent, he'd have never got that shot off!"

"Well, you're not one hundred percent, so pay attention!" Jesús barked. "This is not the time to be playing around!"

Casey drove steadily behind them, holding his revolver with his wrist twisted to the side, aiming carefully with one eye closed. After watching his men fall in battle against Nia and Alvarez, he was more determined than ever to complete his mission, in as painful a manner as possible.

Alvarez stepped on the brakes, swiftly closing the gap between Casey's speeding motorcycle and the rear bumper of the convertible. Casey reacted swiftly and turned his bike hard to the right to escape Alvarez's attack, his knee inches from the speeding ground.

"It's not going to be that easy, Alvarez!" Casey roared, firing his gun at the car. The bullets echoed with thundering booms that seemed to quiver the air. The car trembled as the shots struck.

Alvarez sighed.

"Miss Black…can you shoot, please? We're running out of time."

"He got my good shoulder," Nia replied, grasping her arm. "I can shoot with the right but I can't promise I'll shoot as straight."

"You're left-handed," Jesús ascertained. "But you frequently use two guns—rather accurately…"

"I don't 'frequently' get shot!" Nia screamed. "Just keep the car straight."

Nia climbed on the seat, leaning on Alvarez's shoulder as she fired at Casey with her right hand. Casey weaved his upper body as the bullets zinged past him.

Nia bit her lip. Her recovery from the muscle relaxants wasn't as complete as she'd thought; she was more sluggish than usual, and the near drowning did not help. Nor did being soaking wet, the speed at which they were moving, the constant swaying of the vehicle, or the wound in her arm. Collectively, it was more than enough to disrupt her usual precision.

Billy Casey laughed derisively. But, knowing what she was capable of, Casey knew deep down he was lucky to be alive. He couldn't afford to give either Alvarez or Nia another moment.

He carefully lined up a shot.

I've got you now, you son of a bitch.

A thundering boom preceded a crimson splash eruption in Alvarez's back!

"Damn it!" he roared, snatching his hands from the wheel as he grasped his wound.

"Jesús!" Nia screamed, but it wasn't a scream of concern for him.

It was a warning.

When Alvarez snapped his hands away from the steering wheel, the convertible swerved into the wrong lane.

A pickup truck was barreling toward them, approaching far too fast.

Nia flailed her arms, trying to grasp the wheel but she was too short to reach it over Alvarez in the driver's seat…

The blaring horn of the truck and Nia's strident scream were both stifled as the truck *smashed* into Alvarez's car, sending it twisting in the air! The pickup truck whirled across the road, knocking other vehicles around like bumper cars.

Alvarez's convertible flailed in the air like a centrifuge until it crashed back on the street and continued to slide unstoppably on its mangled tires, passing drivers frantically swerving out of the way. The world rapidly spun and bounced around Nia and Alvarez like a plane crash.

Alvarez's once beautiful red convertible eventually tore through the restraining gate along the side of the highway like a fist through a wet paper bag. It crashed into the woods below, rolling and bouncing downhill, coming to a horrific, crunching stop, lying upside down in the grass.

Casey hit the brakes on his bike and turned sharply toward the edge of the road, driving through the breach created by Alvarez's car. He leapt from the highway with the JTB-36 and landed on the soil not far below. Stopping the machine and leaping off, Casey drew his weapon and stepped toward the wreckage.

"It's a damn shame what happened to your car, Jesús!" Casey shouted aloud with a big smile. "You can have all the drugs and performance enhancers in you that you want, Alvarez. You'll never be as good as I am. Just goes to show you; real warriors can't be made in a lab. They're born."

Casey walked closer to the overturned, mutilated car, the sounds of the dying engine and the endlessly spinning wheels of the convertible playing satisfyingly in Casey's ears.

"And now it's over. I've been wanting to take you out for a long time, Jesús. You're always looking down on everyone when you're not even a real man. Now, while you're lying there, polish your glasses one more time so you can see this bullet coming."

He yanked the door open and extended his gun inside, his grin so wide his cheekbones ached.

213

Then, his jaw dropped.

"No *fucking* way!!"

Billy Casey's angry roar echoed as he stormed away from the empty wreck.

JESÚS ALVAREZ REACHED into his jacket pocket and pulled out fragments of the case he'd been carrying since leaving the storage room in Chelsea Romedrux's island facility. The disc that was inside the case was now nothing more than shards of broken plastic…a result of the car crash.

He sighed, defeat plunging down his face. But then he looked upon the couch next to him and smiled slightly as he looked upon the comatose beauty lying before him, watching her ample chest pulsing up and down as she breathed softly.

The crash knocked Nia Black unconscious. Her once brilliant white leather cat suit was torn everywhere and caked in dirt and blood. Yet, despite the bruises on her body and her wildly mussed hair, the woman wearing what was left of the outfit was no less alluring in her peaceful state, her curves pushing through the holes in her outfit and exposing supple brown skin underneath. Her pendant shimmered brightly as it reflected small glints of light, splayed across her nearly exposed breast like a beacon, beckoning him.

Jesús Alvarez wanted to lie down next to her and sleep.

Nia finally stirred, squirming around and pressing her palm to her forehead. Her vision came into focus and she saw Jesús Alvarez standing over her, facing away. He wasn't wearing a shirt, and he had rags and gauze wrapped around his upper back, covering the wound from Billy Casey's bullet.

"Don't worry," he said. "I'm fine. You should know by now how hard it is to kill people like us."

Nia looked around and took in her surroundings. She found herself inside a small room that looked like an apartment, with wood construction and lots of debris. She lay on a futon, the only thing in the room that was clear of package wrappers, empty water bottles or other junk. The room had two windows, both blocking incoming light with venetian blinds turned up. But enough illumination seeped in between the blinds to let Nia know that it must have at least been mid-afternoon.

Nia saw her guns sitting on a coffee table in front of her. She quickly snatched one and aimed it at Alvarez. She felt its heft and realized the gun was still loaded. She flicked the safety switch off.

He stood still, continued facing away from her, and folded his arms.

"Are you going to shoot me, Nia?"

Nia breathed hard, but tilted the gun away and put it back on the coffee table.

"Where are we? Is this your place?"

"No...but it'll be safe for now."

"Good," Nia grumbled. "Because we need to talk."

"I know."

Nia leaned back and crossed her legs.

"So. Talk. What did you really need to get inside that facility for?"

Jesús chuckled. "Sharp...you're sharp, Nia. I wouldn't have figured you could piece it together so easily."

"Well, evidently whatever you're doing isn't about killing or catching me," Nia retorted. "Otherwise you wouldn't have put yourself in harm's way to get me out. So there's something else you wanted out of there."

"It was a string of fortunate events," Jesús answered. "It all started when you robbed Romedrux Labs. The weapon prototype you stole was Romedrux's finest work, and it would have guaranteed him a position within the hallowed halls of Corp Hudson's Research and Development department. But when you got away with the weapon, Hudson had Professor Kane Romedrux killed that same night for failing to guard it properly. By doing that, and by pinning the blame on you, Hudson turned an otherwise unassuming young assistant into your mortal enemy."

"That girl you told me about...Chelsea Romedrux, right?"

"Right; Chelsea was her father's apprentice—it turns out she had more of a hand in the design of that weapon than her father did. Now, she's Corp Hudson's head of R&D, a position that gives her significant power and prestige. The island facility, where *Hercules* were developed, was renovated to her specifications to begin a new generation of human performance enhancement experiments, and Hudson wanted to start anew with his most passionate project. They don't know where Alexander Black is, or if he's even alive, so they turned their attention to you. This was the key to my plan. I was there for *Hercules*."

"Why?"

"*Hercules* is a defunct project, but I've been in contact with certain parties who would have loved to study its properties themselves. So my job was to get whatever data on the formula I could. As I told you, only the blood that flows through your veins—the blood of Alexander Black—works with *Hercules*. Interested parties want to know how they can make it more...accessible. But by Hudson's own order, none of his regular subordinates is allowed to enter the facility, not even his security agents—no one except for his scientists and his Security Soldiers. This ensures his darkest secrets remain protected. The only way to get to the data I needed was to convince Chelsea to give me access to the facility's storage room. To do that, I had to give her something she wanted."

Nia sighed. "Me."

"Yes," Jesús nodded. "By personally taking you down, I received a bit of an 'honor' by being allowed to join the transfer team tasked with bringing you into Chelsea's lab. Then I spoke with Chelsea and got what I came for."

"So it was never about getting Hudson, was it? You played me from the beginning. You just wanted to get your hands on the *Hercules* stuff."

217

"Not true," Jesús shot back. "It's just that I know it will take more than a brazen attack on the open road to defeat Maxwell Hudson. It must be done systematically...we have to utterly defeat him—make sure no one can rise in his place with equal or greater power and come after us once the fighting's done. Now is simply not the time."

Nia grimaced. "There's something you're not telling me. You...you weren't supposed to come back for me, were you?"

Jesús looked down, and shook his head. "You were the decoy. You were meant to keep the attention off of me. And it worked."

"So, why did you come back then?" Nia wondered. "Why didn't you just leave me there? You got what you wanted, didn't you?"

Jesús said nothing.

Nia hesitated; then spoke again. "And that info about *Hercules*; where is it?"

"Destroyed...I lost it in the crash."

"So you did all that for nothing?"

The remark seemed to send a jolt through the man. He abruptly turned to her.

"No. Not for nothing," Jesús said sharply. "I couldn't bear to leave you there, Nia; not at the mercy of Billy Casey, not with that ditzy, revenge-crazed scientist and her scheming."

"Tell me why," Nia demanded. "Why did you risk your life to save me even though you already had what you wanted."

"Because I..."

Nia lifted herself from the futon, took hold of her outfit by the plunging neckline and dragged it down past her shoulders and back, letting it slide down until it collapsed at her feet.

"If you can't tell me...show me."

Jesús Alvarez looked upon Nia Black, standing before him completely nude except her golden necklace with its opal charm.

He tossed off his spectacles and took her in his arms.

Jesús kissed Nia's breasts, took one hand and slid it down across her chest and belly until he felt the warmth coming from between her thighs.

Nia moaned as his fingers grooved into her, stroking her clitoris up and down as she began to moisten. She wrapped her fingers around his back, threw her head high and gently leaned toward the futon, rubbing him between the legs, feeling his erect manhood fighting against the fabric of his pants.

Jesús followed her. He held her back while laying her down, kissing her across her body until he reached her legs. He took hold of her calves and raised her legs high, spreading them wide open.

Nia looked down at him with a smile.

Jesús smiled back at her and went down, kissing and lapping her in pleasure as she began to gyrate and moan.

He kept it up for what felt like hours to Nia. She hissed and howled, tears of ecstasy trickling from her eyes. Nia's eyes shot open, no longer able to resist her screams of pleasure.

Jesús pulled himself up and unbuckled his pants. He dropped them to the floor and leaned back toward Nia, planting her calves on his shoulders. He wrapped his hands around Nia's curvy thighs and slowly slid inside of her.

And Nia moaned, feeling pleasure she'd never felt before. This wasn't like others she'd been with in the past. Jesús Alvarez was her equal. He was as strong as she was, fully knowledgeable about her power.

Neither had any reason to hold back.

Jesús practically threw himself into Nia, going back and forth like a piston, hissing and grunting as the futon rocked and shook underneath them.

He let Nia's legs down and rolled her over, lying on his back as Nia rode on top of him. He looked upon her splendid body with joy as she put one arm behind her head, leaning on his heaving chest with the other.

Jesús clawed Nia's butt with both hands, his muscles tensing up. She planted both hands on his shoulders, staring into his eyes.

They climaxed together, screaming as loud as their lungs would allow, and then Nia collapsed on his chest, breathing hard. She stroked Jesús cheek and pulled his head to hers, and they kissed passionately.

Nia and Jesús lay together on the futon, naked, his jacket serving as a makeshift blanket. Nia looked upon him, running her fingers through his long, curly auburn hair.

"Jesús, can I ask you a question?" Nia muttered.

"What is it?"

"Why did you show those pictures of me and Bobby to Charlene?"

Jesús quickly released Nia and sat up. "What?"

"I want to know why you felt the need to show those pictures to Bobby's girlfriend."

"I told you before, Nia, I had nothing to do with—"

"Don't try to kid a kidder, Jesús," Nia groaned, sitting up on her knees. "I know you're the one who arranged for them to be kidnapped. I know that Armstrong dude was your dog. I know you were just trying to trap me. That's why you showed up at just the right time and got me out just before Hudson's *other* goons got there. But you ain't have to show Charlene those pictures. Kidnapping them was more than enough to get my attention. There wasn't no reason to put my business with Bobby all out there like that."

"And you're not angry?"

"I was," Nia said. "Then I started to realize that it was for the best. Bobby was holding me back. I know that now. My old man was trying to tell me something like that before, but as usual, I didn't listen. He said 'guard yourself'. I didn't realize he meant guard myself from *Bobby*. I'm slowly getting over him though. I want to know what was going through *your* mind."

221

Jesús took a breath. "I suppose...I suppose I thought you were selling yourself short. You know how strong you are, how skillful you are. You've known this long before I came into your life. But for some reason, you feel content with being someone's plaything; as if you weren't worthy of being with a man who would love you as much as you would him."

Nia scoffed. "You're so full of it. You just wanted me for yourself, that's all."

Jesús looked up, then shot to his feet. He grabbed his clothes and began to dress.

"Where are you going?" gasped Nia.

"You're absolutely right, Miss Black. My feelings for you have become a liability...I compromised everything."

"What are you talking about? It's not over yet. We just have to come up with a new plan and..."

"Wrong," Jesús grumbled as he fastened his belt. "I lost the *Hercules* data. It *is* over."

"So, what, you're just gonna leave?" Nia gasped.

He fell silent.

"I don't believe this shit..." Nia muttered, her voice trembling. "Another one; another man just wants to fuck me and leave me..."

"It's not like that, Miss Black, not at all," Jesús said. "I have no intention of letting you out of my life."

"Then why are you leaving?" Nia sobbed. "And why are you back to calling me 'Miss Black'?"

Jesús looked down. "I must go report to my contact. I let my feelings for you compromise my mission. I don't regret that. But it doesn't change the fact that I lost the data solely because I went back for you. I failed my mission, period. I don't know what's going to happen next, but I can't run. It would probably be better if we separate for a while, for your own protection."

"For *my* protection?!" Nia gasped. "After what we've been through, don't you know there ain't nothing I can't—"

"This one is different," Jesús retorted. "Believe me. There are people out there far more powerful than you can imagine, Miss Black; people who have no interest in you as a beautiful woman or as a useful hired gun. They'll either twist you to suit their purposes, or destroy you. I don't want either of those things to happen."

"Tell me who your contact is," Nia demanded to know. "Who are you working with?"

But Jesús said nothing else. He finished dressing and turned toward the door. Nia called out to him again.

"Look me in the eyes and tell me that I'm going to see you again, Jesús Alvarez," said Nia.

Jesús lifted his spectacles from the floor and slid them over his eyes.

"You will see me again," he responded. "One way or another."

And he was gone, leaving Nia sitting alone on the futon.

A THUNDERSTORM RAGED AS Billy Casey returned to the Corp Hudson-owned laboratory on the man-made island off the coast of the city, escorted by armed Security Soldiers. They walked in double-file, three soldiers on either side of Casey, with rifles at the ready. The doors leading into the facility slid open and Hudson's security chief, Vincent Marks, appeared just inside, facing Casey with his arms behind his back.

"Meeting me face-to-face, Vince?" Casey muttered. "How nice of you."

"It's a special occasion, Casey," Marks replied. "You can thank your own actions for that."

"Don't lecture me, all right? It's been a long day. I get it. I failed. They got away. It sure as hell isn't the first time. Plus, Alvarez took me by surprise. He—"

"Enough, Casey," Marks said. "Look, you don't have to explain it to me. Nia Black is a hard target. And she's in league with Alvarez, which makes her twice as hard. I understand; you know I do. But, here's the thing…"

Vincent Marks approached Billy Casey and lowered his voice.

"Mr. Hudson…he doesn't care. He doesn't like failure. He doesn't like that you had a modified hand cannon, an experimental watercraft and some of our best men with you and still managed to let them get away, not to mention all the accidents and casualties your little escapade on the highway caused. Oh, and Mr. Hudson especially doesn't like that Alvarez managed to get away with the data on *Hercules*, with Dr. Romedrux letting him walk right out the front door along with Nia. Believe me; he let her have it for that."

"Well, how do you suppose Mr. Hudson feels about the fact that his great 'number one' used to *fuck* our little *Target Omega*? Or that the only reason you haven't put a bullet in her head when you had the chance is because you still get a hard-on whenever you see her?"

"This isn't about me, Casey. I've already been through that with the big man. I admitted that my personal bias affected my judgment, which is why I let you and Alvarez handle the Nia Black matter. One of you betrayed us…the other's just incompetent. You know what that means."

Billy Casey gasped. He looked back and forth and saw the Security Soldiers firmly grasping their weapons.

"Hey…wait! Wait a minute! I…I'm loyal! I've done my best! I…"

Vincent shook his head. "We have other guys we can promote. We can recruit. We can *create.*"

The soldiers turned toward Billy Casey and aimed their weapons. Vincent Marks raised his fist.

"Come on, Vince! Don't do this!" Billy cried. "How long have you and me worked together? You can't seriously be…"

Vincent Marks lowered his arm and shook his head.

The soldiers followed suit, lowering their weapons and standing at attention.

"To be honest," Marks muttered, "You're not even worth the bullets. Besides, truth is someone else wants to use you: Dr. Romedrux."

"W-what?"

"Relax, Casey. We're not going to terminate you. However, I do have to make an example of you; boss's orders. So, from this moment forward, you're no longer part of Corp Hudson Executive Security. You're being transferred. As of now you'll be working for Dr. Romedrux."

Billy bit his lip.

"Don't be so upset. Thanks to the doctor, you might just get the chance to redeem yourself. That's why I had you brought here. If Chelsea wants you to go inside, you can. I don't even have that privilege…that's why I'm meeting you in the lobby like this."

Vincent Marks stepped forward, past Casey, heading out into the rain as the double doors slid open again. Billy watched as Vincent left, then turned toward the facility's interior, goaded forward by the Security Soldiers and their rifles.

Billy Casey stormed into Chelsea Romedrux's office and stood by the door in silence. He spotted her sitting in her office chair, facing away from the door. She sat back in the chair with her legs on the desk, casually typing on her computer and waggling the wireless optical mouse. The height of the chair prevented Billy from seeing anything other than her blonde ponytail peeking up from behind. She didn't turn to face him as she heard the sound of the sliding door.

"Come on in, Mr. Billy."

Billy chuckled sardonically. "I didn't think you'd want to have anything to do with me after today's little fiasco. I didn't get you what you wanted. So you called me here just to tease me? Well, forget it."

Chelsea Romedrux dropped her heels from the desk. They came to rest on the floor as she let go of her computer and grasped the arms of her chair. She used her feet to swivel around to face Billy.

Billy's eyes bulged when he looked upon her.

Chelsea Romedrux leaned back in the leather-bound office chair, as calm as could be, wearing her glasses, her lab coat and *nothing* else, except a nearly transparent black lace teddy.

"See, that's the thing, Billy," Chelsea said, "I know it wasn't your fault."

She stood up and walked toward the former security agent until she pressed her chest into his. He briefly scanned her, watched as her cleavage expanded before his eyes and threatened to pop out of her skimpy underwear, and then looked back into Chelsea's emerald eyes.

"I mean, I know you did your best," she muttered, gently running her freshly painted crimson fingernail across his chest. "You're, like, the best Hudson had to offer. You're not love-struck like Vincent, and you're not a nasty traitor like Jesús…you're a real man, a real soldier. You didn't even have to do it…but you went out there on that experimental bike—and for all I knew that thing could have totally blown up under your balls when you tried to transform it…it's not like I had anything to do with the design…"

"Say what?!"

"The point is, you did all of that just for me, and we've only just met," Chelsea smiled slightly. "You're such an awesome guy for that. I was just thinking, maybe I put too much pressure on you. I mean, you're just one man going up against a superhuman freak and her lap dog. Hudson doesn't want us sending out all our security forces like an army because he doesn't want to scare the people. You know the big man's gotta keep looking like an angel. So instead of calling in the troops, he's got lone guys like you running investigations and sneaking around—it's so stressful, I bet."

"I can take them down. All I have to do is…"

"Shush," Chelsea said abruptly. "Didn't Vince brief you on the situation?"

Billy sighed. "Yeah; apparently if I want to keep working for Corp Hudson, I have to do what you say."

"So, like, *do* you want to keep working for Corp Hudson?"

Billy nodded. "I owe those freaks. As long as I'm here, I've got access to the tools that will help me get them."

"Goodie! So I *own* your ass then," Chelsea grinned. "And I do have some instructions for you."

"Yeah?"

"Yeah. The first thing you're going to do is take off that musty uniform, okay?"

That was all Billy Casey needed to hear.

He tore off his clothes and then did the same to Chelsea's skimpy underwear, pushing the lab coat off of her shoulders and dragging her lingerie down until it fell past her ankles. Chelsea collapsed backward on the swivel chair, lifted her legs and spread them wide, resting her calves upon the arms of the chair and throwing her arms high behind her head with a smile. Billy leaned in, kissed her neck, took hold of her breasts and clasped his mouth over her nipples.

Billy took hold of the arms of the chair, using it both as support for himself and to pull Chelsea into him. Instantly he plunged into her as Chelsea wrapped her legs around his waist. Billy stared into her emerald eyes as she whimpered in joy. She pressed her fingertips to Billy's hard glutes and gently dragged her nails up and down his back, moaning and gasping as she felt him inside of her.

The chair rocked on its wheels, bouncing against Chelsea's desk, sending the keyboard flying off and dangling in the air by its cord as the optical mouse slid around, clattering between the monitor stand and speakers like a pinball.

Chelsea's glasses slipped from her face. Billy instantly caught them in his fingertips and gently slid them back against the bridge of her nose.

"Oh, so you dig the glasses?" Chelsea panted. "Most guys do."

"Yeah," Billy chuckled. "Don't lose 'em."

Suddenly the swivel chair slipped off its wheels and tipped backward, leaving Chelsea on her back and Billy on top of her, straddling her with her legs across his shoulders. He and Chelsea smiled together as he leaned forward.

Her high-pitched squeals echoed through the halls of the facility.

The two ended up lying together on a cot sprawled on Chelsea's office floor. Billy Casey rolled over, his fingers limply splaying across Chelsea's bare hips and thighs as she looked at him. She smiled at how soundly he slept and how heavily he snored.

Sweetie, I've got some plans for you, Chelsea thought. *It's like, such a good thing that bitch took the time to knock you out before she escaped.*

Chelsea gently dragged herself from Billy's grasp. She lifted her wrinkled lab coat from the floor and put it on, wearing nothing else except her glasses. She stood the swivel chair back up and sat at her computer, placing the computer keyboard and mouse back in their original places. She turned the sleeping monitor back on and ran a program.

I don't know how I could have gotten a blood sample from you without you knowing otherwise, Chelsea thought as she analyzed the data on screen. *The analysis should be complete by now…good. He's totally compatible; or he will be for as long as it lasts, anyway. But I gotta make sure he doesn't blow it. It has to be perfect. I can't let him screw this up for me. I have to get her back, and I'm only going to have one chance to get it right. I have to get that bitch for what she did to my daddy. And this guy right here…he's going to be my sword. I just gotta run a few more tests…*

Chelsea climbed back over Billy again, opening her first aid kit. She pulled out an alcoholic swab and wiped his shoulder with it.

Billy Casey stirred. He patted the mattress and felt the cold fabric under his palm. Wondering where his partner went, he immediately rose from his prone position and sat up. He saw sunlight seeping through the windows, flooding Chelsea Romedrux's office.

Billy felt a sensation of relief when he saw Chelsea sitting in the chair, steadily tapping away on the computer. Then he laughed when he noticed she was only wearing her lab coat.

"It just never ends with you, does it?" he chuckled as he approached her. "You don't even put on your panties before you get back online."

Chelsea smiled and placed her fingers on his cheek as he leaned upon the back of the chair. She kissed him.

"Hi. Last night was fun. But it's time to clock back in now, okay? We've got work to do."

"What kind of work?" Billy wondered.

Billy glared at the monitor and saw Chelsea clicking and perusing files and folders with expert speed.

"Hey, how can you access that?" Billy gasped. "Only the upper officers can…"

"Because I'm *me*, silly," Chelsea smiled. "Even if they didn't give me access—which, like, totally wouldn't make any sense seeing as how I'm head of Corp Hudson's R&D—these security protocols are *so* last decade. You'd think Corp Hudson would be more up to date. I'll have to do something about that later."

"So what are you looking at?"

"Alvarez's records about *Target Omega*."

Billy grimaced. "We don't need to look at the scraps left behind by that traitor. He probably set all that up to throw us off."

Chelsea rolled her eyes. "You totally need to get over your little jealousy trip because Mr. Alvarez did something neither you nor your precious number one Vincent could ever do. He captured Nia Black. Twice. So like, get over yourself, hush up and pay attention, okay? You might learn something."

Chelsea cleared her throat.

"I was going over the recordings of executive security meetings, and I remembered something Alvarez said about Nia Black during your last get-together. He said that if she were pushed hard enough, she'd probably make plans to run away. You know; like fight-or-flight. If I'm right—and I'm *always* right—then she's so ready to fly. Luckily, Corp Hudson's got men watching all the major exits out of town. No sign of her yet—I'm thinking that she's in hiding right now, waiting for all of this to blow over. Then she's going to skip town."

"Okay," Billy said. "So we gotta find her!"

Chelsea scoffed. "Uh, yeah; good luck with that. The girl's, like, a magician. She's been fooling you guys left and right all this time; what makes you think she'll be any easier to find now that she's actually making an *effort* to hide?"

"Well then, what's your—"

"Dude!" Chelsea bellowed. "Relax! Alvarez totally had the right idea, see. You have to use your head with her. See, that's your problem. You're all 'gung-ho', guts and glory. Kill 'em all and let God sort 'em out and all that. And it's not working. Alvarez succeeded where the rest of Hudson's men failed because he's *smart*."

"There's no way he's any smarter than—"

"Look at this," she interrupted him. "Everything Alvarez did, all the intel he collected during his operation, it's all recorded in his file. He got through to Nia Black not by kicking her ass, but by *outthinking* the stupid bitch. Tricked her into thinking she was going on a legitimate job, and then had an ambush waiting for her at the Hallegan building. Then he set her out to a death trap by tricking her into thinking she'd be able to take out the big man by herself, only to leave her fighting the best of Hudson's security with a couple of pea-shooters, and she ended up getting caught. I'm surprised she still trusts the guy after all that, frankly. But then again, it doesn't take much to trick a trick."

Billy stood straight and folded his arms. He hated to admit it to himself, but Chelsea's words made sense. Every time he tried to take her down with violence, his efforts ended in failure, pain or even death for his men. Yet Alvarez managed to get to her *repeatedly* without as much as a scratch.

231

"That's her weakness, Billy. She's strong; stronger than you, even stronger than Alvarez. But she's not that smart. Of course, you're not that smart either…fortunately for you, you have me."

Chelsea tapped her LCD monitor with her index finger, guiding Billy's glance to a data entry on the screen.

"What's that?" Billy wondered.

"That, sweetie, is how we are going to draw Nia Black out again. You're going to make a phone call."

CHARLENE WRIGHT SAT on the front steps of her home, enjoying a quiet, peaceful afternoon on her block, watching the boys and girls of the block, frolicking in the streets with their bikes and foam rubber footballs and jump ropes.

It was her day off. She listened to the faint hip-hop music flooding from passing vehicles mixed with soft rhythm and blues from residential homes on the block. She relaxed outdoors, at peace for the first time since the hectic events that threw her life in upheaval.

With her rival, Nia Black, out of her life and her man once again her own, Charlene was ready to forgive and forget and move on together with Bobby Styles. She refused to lose her man, a man coveted by many others. He was her prize and with her, he would stay. They put too much time into cultivating their relationship to let one transgression on his part shatter all they had built, she thought.

She embraced a cordless phone as she reclined on the concrete stairs. Not just because she was outside and did not want to miss any calls, but mainly because she wanted to be ready to answer on the first ring, should her boyfriend call and say he was going to be late or something else. She did not want to be distant from Bobby for any reason.

Fortunately for Charlene's nerves, Bobby quickly returned home as he previously told her he would. He parked his jeep directly in front of their home and leaped out, rushing forth to clutch and kiss his lover.

"Welcome home, baby," Charlene spoke between kisses. "I was missing you."

"I missed you too," Bobby sighed. His words belied his true emotions but his tone made them clear; there was more on his mind.

"What's the matter?" asked Charlene.

"It's just...I keep thinking about the club," he said. "If it wasn't for those guys..."

"No, the hell with that," Charlene snapped. "If it wasn't for *Nia*, you'd have got that record deal...but look, she's gone now. We ain't seen hide nor hair of any secret agents or soldiers since we got back the other night. Nia's a skank bitch who can't keep her hands off other people's property, but at least she kept her promise and kept those bastards from messing with us. Forget about all that. I ain't living in fear any more. Let's go out or something."

Bobby replied with a smile. "Yeah, let's do that. Why don't you get out that dress I bought you last month, you know, the short red one, and I'll take you out to dinner? Cool?"

"Sounds good."

The phone rang. Charlene released Bobby and pressed talk. "Hello?"

"Hi. Can I talk to Robert Styles, please?" a male voice spoke.

"Hold on," Charlene said, passing the phone. "It's for you. I don't know him."

Bobby took the phone. "What's up?"

"Robert Styles?"

Bobby shook. The voice was unfamiliar. The caller asked for Bobby by his proper name, his birth name; no one he knew did that.

"Who is this?" he growled.

"I'm looking for someone, Mr. Styles. You know who I'm looking for. Don't you?"

"Who is it, Bobby?" Charlene spoke up.

Bobby pressed his palm to the receiver. "Go ahead and get dressed, Charlene. I'll be right behind you."

234

"Bobby, who is it?!"

"Just give me a minute, okay baby?" Bobby implored her.

Charlene frowned as she turned quickly and stormed into the house. Bobby groaned as he pressed the phone back to his ear.

"The hell you want?!"

"Calm down, 'Bobby'," said the speaker. *"Is it all right if I call you 'Bobby', Bobby?"*

"No it ain't all right if you call me 'Bobby'!" Bobby shouted. "Who the hell are you?"

"Bobby. Pay attention. My name is Billy Casey. I'm with Corp Hudson's Public Security Division. I've got reason to believe you're acquainted with Nia Black."

"Nia…who?" Bobby snapped quickly. "I don't know nobody by—"

"Well that sounded rehearsed. Don't lie to me, Bobby. It's right here in this file. You and Miss Black are real close, or at least you were."

A laugh.

Bobby grunted.

"I'll be frank. Nia Black's a criminal of the highest caliber, a real menace to society. Our benefactor, Mr. Hudson, is trying to do a public service by helping the authorities get her off the streets. She's a public menace. Problem is, she fell off the grid and the trail's running cold. You're the only lead we have left. I figured we'd ask you about her whereabouts, since, according to this, she stays with you."

"All right, listen," Bobby relented. "She did live here, but she doesn't anymore. That's the real."

"So where is she now?"

"I-I don't know. She didn't tell me. We didn't part on good terms," Bobby said.

A heavy snort came through the phone.

"You're lying. You know exactly where she is, don't you? I know she's a cutie, but don't try to protect her. She'll only bring you down with her. Says here she already screwed up your relationship. Not to mention, people everywhere are trying to kill her, you

know. You want to be associated with that? If I were you, I wouldn't do a damned thing for her. You'd better think about yourself for a minute."

Bobby stopped to think. *This guy wants her bad…it's not the same dude from before. What do I do?*

"I'm waiting," the voice on the phone said fiercely.

Nia didn't do her job and get rid of these people, so I would just give her up…but to hell with that, I can't tell him where Nia's living at—I won't do Gallagher like that. I promised Gallagher I would never bring any trouble to his spot. There has to be something else I can tell him so these people will leave us alone…!

The voice on the phone grew loud. *"So that's how it's going to be? I got your address right here, Bobby. If I have to send my boys down to your shabby little ghetto to murder every innocent woman, child and man on your block, I'll do it and it'll be reported as a battle between drug dealers or something. I can definitely arrange it so that you're caught in the crossfire."*

"All right, all right!" shouted Bobby. "I…I can help you find her. Just promise to leave us alone."

"Help me out and you'll never hear from me again. But you don't want to mess around with Billy Casey. I got every piece of info about you and Ms. Charlene Wright, shacking up in that little run-down hovel. I mean, that's rich. Running a nightclub, but can't afford to get married? Really?"

"Why you all up in my—"

"Your girl's a nurse at the Cowlington Retirement Home, right? Works three-to-eleven normally, does a lot of overtime, yeah? And that nice club you play your jazz music at—the Jazz Hall, *is it? Popular spot, isn't it? But you know something? I hate jazz."*

Bobby started seething.

"Yeah, you'd be surprised what we know about you people," the voice on the other line went on. *"I wouldn't want to have to take advantage of all this because you acted foolish. So you'd better give me something, Bobby. Right now."*

A TAXICAB STOPPED in front of Jazz Hall an hour before it was to open for the evening's dining and entertainment. Outside of the club were many of the hangout's common patrons, hoping to utilize the early entrance discount the club's owner offered for the first twenty people.

It was rare to see someone come to the club without their own expensive vehicle, so when the cab stopped and the rear door on the passenger side opened, it captured the attention of the waiting people. The skirt-clad woman who emerged from the taxi caught eyes, as always. Some chuckled with snooty arrogance; others rolled their eyes in repugnance. This time, her beautiful outer shell did nothing to conceal the reputation the woman inadvertently picked up from the tales and events that permeated her from the last few days.

The taxi screeched away as she walked toward the club, surprised eyes following her every step. The woman ignored everyone around her as she charged through, resisting the feelings that this place aroused within her.

Nia Black was certain everyone knew about what happened between her and Bobby.

He was a man; he had to brag about it, how he *tapped that ass* one more time and *smutted* her. She knew it would tear her up inside to revisit this place, but she had to see someone before she would be able to let go of her bond to this, her once favorite hangout. She needed to see him once more before she could leave the dark city behind.

Nia Black entered the Jazz Hall. She found Marc present as usual, cleaning glasses and generally minding his business.

"What's up, Marc? Can I holler at you for a minute?"

237

"I'm glad you're okay," Marc said. "I ain't heard from you since you went to rescue Bobby and Charlene from those people."

"It'd been better if I didn't…" Nia mumbled.

"Now don't be like that," Marc reproached. "You did the right thing—the tendency of a natural born hero."

Nia wiped her eyes, looked about and snatched the closest bottle within her reach. She filled a shot glass nearby sitting on the bar and chugged it.

"You know that's vodka…?" Marc stammered. "You don't usually drink stuff that hard."

Nia slammed the glass down. It cracked as it hit the wooden surface of the bar and left a round dent.

"Sorry…I'll pay for that."

"Don't worry about it," Marc smiled. "Had a rough day?"

Nia sighed. "You know how it is; I got kidnapped, shot, I was in a car accident, got groped by some soldier—just another day at the office."

Marc sighed. "Busy girl."

"Anyway," Nia continued. "I just came here to say goodbye."

"Goodbye?"

"I know Bobby told the whole damn world about what happened between us. Everybody knows we were messing around. I can't show my face around here anymore. I can't…see him anymore."

"Is that the only reason you're leaving?"

"No…" Nia muttered. "That's not even the half of it. After what happened with Charlie that night and after Drakonis played me, my rep's in the toilet. I went from being the baddest girl in the land to the most untrustworthy, volatile bitch with a gun anybody ever heard of. I can't get any work anymore. Nobody's calling me and nobody's taking my calls."

Marc exhaled strongly. "Yeah, I know how that can be. It don't matter how much good you might do for somebody. One little screw-up, one bad word and the next thing you know, you gotta run and hide and change your name and make yourself a new rep for yourself in some other part of the world."

"Huh?"

Marc laughed. "I'm messing with ya. Anyway, I understand. The place won't be the same without you, Nia. Gonna be boring as all hell without your stories keeping me going."

"Sorry. I ain't got much keeping me here. I'm probably going to take care of a few loose ends and then I'm going to leave the city, start fresh. I painted this town red; I can do the same thing somewhere else."

"Damn. Well, at least give an old man a hug."

Marc and Nia embraced, Marc practically absorbing the diminutive Nia in his arms, and she felt at peace.

She wanted to tell him everything about her birth, her abilities and what she'd been through with Jesús Alvarez…she wanted to tell him everything about her.

But Nia reneged. She didn't want to complicate anyone else's life with her problems. She slowly slid away from him, straightening her hair.

"Probably run into you again…" Marc said, walking toward the back of the club. "I get around."

"Hope so," Nia said back as she wheeled around and headed out.

"Now, you take care of yourself," Marc shouted. "And remember everything I told you!"

Nia nodded and turned toward the door. She froze in place when she heard the screech of a jeep coming to a stop outside the club. Suddenly, the last person she wanted to see came charging through the doors like a linebacker.

Bobby Styles stumbled into the hall and doubled over, catching himself with palms on knees as he took in as much air as his lungs would allow.

"Bobby!" Marc roared. "The hell's wrong with you, bustin' up in here like that? You got groupies chasing you or something?!"

Nia sucked her teeth and tried to walk past him, but Bobby grabbed her arm.

"Get the *fuck* off of me," Nia growled, taking hold of his hand. "Unless you want me to put you *through* a wall this time."

"Nia!" Bobby moaned, wincing in pain from the strength of Nia's grip. "I...I just drove halfway across the city from Gallagher's spot...I ran every damn red light...I was looking for you...!"

"Why? What could you possibly have to say to me? I thought we were done. Didn't you say that?"

"Some dude called me! Some dude looking for you!"

Nia flinched and let Bobby go. "What? Who? What was the name?"

"His name...he said it was Casey or something...he said..."

Marc raced behind the bar and filled a glass with water. He came back around and forced it into Bobby's palm. Bobby poured the water down his throat and caught his breath.

"He said he was looking for you," Bobby said to Nia. "I tried to get him off the trail, tried to lie...but then he said something about getting an army...shooting up the block...I had to...had to give him something..."

Nia trembled. "What did you tell him, Bobby?!"

"I couldn't give away Gallagher's spot...he's my friend," Bobby cried. "I gave him the only other thing I knew. I'm...I'm sorry Nia! The dude...he sounded serious! I didn't know what else to do! They knew my phone number...knew about the Jazz Hall, Charlene's job and everything! I had to..."

Nia's blood ran cold. "Oh my God."

She spun around in place like a confused dog. Her taxi was gone. She didn't know what to—

"Nia!" Marc shouted. He tossed a key ring to her; she caught it. It was if he knew what she was thinking.

"Take my bike. Go. GO!"

She raced out the back of the Jazz Hall, where she found a shiny, black sport bike with silver Japanese *Kanji* markings emblazoned on its shell. Nia quickly jumped on Marc's black motorcycle, turned the engine and zoomed off.

The world became a blur around Nia. She darted across the city streets with precision and reaction to traffic that betrayed her superhuman reflexes. She would not stop, not for a red light, not for a cop or a soldier…not until she made it to her destination. Nothing else mattered.

And as the distance between Nia and her destination narrowed, a telltale orange glow began to fill the sky, blending into the hue of the sunset. A plume of pitch-black smoke cut across the sky and Nia began to fear the worst.

Her fears were realized when she stopped the bike in front of Kim's warehouse…or rather, what was *left of it.*

Nia jumped off the bike, snatched her guns from their holsters and raced toward the wrecked warehouse where Kim made his home. She kicked aside pieces of the crumbled walls and jumped inside, screaming out for her mentor.

"KIM!!"

Every one of the dirty windows was shattered, the glass marred with spider-web cracks of gunfire. The doors, torn from their hinges, sat on the ground, and fires flickered inside.

Nia hurdled across the wreckage and rushed into the building. She saw the many crates aground in pieces, the common desk that rested in the center of the room smashed, and the essences of gun smoke and motor oil lingered.

Tire tracks, both wide and narrow, streaked across the floors and led through the many holes ripped through the walls of the simple building.

Nia ran throughout the warehouse, crying profusely. She flinched when the broken table in the room's center moved slightly, followed by a crackled, draining moan.

"K—" Nia began, sheathing her pistols and rushing toward the flat wooden plank. She tossed it aside and saw what she hoped she wouldn't.

Kim lay there, bruised and battered. He bled liberally from his face and joints. Blood, dirt and boot prints marred his body like an abstract painting. Every limb he tried to move trembled and dropped back to the ground.

"My God…" Nia stammered.

"N-Nia…" Kim wheezed. Nia kneeled on the floor next to him, tearing a piece of her shirt off and using it as a kerchief upon his forehead.

"Save your strength…" Nia cried, tears sliding down her rounded cheeks. "Who did this?!"

"Your enemies…" Kim whispered.

Nia looked down and shut her eyes, her tears leaking and dripping upon Kim.

"This is all my fault…I ain't doing anything but ruining people's lives…"

Nia began thinking about everything that happened up until this moment—how it weighed heavily upon her heart.

The death of Professor Kane Romedrux of Romedrux Labs because of her robbery.

The innocents who were injured on that street when Nia destroyed the oil truck while running from the police.

Bobby and Charlene, who were kidnapped, their lives endangered and their peace shattered just because they associated with Nia.

The countless people hurt and killed during her road chases.

Gunner and Armstrong, once normal men who became sick fusions of biology and machinery, giving up their humanity for the sole purpose of destroying her...

And now Kim, the one closest to Nia, lay dying in her arms.

"Nia..." Kim muttered. "You must...go. You have work to do."

"Fu—forget all that!" Nia cried. "You were right. You were always right. Let's just do it like you said. Everything I do is causing problems. Everything's falling apart. It's all because of me! I need to get us out of this city before it gets worse. Let's just leave. I'll get you to a hospital, and then we'll..."

"No, Nia," Kim said with a cough. "You need to understand. Everything you have learned, everything I have taught you...it was not just for you to take it and run away. You are a warrior. You cannot escape your enemies...you cannot run away from your calling. They will follow you to the ends of the earth. You will never be able to live free as long as you ignore them."

Nia sobbed. "Then why did you tell me to..."

"A test, my dear..." Kim stammered. "A test to see if you were as strong of...spirit... as you are of body. And you passed. Time and time again...you passed. Do not fail now."

Nia tightly wrapped her arms around Kim. Even in his sorry state, Kim was always good at telling it like it was.

Kim's staggering arm reached up, his fingers gently clutching Nia's recently repaired necklace as it dangled around her neck.

Kim fell limp in Nia's arms.

"Kim…?" Nia mumbled, tears flowing like a waterfall under her eyes. "Kim?!"

She pressed two fingers to his neck, searching for his pulse.

Trembling almost violently, Nia snatched her fingers away. Tears gushed from her eyes.

She closed his blank eyes with her fingertips and clutched his lifeless body one last time. Nia gently laid Kim's body on the ground, stood and headed for an opening in the wall.

She started hearing the screaming sirens of the ambulance and police vehicles approaching, and darted toward a hole in the wall at once.

"I can't be here when those people show up. You understand. Thank you for everything."

Nia backed out of the building, staring into Kim's motionless face. She wiped tears from her eyes and finally headed back for the motorcycle Marc loaned her, leaving the scene moments before the fire department's emergency vehicles arrived at the torn-down warehouse.

Miles away, she pulled over on a side street. She stumbled off of the bike, fell to her knees and dry heaved on the asphalt.

Nia threw aside the doors of the Jazz Hall. Her eyes were saturated and red, her hair a frizzy mess, her face the definition of sorrow.

She thought it was strange that the Jazz Hall was empty. No customers. She was certain Marc was planning to open that night. But she was glad he changed his mind.

The middle-aged bartender was sitting alone at a table. He calmly shot her a quick glance while going through a ledger and talking on a phone. He then caught sight of the torn piece of denim fabric in her hand, stained with blood. He looked her over, but she had no marks or wounds.

"…All right," Marc said as his expression changed. "I'll call you back. I got a visitor. Uh-huh. Talk to you later."

"Where is he?!" Nia growled. "Was that him on the phone?"

"Who, Bobby?" Marc gasped as he hung up. "No, that was one of my associates. Bobby's not here. He wanted to take a break. Said he wanted to clear his head, so I decided not to open up tonight. He's not home?"

"No. I went there; the house was empty," said Nia.

"Oh. Guess he decided to take Charlene out after all."

"You know where they went?"

Nia stared fiercely at Marc, hoping he realized just how serious and furious she was.

"Look," Marc said, lifting himself from his seat. "Just tell me what happened."

"My…my old man…" Nia sobbed. "They killed him…they killed Kim."

"Aw, damn," Marc sighed, rushing toward her from behind the bar and taking Nia's shoulders in his palms. "I'm sorry. I know that guy meant a lot to you—you used to talk about him all the time."

"It's my fault," Nia cried. "I was so childish...I should have known better. I should have known they would find a way to get to him..."

"So what are you going to do?" Marc said sternly.

"What...? What do you mean...?"

"What are you going to *do*?" he said again with emphasis.

Nia turned away and rubbed her eyes, her skin burning into the irritated flesh of her eyelids like sandpaper.

"You just gonna run away, ain't you?" Marc growled. "That don't sound like the Nia I know. The Nia I know, the girl that took down a whole group of Hudson's goons and a mutant assassin outside my club all in the *same night* wouldn't walk away from this."

Nia turned about and looked up at Marc.

"You need to go after whoever killed Kim, because you know it's not going to stop with him. It's never going to stop until they get what they want from you. You know, Bobby, Charlene...even *I* might be next. I know you ain't thinking of running out on *me*, are you?"

Nia shut her eyes. "I can't...I can't do this anymore."

"What? Can't do what?"

"I'm tired of all this..." Nia said. "I started out being a crook because I saw how strong I was. I knew I could do whatever I wanted. I ain't need to be working in no retail store or nothing simple like that...money came to *me*. I had people fawning all over me, dying to pay me to jack stuff for them. It was fun...but Kim was always trying to tell me I was meant for something more. Kim was the only one who stood by me, and now..."

Marc scoffed. "Yeah. And?"

Nia was startled. "What? What do you mean '*and*?!"

"What you expect from me, a tissue?" Marc snapped. "I'm not going to be a guest at your pity party. You thought you could go around stealing, blowing up, killing, whatever, and didn't think for a second that it would come back to bite you?"

Nia folded her arms and sobbed.

"Stop crying, little girl," Marc went on. "Oh, now that everything come crashing down all around you, now you want to feel sorry? Now you want forgiveness? Now you want to 'change'? I told you before that there ain't no right way to do wrong, but you kept trying anyway. Now look at you...you lost everything you care about and you're an emotional wreck. I...I knew a girl like you once. Crying over every little thing. Couldn't stand that shit...you'd think with her background she'd be tougher inside. But whatever. So let me ask you again. What are you going to do?!"

Nia looked down.

Then a subtle buzzing broke the silence and Nia lifted her pager from her pocket. There was an unfamiliar number on the screen.

"Who's that?" Marc wondered. "Thought you said you wasn't getting any more contacts."

"I don't know who this is..." she muttered back. "Give me the phone."

Marc did so, and Nia dialed the number.

"Hello?" Nia stated as the call connected.

"Hi there. Remember me?"

Nia's face immediately hardened. "Yeah. Casey, right?"

"That's right. I've missed you, Nia. In fact, I missed you so much I tried to pay you a visit. But turns out I couldn't find you at the address I had. Just some old man there. He wouldn't tell me anything about where you were so my friends and I...well, I'm sure you already know the rest."

"It was you?!" Nia growled. "You killed Kim?"

"Killed? Well, that wasn't the plan, but hey…I'm sure he knew how dangerous it was to associate with a loose cannon like you, right?"

Nia slammed the phone on the receiver, nearly shattering it.

"What the fuck did you do that for?!" Marc suddenly shouted. Nia flinched.

"I-I'm sorry! I didn't break it…"

"I mean, why did you *bang* on him? That's who killed Kim, right? Isn't that the dude you're after?"

"What…?"

Marc shook his head. "You was just on the phone with the dude that killed your old man, the guy that got you sitting up in here crying and shit, and you're *still* thinking about running away, ain't you?"

"What am I supposed to do?!" Nia wailed. "Go fight him? Kill him? For what? That ain't gonna bring Kim back! It ain't going to fix my rep! It ain't gonna accomplish anything!"

Nia's pager buzzed again. It was the same number.

"Call him back," Marc ordered.

"What for?"

Marc folded his arms and looked to the ceiling. He exhaled hard as if he set down a heavy load, and then looked at Nia.

"Because *I* need you to."

Nia looked dumbfounded. "You? What the…"

"All right. I guess I ain't got a choice."He looked up and yelled seemingly into the air. "Yo, come on in!"

Nia stopped sobbing as she reacted to the creak of the back door of the Jazz Hall opening. A tall man walked in, and the dim light glanced off of his spectacles.

"What the…?" Nia gasped. "Jesús?!"

"Yes, Nia, it's me," said Jesús Alvarez.

Nia looked back and forth between Jesús Alvarez and Marc Benson, her throat empty.

"I would have thought it was obvious," Jesús went on.

Marc sighed. "I'm disappointed, Nia. I'm disappointed because you couldn't see it. You can't even see it right now. You can't see what's right in front of your face."

"See what?"

"I ain't no damn gunrunner, Nia. I've been on the phone with this guy right here," Marc continued. "We're secret agents, both of us. Alvarez's job was to infiltrate Corp Hudson. My job was to keep tabs on you when you made yourself Hudson's *Target Omega*. Our objective is to put an end to Hudson's science experiments. You were the key. As long as Hudson was pursuing you, we could see Hudson's activities plain as day. The stories you kept telling me helped too."

Nia took a seat at one of the tables in the main hall. She stared at the two men with a blank look.

"You probably got a whole mess of questions..." Marc went on.

"Not really," Nia sighed. "I mean, seeing him up in here confirms a lot. You're the guy he said he was working with. You acted like my best friend, and you hooked me up with weapons when I needed to save Bobby and Charlene. I knew all along Jesús was the one who took them. That big dude was there to keep up appearances, but when he was about to kill me, Jesús stepped in and saved me. It was all a game to gain my trust. The whole plan was to use me to try to get inside that island lab, and it actually worked. But Jesús came back and rescued me and lost what y'all was looking for in the process. So now y'all want to ask me to help you out...right?"

"Something like that," Marc said. "Like I told you, our mission is to take down Hudson, piece by piece. He made you a target, and that made things easier for us. Now I got me an idea as to how we're going to fix..."

Marc shot a glance toward Jesús.

"…Fix *all* our little blunders. But I need your help to do it."

Nia let out a slight chuckle. "You know, I've been played and twisted up so much these last few days that I don't even think I'm bothered by it anymore. I've lost the man I thought I loved…I slept with this guy and then he left me…and the only person in this world who cared about me is dead."

Jesús started to say something, but Marc waved his hand and he fell silent.

"So what are you saying?"

"I'm saying fuck it. I'm in. It's whatever. Give me some orders. But don't get it twisted. I've started killing people for the first time in my life the other night. You know how they say once you do it, it gets easier? It's true. The only reason I'm not busting caps right now is because neither one of y'all attacked me. Let's keep it that way. What I want hasn't changed. Hudson destroyed my family. His little associate tried to rape me, and he killed Kim. I want to make both of them pay…but I guess I can't do it by myself. I sure as hell ain't running no more."

"That's what I'm talking about, Nia," Marc smiled. "Now, call that guy…what's his name?"

"Casey," said Jesús. "Billy Casey."

"Yeah," Marc nodded. "Call Mr. Billy Casey back, Nia. I want you to give him what he wants, but with a condition."

Nia looked at Jesús, then at Marc. "I got a condition of my own."

"Oh yeah, what's that?"

"Tell me how Jesús can do the same things I can do. How come he's…almost…as powerful as I am? I know I was born with my abilities because of my father. I also know that apparently only my dad's body accepted the formula. So what's his story?"

"We outfitted Jesús Alvarez with a performance enhancer that would help him keep up with you in case you didn't trust him and things didn't go the way we wanted them to go," Marc explained. "It was experimental, and he needed regular re-dosing. That's why he had to cut and run, in and out with you. We couldn't risk anyone learning about it. That's another thing we have going on—we're trying this stuff out under field conditions. Turns out it's nowhere near as powerful as you are…guess that's another reason why Hudson wants you so bad. His competitors are starting to rise up."

Nia grimaced.

"Now, if you don't have any more questions, I'd appreciate you making that call. I'll tell you what to say," Marc stated.

Billy Casey sat in Chelsea Romedrux's chair in her office, sulking.

"She's not gonna call back," said Chelsea.

"Yes she will," said Billy, looking down at her.

"I told you not to kill the guy. I told you to just rough him up a bit and grab him, but you just had to take it so far, didn't you?"

"He broke one of my guy's arms in three places!" Billy growled. "No way that guy was going to come peacefully. Besides, he wasn't dead when we left. It's not my fault the old man couldn't take a hit."

"We don't have any leverage anymore. You blew it. Like, again. Guess I'm going to have to come up with something else…" Chelsea began, then her office phone rang.

"It's her," muttered Billy as he reached for the handset. "Don't you move."

He picked up the receiver and answered the call. "Yeah?"

"What do you want from me?"

"Oh, hi, Miss Black. I'm glad you called me back," Billy said, grinning at Chelsea. "What I want is you. Now, you can run away if you want. But I think you know from personal experience what happens when you try to run away from Hudson. Your daddy did that and your mommy paid the price. Now who might pay the price when you try to run, huh? Your buddy Marc and that nightclub? How about I finish off poor Bobby and Charlene?"

251

"So what you saying? You just want to take me on?"

"That's right. Just you and me."

"Why? You know what I can do. Hudson can't be paying you enough to take that kind of risk."

"This is personal, Miss Black. You see, you and your boyfriend Alvarez embarrassed me and ruined my shot at becoming security chief. So I'm going to destroy everything about your life. Whichever way you slice it, you're going down. The only way you're going to stop it is if you come deal with me directly."

"Sounds good to me. It's personal for me too. I ain't forget how you couldn't keep your hands to yourself. But fuck all that. You killed Kim. You know you ain't got long to live anyway since you crossed me. So where and when?"

"Tomorrow morning. The Worthington groundbreaking site. Same place Hudson caught you before. It's wide open and there won't be any passersby. No innocents to get killed this time. I know how much you hate that."

"Fine," said Nia. *"But under one condition. Bring her along with you."*

"Her? Her who?"

"You know who I'm talking about. What's-her-name...Chelsea. Make sure she comes along. I want to clear the air with her."

Chelsea snatched the receiver from Billy.

"You don't have to worry about that. I'll definitely be there. I want to *see* you pay for what you did to my daddy. I'm going to totally watch you suffer and cry and then you'll be all mine. You hear me, bitch?"

The line clicked.

"Are you quite finished?" Billy said with a smirk, hanging up the phone. "Because if I recall, you bet me that she wouldn't call back. Looks like you lost. Time to pay up."

Chelsea sighed with a coy smile. "Okay."

She unzipped Billy's trousers and moved his briefs aside, exposing his penis. She took it in her grasp and opened her mouth, outstretched her tongue, and—the desk phone rang again.

"Don't answer it..." Billy muttered, planting his palm on mop of blonde hair atop Chelsea's head.

Chelsea glanced at the number on the caller ID screen, then yelped. She reached up and took the receiver.

"Hello? Uh...yes! Totally! Be right there!"

Chelsea hung up the phone, lifted herself up supporting herself on Billy's knees, and slid her exposed breasts back into her bra.

"Hey, what gives?!" Billy gasped. "You can't leave a man hanging like that! I'm gonna have blue—!"

"Zip up, Billy," Chelsea shot back, straightening her clothes. "It's the big man. He wants to see us. Like, now."

AT THE NORTHERNMOST POINT of the city stood a lofty skyscraper. This building protruded from the skyline like a sword in a stone, rising over the rest of the city like the seat of an observing god. From top-down view, the building looked like the letter 'H', to represent the name of the man who held that seat of power. The 666-level office building with the penthouse at its peak was none other than the Hudson Tower, the headquarters of Corp Hudson. The penthouse served as home and business headquarters to the chairman of the corporation and the most powerful man in the city, Maxwell Hudson himself.

The Hudson Tower was his pride and joy, used not only as his command center and quarters, but also one of his many sources of revenue. The lowest floors were used for shopping and entertainment while the middlemost levels were used for high-income housing, as well as banquet halls for dignitaries and nobles. Only the highest floors served Corp Hudson's corporate needs, including the penthouse, which doubled as the main office.

The penthouse was divided into two sections; the smaller was the den where Hudson would retire for the night and the larger was Corp Hudson's main office. The den was sectioned off into a separate chamber in the northwestern corner of the room, diminutive in comparison to the rest of the floor but by no means small. Inside, along with a massive Jacuzzi, was a wide and oblong bed with a transparent black and violet canopy overhead and motion sensors tracing a path across all four corners. Fitted inside the walls were drawers filled with scores of designer suits and other fine men's clothing, custom made to fit his unnaturally tall frame.

The office itself appeared more like the throne room of an emperor, with marble flooring, statues of armored warriors brandishing lances standing before the mineral pillars that lined the room and a dome-like ceiling with soft, dimmed lights in an 'H' insignia illuminating the room. Classical music emanated through a PA system, which Hudson enjoyed religiously. At the far end of the office at what felt like miles from the entrance sat a massive oak desk with a gigantic leather-bound swivel chair that itself stood higher than the average man's height, the throne of the emperor, Maxwell Hudson's seat.

The entire level was like another world, a slice of a nobler era dropped into the present.

The front doors of the office slid open and four people stood in the doorway: Billy Casey and Chelsea Romedrux flanked by two eerily silent armored men brandishing next-generation rifles—Hudson's Security Soldiers. The two guards marched backward as Billy and Chelsea stepped inside the office, the gigantic armored doors grinding shut behind them.

Across the expanse of the office, Billy and Chelsea could see Maxwell Hudson's oak desk, his personal chair facing away from them. Three of the four walls of the penthouse were themselves windows that provided a stunning view of the entire city, one that Maxwell Hudson would spend his precious little free time taking in. Rachel Jones, Hudson's personal assistant, and Vincent Marks, the Corp Hudson chief of security, sat on the left and right sides of the desk in large office chairs.

A couch sat a few feet from the oak desk, clearly prepared for this meeting. Billy and Chelsea wasted no time walking to the couch and taking their seats.

The large leather-bound chair behind the oak desk swiveled slightly toward Billy and Chelsea, and Hudson rested an arm on the desktop.

Billy's heart was pounding. This was the first time he'd ever been able to enter Hudson's office.

"You sure know how to decorate, Mr. Hudson," Billy said nervously. "I mean, this place is beyond beautiful. Love the statues. And the view! Amazing…great security too. I mean, seems like you're putting those Security Soldiers to more and more use every day."

Chelsea rolled her eyes.

"Updates," said the deep, guttural voice of Hudson.

"Yes, sir, like, totally…" Chelsea muttered. "You'll have to excuse him, Mr. H. He's like, a total thug. We—"

"We'll have *Target Omega* soon, sir," Billy suddenly said, standing up. "Chelsea and I have worked it all out."

"Have you now?" said Hudson.

"Yes, sir. I promise you. I will be able to do what none of your other men could. With all due respect, you made a mistake when you appointed Vincent Marks as security chief. His military background aside, he's soft. He can't handle this kind of work."

Vincent grimaced.

"You are rather confident," Hudson continued. "…considering your track record."

"I will not just capture Nia Black, Mr. Hudson. I will break her. I will destroy her body and spirit…but I will not kill her. I know she means a lot to you. Through me, you will achieve your goals. I only ask for one thing in return."

"And that is?"

"Once I'm done with Nia Black, you make me security chief. I'll whip your subordinates into shape the *right* way."

Hudson finally turned his chair around and faced Billy Casey, who immediately trembled. He'd never been this close to Maxwell Hudson before. His size, even while seated, was absolutely frightening. There were *buildings* smaller than this man.

Hudson clasped his fingers together and rested his chin on them. "Prove yourself to me then, Mr. Casey. Succeed, and we can certainly arrange a meeting to discuss your future within Corp Hudson."

"I won't let you down, sir."

Chelsea looked longingly at Billy.

Billy gave her a curious glance in response. "Let's go, Chelsea. Don't we have some setting up to do?"

"Yeah...totally."

She lifted herself from the couch and followed Billy as he strolled out without being excused. As soon as they disappeared through the double doors, Rachel Jones turned to Hudson.

"He is a liability," she said. "A cock-sure, full-of-himself joke of a man. He has already failed you once, sir."

"Twice," Vincent added, "If you include the fact that he knew of Alvarez's treachery and did nothing against him until it was too late. He's the reason the *Hercules* data is gone. Pairing him with Dr. Romedrux won't make up for his arrogance."

Hudson turned back toward his vista. "I will let them play their game for now. You know your role in this. No matter what, this game will end the way I wish it to end. As for *Hercules*, it won't be long before my old records are replaced by new ones. Everything is proceeding according to plan."

THE SUN HAD BARELY RISEN when Nia Black arrived at the construction site. Still in possession of the motorcycle Marc loaned her, Nia pulled up a safe distance away from the area and looked around, scanning the circular road that surrounded the grassy field in which she'd battled Hudson's security forces only a day prior. The grass was pristine and scorch-free, as if no vehicles had been blown up in the field; as if no gunfire had torn through the ground. Hudson's clean-up crew was efficient.

Nia pulled the bike closer to the site, and for a second swore she saw Billy Casey himself leaning against a wall, staring at her. She instantly went for her pistol, stuck it out, and saw nothing.

Nia shook her head, parked and leaped off the bike. She was wearing a silk black blouse with only two buttons holding it shut. The bottom fell slightly past her waistline, the unbuttoned lower half exposing her belly and offering a glimpse of the double-belt that was latched around her hips in an X-shape, along with form-fitting blue jeans and boots. Instead of four guns, Nia carried only two this time—her Baby Eagles—and a number of spare magazines in the second set of pockets. She wore small sunglasses with circular frames. She did not want to appear too conspicuous en route, nor did she wish to be too encumbered, so she reneged on wearing any form of body armor even though Marc offered it.

She walked toward the construction site and passed through the gate, her eyes peeled and her guns drawn the entire time. It all looked half-finished; a series of girders stood where the foundation of whatever was to be built would be, cranes and bulldozers sat idle in front of piles of gravel and dirt, and there was a trailer flanked by a pair of outhouses. There were plenty of places to hide; plenty of places one could try to get the drop on her from.

She heard a creaking sound, and immediately outstretched her pistols. She aimed at the trailer door as it flipped open, but saw no one.

What am I even doing here...? Nia thought. *Got me all nervous and twitchy and shit... this ain't like me.*

"Glad you could make it, Miss Black."

Nia gasped and turned around. Billy Casey was standing behind her, not five feet away, wearing a Kevlar vest and baggy cargo pants. He was armed only a knife in a chest-mounted sheathe.

All kinds of alarms were going off in her head. *How did he get behind me? I didn't hear anything! I didn't even hear his footsteps in the gravel...even I was making noise when I walked in here!*

"Don't look so surprised, Nia," Billy said. "I do work for Corp Hudson, you know. Sooner or later, we all have to step our game up if we're going to keep up with the future of human potential."

Nia raised her pistol and opened fire, but her bullets hit nothing but air.

"You know..." a voice uttered from behind her. Nia looked over her shoulder and Billy was again at her back.

"Mr. Hudson thinks you're so special," Billy continued, pacing around. "You're so 'powerful', so important. *'Target*-fucking-*Omega'*. But look at me...if you can."

Nia blinked, and Billy was gone again.

Then a massive force struck her between the shoulder blades and Nia went tumbling into the earth. Her guns bounced away from her and landed in a pile of gravel. She scrambled to her feet and she saw Billy, behind her yet again, fanning his fist.

"Yeah, you are tough. A hard target, just like Vincent said. I didn't think he meant *literally*," Billy laughed. "So not only are you strong, you're also dense. Hard to break."

Nia tightened her fists.

"Well, let's just give it the old college try anyway," said Billy as he slid on a pair of leather gloves.

Nia went into a slight crouch, then dashed backward toward her guns. She threw herself toward the pile of gravel.

An instant before her fingers could reach the grips of her Baby Eagles, she saw a black boot shoot into her face, sending her flying backward.

"Stupid, Nia. So *fucking* stupid!" Billy growled as Nia crashed on the ground and slid on her back. Billy glanced at the guns and shook his head.

Nia spat blood.

Hold up…he actually hurt *me?*

"Don't you fucking get it?" Billy growled. "We're not doing this your way! You're strong, I'm strong. Let's fight like warriors!"

"You're not 'strong'," Nia grumbled. "You're just drugged up."

"Same difference," Billy laughed back. "We can't all be as special as you. You know, at first I wasn't too fond of this stuff Chelsea's been doping me up with. I'm not a big fan of whatchamacallit…being 'weaponized'. But when I realized that it would help me put you in the dirt where you belong, *and* let me keep my good looks, I said, 'Heck, sign me up.' Now let's do this!"

A plume of dust rippled from the ground where her enemy last stood, and before Nia knew what was happening Billy was in her face again. He gripped her hair with one hand and rammed his fist into her gut with the other, over and over, then threw her away like a doll. She crashed into the dirt once more.

Billy walked toward Nia as she pushed herself from the ground. He crushed Nia's glasses under his boot.

"You're not even trying, are you?" Billy growled.

Nia said nothing, and just coughed away the dirt piled up in her face.

"Fight me, Miss Black. Come on! Isn't that why you're here?!"

"What for?"

"So I can prove to everyone who the best really is! Not Vincent! Not Jesús! And sure as hell not you! Hudson doesn't need *Hercules!* He doesn't need you or your coward father! All he needs is Billy Casey and Dr. Romedrux! And I'm going to prove it right now!"

"That's all you care about, isn't it? Proving yourself to everybody?"

Billy rushed forward again, moving in a blur. He grabbed her blouse by the collar, yanked her toward him and slammed his fist into Nia's face, sending her spinning backward, her blouse tearing open in his grip, the buttons popping free of the fabric. He threw the tattered shirt to the ground, leaving Nia topless except for the black, padded sport bra she wore underneath, and her sparkling gold pendant with the opal charm dangling around her neck.

"Who's permission are you waiting for, Billy?" Nia grunted, lifting herself up. "Who are you waiting for to tell you you're good enough? What's the matter? Daddy called you worthless? Mommy didn't love you?"

"Shut the fuck up and fight!"

"Uh oh, I hit a nerve."

Billy grimaced and charged toward Nia again. He raised his fist and roared—until Nia's knee stopped him right in his tracks as it collided with his jaw, forced him into a backward somersault, and the world spun around him. He crashed on the ground and looked straight down at the gravel and rocks under him, as if he were surprised to be there.

"The problem with you is that you ain't got no identity," said Nia. "The only thing you know is what other people think about you. You ain't nothing unless somebody tells you you're something."

Billy shoved himself from the ground and tightened his fists. He rushed forward yet again, slower this time—slow enough for Nia to spin around him, dodging his charge.

She swung out her leg and slammed her heel into the back of Billy's neck, sending him stumbling back to the ground.

"See, me, I'm independent. I don't lean on nobody," Nia continued, bouncing around in her fighting stance. "My strength comes from *me*. It took me a minute to learn that, but I get it now. I don't need a boyfriend and I don't need anybody telling me I'm somebody. I know I am…just because."

Nia walked toward Billy. He stayed low, grinding his fingers into the dirt.

"What, did Chelsea promise you some *pussy* if you beat me? What are you, a virgin? Ain't you a little old to be doing crazy shit just to get some ass?"

Billy flashed teeth. "There's nothing crazy about this."

"All I know is you killed Kim. He meant more to me than anyone else in the world," Nia muttered. "You best believe I'm gonna kill you for that. But not until I 'break' your weak ass."

"We'll see about that…"

Suddenly he swung his hand in the air, and a plume of dirt flew into Nia's face. She shielded her eyes and Billy lunged toward her.

Then a shooting pain lanced from her gut.

Blood dribbled from Nia's lips and she looked down.

A wide blade pierced her belly, her blood oozing out around it.

Nia staggered back as Billy released the handle of his knife. She fell on her butt as Billy approached her again, sweeping himself off.

"For the record, I already fucked her," Billy grunted. "Like I told you before, this is personal."

The trailer door suddenly swung open and a buxom blonde woman came wobbling out, wearing glasses and a lab coat over executive attire, doing her best to balance herself on the thin metal stairs of the trailer in her high heels. She was holding a chrome attaché, latched tightly shut.

"Billy, like, what the hell?!" shouted Chelsea Romedrux. "We're not supposed to kill her!"

"Then hurry up and sedate her," Billy griped. "I've done my job. She's down. You should know by now she's not like normal people. The knife will slow her down but it won't stop her. Get busy."

"What?! Like, whatever!" Chelsea snapped. "There's no way in hell I'm going anywhere near that freak bitch! Cuff her or something!"

Nia dragged herself across the ground as more blood leaked from the wound in her belly. She took hold of the knife and swiftly yanked it free of her flesh, screaming all the while. She found the remains of her blouse, rolled it up in her hand and pressed it on the wound.

A normal person would probably bleed to death from pulling the knife out... Nia thought. *But my shit already started healing. The hole wouldn't close if I left the knife there. I just gotta keep myself from getting fucked up too much more in the meantime and I'll be all right...but I don't know how I'm gonna do that. Where are—*

Then a screeching sound caught everyone's attention. Billy and Chelsea turned toward the street and saw a red Viper speeding toward the area with a rising plume of white smoke trailing it. The car screamed to a halt and two men immediately emerged, one in glasses holding a long range sniper rifle, the other a strong-looking black man holding a Desert Eagle with onyx plates on the handle.

"Is that...?" Billy gasped.

"I can't believe it..." followed Chelsea. "Shit! Shit!"

"Marc? Jesús?!" Nia grunted. "What the...what took you so fucking long...?"

Marc walked toward them, holding the Desert Eagle down. "Useless...you can't fucking do anything right."

"What?"

"All you had to do was kill the motherfucker so we could get to *her*," Marc said. "But you couldn't even beat some punk-ass buster on steroids with a knife?"

"I'll have you know that my high-intensity performance enhancement additive is *not* steroids!" Chelsea hollered. "Like, it happens to be a careful mix of amino acids and experimental chemicals designed to work specifically with Billy's natural—"

"Shut the hell up!" Marc growled, raising the pistol. "You can explain it all to me later, Dr. Romedrux. Right now, just do me a favor and come quietly."

CHELSEA ROMEDRUX WAS FLABBERGASTED.

"Like, what do you mean 'come quietly'?" she squealed at Marc Benson, who had his Desert Eagle trained on her.

"I mean, shut the fuck up, put your hands up, walk towards me and get in the fucking car," said the muscular black 'bartender', wearing a tactical vest and fatigues. "Drop the case and get your pretty self over here, blondie. You're coming with me."

"Um…Billy?" Chelsea mumbled. "Like, do something!"

"He ain't gonna do shit!" Marc laughed, opening fire. Three shots immediately smacked Billy in the chest and his back met the ground.

"Billy!" Chelsea gasped. She glared at him as he trembled in the dirt, clutching himself.

"There. You see, Nia?" Marc growled at her. "You couldn't even do that? I mean, damn, didn't Kim teach you anything? Line up your sight, aim, pull the trigger. You should be able to squeeze off four shots in one-point-five seconds. He should never have gotten anywhere near you."

He turned to Jesús Alvarez. "Keep a bead on her, J. If Nia moves, shoot her."

Jesús flinched. "Sir?"

"You heard what I said," Marc snapped. "Don't make me repeat myself."

Nia winced in pain. The wound from Billy Casey's knife wasn't healing fast enough. She couldn't move.

Nia shot a glance at Jesús.

"So you played me…again…huh?"

"Nia, I'm sorry. It's like I said. Some people are more powerful than even you can imagine. His hold on me is…absolute."

Nia's face hardened. "You're just a coward. You're just a bitch-ass coward. You ain't no different from Billy. You need somebody to tell you you're worth something."

Jesús Alvarez's eyes sank.

Marc turned toward them. "Jesús! I ain't tell you to have no damn conversation! Just follow your orders!"

"—the fuck is going on, Marc?" Nia grunted. "You told me we were going to interrogate them so we could learn about Hudson…"

Marc started laughing. "Yeah, and you believed that shit! This is why you're fun to play with, Nia. Because you're gullible as shit! Why do you think I told you to make sure he brought Romedrux along? This shit ain't got nothing to do with Hudson! It never did! *She's the one we're after!*"

"Huh?!" Chelsea gasped. "What do you want with me? I'm…I'm like, nobody! I'm just a scientist!"

"Wrong, baby," Marc retorted. "You're the brains of Corp Hudson. Not only that, you're talented. Your family has a long history of developing weapons and making advancements in the realm of human performance enhancement. You've always been something of a prodigy. Graduated from college at the age of sixteen, moved into research in your twenties, and now you're researching for the biggest, most powerful defense contractor in the world, and you're not even thirty yet. You're as special as it gets. And as of right now, you'll be working for me."

Chelsea shuddered. "No. I'm not going anywhere with you."

Marc rolled his eyes. "I'm not going to tell you again. Get in the fucking car. I don't have time for this shit."

"Or what? You'll s-shoot me?" her voice started to crack. "Yeah right. You obviously want me alive or you…you'd have totally killed me already."

Marc raised his gun and pulled the trigger. Chelsea felt a vibration through her head as the gunshot's boom echoed.

The frames of her glasses snapped apart from the side and fell to the ground at her feet in pieces.

A tear began to leak from her trembling green eyes.

"Bitch, I can put a bullet anywhere I want to," Marc growled. "Trust me, there are plenty of ways I can shoot you without killing you, but I guarantee it'll hurt like a motherfucker. Don't even try to play tough. The only thing you got going on is that big brain of yours. Soft little thing like you trying to act hard. You believe this shit, J?"

Chelsea felt a nudge at her feet, and she glanced back at Billy Casey, who was still lying on the ground near her. His boot was tapping at her ankle.

Marc approached. "Let's go, doc. Time to move on. You and me got a lot to discuss."

Chelsea grimaced, then opened her hand holding the attaché case. It fell to the ground and popped open like a book. At the same instant, Billy shoved himself from the ground and grabbed the contents of the case—an oblong rifle with a curved shape and a prism inside its barrel.

He pressed the button on the grip and a white cylindrical beam throttled from the weapon, smashing into Marc's chest!

Marc flew backward from the force and crashed into the ground. Jesús immediately turned in his direction.

"Sir!"

"Stop them!" Marc roared.

But before Jesús could react, he was hit by a similar blast, struck in the back and sent flipping to the ground, his rifle swirling away.

Nia looked at Billy as he aimed the weapon at her.

That weapon…it's just like the thing I stole from that laboratory last week. In fact, that's the same gun!

"Kevlar," Billy grinned. "Unlike some people, I came prepared for a situation like this. Now you're on the ground, and I'm on top, again, all thanks to the Romedrux *Crasher* particle beam rifle. A little contingency Chelsea brought along just in case. It's a good thing Vincent managed to get the prototype back from you before you could hawk it, huh? How do you like the finished model?"

Nia sat still, waiting for him to make his move. *That's right, Billy. Do your thing. Keep talking.*

"It's been fun, Nia…" he said as he raised the rifle, lining up the barrel with Nia's head. The weapon began to make an unsettling hum as light started glowing from inside it.

Shit. Too soon…

"Billy!" Chelsea screamed. "We gotta get out of here!"

"Not until we finish them off!"

"No! The Crasher's only set to incapacitate! I didn't have time to reconfigure it! They're going to get back up! We're outnumbered! We gotta call Mr. H and get some help!"

"Fuck that! She's dying today, and I'm gonna do it! I don't need any of them damn drones to help me!" Billy growled.

But Chelsea grabbed Billy by the arm.

"Dude! Get me out of here now! Didn't you hear what that big guy said? They're after *me!* Do you know what Mr. Hudson will do to you if you let anything happen to me?!"

Billy grunted, then sighed.

Marc pulled himself up and snatched his dropped pistol from the ground. "Fuck! That shit hurt! Yo, J! Get your ass up! They're getting away!"

Jesús Alvarez obeyed, climbing to his feet, collecting his rifle. Marc opened fire toward Billy and Chelsea, but they already made their way behind the construction site and Marc's shots only struck metal beams.

"Jesús!" Nia hollered, still grounded and clutching the wound in her belly.

Marc turned in Nia's direction, shaking his head.

"J…kill her. I got no more use for her."

"But sir! She's…how can you do that to your—"

Then they all heard Chelsea's car, a pitch black Porsche, peel out. Marc and the others watched as it zoomed away from the construction site.

"Fuck!" Marc griped. "Come on!"

Jesús Alvarez gave Nia one last lingering look, then rushed to the driver's side of their Viper. Marc climbed into the passenger side, checking his pistol as he did, and the two drove off after Chelsea and Billy.

Nia lay on the ground, wincing in pain, alone in the dust and gravel.

What the fuck just happened…? Nia thought. *Marc was after Chelsea the whole time. Chelsea! But why? What's he want with her…and how did he shoot like that? He popped Billy in the chest before he could even move; I couldn't even see Billy when he was running around! And he broke Chelsea's glasses with a bullet, without even nicking her face! Whatever Jesús is on, he must be on it too…no, there's something else. Marc made me look like a fucking amateur. What was Jesús trying to say…?*

Nia finally climbed to her feet. The pain was starting to go away. She lifted away the makeshift bandage she'd made out of her blouse. Her wound was smaller than it was before. Strength returned to her body.

She looked ahead and saw the black and silver motorcycle Marc loaned her. It sat untouched, shining in the morning sun…

Beckoning her.

I need me some answers. They ain't just gonna leave me in the dirt.

Nia tied the tattered shirt around her abdomen, dislodged her Baby Eagles from the pile of gravel and ran toward the sport bike.

JESÚS ALVAREZ STEERED the Viper with precision, its powerful engine growling like a beast as he swerved around traffic and struggled to catch up with Billy and Chelsea's Porsche. The Viper was the faster vehicle, but the narrow streets and multitude of intersections, as well as Chelsea's lead, enabled them to keep ahead of Marc and Jesús by constantly turning.

"Don't you ever fucking question me again, Jesús!" Marc roared. "We don't need Nia getting in our way anymore. She got Chelsea Romedrux out in the open. That was the plan. That was all we needed her for!"

"Then why did we hesitate?" Jesús retorted. "I could have taken Casey out from a distance had you asked me to. But you would not let me. I thought that's why we brought the rifle."

"You still questioning me?" Marc growled. "The rifle was a contingency. I wanted to give Nia one more chance…see if she had what it took to be a part of this. She up in there getting her shit punched in by a normal guy with a little medicine pumped into him…ain't no way she'd stand a chance against the kinds of targets I'm gonna be going after once we're up and running."

"And Casey? Why did you choose to spare him? Either of us could have shot him in the head."

"Hell, he beat Nia. I was thinking about asking him to sign up with me," Marc sighed. "Lord knows Corp Hudson ain't gonna be employing him for much longer, from what you tell me about him. But he's too pussy-whipped. Fuck him. Just get us close enough and I'll get the boy out of the way."

"There was no reason to do that to Nia," Jesús said. "She is a good person. She did not deserve this."

"'A good person'?" Marc laughed. "The girl is barely in her twenties and she done already killed more people than most soldiers, robbed more companies than any burglar and probably been fucked by more dudes than the most turned-out prostitute. She ain't worth a damn thing."

"You don't know anything about her. She did what she had to so she could survive, without the guidance she needed."

Marc grimaced. "You got one more time to talk out of line. Watch the fucking road and shut the fuck up."

Jesús Alvarez flashed teeth, then turned the wheel. The car changed direction and pulled away from the chase.

Marc grew furious. "Are you fucking crazy? Do you know what I can do to you?"

"Yes sir. You can take away everything you've given to me. I know that you are the only reason I am strong. But she has become the only reason I care about my life, and I can't sit by and watch you continue to treat her like she's just some object. I would rather betray you for her sake than cross her for yours another second."

"I cannot believe this shit! The stuff I got pumping through your veins is supposed to help you repress that weak emotional shit…but Nia still managed to get you pussy-whipped after one damn lay."

"She is special, sir. You should know that. I would do anything for her. She's worth it."

The Viper rounded a corner and sped forward. The two looked up the street. They saw Chelsea's Porsche sitting idle.

Chelsea was in the driver's seat, looking straight ahead.

Billy was standing in the passenger seat, sticking out of the car's sunroof, holding the *Crasher* rifle. He had them dead to rights.

Both Marc and Jesús stared in horror as Billy pressed the fire button.

271

The beam of light throttled forth and struck the head of Jesús Alvarez…cutting through the windshield and searing *right through his skull.*

As Jesús Alvarez's eyes rolled back, the Viper skidded out of control, flipped sideways and smashed upside down into the front entrance of a grocery store.

Billy nodded and sat back down in the seat. Chelsea leaned over and planted a kiss on his lips, shifted the car into reverse and drove away.

Seconds later, the windshield of the mangled Viper flew away from the wreckage, forced off by an outstretched foot.

Marc Benson tore himself free of the wreck and stood up. He swept himself off. His skin was singed from fire and smoke, but he had no marks or wounds.

He glanced at the wreckage and looked at the blood pouring from the broken body twisted and mangled in the driver's seat.

Jesús Alvarez was dead.

Marc glared down the street and looked at the slowly-disappearing plume of smoke, rising from where the Porsche once sat.

He took a breath and started running forward. With each step, his muscles began to expand. Soon he was running so hard and so fast he was outpacing other vehicles, cracking the asphalt underneath his feet.

Billy Casey laughed.

"You mean to tell me that's all we had to do? Put in a little code in this keypad and it turns the gun into a lethal weapon? Why didn't you do that in the first place?"

"Because," Chelsea whined, "The whole idea was to bring in Nia Black alive, wasn't it? The *Crasher* was meant to incapacitate them, but it can go lethal as a last resort. Those freaks…they dodge bullets. But they can't dodge a sophisticated laser targeting system. I just wasn't expecting *him* to show up. Alvarez, yeah, but…not him."

"It doesn't matter. We got rid of the peanut gallery. Frankly I'm shocked he went down so easily. Now let's swing back and get Nia before it's too late."

"Billy, we already screwed up! There's no way she's still there! She's totally on her way to Puerto Rico or something by now. We're done!"

Billy grimaced and looked out the window. Watching the surroundings speed by, he looked skyward and stared at the Hudson Tower soaring above the skyline, looming above everything.

Billy took a deep breath.

"Then let's keep driving. Don't go back, Chelsea. Let's just run. I've got some cash tucked away and I've got a safehouse. Between your brains and my skills, we can start something new."

"You just don't fucking get it, do you Billy? The minute you were assigned to executive security, you became Corp Hudson's *property*. We know too much. We can't run. We just need to go face the music. Either way—"

"What's that?" Billy gasped, looking through the rear view mirror.

The two stared into the reflection with bulging eyes, looking at what appeared to be a large black man running down the road, jumping between, over and around cars…

Gaining on them.

"Fuck!" Billy growled. "Floor it, Chelsea! Floor it!"

"Fine…" Chelsea griped. "But you know where I'm going."

"Whatever. Just go!"

Marc's heart rate was immeasurable. His eyes were glazed over, blank. His muscles expanded.

He raced through traffic, running past cars and trucks and buses. He darted across the asphalt on foot, closing in on the Porsche.

He slammed his feet into the ground, leaving cracks in the street, and lunged into the air. He outstretched a hand...

And grabbed the roof!

He curled his fingers around the border of the sunroof, clawing the roof with enough pressure to bend the chassis.

Chelsea swerved the Porsche back and forth, speeding past red lights, frightening crossing pedestrians into staying on the sidewalk.

Onlookers glared in shock at the sight of a muscular man wearing a vest and fatigues dangling from the roof by one hand, his legs flailing, pulled in the wake of the zooming vehicle.

Almost as frightening and twice as loud was the motorcycle that zoomed right behind them at ridiculous speed.

"Will you give it up?!" Casey shouted. "Can't you see it's not worth it by now?"

But Marc wasn't listening. All he knew was that Billy Casey just killed his longtime partner, associate...brother-in-arms. And he would make Casey pay.

However, Marc lost his gun in the crash. He only had his bare hands. He just wanted to get them around Billy Casey's neck.

Logic no longer figured into his objective; only blind fury. And in his rage, he neglected the *Crasher*.

Billy Casey did not.

He lifted the rifle, watching as the desperate-looking Marc Benson did everything in his power to keep his grip. He brought his other arm about and managed to take hold of the car with both hands. Slowly, Marc began pulling himself up.

"Shoot him, Billy!" Chelsea screamed.

"Well isn't this a sight...?" he muttered mockingly as the hum of the *Crasher* grew louder.

"Billy! Just shoot him!" Chelsea bellowed again.

"Here I am, face-to-face with the so-called 'world's greatest physical specimen' …the 'most dangerous man alive'… and he's completely helpless. I do believe I'm going to enjoy this."

Casey pressed the button—

Just as a bullet tore through the window in the back of the Porsche and struck the *Crasher*.

The futuristic weapon jerked skyward on impact, the beam missing Marc's head by an inch. Sparks crackled everywhere as Billy frantically tossed the broken weapon aside.

"What the…?"

Two more shots sped through the glass-less rear opening, pounded into Billy's Kevlar-covered chest and forced him back into the passenger seat. Billy clutched his torso, flashing teeth as he glared at the road behind them.

He saw a motorcycle speeding toward them, a small woman at the handles with a Baby Eagle in her left hand, aimed directly at him.

Nia Black.

The Porsche swung around a corner and sped through the uptown district like a missile. Nia kept chase, finally realizing what was going on.

She'd thought Chelsea was merely whipping the car around the city, trying to shake Marc from the roof. But when she saw a massive, soaring building looming ahead, she realized they weren't driving randomly at all.

The chase was speeding directly toward the Hudson Tower.

Marc Benson stood up on the roof of the Porsche. He held his balance amazingly well, considering how fast the car was moving. He glared down at Billy Casey and Chelsea Romedrux, and got ready to force his way inside the car through the sunroof.

But Billy and Chelsea didn't look worried. Marc wondered why they were so confident.

Then he looked ahead, and saw a large metal beam careening toward him—an overpass that stood over the driveway leading inside the Hudson Tower's front lot.

Marc dodged out of the way in an instant, but when he did, his center of gravity shifted and he finally fell from the car roof, flung by the sheer force of the swift-moving vehicle. He tumbled and rolled on the ground, and by the time he caught himself and bounced back to his feet, Billy and Chelsea had already leaped out of the car and rushed toward the soaring skyscraper's executive entrance.

Marc fished in his pocket, but found his gun was gone. He realized he must have lost it when his Viper crashed or while he was running. He was empty-handed.

He sighed and started walking toward the Hudson Tower. He stopped in his tracks though, when a black sport bike growled into the lot and skidded to a stop right in front of him.

"Where you going?" the young, beautiful and battle-scarred female rider grunted at him.

"I GOT A BETTER QUESTION, NIA," Marc shot back. "What the hell are you even doing here? Ain't you had enough yet? I mean, fuck…you weren't strong enough to get your revenge for Kim. Jesús is dead so ain't no point holding out for him to come back to you either. They ain't after you anymore. So why don't you do what you said you was gonna do and just run your ass away?"

"You got Jesús killed?!"

"No. *You* did. You made the boy fall in love with you. I mean, if he wasn't so infatuated with you, we could have just done what we originally set out to do, get the *Hercules* data—"

"And leave me to die," Nia whined, her eyes welling up with tears. "Right?"

Marc paced around the parking lot.

"That's right. I used you, Nia. From the beginning, I've been using you, because you're weak and gullible, naïve and fucking predictable. I've been working on this for a long time. I'm the one who sent Jesús Alvarez into Corp Hudson to begin with. I knew it was time to act after you beat the shit out of that Gunner dude outside of the Jazz Hall. I needed an in with the Corp, and they had an opening on their security team, so I sent Jesús in there as their newest executive security member. He needed to impress them, so I've been supplying him with a special additive to make him stronger."

"'Special'?"

"Yeah. But the problem is, it was only a temporary boost," Marc went on. "And it started getting less and less effective, so I needed to get some insight into how it works and how I could improve it. I needed the best

277

resource I could get…Hudson's records. And when Jesús fucked that up, I had to go for the next best thing. Little miss prodigy Chelsea Romedrux. So I made Jesús befriend you so you would trust him enough to put yourself in bad situations for him. Having him kidnap Bobby and Charlene, telling you how to get to Hudson…even when I hooked you up with weapons…it was all to keep you focused on what I needed from you."

"Why?" Nia growled. "Why do all this? What are you trying to accomplish?"

"I'm gonna make the perfect mercenary force—a team of invincible soldiers who solve problems all over the world, independent of corporate bosses or corrupt government; a team of mercenaries who follow their own rules and set their own prices. I'm building my own personal headhunters' guild, signing up the best of the best and making them even more powerful using my additive. They're gonna need to be more than human to take down the kinds of targets I'm looking at. I needed Hudson's files to perfect this additive so it can be just as permanent in them as it is in the source."

"And what 'source' is that?"

"You should know by now, Nia," Marc snapped back. "The additive that strengthened Jesús was made from the same stuff running through you."

Nia staggered back.

Marc smiled. "Now you get it. Finally."

"Who are you? What was Jesús trying to say?"

"You know what he was trying to say."

He reached in his pocket and pulled out an old Polaroid photo. He tossed it on the ground. Nia slowly stepped forward and picked it up.

She stared at the picture of four people: a man—clearly a younger looking Marc—along with a woman and two young, identical twin girls. Both girls were wearing gold necklaces with opal charms, identical to the jewelry Nia always wore around her neck.

"You saw what I can do," he continued. "You're at least smart enough to know that I'm way more powerful than Jesús and way more powerful than *you*. You already know Hudson has yet to figure out how to get his creations up to your level, so how do you suppose I'm already past you?"

A tear leaked from Nia's eye.

"No way. No fucking way!"

"Do you know why they call you *'Target Omega'*? Because you were meant to be the end of the *Hercules* project, Nia. You...and your sister. But for there to be an end, there had to be a beginning. There had to be a *'Target Alpha'*. That's me. I'm your father, Nia. I'm **Alexander Black.**"

Nia started breathing hard, shaking her head. She tried to resist, but she couldn't hold her tears back.

"You're lying! You've been lying to me from day one. I ain't got no reason to believe you now. None of this is making any sense. If you are my pop, why did you hide it? Where were you all this time?"

"You want the truth? Here it is. A long time ago, I met a woman named Shauntee Lawson. Remember last night when I said I knew a girl like you once? That was your mother. She used to be an assassin working for the Phoenix Group. We hooked up and she got pregnant with twins: you and Shauntia. That was *after* I escaped from Corp Hudson; after my body was changed by *Hercules*.

"But Shauntee and I stopped getting along. She left the Phoenix to build a life with me, but I wanted to go back to war. So I left her—and you— behind. I found out later that Hudson was still looking for me, and they attacked the house while you and Shauntia were at school, and Shauntee was dead. They must have spared you hoping I could come try to rescue y'all or something. But I washed my hands of you and went about my business. I never came back so they just let you two go. That sound about right?"

Nia grew even more furious.

"Then come to find you and your sister were alive and growing up in an orphanage, and I heard rumors about twin teenage girls who were 'athletically gifted' or some shit. It hit me—what if my daughters grew up just as powerful as I was, or even more powerful? So I came back to check it out. I sent Kim to look into it to keep myself under cover, but by the time he got there, Shauntia was already gone."

"Where is Shauntia?" Nia asked.

"Hell if I know. If the Phoenix Group got her, she's probably following in her mom's footsteps…becoming a contract killer."

"A what?"

Marc—Alexander—turned away from Nia. "I've wasted enough time. For all I know the big man's got a private helicopter waiting on the roof to fly Dr. Chelsea to the Barbados or something. I'm going up there."

"The *fuck* you are!" Nia screamed, raising her pistols. "After you put me through all this shit, you think I'm just gonna let you walk away and go about your business? You put Bobby and Charlene in danger, got Jesús killed, and you made a fool out of me!"

Alexander turned back toward Nia. "No, little girl. You made a fool out of *your damn self!* Walking around wearing tight shit, carrying guns like you some kind of dumb ass cowgirl, not doing nothing but making smart people shake their head at how fucking stupid you were. Drawing the cops to you because you like being chased. No kind of style. No kind of stealth. Why, because it was fun? You like being shot at, like your face being on wanted posters, like having to watch your back all the time? You wondering why so many people treat you like shit…because you treat *yourself* like shit!"

Nia held her guns steady. "I will shoot you."

He turned away again, waved and started walking away.

The wind moaned around her and silence filled the air.

The silence was broken by Nia's scream, and then a gunshot echoed.

280

Alexander shifted his head sideways, the bullet narrowly missing his ear. He neither broke his stride nor turned around.

Nia fired again, and this time Alexander had to duck to avoid it. He stopped.

"Okay, Nia," he said, turning around once more. "I see you're not going to let this go."

"You damn right I'm not. You owe me some answers, some real answers. You knew from the gate that I was your daughter, and even so…you let me get shot at, kidnapped, chased, damn near raped and dissected and all that shit…you ain't care about me at all."

"You finally get it!"

Alexander started running at Nia with his fists raised. Nia opened fire, but he swayed *around* the bullets and slammed his knuckles into Nia's chest.

She soared through the air like a rocket and collided into a parked minivan, her back smashing the doors in and cracking the windows.

Nia crumbled to the ground and fell on her hands, letting out a hard cough at the same time. Blood spattered from her mouth onto the asphalt.

"Yeah. You ain't used to that shit, are you?" Alexander said with a laugh. "That's always been your problem, Nia. You ain't never know what it was like to be 'normal'. You always had this strength, so to you it's natural to heal quick, to dodge bullets, to know what's coming. But the problem is that same strength that makes you think you're such a badass is actually the reason you're weak. You're only good at taking out those enemies beneath your level, like a gamer who refuses to stop playing on 'Easy'."

Nia clawed the ground reaching for her dropped pistols, but Alexander closed in and kicked them away from her.

"I'm different, Nia. See, I know the best of both worlds. I was once a regular guy, before you were born. Then *Hercules* made me this way. But I was a soldier before that. And you know what soldiers do when we're not fighting wars? We drill. Constantly. I trained myself to take the best advantage of this new power. I learned how to make myself invincible with these powers, because I trained myself to be damn-near invincible *without* them. But you, all you know is the power. That's why you cry so much. As soon as something—anything—happens to you that you ain't ready for, you break down like a baby. You go for your guns, you run, you hide, you look for somebody to love you. Because you're weak."

"Shut up," Nia mumbled. "All you do is talk down on people like you're so much better. But think about this, 'pop'. Who's fault is it that I'm the way I am? Who's blood do I have flowing in me? And who *wasn't* there to help me learn what I needed to learn? You're the reason I have this power. You're the reason that it's all I know."

She finally stood up. "Everything you ever said about me is the truth. Everything that happened to me and the people around me was because of the things I did. I don't deny that. But what you expect? I grew up with no parents. Worse, my own dad watched me continually fuck up and didn't do anything about it but sit back and laugh and think of ways to use me."

"You making excuses now? You're a grown-ass woman, Nia!" Alexander shouted at her. "Take some fucking responsibility for yourself for once!"

"I intend to. It would be fucking irresponsible for me to let a man like you continue to walk this earth," Nia stated, tightening her fists.

Suddenly her muscles expanded. She looked like she gained double her original mass—all muscle.

"Oh!" Alexander laughed. "So you finally know how to do the Breach, huh? Maybe there's hope for you yet. Maybe."

She rushed forward in a fighting stance. Alexander just stood there, watching her as she closed in.

Nia swung her fists back and forth at her father. He folded his arms behind his back and tilted his torso from side to side. Nia hit nothing but air.

She swung her feet out, performing a sequence of roundhouse kicks, swirling like a dancer. Her feet cut the wind but did not come anywhere near her target.

Nia sprang up after the third kick and launched into a knee strike combo. Alexander raised a palm and caught her left knee, deflected the right follow-up and had time to duck when Nia outstretched her left leg again before gravity took over and she landed.

Pressing her fingertips to the ground, Nia started to breathe hard. She looked up at her father, who appeared to tower over her, the morning sun silhouetting his muscular frame.

"Finished?"

Before Nia knew what was happening, Alexander's fist smashed into her cheek. Her skull made an impact crater in the ground. Her muscles trembled and shook, and her body returned to normal.

Alexander stood straight up and turned his back. "Do yourself a favor, sweetheart. When you finally get up, get ghost. Get out of the city and disappear. Breach or no Breach, you ain't got what it takes to be a part of this world. Oh, and you can keep that bike. Consider it me making up for all your missed birthdays or something if it makes you feel good. Just do what I told you to do."

Nia craned her neck to look up, watching her father as he walked further and further away. Soon he disappeared into the main entrance of the Hudson Tower.

Then everything went dark.

BILLY CASEY AND CHELSEA ROMEDRUX rode inside a private elevator deep within the Hudson Tower, reserved only for the highest-ranking executives and associates.

"What do you think he'll say?" Billy muttered.

Chelsea stayed silent.

"That's not like you," he went on. "You always have something to say."

"You tell me," Chelsea finally said. "What does he usually do to people who screw up as badly as you did?"

"Me?!" Billy growled. "You're the one who had your fancy gun set to stun! You're the one who arranged for me to take Nia alone."

"We couldn't get the Security Soldiers, Billy. Like, Hudson doesn't *trust* you to command them, and I'm not a member of security. It was up to us by ourselves. You forgot, didn't you? Vincent failed and Jesús betrayed us. You were the last member of security we could even hope to rely on."

"What about Jason and the others?"

"They're…they've been transferred to another department."

"The odds were against us from the beginning," Billy griped. "We were on our own out there."

"You're the one who said you could handle it. You wanted to prove you were so much better than Vincent," Chelsea sighed. "You could have humbled yourself and said 'Uh, like, Mr. Hudson, I totally suck. I need you to back me on this one.' He would have given you what you needed. But no…you had to be cocky. You had to be *you*."

The elevator chimed and they arrived on the 50th floor of the tower.

284

"Well, time to face the music," Billy mumbled. "But I'll be damned if I'm taking all the heat for this."

Then the doors slid open and Billy looked down the awaiting corridor…

And his heart started pounding.

Six of Hudson's armored Security Soldiers stood in the hall, holding rifles.

Chelsea started trembling.

A digitized voice emanated from one of the Soldiers.

"RESEARCH AND DEVELOPMENT DEPARTMENT HEAD, DR. CHELSEA MARIE ROMEDRUX. PLEASE COME THIS WAY."

Chelsea gulped, but slowly did as she was told. Billy started to follow her.

"WILLIAM ROBERT CASEY. PLEASE REMAIN STILL."

The Soldiers leveled their rifles and aimed them at Billy, all at once like automatons. He stopped in his tracks.

"What?! What the hell's this about?"

One of the Security Soldiers took Chelsea by the arm and guided her behind the group. Heavy footsteps approached from the other end of the hall. Chelsea looked ahead and saw the towering Maxwell Hudson himself emerging from the shadows.

Hudson stopped behind the group of Soldiers and glared at Billy with no expression, like a being without a soul.

"Mr. Casey. I've decided to move up our discussion regarding your future with Corp Hudson."

Billy started to say something. Then he looked at Chelsea. She looked in his eyes one more time, then moved behind Hudson, turning away.

Billy's blood ran cold.

He immediately reached for his gun holster. He grabbed nothing but air. He forgot that the only weapon he'd carried that day was the knife…the one he left in Nia's belly.

He slapped at the elevator buttons, but they did not respond. He huffed a chuckle at the fact that Hudson and the Security Soldiers simply waited for him to go through all that…waited for him to discover for himself that there was no escape.

Billy Casey took a deep breath, turned back toward the people in the corridor facing him, and closed his eyes.

"Well I'll be damned."

Then the deafening scream of automatic gunfire filled the air and the muzzle flashes played on the reflective walls of the corridor and on Hudson's opaque glasses.

Chelsea stood still, facing away, pressing her palms to her ears, her eyes shut tight.

The Security Soldiers stopped firing and lowered their rifles, smoke rising from their barrels. Billy's body slumped to the floor, blood spilling out everywhere.

Hudson spoke, "My apologies, Dr. Romedrux. I am aware of how you hate the sight of death."

"It's not that, Mr. H," Chelsea muttered. "I kind of liked him."

"Did you?"

"Yeah. His body was totally awesome for experimentation. Great biology. It's a shame he didn't have the brains to match."

The two started walking away from the executive elevator. The Security Soldiers moved in and picked up Billy Casey's body as Hudson ordered one of them to summon a clean-up crew to replace the damaged walls and blood-stained carpet. They dragged Billy's corpse into the elevator; one Soldier pressed a key and the doors immediately closed with a chime.

"Perhaps the others will be more to your liking," Hudson went on. "While you were away, your staff completed the initial analyses of Jason Priest, Don Thompson and Cherie Wilson. The results have been sent to the terminal in your laboratory. The HEX project can proceed as planned."

"Coolness," Chelsea smiled. "You'll at least be glad to know Billy got one thing right. Jesús Alvarez is totally dead. Now, about that other problem..."

Maxwell Hudson and Chelsea Romedrux reached the end of the hall and entered another private elevator, one more narrow than the executive elevator. There was a single button on the panel inside. Hudson pressed it and the doors gently closed.

There were several small monitors on a wall in the elevator. Each monitor showed images around the exterior and lower floors of the Hudson Tower. Hudson and Romedrux examined them.

"You did well. You have flushed out *Target Alpha*, doing what I could not after all these years," Hudson said with a small smile. "It was clear that if we paid enough attention to his daughter, he would eventually show himself. And now, if our security cameras are any indication, he is coming to see us."

"After hiding and pulling strings all these years, he just, like, decides to deliver himself to your doorstep?" Chelsea laughed. "This is gonna be so awesome. Now, what about that bitch?"

"Doctor," Hudson grumbled. "Language."

"Sorry. I mean Nia Black. She's still out there. Her father gave her an old fashioned spanking, but she'll get up. She always does."

"I have taken care of that."

"You mean *him*?" Chelsea gasped. "Like, no way. He can't do the job. You know he can't, Mr. H."

"We're moving on, Doctor," Hudson retorted. "With everything. I've also sent second-generation Security Soldiers."

"But he—oh. Okay, cool. Then I guess it's back to work then. Like, onwards and upwards!"

The elevator chimed again and the doors slid open. Dr. Chelsea and Maxwell Hudson stepped out of the elevator, arriving in the expansive and opulent penthouse at the peak of the Tower.

The strident sound of shifting metal finally reached Nia Black, and she regained consciousness.

She lifted her head from the warm asphalt she'd been laying on—for how long, she had no clue—and looked up as crumbs from the street fell from her cheek and hair.

There was a gun barrel pointing at her head...the barrel of a familiar Beretta.

"Get up, Nia," said Vincent Marks. "It's time to go."

NIA DRAGGED HERSELF UP from the ground until she sat cross-legged. It was still morning, or probably early afternoon. She couldn't tell for sure. She was still in the lot surrounding the Hudson Tower, where she'd confronted Marc Benson—who turned out to be her father Alexander Black—a short time earlier.

Nia looked around and saw six of Hudson's Security Soldiers standing behind her one-time beau.

"Hey, Vince..." Nia mumbled.

"You look like you took one hell of a beating," he went on. "I didn't think anything could take you down like that."

Nia climbed to her feet. Vincent backpedaled, keeping his aim on her.

"This time I've got you, Nia. I mean it. We're going to pay a visit to Mr. Hudson. You resist and they will shoot. I won't have to."

Nia sighed, sweeping dirt from her face and flicking debris from her hair.

"Fine. Take me away."

"Huh? What...you're not going to..."

"What, fight? For what? I ain't got nothing to get away for no more," Nia moaned. "I don't have anyone to go back to. I don't have any contacts to fence shit to. I don't even have a father. I'll probably be better off as a guinea pig."

Vincent looked confused.

"But can I ask you something, Vincent?" Nia continued. "Do you even know why Hudson wants me so bad?"

"It doesn't matter to me, Nia," Vincent retorted. "When we were dating, I had no idea you were the woman who was hassling Corp Hudson's holdings so much in the beginning. But you knew I was the head of Hudson's executive security detail. You were playing me from the start. How could you not expect it to come to this?"

"Don't change the subject, Vincent. I know you still care about me, at least enough to wonder why I'm so important to your boss. You ever ask yourself why he was willing to put you and your co-workers on the line time and time again just to get at me? Little ol' me?"

Vincent rolled his eyes. "Enlighten me."

"EXECUTIVE SECURITY CHIEF VINCENT JAMES MARKS," said one of the Security Soldiers. "PLEASE DETAIN TARGET OMEGA NIA SHAUNTEE BLACK IMMEDIATELY."

"Hey!" Vincent growled. "I'm the head of security! You don't tell *me* what to do!"

"WE ARE UNDER ORDERS FROM THE CHAIRMAN TO BRING IN TARGET OMEGA NIA SHAUNTEE BLACK," the Soldier said. "DISSENT SUSPECTED. PLEASE COMPLY."

"And we will!" Vincent snapped. "We will when I'm ready!"

"'Dissent suspected'?" Nia spoke up. "Look at them, Vincent. Listen to them. They look like men, but they're not. They're machines. They're made to follow Hudson's orders without offering a word of resistance. Ain't you noticed that while your numbers are going down, the number of those Security Soldiers is going *up*?"

"What's your point?"

"Hudson's plan this whole time is to make an army out of these things. He wants to figure out how the powers in my body work so he can make a whole army of soldiers who can do what I can do."

"How do you figure—"

"I figured it out when I was on that island of Chelsea's. Billy Casey told me Chelsea was going to do all kinds of experiments to figure out 'what makes me tick'. Jesús told me he needed to use me to help him get on the island because regular guys like you weren't allowed."

"So that was his game," Vincent mumbled.

"You ain't listening, Vincent!" Nia squealed. "Goons like these Security Soldiers were all over the island. Meanwhile he's sending guys like you, Jesús and Billy after me, not giving a damn about whether you win or lose. Don't you fucking get it?"

Vincent started breathing hard.

"Look around you, Vincent."

Vincent stared into Nia's eyes, and then slowly turned around.

All six Security Soldiers had their rifles trained on Vincent Marks.

"EXECUTIVE ORDER FROM CHAIRMAN MAXWELL ADRIAN HUDSON. TERMINATE *TARGET OMEGA* NIA SHAUNTEE BLACK AND *FORMER* EXECUTIVE SECURITY CHIEF VINCENT JAMES MARKS."

Vincent's heart pounded in his chest.

Then everything happened at once.

Vincent swung around, raising his Beretta, then he felt a weight on his head, forcing him to the ground. He looked up and saw Nia. She'd sprang into the air, vaulting over Vincent and pushing him down at the same time. He crashed down, catching himself with his arms an instant before his chin could collide with the asphalt.

The Security Soldiers opened fire, but their shots passed over Vincent's head and under Nia's legs.

Her legs went wild after that, swinging into the Security Soldiers' heads like baseball bats, putting cracks in their helmets, sending them tumbling all over the ground. Nia took down three of them with two kicks and sent the others falling with two more sweeps. She rolled on the ground, snatched two dropped rifles up, shot to her feet and screamed "Move!"

Vincent did as he was told, bounding out of the way as Nia squeezed the triggers, riddling the Security Soldiers' armor with automatic gunfire.

The gunshots glanced off their armor, sparks flailing all around them. They were bulletproof.

Nia grimaced and turned the rifles around, swinging them like batons into the skulls of their enemies. The rifles shattered on impact, along with their helmets.

Vincent gasped when he looked at the unmasked Security Soldiers.

None of them had hair. Their faces were blank, lifeless. Computer chips were imbedded in the backs of their heads right through the skin.

Nia bolted away from them as their armor crumbled. She darted across the parking lot and scraped her Baby Eagles from the ground.

Then gunshots crackled and the soldiers' heads shattered like coconuts one by one.

Vincent took deep breaths as he turned to Nia. "What the...what the hell..."

"I tried to tell you," Nia sighed. "I tried to tell you from the beginning. Hudson ain't somebody you need to be devoting yourself to. You're too good a man for that."

"Hudson told me these guys were volunteers. They led normal lives. They just did this during their eight hours...these people are..."

"They ain't even alive," Nia shook her head. "I can't explain it. All I know is this shit ain't cool. Hudson's looking to get rid of everybody who he doesn't trust—everybody who might disagree with him. Who else is on your security team?"

Vincent shook his head. "There was Jason, Cherie and Don...but they decided to join the weaponization program...they mean to become like Gunner and Armstrong. Then there was Jesús... and Billy; Hudson had him terminated. Good riddance too..."

"Then that's it. You're the last one, Vincent; the last one Hudson needs to kill before his whole security team ain't nothing but these drones. You're the last one with a brain of your own. Hudson's trying to lay your ass off—the hard way."

Vincent's face turned furious. "I can't believe this. All this time, I trusted him. I believed in him. I thought Hudson was trying to bring peace to the streets. I thought he wanted to take out superhuman criminals...like you...but he's not. He's trying to corner the market on them!"

Nia nodded. "Uh-huh. And there's more. My father's on his way up to Hudson."

"What?! Your father...you mean *Target Alpha?*"

"You know about him?"

"Hudson's been looking for Alexander Black for years. No one else was ever compatible with *Hercules*. Eventually Hudson gave up on the formula, but he didn't give up searching for the man who made it work. We'd been tracking him for a while, then he disappeared a couple of years ago...right around the time you started making waves."

"He came back here when he heard about me," Nia explained. "He wanted me to take his side. He wanted to understand *Hercules* himself, so he used Jesús to get to me, so he could get to Hudson's secret files or something. When that didn't work, he decided to go after Chelsea. He used me to draw her out, and if it wasn't for Billy, my dad would have had her, and I would be dead."

"Dr. Romedrux doesn't deserve this," Vincent shook his head. "She's just doing her job. No way she's a part of this."

"What, you like that crazy bitch or something?"

Vincent looked flustered. "No, it's not like that! She just seems so innocent. Like she was brought into this bad situation and tainted by him..."

"Whatever," Nia said, looking up at the Hudson Tower. Its peak was so high it was hard to see in the haze of clouds up above.

"All I know is she's my dad's target. You want to save her, fine, whatever. I need to get at my father."

"If he's going up there, Hudson knows he's coming. Hudson's probably got a plan to deal with him. Wait…that explains it!" Vincent gasped.

"What?"

"Hudson insisted upon sending Security Soldiers with me, even though I'd planned to use my own men to get you. Now I get it."

"Come on, Vincent!" Nia squealed. "Spit it out!"

"Hudson's not after you anymore. He's got *Target Alpha*. Hudson just wanted to cut us both down and be done with it. Hudson's got your father, so you're of no more use to him. Neither of us are."

Nia started pacing around the lot, looking at the ground.

"'No more use', huh?" Nia muttered low, as if talking to herself. "After all that shit they put me through, now I'm 'of no more use'?"

"Nia?"

She started breathing hard. "My father said the same thing to me earlier. He made Jesús put a gun to my head and told him with a straight face to kill me because he had no more use for me. My fucking *father* said that to me while I was sitting on the ground with a damn hole in my stomach from Billy's knife, my blood spilling all on the ground."

Vincent's face lit up. "And that pisses you off, doesn't it?"

"You damn right it does. I ain't even get no money for this shit. To hell with that. We're going in."

"You sure? You sure you don't just want to escape? There's nothing stopping you anymore…least of all me."

Nia shook her head. "Like I told you, I don't have anywhere to escape to. It was all good when y'all was just trying to capture me. I could always get away. I could always come back and mess his stuff up a little more. But it's different now. I'm worthless to him, which means I'm a target. I let my guard down for one second, and I'm dead. I'm sick and tired of having to

294

watch my back every waking moment of my life. I'll be damned if I'm gonna let Hudson do me like he did my mom all those years ago."

Nia reloaded her Baby Eagles and looked toward the Hudson Tower.

"Plus, if Hudson does beat my dad, it'll be just as bad as if he got me…worse. My father's *way* stronger than I am. I can't even imagine what those Security Soldiers of his will be like if they're all juiced up like my pop."

Nia looked Vincent in the eyes.

"You know what I really hate about your boss? It's not even about mom anymore. That's just what got me started. I can't even blame Hudson for that, not entirely. It only happened because my father crossed Hudson, and then he abandoned my mom, left a damn bulls-eye on her back. My father's the one who didn't protect her. And to be honest, I barely remember my mom."

"So then, what?" Vincent wondered.

"The thing that *really* pisses me off about Hudson is how he just don't give a damn about life at all. He thinks living people are his toys just because he's a rich man. He takes these people and turns them into robots. He goes putting chemicals and drugs into people's bodies so they can become weapons just so he can get his kicks watching us shoot at each other. My biggest fear was that you were next, Vincent. I was always afraid the day would come when you would have some mutation in your body or guns on your arms or some shit, and we would have to fight for real. I'm glad it didn't happen."

"Yeah," Vincent nodded. "Me too. So does this mean we're partners now?"

"Don't get it twisted," Nia smiled small. "I'll help you out this time for old time's sake. The next time, it's going to cost you."

"That's the Nia I remember," Vincent said with a smile. "All right, let's do this."

Suddenly an ominous beeping filled the air. Nia and Vincent glanced at the bodies of the Security Soldiers, their eyes immediately drawn to a flashing red light on one of their gauntlets.

"Oh no…" Vincent mumbled. "This is bad."

"What?" Nia grunted. "Can you just say what's on your mind?"

"That's the distress beacon," Vincent explained. "I didn't think it was active yet. It alerts other Security Soldier units and calls them to their location in the event a unit is defeated."

"Oh yeah? Well, I'm fired up now. Let's have it then! How many units we talking about?"

"Based on the light pattern…" Vincent looked longingly at Nia. "All of them."

Nia gasped. "A-all of them?! And how many would that be?"

"I think R&D has completed about three dozen units."

Nia looked dumbfounded, then raised her fingers.

"Um…a dozen is twelve…multiply by three…carry the…"

"Thirty-six units," Vincent sighed. "*Two hundred sixteen* Security Soldiers, total."

Nia flinched. "Two hundred what?! We barely took out six of them just now! You tryin' to tell me we're gonna have to fight two-hundred-something more mindless dorks with bulletproof armor on? Ain't no way we can deal with all that!"

"There's only one thing we can do," Vincent said as he checked his Beretta. "We stop them at the source. Come on, let's go."

Without another word, Nia Black and Vincent Marks ran toward the Hudson Tower.

ALEXANDER BLACK HURDLED the stairwells, avoiding the elevators. He was speeding like a man running a marathon.

He dashed past the entertainment multiplexes that littered the lowest levels of the Hudson Tower, bolted past bellhops and ushers who maintained the luxurious upper class housing that made up the middle levels, leaping through gaps in the crowds with precision. He didn't knock a single person down.

He darted past professionally-dressed employees who milled about the upper levels, sending manila folders and papers flying in his wake like leaves rustling in the wind.

He skidded to a halt before a pair of heavy doors that read 'AUTHORIZED PERSONNEL ONLY' in large block lettering.

He shoved his fingers between the doors, penetrating them like railroad spikes. He spread his arms apart, tearing the doors apart like they were tinfoil. He stepped into the yawning corridor ahead.

A droplet of sweat trickled down his temple.

Alexander took a deep breath, as he felt the tension in his massive muscles subsiding. With a full day's worth of action already behind him, as powerful as he was, Alexander Black started to feel the burn. Ascending the heights of a skyscraper from ground level while avoiding the elevators didn't help matters.

He finally reached the highest level accessible by stairwell, and found himself in a corridor lined with paintings of distinguished gentlemen and awe-inspiring landscapes on either side.

Stopping to consider why he did not meet any opposition, Alexander chuckled when five gold-and-black armored men appeared at the far end of the hall.

"*Target Alpha*. Please surrender and accompany us," said one of the Soldiers.

"So, you're the famous Corp Hudson Security Soldiers," said Alexander. "So glad I finally get to meet you flunkies face-to-face. Don't nothing beat selling your soul to a tyrant, huh? Oh well, here we go."

They each raised their gauntlets, electrified batons jutting out from inside their armor. But the Soldiers never even had the chance to assume fighting stances. In the blink of an eye, *Target Alpha* was already upon them.

One Soldier's head ended up caught in Alexander's flexed arm like a walnut in a nutcracker, garroted unnaturally to the left until the bones snapped and the muscles tore, blood squirting through his twisted flesh like a soaked washcloth.

Alexander's fist exploded into the next Soldier's chest, clear through his armor, vertebrae segments ripping through his back.

A swift kick struck another Soldier so hard his ribs pierced the back of his torso, skewering his innards and ripping through the armor like spikes.

The fight ended as gruesomely for the last two, their bodies torn apart like chicken wings.

Alexander stood in the center of the pile of mutilated men, their bodies rent and torn, their blood coating his hands like latex gloves. He flicked his fingers in the air and wiped his hands on his pants.

Walking a little further down the corridor, he found a smaller elevator. The door was open, there were video monitors on a wall and a single button on a panel.

Alexander shrugged, stepped into the elevator and pressed the button. He heard a chime, the door gently closed and the elevator ascended.

Alexander had no idea how fast the elevator moved or how far it went up, but the ride felt brief.

The elevator opened again, and Alexander found himself facing another long corridor with a set of double doors that were reflecting him and the entire hall, most likely a one-way window, he figured. He walked forward, and subtle classical music started to fill the air. Beethoven's Ninth Symphony.

The mirror doors creaked open and filled the hall with light. Alexander shielded his eyes, startled by the sudden illumination, and then when his vision focused, he smiled.

Stone pillars with statues of knights lined the path ahead of him. On the opposite end, there was a massive oak desk inside the room ahead behind the reflective doors. Seated there was a large, suited man wearing opaque sunglasses with his arms folded. A blonde woman in a lab coat sexily parked her rear on one edge of the desk, her legs crossed, with a huge smile on her face. Three of the walls in the room were like windows, revealing a glorious view of the city thousands of feet below.

Alexander Black finally reached Maxwell Hudson's penthouse office.

Nia Black and Vincent Marks rushed through the lower levels of the Tower. Vincent's access card still worked, and he was able to make use of the building's executive elevators. It didn't take long before the two were in the corporate levels of the Hudson Tower. They stormed past frightened employees, who gasped and backpedaled when they spotted the twin Baby Eagles in Nia's hands and the Beretta in Vincent's grasp.

"Okay, here's the plan," Vincent stated. "The Security Soldiers go out in units. Each unit receives a specific command. Orders are issued from the control room. We have to get in there, take control of the system and shut it down completely. We basically order every unit to cease operations."

"I'm not all that good with computers," Nia muttered.

"That's okay; I can handle it, even if they revoked my access. All I need you to do is make sure I don't get shot while I'm in the middle of it."

"Yeah, okay…" Nia mumbled.

Then Vincent took Nia by the arm and yanked her down, raising his Beretta with the other hand at the same time. He let off two rounds down a corridor and they smacked a Security Soldier in the helmet, sending him tumbling to the floor.

Nia looked up from the floor, staring at Vincent standing over her.

"I knew he was there."

"I'm sure you did," Vincent nodded, helping Nia to her feet. "I guess I just wanted to show off a bit. I may not have *Hercules*-enhanced DNA like you do but I can hold my own. I can't let you have all the fun."

"Didn't you say they come in units of six or something?" Nia said.

Then five more Security Soldiers appeared at the end of the hall, holding assault rifles.

"And didn't we discover outside that their armor is bulletproof?"

The sixth Soldier stood back up and took his place alongside his counterparts.

"You're gonna need something a little bigger than that Beretta," Nia suggested.

"The heavier artillery isn't kept here, for obvious reasons," Vincent grumbled. "Can't endanger the civilians who work here. I could probably get my hands on an assault rifle from our weapons locker, but we already know that won't be enough."

"Then we're going to have to take the direct approach."

Nia put her guns away and cracked her knuckles.

"What are you doing?"

Nia looked back at Vincent with a smile. "Just get to the control room. There's more to having enhanced DNA than being able to shoot straight."

The Soldiers wasted no time. Each leveled their rifles and aimed square at Nia and Vincent.

But even that took too long.

In the time it took each Soldier to lean their guns forward, Nia had already crossed the distance of the hall.

Vincent darted out of the way as triggers were pulled. Automatic gunfire rattled in the air and sparked on the walls. Nia sprang in the air and sprinted toward them *along the walls* as all the shots passed underneath her.

She leaped off and slammed her knee into one Soldier's helmet. Upon impact, her leg muscles doubled in size, her leg becoming hard as cement. The helmet shattered like glass and the skull inside burst like a grape.

Nia kept a tight grip on the body of the Soldier she defeated first, outstretching her legs and smashing her heels into two throats. The armor protecting their necks was dented, and both Soldiers gasped for air, collapsing to the ground, trembling until they stopped moving.

Nia landed and outstretched her arms, throwing herself forward, tackling the other three Soldiers to the ground. Their guns flew away. They all raised their fists and started pounding Nia in the head.

Nia shot a glance down the corridor and saw Vincent was still standing there.

"GO!!" she screamed.

"But..." Vincent mumbled.

"I got this! But I don't know how long I can hold them!"

Vincent flashed teeth, then he ran past Nia and the Soldiers, disappearing down the hall.

Nia suddenly forced herself to her feet, throwing the last three Soldiers in three different directions. One crashed into the fire alarm, and a shrill ringing followed. Ceiling-mounted sprinklers shot on and it looked like torrential rain inside the building. Nia tightened her fists. She looked back and saw six more Soldiers appear behind her, ready to fight some more.

She then noticed something near the fire alarm. A fire extinguisher.

Nia quickly dashed away from the new unit, skipping over the fallen bodies of the first set, and snatched the fire extinguisher from the wall.

The Security Soldiers leveled their rifles and took aim, but the fire extinguisher was already swirling in the air toward them. They held their fire.

Nia Black raised a pistol, winking at the Security Soldiers with a smile.

Maxwell Hudson and Chelsea Romedrux just stared at Alexander Black with strangely calm eyes.

Alexander couldn't believe them. He was the strongest man on earth, standing face to face with his nemesis in the only doorway out of the room, and Hudson didn't even so much as have armed guards waiting.

He approached the desk. The doors creaked shut behind him. Alexander looked back briefly, then shrugged at Hudson.

"I always knew you were bold," he started. "But I didn't know you were insane. I guess you finally got it through your head. You created a monster. Raised one too many devils. I've come here to pick up your lady friend. But as long as I'm here, I might as well tear a new hole in your ass too."

Hudson didn't react.

Then Alexander noticed something. He didn't even realize it before, but while he was talking, the music stopped. In its place was a high-pitched sound that started out faint. It was starting to get louder. And louder.

It felt like pins and needles in his head.

He couldn't hold back his screams any longer. The pain became unbearable—a sensation he hadn't experienced in a long time. Blood began leaking from his ear canals. He fell to one knee, clutching his temples.

The doors opened again and six Security Soldiers rushed into the room, four of them holding shackles that looked like they were meant to restrain a rhino. The other two each held large jet injectors that they immediately stabbed into Alexander Black's deltoids.

They pulled the triggers and Alexander suddenly felt wobbly and feeble.

It was sedative, and a powerful one.

As Alexander stumbled all the way to the floor, unable to support his own weight any longer, the other Soldiers latched his arms and legs together using the shackles.

Maxwell Hudson stood up, and Chelsea Romedrux hopped off of the desk, standing up as well.

They both pulled high-tech earplugs out.

Rachel Jones stood at a computer terminal in a sealed room deep within the Tower's corporate levels. She darted back and forth, looking at camera monitors, taking in the bedlam. Then a thundering BOOM from outside the room startled her. It was loud enough to penetrate the supposedly soundproof walls of the control room.

"Where are they?" she shouted into a microphone. "We need backup now! *Target Omega* is here and she's taken out three units already!"

"Sorry, Ms. Jones," a voice crackled over the mic. "We got held up by a traffic jam. Cops are all over the place out here. Something about a car crash. There's a mangled Viper sitting here, people are all over the place, ambulances, cops, reporters…"

"Damn it!" snapped Rachel. "Go around! Get here as quickly as you can!"

Then the room's only door swooshed open. Rachel looked behind her and saw Vincent Marks standing there with his Beretta out.

"What are you doing, Vincent?" Rachel asked him. "You should be out there investigating that blast…"

Vincent stared firmly at her, writhing his gloved fingers around the handle of his pistol.

"Don't play dumb with me. I know everything now. You made those Soldiers turn their guns on me. Shut them down. You know this is wrong."

"No, Vincent," she said, "You're wrong. Your whole existence is wrong. Mr. Hudson is trying to solve the problem created by people like you."

"By replacing everyone who works for him with an automaton?"

Rachel slowly paced around the room, navigating around the various terminals and keeping her distance from Vincent.

"No…just you soldiers. You with your morals and your free will…you should understand this better than anyone, Vincent. After all, your weak little heart is the reason we haven't been able to capture *Target Omega*."

Vincent took his pistol in both hands. "You think Hudson's going to spare you? What happens when you stop being useful to him? Just like his executive security, you can be replaced too."

"I provide services for Mr. Hudson that no mere machine can ever compare with," Rachel said with a grin, sliding her hand under one of the terminals. "I could provide that service for you too, if you want."

"Rachel…" Vincent mumbled.

Then a gun went off.

Rachel's eyes rolled up to the hole in her forehead. Blood rolled down the middle of her face and she fell dead.

"She's right, you know."

Vincent spun around and saw Nia. She was soaked from the fire sprinklers and scarred from battle, holding a smoking Baby Eagle.

"Those morals of yours almost got you killed," she said as she walked past him, approaching Rachel's corpse. "There is a such thing as being too honorable, you know."

A revolver sat barely grasped in her hand.

"You couldn't tell she was going for a gun? I mean, that's the oldest trick in the book. We put a little more breath in our voice and talk all slow, and you men just look and stare and think about how much fun it would be to fuck and *bang!*—you're dead."

Vincent scratched his head. "I have an issue with shooting women."

"Yeah, I know," Nia said with a smile. "Now, you do know how to turn off those Soldiers, right?"

"Might take a while," he responded, looking over the computers. "Rachel locked her terminal. I need to break through so I can log her out and log myself in. She had administrator access so it might be tough..."

"I ain't understand a word you just said," Nia sighed, starting for the door. "Just do it, all right?"

"Where are you going?"

"You should be cool in here. Just seal the door. I've got unfinished business to deal with upstairs."

"What do you plan to do? Hudson...you're going after him? He's not worth it, Nia!"

Nia took a breath. "Even if you shut down the Soldiers, he'll just start the project up again later. He'll come after us. This has to stop, today. I have to end it. For me, for you...for my father and mother. For everybody. Hudson's got to be stopped."

Vincent crouched down at Rachel's corpse and dug into her jacket pockets. He drew a small card with a magnetic strip on it.

Tossing the card to Nia, he said, "Here; that's Rachel's key. She was the only one with direct access to Hudson's penthouse besides the big man himself. You should be able to get up there easily now."

"HELLO, MR. BLACK," Hudson said, approaching his quarry, looking down at Alexander as he trembled on the floor. "The moment you entered the room, you were under the assault of a high-frequency sonic wave bombardment. Much like a dog whistle, only more potent. Everyone else was wearing specially-designed earplugs that filtered out the tones. They did make us deaf to your babbling, but I'm sure you weren't saying anything terribly important."

Alexander could barely move. It took matchless effort just to make a grimaced face. Chelsea Romedrux walked close and crouched low, looking into his eyes.

"Aw...you're like a little puppy who knows he's about to be put to sleep," she laughed.

"H-how..." Alexander stammered.

"Heightened senses...that's like, your greatest asset, you'd think," Chelsea continued. "But I figured out that they're also your Achilles' Heel. You're like, super-sensitive to extremes. High-pitched sound, super-bright high-beams, subzero temperatures; you name it. And the stronger you are, the more effective it is. I had to shut the sonic defense system off before it made your brains explode. After all...I need your heart pumping for my experiments."

The Security Soldiers took Alexander by the arms and lifted him to his feet.

Then they released him and he fell back to the floor.

"Hey...what's going on?" Chelsea mumbled. "Like, pick him up!"

"Negative. Threat imminent," said one Soldier as he and the others turned away from Chelsea and Hudson, facing the open doorway and looking down the end of the hall.

The elevator door chimed and slid open, and a woman stepped out.

Chelsea gasped. "Like, how in the hell did you get up here?"

Nia Black presented the key card, holding it between two fingers.

"Rachel..." Hudson mumbled.

"Yeah, she's pushing up daisies," Nia said. "She was about to shoot a friend of mine so I had to stop her. You know how that is."

Hudson looked at Chelsea. "Dr. Romedrux, if you would."

"Yes, sir."

Chelsea pressed a key on top of Hudson's desk, and the six Security Soldiers immediately assumed fighting stances, producing electrified batons from inside their gauntlets.

"This again..." Nia sighed.

The Security Soldiers ran toward her like rhinos, their thunderous footsteps quivering the carpeted floor. Nia just stood her ground, tightened her fists, and took action.

Nia swung her forearm into her first opponent's throat, sending him somersaulting backward, his own momentum throwing him forward to the ground.

The second swung at her with his electrified baton. Nia ducked, shot her elbow into his gut and connected with the force of a shotgun blast. She followed with a rising kick that sent the soldier flying backward, his helmet shattering to pieces.

The third thrust his gauntlet toward Nia. She caught it, swung him around and slammed him face-first into the office door. He collapsed to the floor and didn't move.

Nia spun around as the fourth Security Soldier rushed forward, wrapping his arms around her waist. He pushed forward to slam Nia to the ground. She dug her heels into the floor and halted him in his tracks. She raised her arms and barreled her elbows down to the Soldier's back, smashing into him like an anchor, leaving dents in his armor as he fell in front of her. Finally, Nia took hold of his torso and swung him around like a sack of potatoes, throwing his body into the air.

Nia was grateful for the high ceiling in Hudson's penthouse.

She suddenly took off into a sprint, sprang into the air and swung her foot into the flailing Soldier, the collision hitting him so hard he changed direction in midair, hurtling into the last two like a missile. They all crashed to the floor. Nia charged toward the pile of men, grabbed their gauntlets and jammed their stun rods into each other's helmets, breaking through them. They all violently thrashed about as the electricity lanced through their bodies.

Smoke hissed from them as Nia stood back up and swept her hands of dust.

She stepped over the fallen guards and yanked her Baby Eagles from their holsters.

"It seems more experimentation is necessary," Hudson said. "Apparently even our second-generation Security Soldiers aren't enough to stop her. Perhaps with *Target Alpha*'s DNA, the third generation will—"

"You ain't ever gonna get the chance to find out, big man," Nia said, determined. She raised a pistol.

"NO!!" Chelsea squealed, standing in front of Hudson, outstretching her arms. "You can't do this! The world needs him!"

Nia sighed and shook her head. Then she opened fire.

Chelsea shook.

Three bullets smashed into Maxwell Hudson's forehead—that towered well above Chelsea's feeble height—and he fell backward over his desk.

Chelsea flashed teeth, staring daggers at Nia.

"You...you bitch! Like, how could you?"

"If you're going to use yourself as a human shield for somebody that big, at least have the good sense to get a chair or something, shorty. Damn. You corporate types can't even go take a piss without somebody giving you time off to do it. Don't worry; somebody else will get promoted in his place. I just had beef with him."

Chelsea started sniveling. She looked over at the fallen body of Maxwell Hudson, his legs sitting lifelessly on top of his desk, the giant chair flipped over his face.

"Like, go ahead then," Chelsea sobbed, furiously wiping her eyes. "Finish what you came up here to do. Kill me like you killed my father. Here, I'll even turn around so you can put two in my back just like you did him. Like, that'll make it easier, right? Don't have to look me in the eyes?"

"What the hell are you talking about?"

"You know what I'm talking about. Romedrux Labs. You went there to steal our prototype, and you killed my father on the way out. Two rounds in my father's back. That's what I was told."

Nia rolled her eyes. "Look, I didn't kill anybody that night. Your father was alive when I left. Did you even look at the tapes? Or were you just trying to look for somebody to blame? You know damn well what happened to your father for real. You keep on blaming me but you know it only happened because of your boss."

"Liar!" Chelsea screamed. "Even if...even if you *didn't* shoot him...it was still your fault!"

"My fault? It's my fault you work for a crime lord who hands out gunshots instead of pink slips when his employees screw up? Ain't that why your boy Billy's not around anymore?"

Chelsea wiped her eyes again. "If you didn't go to my daddy's lab that night, it never would have happened. He would still be alive!"

"Cry me a river, build a bridge and get over it," Nia said as she shrugged and looked around the room. "Well, let's see. Hudson's done, these goons are down…"

The Security Soldiers started to get back up. Nia frowned.

"I'm getting so tired of beating up these things…"

They assumed fighting stances again, produced the stun rods again…

And then they collapsed again, this time like corpses.

Both Nia and Chelsea looked dumbfounded as a voice filled the air over the public address system.

"Nia, it's Vincent. I've done it. I ran a failsafe code through the entire Security Soldier network. Their circuits are fried for good. They won't be getting back up. I'm on my way up there…but you've got the only good key so it might be a while."

"Take your time," Nia said with a smile, even though she knew Vincent couldn't hear her. "So, like I was saying, I'm pretty much done here. Just one more loose end."

She looked toward the floor and saw her father, still sedated and trembling, shackled and unable to move.

She scoffed. "How the mighty have fallen."

Alexander struggled to crane his neck toward his daughter, and his lips started trembling.

"Oh, now you want to talk rational, pop?" Nia said with a giggle. "I don't even care anymore. Hudson's down and out and Vincent stopped the robots. I think I'm going to let Miss Chelsea over there do whatever she wants to you. Because you know, if it *is* my fault her father's dead, I figure, she can just have mine. How's that for a 'right way to do wrong'? Punk-ass."

"N-Nia…" Alexander stammered.

"What? You got something to say? Say it quick because I'm about to be out."

"Behind…"

Nia gasped and spun around, just in time to duck a particle beam blast from across the room. It cut clear through the double doors of the penthouse and left a smoldering hole.

Nia rolled and caught herself, looking toward Chelsea. She was holding the *Crasher* rifle, the same one that Billy Casey used against her, Alexander and Jesús earlier, complete with the damaged chassis from Nia's gunshot.

"Girlfriend, you better think about what you're doing," Nia said. "The only reason you're alive right now is because I didn't think you were a threat. You do *not* want to fuck with me. You seen what I did to all your little soldiers and all your little weapons and your boss. Think about it."

"There is, like, *no way* I'm gonna just let you walk out of here after what you've done," Chelsea wailed, her eyes flickering with tears, her voice cracking. "You're so lucky you disabled the targeting system when you shot it before; you'd totally be dead otherwise. But that's okay! Like, where there's a will…"

She fired again and again, forcing Nia to bound out of the way as the beam scorched the walls and the floors and the statues. Chelsea walked forward, holding the massive weapon in both hands and firing with reckless abandon.

"The *Crasher* never runs out of ammo! It never needs to be reloaded! The battery lasts for hours! You can't keep this up forever!"

Nia took cover behind a statue and raised a pistol.

She's actually right about that. I'm getting kind of tired. If Vincent thinks this bitch is so sweet and innocent, he must not know her all that well. It won't take much for me to take her out. One bullet and that's it. But I don't feel right about this. She's not evil. She's just angry. She's doing this because she feels like she has to. Revenge, that's all that is.

"Come on out!" Chelsea screamed. "Like, you know you deserve this! You'll get to be with Alvarez! Your life is totally worthless anyway!"

Nia grimaced. She sprung from behind the statue and leapt toward Chelsea. Chelsea aimed and fired again, but Nia ducked the shot. She continued to swerve and sway, closing the gap between them.

Before Chelsea realized what was happening, Nia rose up from directly below her, wrapped one arm around the *Crasher* and raised the other—with a Baby Eagle barrel pressing into her throat.

Their eyes met.

Nia flexed her arm around Chelsea's weapon until she started crushing it in her grasp. Sparks sputtered out of the mangled gun and Nia forced it out of Chelsea's hand. It clanged on the floor like a bent tire rim.

Chelsea forced a swallow past the lump the gun barrel made in her throat. She never looked away. Tears didn't even well up in her bright green eyes. Her face grew a furious red as she furrowed her brow, pursed her lips and just stared.

Nia looked calm…and sad.

"What are you doing this for?"

"Don't talk to me. Just shoot," Chelsea grunted. "You won. You got me, okay? One more notch on your belt."

"Ain't you ever asked yourself why you're alive?" Nia said. "You said my life is worthless. My dad said that too. Bobby even said something like that. I'm up in here because I'm trying to prove everybody wrong, everybody who ever said that about me. But you…working for Hudson, even after he did what he did to your father, even how he treats his loyal people…he even got you up in here fighting me yourself. You're the one acting like you don't care about your life."

"Don't lecture me! Don't you want to kill me? Just do it! I've got nothing without Mr. H anyway…"

"I never wanted to kill you," Nia sighed. "But you brought this on yourself. If you could have given me a straight answer, I might have let you go. But you're just another one of Hudson's slaves after all, and you ain't even got a chip in your head...just one on your shoulder. I'm sorry...but I'm done being worried about watching my back."

Chelsea took a deep breath, then closed her eyes. Tears began to escape her eyes.

Nia slid her finger around the trigger.

Then a massive hand yanked Nia's forearm to the sky. A bullet struck the ceiling and echoed in the air.

Nia and Chelsea looked up and gasped at the same time.

A large man was looming over them, tightly holding Nia's arm, his fist like a clamp. Then Nia saw the world spin around her as she found herself torn from the floor and hurled across the room!

She crashed into the reflective doors, the force of her body shattering them completely.

Satisfied for the moment, the man looked toward his head of Research and Development.

"Dr. Romedrux," Maxwell Hudson said, peeling Nia's flattened bullets from off his unharmed forehead. "You may take the rest of the day off. I shall attend to our guests personally."

NIA BLACK PUSHED HERSELF from the floor, struggling to recover as Chelsea Romedrux hurriedly trotted by. Chelsea glanced at Nia, and at her shackled father Alexander, before disappearing from the penthouse.

The doors closed behind her as Maxwell Hudson took off his suit jacket.

"*Alpha* and *Omega*...the beginning and the end," said Hudson. "I was always certain I would get one or the other. I never imagined I would have both of you here."

Hudson glanced at Alexander, who was forcing himself to sit up.

"Ah...I suppose the sedative is starting to wear off. Well, we can't have that."

Hudson picked up one of the jet injectors dropped by the Security Soldiers. He immediately slammed his loafer-clad heel on Alexander's head, forced him to the floor and squeezed the trigger as hard as he could, injecting the entirety of sedative in its chamber directly into his neck.

"There, that should do it."

Alexander slumped back down to the floor and ceased moving.

"How..." Nia Black coughed out. "H-how the hell are you still alive? I put three bullets in your head."

"Remember my experimental bio-weapon projects, 'Gunner' and 'Armstrong', Miss Black?" Hudson took off his glasses, revealing his burgundy eyes. "Before I tried my weaponization procedures on them, before I had the resources to do so, I decided to use myself as a guinea pig. As you can see, I became a success by taking the greatest risk of all, and it has benefited me spectacularly."

Nia finally rose to her feet. "It doesn't even matter. Your army is shut down. You went and killed all your regular people, replaced them with those zombies, and now you ain't even got them. You're through."

Hudson chuckled. "Indeed? You may have disabled the existing Soldiers, but the data that created them still exists. I need only start acquiring new subjects. And as soon as I'm through with you, it will be back to business as usual."

"What's the point of all this? Why would you take the people who work for you and turn them into weapons?"

Hudson turned his back and looked out the window-wall. "Tell me, Miss Black. What do you think is a soldier's greatest weakness?"

Nia wanted to shoot Hudson in the back, but remembered it was useless, no more effective a use of ammo than firing at a brick wall.

Hudson went on. "As the head of a defense technology firm, I have seen much of the military. Armies around the world train their soldiers to fight, watch the backs of their fellow men, and survive at all costs. They continuously try to create modern means of training new generations of soldiers to make them more efficient."

"Yeah? So what?"

"No amount of training guarantees absolute discipline. No matter how well-designed the weapon in their hands, the will of the soldier is always a liability. No matter how well they're trained, eventually a weak-willed soldier will defect. He will start to doubt his conviction or his patriotism. He will want to run from his duty. One soldier's accidental friendly fire can end the life of another, give away a position, and compromise an entire operation. Wartime suicides continue to occur, unabated, and far too many lives—too many skirmishes—are lost. The weakness, Miss Black, is *free will*. Remove that liability and a soldier becomes unstoppable."

"So you just trying to control everybody, huh?"

"There has never been a guaranteed way to ensure a soldier's perfect obedience and discipline, never a means to completely eliminate human error, until now."

"By making soldiers into robots," Nia grunted.

"A crude term, but accurate enough. The idea is simple. By planting control chips in the central cortex of the brain, we can use electronic signals to suppress independent thought, enabling the Security Soldiers to focus solely on their mission by receiving commands from a remote location. You've already seen how efficient they are. We only need to improve their physical prowess."

"And that's what you need my dad for," Nia grumbled.

Hudson turned back around. "Precisely. When your father escaped me so long ago, I left him a message he would never forget…a message for you as well. Yes, Nia Black. I ordered the death of your mother, Shauntee Lawson. I did this because I wanted to make sure at least *one of you* came for me eventually."

"One of us…? Then, you knew? You knew about me the whole time?!"

"Of course. I personally led the *Hercules* project. I knew its mutagenic properties. I only needed the right host, the right biological makeup that could produce the powered offspring. There were many failures, but only one…or rather, two, successes. That is why I named the formula *Hercules* in the first place; it was designed to create super-powered offspring like the mythological demigod."

Nia looked at her own hands, her own body, disgusted by the thought that everything she was, everything that defined her—was planned, designed, *orchestrated* by the man she despised most.

"You were my backup plan, Miss Black…my *Omega*. Now that I have my property back, my *Alpha*, I can pick up where I left off. I will study your father's DNA closely, with modern technology. I will finally learn why *Hercules* only affected him. Then I will redesign it so it will work on all of my Security Soldiers. The next step: to sell the services of my perfected Soldiers to the highest bidders around the world. Terrorists, rebels…it's all the same to me as long as they pay."

"You're crazy…" Nia gasped. "You're fucking crazy. These are people. People with lives. What if they don't want to be Soldiers anymore? What if they want to stop serving?"

"Through my Security Soldiers, I will control the ultimate private military corporation," Hudson bellowed, ignoring her outburst. "I will decide the outcomes of the world's conflicts. In time, Corp Hudson will control everything. But first…"

Hudson started walking toward Nia.

"I no longer have need of you, Miss Black."

"So, what you're saying is…I'm *worthless?*"

"Understand. The entire reason you exist was an experiment. You were allowed to live only for me to see what *Hercules* would do to a body when it's part of your natural chemistry from birth. This was only because I thought your father was lost. You hate your father for leaving you, but if he hadn't, you would have been dead years ago. You were a substitute, a hypothesis that worked out. Now, the source of the original phenomenon is here. I have no need of a substitute anymore, especially one that would defy me. Accept the truth of your life. You serve no purpose to anyone. You have no meaning. You should *want* to die."

Nia flashed teeth. She raised both her Baby Eagles and opened fire, emptying the clips into Maxwell Hudson's chest. He stumbled and staggered back, but stood his ground.

Hudson took hold of the collar of his dress shirt, shredded and perforated from Nia's gunshots, and tore it away from his torso. The bullets sat flattened on his broad chest. Aside from burn marks, he was unscathed. Hudson swept the bullets off like they were pieces of paper stuck to his skin.

Nia kept pulling her triggers, then the guns clicked.

"Let me tell you something," Nia grunted, tossing her guns away. "I've been beat up, insulted, played, shot, stabbed and told over and over that I was worthless. But I'm up here, now, standing on my own two feet, here because I want to be here. I'm not like that dumb-ass laying on the floor who walked into your trap. My pop's getting old, Hudson. He's slipping. Meanwhile, I'm getting stronger. I just figured it out. My dad, he's the one that's a substitute. He's the artificial one. I was born with it. *I'm the real deal!*"

"Is that a fact? Then by all means, show me. Show me what you're worth, *Target Omega*," Hudson cracked his knuckles.

Nia inhaled sharply. She wiggled her fingers, formed fists, and shook her shoulders.

Running toward Hudson, Nia leaped in the air, stretching her knee toward his belly, her movements a blur.

Maxwell Hudson calmly opened his left hand and outstretched his arm.

Nia froze in the air with a thump.

Her face landed in his palm, her knee falling far short of his body, her legs dangling like loose threads.

Hudson looked back upon the little woman in his grip with condescending eyes. He inhaled, raised his arm and hurled Nia away.

Nia flew through the air until her back crashed into one of the pedestals, hitting it so hard the stone knight standing on it fell off and shattered on the carpet only inches away from her.

Nia clutched her torso when she felt a shooting pain in her side. One of her ribs was cracked.

Hudson walked toward Nia, his shadow looming over her like a colossus, his footsteps shaking the floor.

Nia rolled over and tried to push herself up, but Hudson took hold of her ankle, scraped her off the floor, swung her by the leg and tossed her into a window-wall, her back crashing into the Plexiglas as the whole room seemed to shake.

Nia rolled to the floor and coughed blood.

She forced herself to her feet again, defying the pain racing through her body, and ran toward Hudson. Hudson reached for her as she closed in, but Nia reacted this time. She knocked his hand aside with an elbow and followed up with a roundhouse kick, slamming her heel into his belly.

Hudson stumbled back with a sigh. "As I was saying—eh?"

He appeared to choke for a moment. He pressed his fingers to his lip and raised his hand to examine it. Blood.

Hudson smiled.

"That was quite a blow, Miss Black. That means you must be getting there. A little more."

He took hold of Nia's torso faster than she could blink. Hudson clawed her abdomen in both hands and lifted her in the air.

"So small..." he muttered before swinging his body backward, smashing Nia through his desk headfirst!

Nia risibly tumbled and landed prone on the carpet, laying in a pile of wood and metal shards. She stared as the upside-down Hudson walked toward her again, raising his foot.

He thrust his heel into her face, the floor rumbling underneath her skull.

"I was actually expecting a workout," Hudson sighed. "But all I've gotten out of this is a need for new furniture. Pity. You said you were superior to your father's strength. I disagree."

He smashed his foot into Nia's face again.

And again. And again.

319

Blood shot out from her mouth and nose like fireworks with every thunderous stomp. The world shook around her, her head throbbing as Hudson's foot pounded her head like a drum.

Hudson raised his foot one more time and barreled it down. Then Nia jutted her hand up, caught his shoe in her tiny palm, and swung her arm, sending Hudson stumbling backward.

She sprung to her feet and wiped the blood from her mouth, staring at Hudson with, dilated pupils, blind rage written all over her face. Her muscles were larger, pushing the seams of her clothes to the limit.

Hudson regained his balance and smiled.

"Ah, there it is."

Nia seethed through her teeth and stormed toward Maxwell Hudson, slammed her fists into his chest, leaped and kicked his belly, swirled around and slammed her knees into his sides.

Hudson staggered around the room, each blow sending him in a different direction like a punch-drunk boxer.

She continued to hit Hudson, her bloodied fists leaving prints all over him. She sprung in the air and smashed her elbow into his chin, blood squirting from between his clenched teeth.

Hudson slipped backward. He thrust his heel into the floor, his leg bracing him like a pillar. It was as if he adamantly *refused* to fall.

"Enough!" he roared like a bear. He swung out his arm as Nia charged forward again, the back of his hand colliding into her face. She was sent spinning in the air before collapsing to the floor once again.

Pushing herself from the floor, Nia glanced at her father, who was still in chains. He'd come around again, and started lurching toward her at a snail's pace.

"N-Nia..." Alexander grumbled. "Hold onto it...!"

Nia gasped. Her muscles were relaxing. The Breach had subsided. The pain she'd already endured was too great—she lost her focus.

Hudson suddenly reached out and took hold of Nia's face and lifted her whole body by her head, her legs swaying wildly in the air. He held her away from him, her diminutive limbs unable to do more than meaninglessly slap his forearm.

Hudson walked toward the window behind his dilapidated desk. He took a deep breath and thrust his left hand—and Nia's back—*through* the Plexiglas pane, breaking the panel from the frame. It flip-flopped through the wind and fell from sight.

Hudson held Nia dangling in the air outside his penthouse office. The wind moaned all around her as the clouds grayed and the air grew moist.

Alexander Black flashed teeth, calling upon every ounce of strength he could, fighting the sedative coursing through his veins and the chains that bonded him.

Nia grabbed Hudson's wrist, pulling herself up, until her eyes peeked above his palm, struggling to break his grip. She stared into Hudson's dark red pupils as he cracked a smile.

"It's been a good meeting, Miss Black. Good day to you, now."

Hudson arched his arm back, ready to hurl Nia into the heavens like a baseball pitch. Nia wriggled in Hudson's grasp, desperately trying to escape her fate. But it was no use. Hudson's grip was like a steel clamp, locked in place. Nothing would stop him from sending Nia Black's small body hurtling through the sky...

The sound of a metallic pop snatched Hudson's attention. Then the floor shook, then a massive force hit him in the small of his back.

Hudson stumbled forward, flashed teeth and looked down behind him. A pair of dark, hulking arms with bulging muscles, beads of sweat, and engorged veins coiled around his waist. Alexander Black glared at Hudson from behind, with insane eyes, the metal cuffs still latched to his wrist—connected to broken chain links.

Nia's fight against Hudson gave Alexander the time he needed to recover his strength. He overcame the sedative and broke the chains. He initiated the Breach. And he pushed against Hudson with all his might.

Nia slipped free of Hudson's grip and crashed on the floor inside the office, her legs dangling outside the building as she clutched the window's edge.

Maxwell Hudson felt his equilibrium shifting. The force that struck him from behind had also robbed him of his balance. He saw nothing but the open sky before him. Hudson outstretched his arms and reached to grasp the edges of the window opening, but only grazed them with his fingertips as he fell forward.

He found himself surrounded on all sides by open sky.

Nia bellowed out to her father at the top of her lungs, her eyes awash with tears. She reached out of the window with no regard for her own safety, grasping nothing but air as she watched the two figures vanish into the gray mist of the clouds that surrounded the Hudson Tower's peak.

A pair of hands wrapped around Nia's forearm at the last second and she found herself being yanked back into the building. She flopped on the floor, safe.

Paying no attention to what just happened, she scrambled on all fours, looked back through the opening, and saw Alexander Black hanging by one hand penetrating a lower level window.

Hudson was gone.

"Nia…" Alexander muttered. "You did pretty good."

"Pop!" Nia screamed. Just hold on! I'll find a ladder or something…"

"Do yourself a favor, Nia," Alexander went on, looking down. "Find your twin sister."

"What?"

"You're incomplete! You need balance! You gotta close that hole in your heart. My way was to seal it all off—how I felt about you, your sister, even your mother—and go cold. You're not like me. You need somebody in your life. I get that now; that's why you have so much trouble committing. You need something…some*one* to fight for. Find Shauntia!"

"All right, whatever, I'll do it, but let me go get something to pull you in with!" Nia stammered.

"Just do what I told you, and everything will be cool," Alexander said. "See you."

Alexander Black thrust his other hand into the building, as easily as a hammer drove a nail. Taking hold with both hands, he kicked off and swung his feet away outward. He brought his feet together and barreled them into the Plexiglas, crashing through the window and swinging himself inside the Tower on a lower level.

Nia jumped up and darted past the man who saved her, still paying him no heed.

"Nia!" shouted Vincent. "Wait!"

She raced through the penthouse, leaping over the shards of the oak desk, the still-collapsed Security Soldiers and broken statues. Nia reached the elevator and hammered the lone button that controlled it to the point of flattening it into the panel. The door chimed open after what felt like ages and Nia darted in. The doors started to close and a hand grasped the door, forcing it back open.

"Get off the door!" Nia screamed. "I have to go!"

Vincent pulled himself into the elevator. "Forget it, Nia. It's over. He's gone."

"I have to find him," she said. "I need to talk to him."

"Look," Vincent pointed to the monitors inside of the elevator. "See? These monitors show views all over the building. There's no sign of your father anymore. You know how fast and strong he is—we all do. You'll never catch up to him."

"Yes I can," Nia said. "I'm fast and strong too. I'm—"

Her vision started to blur as her voice broke. Nia pressed both hands on the wall, trying to hold her balance, but her knees wouldn't cooperate. She slumped down and Vincent put his arms around her back just in time.

She fainted.

Vincent looked at Nia's peaceful, soft face, and couldn't help but smile.

"Yeah…that's what I thought. You've had enough excitement for one day."

He took the bruised, battered and blood-covered Nia in his arms and pressed the button inside the elevator. The doors closed with a chime and the elevator descended.

NIA ROLLED OVER, squirming under in a thick comforter with a smile on her face. It was like being wrapped up in cotton candy. She couldn't remember the last time she slept so comfortably.

And then she did remember. It hit her like a magnum load. She was somewhere familiar.

She forced herself up from the queen-sized bed, looking through the nearby window. She saw the array of identical windows across from hers, the brick construction and the lush green grass of the courtyard below, and the tall gate that sealed the high-class condominiums from the outside world.

Nia sighed. *I can't believe him. No he didn't...*

She threw the comforter off and swung her legs out of the bed, and that was when she noticed she was only wearing her panties. Her skin was healed of all marks and wounds. Even the hole Billy Casey's knife made in her belly was closed up; only a scar remained.

Her eyes darted around the room. It was a square room with plain décor; some posters of rock stars and movies that had long since been out of the theaters were tacked to the walls, but little decoration aside from that. There was a soft, oval-shaped rug in the center of the room covering a small part of the wood floor, and a pair of dressers, one tall with a T-shirt and a pair of boxers left hanging out of the top drawer as if beckoning her, and a shorter, wider dresser sitting across the room with a prominently-placed photo in a frame.

Nothing's changed at all, she thought.

But one thing did catch her attention. Her golden pendant with the opal charm was dangling on a post at the foot of the bed. It looked like someone had cleaned it and restored its luster.

Nia couldn't help but chuckle as she retrieved the necklace and clasped it around her neck. *That's exactly where I would leave it when I used to spend the night here. He was the only one who could get me to take it off. He thinks he's slick.*

With no sign of her own clothes, Nia grabbed the shirt and boxers and dressed. She remembered the fit; her hips stretched them out. She approached the dresser and picked up the photo frame.

It was a photo of herself and Vincent Marks, arms around each other. They were smiling and embracing in a park on a bright, sunny day not different from this one.

Then the door creaked open and Vincent stepped in carrying a bag from a designer clothier.

"Hey," he said. "Sorry. I know this is probably the last place you'd want to be, but I didn't know where else to take you."

"That's okay, I understand. But…"

"Your clothes? Well, they were torn up and covered in blood and dirt, so I had to get rid of them."

Nia twisted her lips. "Don't go acting like you got special privileges or anything just because you were my first boyfriend. You better not have been all touching me."

Vincent laughed. "You know me better than that, Nia. But the way you were sleeping, you wouldn't have known the difference. Haven't you noticed? You were out for a whole day."

Nia gasped. She remembered…it was raining when she saw her father tackle Maxwell Hudson through his penthouse window. It was afternoon when everything ended. But now it was early morning.

"I slept that much?"

"You're lucky you woke up at all after what you went through. But I'm glad you did. Hungry?"

"Hell yeah."

"I'll warm something up. And here," Vincent said, handing Nia the designer bag. "I bought you an outfit. Pretty sure I got the right size. I read the tags on your old clothes before I threw them out."

Nia took the bag, opened it and glanced inside. "Oh uh-uh…you done lost your mind if you think I'm wearing this."

"I don't know what to tell you then. I kind of need my underwear back and I don't keep a lot of women's clothes in my drawer these days," Vincent shrugged, turning toward the door. "Come out into the living room when you're ready."

Nia rolled her eyes and pulled the outfit out of the bag, laying it out neatly on the bed.

Vincent stood by his electric stove, stirring the contents of a large, steaming pot. Then he heard his bedroom door creak open and he spun around. He dropped his ladle inside the pot and smiled.

Nia stood in the hallway wearing a black and white dress that flared out from her waist and fell down to just above the knees. It was a far cry from her usual attire, and based on Vincent's expression, a pleasant sight indeed.

At least for him.

"What kind of mess you got me wearing?" Nia griped. "One strong wind and this dress will be all up around my neck and I'll be giving the world a show."

"It's not windy today. I figured something a little more loose-fitting would be more comfortable than a vinyl skirt and a tube top, since you're recovering and all."

"Stop trying to be funny. The stuff I normally wear isn't that skimpy."

Vincent scoffed. "It's a hell of a lot tighter and more revealing than what you'd wear when we were dating. Or were you just putting on another act for me, just like the whole story about you being a bartender instead of a criminal?"

Nia quickly changed the subject. "So, what smells so good?"

"Oh, this?" Vincent turned back to the pot on the stove and retrieved the ladle. "It's just some beef stew my mom dropped off the other night. She's always cooking for me because she thinks I can't take care of myself. Problem is she always makes enough to feed an army. I used to have Jason and the other security guys come over for dinner every now and then, but...well, I have a lot of leftovers now."

Nia grabbed a spoon and tasted the stew. "It's good."

"Glad you like it."

Nia took two more sips, then put the spoon down. She looked into Vincent's bright blue eyes.

"So what did I miss?"

"Needless to say, I left Corp Hudson," Vincent replied. "I got lucky. Hudson never officially fired me or anything; I guess he didn't have time, or maybe he was waiting until he was sure I was dead. I had time to go around and do what I could to clean up the mess. The Board of Directors doesn't know anything outside of a story I managed to concoct about the Security Soldiers going haywire. I told them that Rachel, Hudson and other employees died in the carnage, and that I didn't want to stay with the company under those conditions, so I left."

"I'll bet the Corp's still going to be trying to mess with me, huh?"

"The whole *Hercules* thing was Hudson's private deal. With him gone, it's not a profitable venture according to the Board. From what I heard they decided to shelve it all indefinitely. Since they have to restructure everything including executive security, not to mention deal with investigations and injunctions, not to mention figuring out what to do with all those shut-down

Security Soldiers just lying around, I'm sure the Board has bigger fish to fry than worrying about you, especially since you're not the one who killed Maxwell Hudson. As far as they're concerned, he brought it on himself. Who knows…maybe they were looking for the chance to get him out of the way."

"And what about Chelsea?"

"Yeah…I don't know," Vincent said with a sigh. "Last I heard, she confined herself to the island facility. She's still working for the Corp, but there's been no word from her at all. She's got to be pretty messed up about all this."

"Damn," Nia grunted, standing up. "So I guess I really will have to be watching my back some more. She ain't gonna let this go."

"You've made some enemies, Nia, no mistaking that," Vincent said with a shrug. "But you can change your path for the better if you want to."

"Tell that to everybody else," she said. "Turning around and being a good girl ain't gonna get that bulls-eye off my back."

"Well, you never know," Vincent went on, filling a bowl with stew and setting it on a table. "So, where do you go from here?"

"I'm going home. I do have my own place now," Nia retorted. "I'm not that immature little girl you used to date anymore, you know. I can take care of myself."

"I see that. But you know what I mean. What are you going to do next?"

"Where are my guns…my bike…?"

Vincent raised his hands to reassure her. "I took care of all that. I had your bike towed here. Speaking of, why did you have to be so careless with the bike I bought you? Do you know how pissed off I was when I heard it got blown up while you were out there fighting Hudson's private security the other day? Do you have any idea how much I paid for that bike?"

Nia shrugged. "You should have taken the keys from me when you threw me out if you cared about the bike so much. You gave it to me; it was mine to lose, so get over it."

"Whatever you say. Just don't expect me to buy you another one."

Nia fell quiet. The bike was the only thing she had of her father's, the only thing he'd ever given her. It was quite a present; although it didn't make up for what he'd put her through, it would have to do.

"Nia?"

She sighed. "Don't worry. I'll take good care of the one I've got. You ain't even gotta worry about it. So what about my Babies?"

Vincent slid open a drawer in the kitchen and Nia's pistols sat there waiting, the chambers still empty. The keys to her bike were also there.

Nia looked at the guns with a slow smile. "I remember when you caught me holding them for the first time. That's when you put two and two together and figured out that I was that crook messing with your boss' company, the young female thief with the dual Magnum Baby Eagles. I tried to creep back in here but you were up late and caught me. We broke up that night. I'm surprised you ain't throw them away."

"Believe me, I wanted to," Vincent muttered. "But then again, I've had enough of the two of us being enemies...rather not have you hunting me the way I used to hunt you."

"Yeah, but...I know you hate them. I know how they make you feel."

"Those guns don't just represent how we ended. I think they represent all the bad choices you ever made. You hold those guns and you act like you can do anything you want. But the world doesn't work like that, not even for someone as strong as you are."

"Yeah, I know that now," Nia sighed. "I thought I was so badass, but I ended up losing so much...and I ain't got nothing to show for it except these two guns."

"You haven't answered my question, Nia. What are you going to do next? Back to the streets? Back to working for others like Charlie? The same old, same old?"

"I guess; I mean, I'm not sure I even want to go calling around looking for jobs anymore. That life…it just doesn't seem like it means anything—but I do still need to eat, and I lost every dime I had in Kim's place."

"If you don't have any ideas…well, I do. I've been doing a lot of thinking. I was thinking the two of us could make the most of this situation. I don't work for Hudson anymore, and if you're done being who you used to be, maybe the two of us could go into business together?"

Nia looked confused. "What kind of business? I mean, look. We're cool and all, Vince, but …the past is over. I'm not trying to go backward."

"That's not what I meant…" Vincent's voice trailed off. He walked toward a cupboard and pulled out a manila folder. Laying it out on the table, he spread out several photos and papers with all kinds of statistics and data before Nia's eyes.

They were men and women, wielding all kinds of weapons, bearing all kinds of disfigurements: a muscular, hairy man with giant metal gauntlets and claws where his hands should have been; another man, bald and shirtless, with red skin that looked rough like sandpaper, his fingernails like swords; a woman with giant boots that looked like the legs of a walking robot.

"Underground mechanics and disgraced scientists are copying Hudson's technology to make more and more criminals like Armstrong and Gunner: living weapons. Hudson may have started this, but his death didn't end it. The world can't have people like this roaming free. Local law enforcement is stretched to the limit. There aren't enough people out there who are strong enough to take the fight to them…people like you."

Nia shook her head. "Nah-uh. You're asking me to be some kind of super hero? I don't do the charity thing, Vincent. Didn't I just say I gotta eat?"

331

"Did you read it, Nia? Look again."

Nia did so, and saw numbers in bold type at the bottom of each page. They were dollar amounts.

Bounties.

"Like I said, the police are at their limit…they'll do whatever they can to get some help. We can be that help. I handle the administrative part, you do the heavy lifting with my support; we split the cash," Vincent explained. "Come on, what do you say?"

The conversation reminded Nia of what her father said to her outside of the Hudson Tower. She remembered his story about forming his own mercenary group.

"They're gonna need to be more than human to take down the kinds of targets I'm looking at."

Nia immediately snatched the guns and keys from the drawer and ran toward the door.

"Nia? Nia! Where are you going?"

"I need some air, Vince," Nia mumbled back. "Give me some time and space, okay? I got your number. I'll call you."

"Nia, wait!" Vincent yelled, starting to follow her. Then he stopped in his tracks, spun around and turned his stove off. As soon as he turned back toward his apartment door, he heard the sound of a motorcycle engine growling to life, and knew there was no point chasing her.

"Damn," he said to himself. "I forgot how fast she can be."

CHELSEA ROMEDRUX SAT in her private office, nestled in the highest level of the laboratory facility on Corp Hudson's manmade island. She was leaning on her computer desk, head in her palm, mindlessly browsing the web, rubbing her pantyhose-clad feet together. Her eyes were red from being rubbed too much, her hair was unkempt, she wore no makeup...it was as if she'd lost interest in life itself.

She hadn't spoken to anyone for days, not since she learned of Maxwell Hudson's fate. The corporation's board of directors kept her on duty but gave her space so she could recover from the stress of the experience.

But Dr. Chelsea wasn't just stressed. She was furious.

Her father died for nothing. The man who gave her everything was thrown from his own penthouse. She'd even lost a potential lover. And the woman who caused it all was still alive, roaming free.

For all her knowledge and power, all her funding and access, Chelsea Romedrux never felt so lost, so defeated. Was there nothing she could do against Nia Black?

A tone snapped Chelsea out of her stupor. She straightened her recently-replaced glasses and looked at her intercom, where an LED was beeping.

She ignored it. Chelsea wasn't interested in taking any calls.

Then her smartphone vibrated.

With that, Chelsea groaned. She snatched it from her pocket and glanced at the glowing touch screen. A text message read:

"HEX PROJECT HAS ENTERED THE SECOND PHASE. PLEASE REVIEW."

Like a dim light slowly cranked to full luminance, Chelsea's face brightened up. She leaped out of her seat and literally ran out of her office, leaving her high-heeled shoes behind on the floor.

Chelsea made her way to a large chamber deep in the lower levels of the facility, a synthetic cavity dug under the surface for housing projects too dangerous and grandiose to experiment upon within her small laboratory in the halls of the Hudson Tower. She walked inside, wrapping her long golden hair into a ponytail as she entered the room.

In the center of the chamber were three capsules, each large enough to house a fully-grown human being. The capsules were connected to all manner of life support mechanisms, computer terminals and generators. Each capsule was labeled with a different name; "Alpha", "Beta", and "Gamma".

Chelsea glared at the chambers as her subordinates darted back and forth across the room, accessing terminals and recording data and doing numerous other things. One of the aides stopped in his tracks and approached.

"Dr. Romedrux," said the young researcher, "You never gave us your feedback about the progress of the Hudson Exceptional X-terminator project. When we lost contact with Mr. Hudson and we didn't hear from you, we figured we would just go ahead and begin the second phase. We've attached the prosthetics and we're currently monitoring their vital signs, making sure there aren't any bio-electric compatibility issues. Everything seems fine so far."

Chelsea placed a hand on one of the chambers, looking through its tempered glass shield, analyzing the figure within. Laying in silence inside the capsule was Jason Priest, one of the three remaining members of Hudson's executive security. He realized that the normal humans in Hudson's employ were on the verge of becoming obsolete, long before Vincent Marks or even Billy Casey knew it, and he must have convinced Cherie Wilson and Don Thompson to take action along with him.

They chose to live as Corp Hudson's newest weapons.

Jason's arms were covered by heavy armor and circuitry, wiring feeding directly into his spinal cord and brain stem. Cherie had similar additions on her legs. Don, in turn, had armor on his torso, with wiring and circuitry feeding from his trunk into his limbs.

We supplied them with the modified formula you devised, Doctor," the researcher went on. "It's the same base formula that was used to give the previous projects increased density and strength, but we've managed to greatly reduce the possibility of erratic aggression. We implanted microchips in the brain that will stimulate higher functions of the prefrontal cortex, just as you ordered. That will help them stay clear-headed, and focus on their mission. They'll be a perfect team, but they'll also maintain independent thought. No one will be able to take advantage of them like robots, like those flawed first generation Security Soldiers."

"Don't you dare insult Mr. Hudson's dream," Chelsea grunted. "The Security Soldiers were brilliant. He needed more time to perfect them, time that...*that woman* took away from him. Mr. Hudson's dream of a peaceful world, protected by the perfect army, will be realized through me."

Chelsea paced around the capsules again, looking upon the three figures with glee.

"But, like, while we're waiting to get that project up and running again, these three will do. Totally."

NIA KNELT DOWN in the wreckage of an old warehouse, standing in the center of a pile of scorched wood and crumbled cinderblock as the sun began to set. The grass surrounding the area was browned, the dirt and roots blackened and dried. There was no sign of the building's former glory, no evidence that anything worthwhile ever stood there. Yet to Nia, it felt like homecoming.

"You told me to stop being so selfish, Kim..." she whispered, laying carnations on the ground in the center of the pile. "You told me that doing dirt would just lead to more dirt being done to me. I would have been all right with that, if it wasn't for what happened to you. I never meant for this to happen to anybody I cared about. You ain't deserve this...I'm so sorry."

She stood there for what seemed like hours, the dress Vincent Marks bought her fluttering in the soft breeze. Nia touched the sparkling necklace around her neck as a tear rolled down her cheek.

"My dad told me to find my sister. You know, Shauntia? She ran off before you could get her along with me, remember? I wonder how things would have turned out if we were both here at the same time. Would I be the same person? Was I wrong for letting Tia go?"

Then Nia shook her head.

"Enough of that, right Kim? Let go of the past. That's probably what you would say. I'm gonna do that. I'm going to do something new. I don't know what yet. But there's something I need to do first, because I need closure."

Nia turned and started walking toward her bike, parked just off the edge of the street.

"I know you wouldn't approve of this, Kim. But he's the one who caused this. He's got to get dealt with."

Nia took off on her bike and zoomed across the city, speeding uptown. She made a beeline for the one place she knew her final target would be.

She sped toward the Jazz Hall.

She parked her bike in the alley across the street from her destination, grasped a handgun and charged toward the building, her grip on her pistol as strong as her resolve to get revenge for herself and for her mentor.

The truth was clear: Bobby Styles was the one who told Billy Casey about Kim's hideout. After all, he was the only other person who knew about it. Nia didn't care why Bobby did it. She'd come to accept that the way Bobby treated her in her apartment was her just desserts. But pointing an enemy of hers in her mentor's direction—a move that cost Kim his life—Nia viewed that as a baseless, personal attack. And no one attacked Nia Black without retribution.

She drew her semi-automatic pistol and stepped closer to the nightclub. Faint jazz music seeped into her ears; with every step, the music grew louder, and chipped away at Nia's hardened disposition. Soon, the languorous and tranquil tunes of the expert saxophone player began to soften Nia's heart as she peeked inside the doorway of the Jazz Hall like a curious feline. She held her gun behind her back as she analyzed the club interior.

Everything was smooth and peaceful, the way an upscale jazz club should always have been. No danger of gunfire or police raids, no secret gangster meetings, no espionage; only nicely dressed patrons from all walks of life chilling out under dim lights to enjoy fine dining, good drink and smooth jazz in a laid-back atmosphere. It was as if all the darker element that used to frequent the Jazz Hall vanished along with Alexander…and with Nia.

It was as packed as it had ever been. In the wake of "Marc Benson's" vacancy, Bobby Styles seemed to be able to perform as a club manager and as the main entertainment at the same time quite well. They hired a new bartender. Silk was there talking with some lively friends. The club was the same, and yet it seemed so much more pleasant...more alive.

Nia looked toward the table nearest to the stage and caught a sight that shocked her.

Charlene was there, in the seat most often reserved for Nia, wearing a sleek red dress and high heels, staring at her man as he smiled back at her. It was the first time Nia ever saw Charlene in the club. What Nia couldn't take her eyes off though, was the diamond ring that sat on the third finger of her left hand, sparkling like a prism under the dim ceiling lamps and candles that made the Jazz Hall glow from inside with an iridescent golden orange.

Nia sighed.

Bobby Styles and Charlene Wright had moved on with their lives. It was time to let them live, to let them be. They looked like they had a bright future ahead of them.

It was time for Nia Black to create the same thing for herself.

She drove away from the nightclub, keeping her vehicle under the speed limit. She looked to her side and watched the steel towers of the city pass by in the distance, her eyes focused on the soaring tower that seemed to drift more slowly than the other buildings, as if to ensure everyone saw it, protruding above the city's skyline with its arrogant H-shaped roof marring the sky like a bad tattoo.

Corp Hudson was more than just its fallen gigantic chairman. Maxwell Hudson was the most powerful man in the city—but he was just the head of the corporation. His empty seat would be filled. Those under him would move up, taking control of the Corp's vast resources, following the same ideals and the same objectives as their recently-deceased boss.

Nia knew the fight wasn't over. The fight would never be over. And she knew that even if she tried to avoid it, she would end up being dragged back into it. Hudson's supporters and loyalists were numerous. And if Vincent was to be believed, there were new threats rising up by the day.

But for the first time, the hunger for petty revenge or desire to simply piss off Hudson's emissaries wasn't what fueled her will to fight back. Her selfishness created more problems than it solved, and she was tired of seeing others suffer.

The downfall of Maxwell Hudson was only the beginning, and Nia wanted to end it. No one else would suffer the way she and her family did. No one else would lose their humanity to Hudson's—or anyone's—ruthless experimentation. She felt she had a responsibility to everyone who came to harm because of her.

And, she realized, she had nothing better to do.

Nia gently steered her bike between a pair of parked cars and cut her engine. She pulled her goggles away from her eyes, unclipped her cell phone from the waistband of her dress, and dialed a number.

It only rang once.

"Nia?"

"Damn, Vince, were you waiting by the phone?" Nia laughed. "Are you busy? I was thinking I would stop by and we could talk some more about this whole bounty hunting thing."

Some time ago…

Night fell. Under chilly and rapid winds in the autumn night, four women crouched on a rooftop some distance from a hotel with golden lights sparkling against the shadow-laced cumulus clouds. They all wore navy blue combat armor with ski masks, their eyelets masked by night vision goggles.

"Target located. The information was right on the money."

"Acknowledged. The treasure is our primary objective."

"So why the heavy artillery then?"

Each carried an MAC-11 submachine gun with a silencer attached, in addition to a secondary sidearm, a knife and first aid kits.

"Intel says we're dealing with a hard target. We're authorized to engage if necessary. Only if necessary. He doesn't want any harm to come to the treasure."

"Let's see what's going on in there."

One of the women pulled out a pair of binoculars and analyzed a room of the hotel directly across from their position. She pressed keys on top of his binoculars, and her view zoomed and focused until she was able to see the interior of the posh hotel room in crisp detail.

Her eyes went wide.

"What? What is it?"

"She's there."

In the electronic green screen of his binoculars, she saw the heat signature of a slender, fit woman with long black hair sliding a cloth robe from her shoulders. Dropping the robe to the floor, she stepped across the room in the nude and opened a door, fluorescent light and steam emanating from the other room.

"She's taking a bath."

"Stay focused. Any sign of the treasure?"

"Negative. We can't see the entire room from this vantage point. It's likely she has it in the bathroom."

"The bathroom? What the heck...?"

"Our info said she considers it extremely valuable. No surprise she wouldn't let it out of her sight even for a moment."

"So we're going to engage?"

"Affirmative."

The four women moved across the rooftops like inky blobs against the gray-blue sky, rappelling across the expanse until they reached the balcony just outside the hotel room.

They used power screwdrivers to breach the sealed window between the balcony and the hotel room, and stepped gently across the soft carpet. They tiptoed past the plush bed and dresser, approaching the far end of the room where the bathroom awaited them just adjacent to the room's front door.

The women took positions outside of the door. The first two stood on either side of the door, the third retreated behind the bed and knelt; the last one stood directly in front of the door. They nodded to each other, waiting patiently as they listened to the sounds of a body slowly breaking the surface of hot water that filled the tub behind the door.

All fell silent.

The women traded nods again, and the fourth raised her leg and kicked through the bathroom door.

She threw himself in with both hands on her MAC-11 and opened fire, three rounds at a time tearing through the bathroom tiles and the tub, the mirror, the sink and the shower curtain, decimating everything in the room.

Then the fourth let go of the trigger and raised her gun high. Smoke wafted away from the suppressor as she looked around.

There was no sign of anyone. Only broken tile and ruined caulk, cracked porcelain and shattered glass, and water gushing from the holes in the tub and creating a small lake on the floor.

"What the—?"

The second and third mercenaries flanking the door stood up and looked inside the bathroom as well.

"That's impossible…we saw her come in. Heard her get in the tub…"

Then a droplet of water hit the fourth shooter's goggles. It took her a moment to realize it came from above.

She craned her head toward the ceiling, and that was when she saw her.

A drop-dead gorgeous woman with caramel brown skin, glistening wet and naked, her long pitch black hair—with one blood red highlight in front—cascading across her face like a hood. All she wore was a golden necklace with an opal charm around her neck. She was holding herself aloft with her fingertips atop the door frame and her feet on the fluorescent light at the center of the ceiling. And she was holding a *katana* sheathed in a red and gold scabbard in her thumbs.

Her face showed no emotion as she let go of her supports and took the sword in both hands, unsheathing it as she descended from the high ceiling.

She landed kneeling in front of the fourth assailant, and with an almost inaudible whistling sound, the blade came to gentle rest on the floor between the woman's legs, her hair fluttering down and cascading across her back like a cloak.

Everything was still. The women flanking the door didn't know what to think.

The shooter was standing there, trembling.

Then her body fell apart, *split in twain*, blood gushing from her in all directions.

The target stood up and held the sword in front of her while her first victim's entire body practically spilled on the floor. She looked at the second woman, and then the third, her face as calm as death.

"Shit! Shit!" one of the mercenaries hollered. "Engage! Engage!"

The woman twirled the blade in the air, its reflective edge leaving trails of light in its wake, and she dashed past them, swinging her sword as soon as they pulled their triggers.

Their gunfire radiated outward, cutting up more of the bathroom and the surrounding walls. Then their bodies collapsed on the carpet, their heads sliding from their necks at the same time.

It would have taken an electron microscope to tell, but the blade was actually vibrating many thousands of times per second, fast enough to disrupt the molecular structure of whatever it met. Each time the blade moved through the air, it let out a high pitched whistle. The sword had no more difficulty slicing through flesh and bone than it did thin air, and it was in the hands of a young woman born with superhuman strength and agility.

"You...you crazy bitch!" the first mercenary popped up from her hiding place behind the bed. But as soon as her head emerged, the red lacquered scabbard shot through the air and smashed into her night vision goggles like a bullet, shattering the lenses as she reeled back.

She staggered and regained his balance, pulling the destroyed goggles away from her head so hard she snapped the elastic strap securing them to her face. She gave the target an insane glare through the eyelets of her ski mask.

The sword wielding target-turned-hunter stood still and watched her foe the entire time, her face as calm as the night wind.

The mercenary outstretched her gun with one arm and squeezed the trigger. But her opponent swung her sword in a circle, the blade spinning like a propeller, the gunshots pattering in front of her. The first assailant stopped firing when she saw the futility of it.

Bullets fell to the floor, cut to shreds as the woman lowered her blade.

Then the mercenary lost her temper. She flipped the switch on the side of her MAC-11, setting her gun to full auto. Barely able to control the gun and blinded by rage, her concerns about accuracy and discretion were forgotten and automatic gunfire shredded everything in the room...

Except the target.

The mercenary watched in awe as the assassin pounced forward, planted both her bare feet on the bed, somersaulted off it and overhead. The wildly-aimed bullets whizzed over her and under her but never touched her. She landed in back of the soldier, the wind whistling as she moved past.

The first mercenary screamed as her firing arm plopped on the floor, her trigger finger locked on the gun, suppressed automatic gunfire tearing up the bodies of her comrades even more until the clip was finally expended, the chattering sound of the automatic mechanism repeating endlessly.

The target stood up and spun around to face her victim, her sword arm moving with her. The look of shock was frozen on the first mercenary's face as a diagonal cut as fine as a razor's edge divided her skull from brain to jaw, and she fell dead.

The woman flicked her blade in the air, swiping the droplets of fresh blood from its heat-tempered edge. She picked up the scabbard and sheathed the sword.

She drew a fresh robe from a drawer, since the blood of her would-be killers had spilled all over the one she'd dropped by the bathroom floor. She put the robe on over her shoulders, but didn't bother to wrap or tie it around her body.

The woman walked toward the balcony and opened the glass doorway. She stood outside the hotel room, her hair and the open robe gently flying in the breeze of the high altitude. There was no point in hiding anything—she knew she was being watched the entire time.

She glared straight ahead, her superhuman eyesight focusing on a figure several blocks away—a man standing on a rooftop, wearing a gray overcoat, with a cashmere sweater and slacks underneath. He carried a *katana* as well, sheathed inside a black and silver scabbard.

The man across the way lowered his binoculars, swept a hand through his albino hair and smiled calmly as he stepped off the rooftop.

"So beautiful…" Darien Drakonis muttered to himself. "I'll be seeing you again soon, Miss Shauntia Black."

Jonathan Price lives in Philadelphia, PA with his wife and four children.

The author's creative pursuits go beyond just writing and transcend into visual arts as well. Please peruse Jonathan Price's artwork at http://dualmask.deviantart.com.

The author is available on Facebook at http://facebook.com/DualmaskArt and is also on Twitter and Tumblr under the name Dualmask.

Thanks for purchasing this novel!

www.ingramcontent.com/pod-product-compliance
Lightning Source LLC
Chambersburg PA
CBHW030405180626
46812CB00005B/1936